By Anne Rivers Siddons

Fiction
OFF SEASON
SWEETWATER CREEK
ISLANDS
NORA, NORA
LOW COUNTRY
UP ISLAND
FAULT LINES
DOWNTOWN
HILL TOWNS
COLONY
OUTER BANKS
KING'S OAK
PEACHTREE ROAD
HOMEPLACE
FOX'S EARTH
THE HOUSE NEXT DOOR
HEARTBREAK HOTEL

Nonfiction
JOHN CHANCELLOR MAKES ME CRY

ANNE RIVERS SIDDONS

FAULT LINES

wm

WILLIAM MORROW
An Imprint of HarperCollins*Publishers*

A hardcover edition of this book was published in 1995 by HarperCollins Publishers.

FAULT LINES. Copyright © 1995 by Anne Rivers Siddons. All rights reserved. Printed in the United States of America. No part of this book may be used or reproduced in any manner whatsoever without written permission except in the case of brief quotations embodied in critical articles and reviews. For information address HarperCollins Publishers, 10 East 53rd Street, New York, NY 10022.

HarperCollins books may be purchased for educational, business, or sales promotional use. For information please write: Special Markets Department, HarperCollins Publishers, 10 East 53rd Street, New York, NY 10022.

ISBN 978-0-06-200468-0

11 12 13 14 15   OV/BVG   10 9 8 7 6 5 4 3 2 1

This book is dedicated to the memory of my mother,
KATHERINE KITCHENS RIVERS,
who goes with me on every journey,
and to PETER WARD, who lit the way for this one.

Acknowledgments

Special thanks are due, as always, to Ginger Barber and Larry Ashmead, agent and editor respectively, who are truly a dream team for any author. Martha Gray, who translated and processed, is invaluable and knows it—or should. Two writers to whom I owe much are John McPhee and Kenneth Brown, whose books informed and enchanted me. And Dr. Peter Ward of the U.S. Geological survey in Menlo Park was generous beyond expectation with his time and expertise. The facts are his, the errors mine. And thanks to Heyward, who loved *Fault Lines* unconditionally down to the last word—because someone's got to.

FAULT LINES

1

On the day of my husband's annual fund-raising gala, I was down by the river liberating rats.

There were two of them on this day, massive, stolid, blunt-snouted beasts who bore no more resemblance to common house mice than beavers, or the nutria from the bayous of my childhood. *Rattus rattus* they were, or, more familiarly, European black rats. I looked them up in *Webster's Unabridged* when Pom first designated me their official executioner. I figured that if you're going to drown something, the least you can do is know its proper name. That was a fatal mistake. Name something, the old folk saying goes, and you have made it your own. *Rattus rattus* became mine the instant I closed *Webster's*, and after that I simply took the victims caught in Pom's traps down to the river and, instead of drowning them, let them go. Who, after all, would know? Only the dogs went with me, and, being bird dogs, they were uninterested in anything without wings. The leaden-footed, trundling rats were as far from the winged denizens of God's bestiary as it was possible to be. My hideous charges waddled to freedom unmolested.

There were two and three of them a day in those first steaming days of June. Pom was delighted with the humane traps. The poison put down by the exterminating company had worked even better, but the rats had all died in the walls and for almost a month before we tried the traps the house smelled like a charnel house, sick-sweet and pestilential. We'd had to cancel several meetings and a dinner party. The exterminators had promised that the rats would all go outside to die, but none of them had, and Pom was furious with both man and beast.

"Why the hell aren't they going outside?" he said over and over.

"Would you, if you could die in a nice warm pile of insulation?" I said. "Why on earth did either of us believe they'd go outside? Why would they? They probably start to feel the pain almost immediately. They're not going to run a 10K with arsenic in their guts."

I hated the poisoning. I hated the thought of the writhing and the squeaking and scrabbling and dying. I never actually heard it, but somehow that was even worse. My mind fashioned grand guignol dances of death nightly behind my Sheetrock. I took to leaving the radio on softly all night, in fear that I would hear. The only result of that was that I would come awake at dawn with my heart jolting when the morning deejay started his drive-time assault and would lie there blearily for long seconds, wondering if it had been the phone I heard, or Pom's beeper, or Glynn calling, or some new banshee alarm from Mommee upstairs. Only when I had listened for a couple of minutes did it sink in that I was hearing Fred the Undead blasting Atlanta out of bed and onto the road.

As early as I wakened on those mornings, Pom was invariably up earlier and was almost always gone to the clinic by the time I padded into the kitchen in search of coffee. I would find his usual note propped up against the big white Braun coffeemaker: "Merritt: 3 more, 2 in lv. rm. and 1 in libr. Call A. about Fri, I think there's something. Blue blazer in cleaners? Worm capsules, 2 @. Mommee restless last night, check and call me. Home late, big bucks in town. See you A.M. if not P.M. XXX, P."

Translated, this meant there were three new captives in the rat traps, and I was to dispatch them in the river. Then I was to call his secretary, Amy Crittenden, who loved him with the fierce, chaste passion of the middle-aged office wife, and see what our plans were for Friday evening; Pom frequently made social arrangements for us and forgot to tell me, so Amy became a willing go-between. I liked and valued her and seldom chafed at her fussy peremptoriness, though I was not above a moment's satisfaction when I was able to say, "Oh, Amy, he's forgotten we have plans for Friday. You really need to check with me first." Then I was to locate his blue blazer and fetch it from the cleaners if it was there, which meant that the Friday mystery evening was casual and funky, like a rib dinner down in the Southwest part of the city, to show the flag in the affluent black community there. Much of Pom's clinic's work was done in and for the black communities south of downtown, and he endured the socializing as coin that paid for the free clinical work that was his passion. Pom was as impatient with the River Club as he was with the rib dinner, but knew better than anyone the necessity for both. In the twenty years that the network of Fowler clinics had been in operation, he had become a consummate fund-raiser. He was an eloquent speaker, a tireless listener to fragile egos, and without vanity himself, a rare thing indeed in a physician. The day his board of directors and auxiliary discovered this was the day that he began to move, imperceptibly at first, out of the office and onto the hustings. Because he was unwilling to surrender even a moment of what he considered his real work, diagnosing and healing the poor, he solved the conflict by simply getting up earlier and earlier to get to the clinic and coming home later and later. Now, two decades later, I virtually never saw him by morning light and often not by lamplight, either. Of course he didn't have time to get his blue blazer out of the cleaners; of course I would do it for him. It was in our contract, his and ours. He would care for the poor and the sick; I would care for him and our family. If this grew tedious at times, I had only to remind myself that Pom and I were in a partnership beyond moral reproach. Caretaking, any sort of caretaking, was my hot button. The smallest allegation of moral slipshoddiness was my Achilles' heel.

Next, the note bade me give the two bird dogs who lived in the run down by the river their worm capsules, two each.

Samson and Delilah were liver-spotted setters, rangy and lean and sleek, seeming always to vibrate with nerves and energy and readiness. Pom had grown up bird hunting with his father, the Judge, on a vast South Georgia timber plantation, and he thought to take the sport up again when we bought the house on the river five years before, so he kept a brace of hounds in the river run at all times. But he had yet to get back out into the autumn fields with them, even though he belonged to an exclusive hunting club over in South Carolina, on the Big Pee Dee River. He did not spend much time with the dogs, and did not want me to make pets of them. It spoiled them for hunting, he said, and it wasn't as if they were neglected or abused. Their quarters were weatherproof and sumptuous, their runs enormous, and he ran them for a couple of hours on weekends, or had me do it, if he couldn't. Besides, they were littermates, brother and sister, and they had each other for company. I will take them the pills in late afternoon when I decant the rats, I would think. Then I can spend some time with them and no one will be the wiser.

It had not yet struck me, at the beginning of that summer, how much of my time was spent doing things about which no one was the wiser.

Mommee restless: Nothing ambiguous about that. Glynnis Parsons Fowler spent her entire married life in her big house on the edge of the great plantation and ruled her husband, sons, and household help with an iron hand in the lace mitt of a perennial wiregrass debutante. As far as I know she was never called Glynnis in her life; her adoring Papa called her Punkin, her sons called her Mommee, and her husband Little Bit, but despite the cloying nicknames and her diminutive stature, she was a formidable presence always. Even now, ten years widowed and five years into Alzheimer's, two of them spent under our roof, she ruled, only now with mania instead of will and wiles. A restless night meant muttering and shuffling around her room at all hours, which Pom, no matter how weary, never failed to hear and I, no matter how well rested, seldom did. The note meant that he had had to get up and calm her again, and I whose task this was, had not . . . again. I knew that Pom had no thought of shaming me about this. The shame I felt was born entirely within me. I should have heard her. I will spend the morning with her, I would think, and Ina can go for the groceries and dry cleaning.

Finally, the note told me that someone with the potential for major financial support for the clinic was in town, and Pom was wining and dining him, and might be taking him somewhere afterwards for a nightcap. Many of the clinic's benefactors were from the smaller cities across the South, and liked to see what they thought of as the bright lights of the big city when they came to Atlanta. Not infrequently, that meant one of the glossier nude dancing clubs over on Cheshire Bridge Road. The first time Pom had come in very late from one of those evenings I whooped with helpless laughter.

"Oh, God, I can just see you with huge silicone boobs on each side of your face, hanging over your ears," I choked. "Even better, I can see you with huge silicone boobs over your ears and half an inch of five o'clock shadow, glaring out from the front page of the *Atlanta Constitution*. 'Prominent physician caught in raid on unlicensed nude dancing club.' What would Amy say?"

Pom's square face reddened, and his black hair flopped over his eyes as if he had spent the evening shimmying with a parade of *danseuses*, but he grinned, a reluctant white grin that split the aforementioned five o'clock shadow like a knife blade through dark plush. By the end of a long day Pom frequently looks like a pirate in a child's book.

"She'd say it never hurt a real man to sow a few oats," he said, leering showily at me and twirling an imaginary mustache. And I laughed again, because it was just what she *would* say, and because he looked, in the lamplight, so much like the much younger and far lighter-hearted man I had married eighteen years before. That man was intense and impulsive and endearingly clumsy, and somehow astonishingly innocent, though he was certainly no stranger to strip joints and bovine boobs. I had not seen that man in a long time. I held out my arms to him that night, and he came into them, and it was near dawn before we slept. That had not happened in a long time, either.

* * *

Pom has amazing eyes. They are so blue that you can see them from a distance; you notice them immediately in photographs, and the times I have seen him on television they dominate the screen as if they were fluorescent. It may be because they are fringed with dense, dark lashes and shadowed over by slashes of level black brows, and set into flesh that looks tenderly and perpetually bruised. His thick black hair is usually in his eyes. All of this darkness makes the whites extraordinarily white, and very often they seem so wide open that the white makes a slight ring around the irises. All that white should, I tell him, make him look demented, a mad Irish visionary, but it is the genesis of his apparent innocence, I think. Much of the time Pom seems wide-eyed with surprise at the world.

The rest of him is solid and muscular, and he moves lithely and fast on the balls of his feet, a tight package of coiled energy and strength. He has always reminded me, in his stature, of one of the great cinema dancers, Jimmy Cagney perhaps, or Gene Kelly. But Pom is an abysmal dancer. He is always in a hurry, and frequently stumbles and bumps into things. Oddly, he is an awesome tennis player, fast and savagely focused and powerful. He shows no mercy. I hate playing with him.

He is short, or at least not tall: five nine. My height almost exactly. He pads when he walks, like a tomcat or a street punk, and looks as disheveled as if he had been in a fist fight an hour after dressing, no matter how carefully his shirts are done by the specialty cleaners over in Vinings, or how perfectly Clifford at Ham Stockton's fits his suits. The shirts and suits are my arsenal, my weapons against the sartorial entropy with which he flirts daily. Pom doesn't care what he wears. He remembers the blue blazer because his father told him when he sent him off to Woodbury Forest that a man needed nothing else but a good dark suit and a tuxedo to dress like a gentleman. I think his heart leaped up when he discovered white medical coats. He would wear them everywhere if he could, not because he considers them becoming (they are), but because they are comfortable, correct, and there is a seemingly inexhaustible supply of them both at home and at the office. Amy sends them home to be washed twice a week, tenderly folded in tissue paper. She would wash and iron them herself if she could, I am sure. Pom said he saw her polishing his stethoscope once.

Mommee has always insisted that the Fowlers are of old Saxon stock, but both Pom and his brother, Clay, have Celt written all over them, as did his father before him, and his oldest son Chip is the same small, powerful dark creature of the Cornish caves or the wild cliffs of Connaught. Mommee herself is small and birdlike, with a thin, high-bridged nose, pale hazel eyes, and the jaw of a mastiff. A little Teuton in the Tudor gene pool there, no doubt about it. I think Jeff, the younger boy, looks like her, but since Pom's first wife, Lilly, is short and gilt-blond too I can't be sure of that. But in Lilly's case the smallness is of the small-town high school cheerleader variety, not the Blanche du Bois sort, as Mommee's is, and runs now to thumping curves that strain at her Chanels and Bill Blasses. And even I, with no eye at all for such things, can tell that the polished hair comes weekly from Carter Barnes. English or Irish, the Fowler provenance matters not at all to anyone but Mommee. Atlanta, and indeed most of Georgia except the old Creole coast, is far too raw and new and self-involved to make much of a distinction, requiring only strong Caucasian chromosomes and good teeth.

I met Pom at a fund-raising party for the new outpatient diagnostic center at Buckhead Hospital, on a spring afternoon in 1978. It was an old-fashioned all-day barbecue on the enormous back lawn of an estate on Cherokee Road in Buckhead that had been built in the early twenties for a former governor of Georgia and had just been renovated by the New Jersey–born administrator of the hospital. There was a gruesome whole hog turning on a spit over a pit of banked coals, hams and pork shoulders on grills, huge iron pots of Brunswick stew, and great bowls of potato salad and coleslaw iced and waiting in the pantry off the cavernous kitchen. Sweating black men and women in starched white and chef's hats stirred and carried and grinned, looking for all the world like devoted family retainers, but they were, I knew, the cream of the cafeteria staff from the hospital. Others, bearing trays of drinks and hors d'oeuvres across the blue-shadowed green lawn, were waiters and bartenders from the Piedmont Driving Club, imported for the occasion not by the New Jersey administrator, who was not a member, but the silver-haired chief of Internal Medicine, who was. The miniature carousel and the aging clowns and the mulish Shetland pony and crisp young attendants minding the shrieking small children in the blue, oval pool at the far end of the lawn were from the city's oldest and most favored party-planning establishment. The same sagging clowns had doubtless frightened many of the adults present and the same evil-tempered pony had certainly nipped them on their short, bare legs when its tender was not looking twenty years before.

I knew all this because I had planned the party, or at least had helped. My advertising and public relations agency had long had Buckhead Hospital for a client, and had long done the PR and printed materials for its various fund-raisers without billing anyone's time. Most agencies had these gratis clients, whose work was handled solely for the prestige and worthiness of their causes. I had been at the agency for four years, long enough to work my way up to copy chief and be in line for associate creative director, and this was my fourth Buckhead Hospital fundraiser. We had had a Parisian Street circus, a Night at the Winter Palace ball, and an Arabian bazaar. This time the board wanted to include families, and so Christine Cross, my art director friend, and I had suggested the barbecue and modeled it partly on the barbecue at Twelve Oaks from *Gone With the Wind*.

"Hell, it won't be any work at all," Crisscross said, dumping the ashes from her Virginia Slim into my tepid coke. "The board's got ten Twelve Oakses between 'em, and about a thousand slaves. We won't have to lift a finger."

And we hadn't, hardly. When I walked around the side of the big white house and stood looking down from the veranda at the barbecue in progress, it seemed to be surging and swarming along under its own volition, with everyone knowing exactly what part they were to play, and doing it faultlessly. The lawn was a sea of pink linen tablecloths and green tents and seersucker suits and pastel cocktail dresses and butterfly pinafores and sunsuits. The only jarring note was a thick-shouldered, dark-faced young man with his hair in his eyes and a red-splotched white physician's jacket, crouching on one knee at the bottom of the veranda steps and attempting to mop a veritable bath of red off the furious purple face and arms of a bellowing, struggling small boy. The red looked shockingly like blood but a vinegary tang in the still air told me it was barbecue sauce. Behind the man a slightly older boy was dancing up and down, stark naked and dripping, waving a tiny wet bathing suit in his hand and shrieking, "Dry me off! Dry me off! Jeff peed in the pool and it's all over me!"

The man raised his face to me, and there was such a look of desperation and entreaty on it, such utter helplessness in eyes of a color I had literally never seen in a human face before, that I ran down the shallow stone steps and reached for the wet, naked child before I even thought.

"If you don't stop right this minute you're going to turn to stone, and you'll have to spend the rest of your life naked in this backyard, and pigeons will crap all over you," I said, pinning the slick, small arms firmly. The child stopped dancing and looked at me. The smaller child stopped bellowing and looked, too.

"Oh, God, are you married?" the man said. "If not, will you marry me in fifteen minutes?"

"So tell me about his eyes again," Crisscross said the next day at lunch. She had pleaded cramps and missed the party. Crisscross did not go to parties where no recreational drugs were offered. It was a matter of policy with her; I knew she did not indulge. She had gone to Bennington, and regarded the social doings of old Atlanta society, or what passed for it, as she might the ponderous frolicking of dinosaurs. Once was interesting, more was grotesque.

"I never saw eyes that color," I said. "Such an intense blue they could burn you—"

"What kind of blue? Be specific."

"The blue of . . . of . . . the blue of those lights on the top of police cars," I said.

"Jesus," Crisscross said. "How utterly charming. Is his last name Mengele, by any chance?"

"No. It's Fowler. Pomeroy Fowler. *Dr*. Pomeroy Fowler. Pom to his friends."

"Of which you are now one."

"I guess I am."

"So. Two kids, both brats. Cop car—blue eyes, five o'clock shadow, slept-in clothes. Wife at Sea Island, or Brawner's?"

I glared at her. Sea Island is where much of old Atlanta goes to re-create itself. The Brawner Clinic is where it goes for its breakups, breakdowns, and substance addictions. The latter, Crisscross maintained, ran primarily to booze and Coca-Cola. The sixties never quite got to Atlanta, she said, much less the seventies.

"Why should it be either one?" I said.

"Because no Nawthside Atlanta matron goes anywhere else and leaves her chirrun behind, don'chall know? Especially during the Little Season."

Crisscross had not been in the South long. Her southern accent, even in parody, was execrable.

"As a matter of fact, she's on Hilton Head," I said. "She ran off with the architect down the street when he decided to go live on an island and free himself of conventional restraints. Pom got the children without even going to court."

"I'd give a lot to know how you free yourself from conventional restraints on Hilton Head," Crisscross grinned. "What do you do, join the Young Democrats? Violate the landscape code?"

"He wanted to build experimental low-cost housing for the Gullahs," I said, grinning back at her. "But none of them would move into the prototype. The one family that finally did tacked tin over the cedar shake roof and painted the door blue. That's to ward off evil spirits. You still see it on the Gullah shacks down there."

Crisscross folded her arms over her stomach and bent over laughing. I began to laugh, too.

"Maybe they'll find out it wards off Republicans, too," I gasped. Despite our seeming lack of anything at all in common, Crisscross and I became instant friends when she joined the agency, and we spent much of our billable time laughing. Of all my old advertising crowd, she is the only one I still see with any regularity. She has her own agency now. We still laugh.

"So after you shut his kids up what happened?" she said on the day after the barbecue.

"I took both of them into the house and bathed them and got clean clothes on them and we left and went back to his house. He made supper for them and I put them to bed and we had a drink. We had several, in fact. And then we ordered in pizza because all he had in the house was hot dogs and stale potato chips and strawberry Jell-O, and the kitchen looked like an army had been camping in it for weeks. The whole house did, for that matter. It's a nice Cape Cod in Garden Hills, but his baby-sitter doesn't clean, and he doesn't get home until late from the clinic most nights, and he thinks it's more important to spend what time he has with the boys, instead of cleaning. I sort of straightened things up for him; it looked a lot better. I'm going to see if Totsy Freeman's housekeeper has a free day or two. I think she said she did. It could really be a pretty house."

Crisscross looked at me silently for a time. Then she said, "Oh, Merritt. Merritt Mason. You did it again. There is absolutely no hope for you; you're a goner."

"Did what?"

But I knew what she was going to say.

She said it.

"Saw somebody in need of something and loped right in to fix things. Spied a creature in distress. I know you. 'Oh, Lord, there's something over there moving and breathing and looking like it might need help. Let me at it!' What did you get out of it this time? A chance to go back next week and clean his basement?"

"I got asked out for dinner this weekend and one hell of a goodnight kiss," I snapped.

"I'm glad about the dinner," she said. "I hope the kiss was worth all the fussing and nurturing you're going to do. For that he could at least have screwed you."

"The kiss was terrific," I said, reddening. "The other comes next week. I can tell."

"Thank you, Jesus," she said, and folded her hands as in

prayer, and rolled her wicked brown eyes heavenward. She looked back at me, waiting.

I looked away from her sharp, expectant little fox's face. I was not a virgin when I met Pom, but I had slept with very few men. I had not even been out with many, and in the Atlanta of that time, with singles' apartments sprouting like weeds and young men pouring in to catch the city's soaring comet's tail, that was downright difficult to accomplish. Every woman I knew dated all the time. It wasn't that I wasn't attractive; I am not pretty, but I am tall and thin and wear clothes well, and I know that I have an appealing smile. One of my last boyfriends had told me, "You're just a tall, skinny drink of water with exploding hair until you smile. Then there's nobody else in the room."

It was nice to hear, but it did not make me feel any more comfortable with the young man who said it, and gradually I stopped seeing him. It was what happened to most of my relationships. I had slept with one man at LSU, after a rock concert, where the pot smoke had drifted thick and sweet, and had lived in mute terror of pregnancy and other things until the next month. The next man I slept with, years later, was a rock-climbing, sports car–driving investment banker who told me flatly that there was absolutely nothing attractive about a twenty-eight-year-old virgin. By then I was on the pill, because you never knew when, et cetera, et cetera, but I might as well not have been, because I enjoyed the sex so little that after being shamed into bed by the investment banker I did not do it again, and he stopped calling. I was thirty when I met Pom. For the first time, I wanted, with no reservations, to go to bed with a man. I could hardly wait, in fact. If he did not initiate it on our next date, I was going to. When he had first kissed me my whole body ignited. When we finished it was near meltdown.

It was the first time in my life I had not heard, in my mind, my mother's bled-out voice saying bitterly, "Go ahead and do it with the first boy that tries it, if you're ready to die, because doing it will kill you. It will hurt you and hurt you, and then it will kill you."

My mother died of ovarian cancer when I was thirteen

and my sister Laura was three. She was terribly sick for a year before that. I used to pull the covers over my head at night so that I could not hear her crying. She died thinking that she had gotten the cancer from having sexual relations with my father, who, she said, wasn't satisfied unless he was on her every night. By that time, he had moved into the downstairs guest room and they seldom spoke. Our maid, Felicia, took care of her and my sister during the daytime, and a succession of Felicia's relatives from the bayou came in and cooked. I took care of mother after school and at night. I didn't miss much of the progress of the cancer as it chewed its way through her vitals. Later, when I got close enough to someone to want sex, or had necked in the back of a car until it seemed inevitable, I always stopped things abruptly. I knew with the top part of my mind that whatever else I got from the dirty deed, it wasn't going to be cancer, but the bottom part of it didn't know that. Whenever a hand touched my bare breast, or found the warm dark between my legs, I heard her voice: *It will hurt you and hurt you, and then it will kill you.* None of my relationships overrode that voice.

Pom silenced it with one kiss. Or perhaps the sheer need I saw in him overrode it. I knew, somehow, that I would not hear the voice again. I would sleep with him. I would marry him if he asked me. I would make him ask me. I would make such fine love with him that he would ask me; I would make such a good and orderly world for him and his children that he would ask me. I knew just how to do that.

After my mother died I took care of my sister and my father. It pleased him that I wanted to. It pleased me that it pleased him. He was a lawyer, a remote man who lived among paper and dust, or so I thought. Later I would learn that he lived most fully in the company of attractive women; my mother had been right about his sexual appetite. But he was discreet about it, and only remarried after I started college. Perhaps he was remote only to me and my sister; to Laura, especially. I knew she had not been a planned baby because I overheard the hushed, hissing quarrel over my mother's pregnancy. Laura sensed it, long before Mother died. She cried inconsolably for much of her babyhood, and only I could seem to soothe her. By the time she was walking Mother was past caring for her. The only real approbation I remember seeing in my father's eyes was when I had ministered particularly well to his second, changeling child.

I soon learned to care for him as well, acting as a grave, correct young hostess for him when he required it, seeing that his house was orderly and polished and quiet at all times. He would compliment me and I would feel my entire face light up, would grin from ear to ear despite myself. He was the first to tell me I had a wonderful smile. It earned him years of comfort. It earned me years of what amounted to servitude to my sister and father and our big house in Baton Rouge. I didn't mind. I thought that it would keep him with me forever. When he remarried and moved into the perfectly run home of a rich seafaring lady who lived in Pascagoula, I was stunned, lost. But I still took care of Laura, because by that time it was what I knew best, was most comfortable doing. Caring for. Tending. I brought her to live with me in Atlanta when I came here after college to try my wings in advertising, and when I met Pom she was still living with me and attending sporadic classes in theater arts at Georgia State University downtown. Up until that time I could not imagine a world in which I did not care for Laura.

Fragile, lovely, hungry Laura. Edge-dancer, wing-walker, windmill-tilter, limits-pusher. From babyhood she could stand no boundaries, tolerated none. In the airless world of a small Louisiana city, even in the volatile sixties, boundaries swarmed thicker than June bugs. Her entire life was a starved scrabble after two things: freedom and love. Since the two are mutually exclusive, she achieved neither, except minimally, but she never abandoned her hectic quest. Freedom of a sort she might have had if she had been a less difficult child; Felicia was too old to keep up with her, and my father simply did not seem to see her. I was a nurturer, but no real threat as a disciplinarian. She might have soared like a small butterfly in an empty blue sky except that her need for love was visceral and unending and dragged her down out of the air, time after time, to dog the footsteps of those who could not seem to give it to her. Ravenous for love, she pursued it shrieking; repulsed, love fled her.

"Hush up that yellin', Laura. I ain't studyin' you," Felicia would say over and over. "You looks like a little ol' baby bird, with yo' eyes squoze shut and yo' mouth open a mile wide. Cain't nobody fill you up. Go on and find yo' sister and tell her what you want."

"Laura, get down now and let Papa work," I would hear my father say stiffly from his study. "You're getting that jam all over my shirt. You're far too big to sit in laps. You should see yourself; it's really very unattractive. And don't *cry*! You cry more than any little girl your age I ever saw. Your sister doesn't cry. You should take a leaf from her book and try smiling every now and then. People would treat you a lot better, I can tell you. Oh, for heaven's *sake*, Laura Louise! Merritt! Come in here and get your sister, will you please?"

And once again I would take my beautiful, fragmented little sister, dancing and sobbing her rage and hunger, up to her room and cuddle her and shush her and whisper silliness to her, and soon she would let me dry her tears and wash her face and brush out the tangled chestnut curls that were so like our mother's, and in an hour she would be off again, flouting rules, testing limits, pushing, pushing, pushing.

"It's not really fair to you," my father said in the spring of my last year in high school, after I had come back downstairs to watch TV with him after settling a wailing Laura into bed. "You're only seventeen. You don't have much of a life of your own, do you? It's mostly studying and Laura. But I don't know what I'd do without you. You're the only one who can handle her. I admit she's too much for me. I don't know, maybe if her mother had lived . . . what in the world are we going to do next year when you go to school? Should I put her in boarding school?"

"Oh, Papa, she'll only be eight then," I said.

I was flattered at the adult tone of the conversation and felt mature and important to be consulted about the future of my little sister. I knew that for once I had his entire attention and that he would probably take my advice. I was the one, after all, who knew her best. I sensed suddenly what sort of relationship we might have had if I had been alone with him in the house, without the hovering, importunate Laura to define and absorb me and isolate him. I knew too that I could probably create that relationship if I told him to send her away.

But in my mind there was the white rush of wings beating at windowless walls and a thin silver wailing from an empty, dark place. I knew that boarding school would send Laura mad or kill her. My stomach literally turned over. My first taste of power frightened me badly.

"No, I don't really think that would be good for her," I said judiciously, hoping he could not hear the pounding of my heart. "Maybe we should get someone to come in and take care of her, a live-in housekeeper, or something. Somebody younger, closer to my age so she wouldn't seem strange. Then Felicia and the others could go on and do their work. I could ask our guidance counselor at school about it. She knows about things like that. I could even interview people, if you wanted me to."

"See? You always know just the right thing to do," my father said in relief, and smiled at me, and I felt the tremor of my answering smile begin on my mouth. We turned back to John Chancellor with relief, like two old married people who had just settled, indulgently, the problem of a troublesome child.

I found a young black woman to come and stay with Laura after school and half-days on Saturday. Matilda was a lunch server at my high school cafeteria and had the same hours free that Laura did. She was only two years older than I, but she seemed far ahead of me, across a chasm of adulthood. She had cared for a half-dozen younger siblings and cousins, and she had a matter-of-fact, cheerful firmness about her that soothed me and seemed, for a while, to be just the anchor to earth that Laura needed. She stopped a good bit of the acting out at her elementary school and much of the needy fussing at home. During that time it was easy to love Laura; her awful emptiness seemingly filled, we saw more of her quicksilver charm and the vein of whimsy that lay deep inside her. Her imagination was lightning quick and her ability to mime and posture was funny and true. And, her face unbloated by tears and rage, she was beautiful enough to turn heads in crowds.

She was all my mother, with pale, thick, magnolia-petal skin that she never allowed the sun to stain, and Mother's slanted sherry-colored eyes and rich spill of chestnut satin hair. Laura's hair was glorious. She wore it tied in a high ponytail, cascading down her back, or let it fly free in shining curtains around her face. She never let anyone cut it past shoulder length, and even that was an occasion to be feared, fraught with tears and temper. The first time she had it bleached, when she was a sophomore at Westminster, I cried.

"It's not you anymore," I said.

"Au contraire," she said, trying out her appalling first-year French. "It's exactly who I am. The other was somebody else."

But when I went away to LSU she changed again, back to the frantic, hungry small bird we had known, and began the trapped-bird battering at everyone and everything once more. We could get no sensible explanation from her for the change, except that she didn't feel safe.

"I feel like I'm walking way up high with nothing to hold on to," she would cry over and over. "I feel like I'm going to fall forever and ever."

"What would it take to make you feel safe?" I said desperately. Matilda was threatening to quit if Laura did not stop shrieking and plucking at her and dogging her every step. My father had the boarding school brochures out again.

"You! I want you! I want you to come back home," Laura wept. She was shuddering with sobs and retching. There was no doubting her sincerity. At Christmas I moved back home and began attending day classes. My father's gratitude and Laura's subsequent blooming were enough, I thought, to make up for the dorm and campus life that I forswore. I made a number of new friends anyway. I dated a good bit. I joined a sorority. And my grades undoubtedly benefited. I made Phi Beta Kappa, and basked in the modest glow of a number of minor achievements and awards. At my graduation, my father's proud smile and Laura's shining eyes gave me a salt lump in my throat and a tickle in my nose.

My graduation picture shows a tall, arresting, stooped man with thick brown hair just beginning to go gray at the temples; a tall, slightly stooped young woman in a cap and gown who looks ridiculously like him, down to the unruly shock of curly ash-brown hair and the tilted nose and sharp cheekbones; and a young girl of such vivid, blinding beauty that you cannot look away from her. She might be a budding movie actress graciously posing with tourists. Her presence captures the camera and eclipses the other two. I noticed anew that spring Saturday how eyes followed her, in her new mini that showed a great deal of white leg at the bottom and a precocious swell of white breasts at the top.

I also noticed that she was aware on every inch of her of the eyes. I remember feeling a small *frisson* of dread. Despite the calming presence of Matilda, there had been enough transgressions, tears, conferences with teachers, trips to smooth things over in her principal's office, promises. Always, Laura insisted that she had been wronged and misunderstood; always the contrition was heartfelt and her fear of reproach real. And always I was the one who went, who apologized, who smoothed, who promised. I did not need trouble of a sexual nature from her, but on that day I knew, as portentously as if I had read it in sheeps' entrails, that I was going to get it.

That night, after he had taken us to dinner in a new, baroquely awful French restaurant to celebrate and Laura had gone, reluctantly, to bed, my father told me he was getting married again. I sat still and looked at him, feeling a sort of percussion against my face as if there had been a silent explosion in the room. My mind was empty and ringing with it.

"I didn't know you knew anybody," I said stupidly.

"A nice woman," he said, looking away. "Her name is Andrea. I call her Andy. She's a widow. She lives in Pascagoula and she has a great big sailboat. She and her husband used to go all over the world in it. You and Laura will have a good time on that boat."

I was silent, staring at him. I could think of nothing to say. A boat? All of us, him and Laura and me, on a huge boat with a woman from Pascagoula called Andy? I had never known my father to call me by any sort of nickname, nor Laura, either. Not even Mother. I had never known him to evince the slightest interest in boats or the sea. When we vacationed, we usually went to Highlands, North Carolina, where he played golf and bridge with other lawyers. I could find no picture of us as a merry, seagoing family in my mind.

"But who will run it?" I said. "Can you? Have you learned to run a boat?"

He smiled. "She has a captain who looks after it and does the actual sailing and a crew to help him. We won't have to do anything but lie back and get suntans and eat great food and sleep with the waves rocking us. Forget the world for weeks at a time. You could get used to that, couldn't you?"

I felt my face redden at the thought of my father and this Andy woman, in a bed rocked by the waves. In my mind she was massive and blond, and very tanned, and walked in a rolling swagger.

"When did you . . . I mean, I never knew you even were . . . you know, seeing someone," I said, feeling the sofa rock under me as if I were already riding waves.

"Well, for some time now," he said. "She has a little place here and one in New Orleans, too. Say, you all will really like that. It's in the Quarter. I guess I thought you knew. Laura does."

"Laura does?"

Nothing seemed to connect, to fit together, to make any sense.

"I told her a while back," he said a shade too casually. "I was sure she would have told you by now."

"I wish you'd felt you could tell me, too," I said thickly around the tears that were pooling in my throat. "I thought you told me everything—"

"I told her because I had to talk to her about something else, and I want to tell you about that now; see what you think," he said. "You were in the middle of your thesis when it came up. I didn't want to bother you then. This all depends on you, Merritt. If you're uncomfortable with it in any way, at all, we'll make other arrangements."

"Uncomfortable with what? You mean you wouldn't get married if I didn't want you to? I'd never interfere in that, Papa, if it's what you really want—"

"No, no. We're definitely getting married. Too late to

back out now." He laughed, and then coughed and went on. "Here's the thing. Andy has never had children of her own, and while she's really looking forward to getting to know you two, she feels . . . we feel . . . that she needs a little time to get used to me and my strange ways before she takes on Laura. Laura isn't the easiest . . . well, you know. We thought we might take a long honeymoon cruise, maybe down around South America, maybe even as far as the Galapagos. Take our time, just bum around . . . and I thought it might be fun for both of you if Laura came with you to Atlanta for a year or two. I'm prepared to pay her way, of course, and she's already accepted at Westminster. It's the best private school up there. I had a couple of friends in the Georgia Bar Association look into it; their kids go there, too. They pulled some strings. She's already accepted, and I've made all the arrangements. She starts this summer because she needs to get up to speed with the rest of her class. I know it sounds like a big responsibility, but they've got a bus that picks students up and drops them off, and there's a program for students who need to stay until six or so. I'll give her a clothes and living allowance as well as her tuition, of course. All you need to do is keep an eye on her in the evening and on weekends. You know you can handle her; you always could. And of course she'll make friends and be out of your hair a lot of the time, and she's surely old enough to stay by herself occasionally when you want to go out. And you will, because you're going to knock 'em dead in Atlanta. She isn't going to be any trouble. I've already talked to her about it."

"No trouble," I whispered. "Papa, that's all she knows how to be. In a new city, a big one, with all those new kids and . . . I don't know, the drugs and the rock concerts, and the hippies and the war protests and civil rights . . . she'll be like a bomb with the fuse lit. I can't work and run around bailing Laura out all the time; it's going to be different up there. I'll be trying to get a career going—"

"And fighting off the guys. I know," he said jocularly. But he would not look at me.

"She promised," he said. "I told her all that, and she swore on her mother's Bible that she would do everything her teachers and you told her to do, and not make any trouble at all. I believe her. She knows I'll have her out of there and in Saint Ida's before she can blink if she makes one misstep. And I will. That's a promise. But of course, if you really think it's too much—"

Saint Ida's. A New Orleans convent school so thoroughly and murderously cloistered that not even fathers and brothers were allowed to go further in than the beautiful old courtyard. Academically first rate, socially beyond reproach, culturally luminous in matters pertaining to the late Renaissance and backward from that. The nuns of Saint Ida's had no truck with Rousseau and his kindred romantic *sauvages*, nor with much that followed them. The sixth and seventh decades of the twentieth century simply did not exist. Little outside the thick, high walls did. I had known three girls at LSU who had gone there; two were said to be lovers and the other dropped out pregnant during her first year. Stories of suicides and breakdowns among its alumni made the rounds regularly. Laura would not last a month there.

"It's not too much," I said in a low voice, looking down at my new rope-soled wedgies. "I wouldn't want her at Saint Ida's."

"Neither would I, really, but she's as good as there the instant she causes you any trouble," my father said.

"Private school must be awfully expensive in Atlanta," I said, only then feeling the heat and anger. "Are you sure you can afford it?"

He flushed.

"I can handle it," he said. "Don't you worry about that."

"I won't, then," I said, and thought with a small curl of malice that I knew just how he could afford it. Cap'n Andy, or whatever he called her, obviously had truly big bucks, and counted them well spent if they kept a troublesome adolescent out of her venue. I would, I thought, be harboring a remittance sister.

"Why didn't you tell me?" I asked Laura later, when I had gone upstairs and found her crouching at the top of the stairs, listening.

"I didn't want you to worry," she said, looking up at me through her thick gold lashes.

"Bullshit," I said, forgetting my resolution not to use sorority language in front of her. "That's *just* what you want me to do. C'mon. Why didn't you tell me?"

She was silent. The skin at the base of her nostrils whitened. Finally she said, "I was afraid if you had time to think about it you wouldn't let me come to Atlanta with you, and I'd have to go live with him and *her*. I know she doesn't want me, but I was afraid he'd have to take me if you didn't, or put me in some boarding school. If I had to go to Saint Ida's I'd jump out the highest window there. If I had to go on that stupid boat with her I'd drown myself. I really would, you know."

I didn't know, not really, but I did know that Laura had long been half in love with easeful death, a line she espoused after I read *Ode to a Nightingale* to her when she was six. I thought that the darkness of death called out to a corresponding darkness in her, without her understanding its import in the least. I have always been afraid that the part of Laura that dances with self-destruction might one day win. That, knowing nothing of halfway measures, she might well jump onto broken old paving stones or into the warm, deep Gulf.

"Well, you don't have to jump because I said you could come, as you well know, since you've been listening," I said. "What about it, Pie? Do you think you can hold it in the road so I can have a job and live like a grownup? I really will have to call Papa if you can't. This is the real world now."

"I can," she said fervently. "I will. I'll grow up fast. I'll be so grownup and responsible you won't believe it's me. You can get to be president of the world and I'll be a great actress. Westminster has a super drama department. They win stuff all the time. They'll be auditioning in September for *Li'l Abner*. I'm going to be in that play, Merritt. The brochure says eighth grade and up is eligible."

I had to smile at her, even though I did not for a moment believe she would be capable of keeping her promise about responsibility. But I did believe that she would try. And her ardor was infectious; it always was. And there was something else. Much later, a continent away, she would fling it at me: "It wasn't all give! You got your kicks for years through me! You lived a life through me you never could have had on your own!" Her words stung, but even in my anger I had to admit there was truth in them. During the years with Laura I soared to heights and sank to depths that I would never have reached on my own. It was as powerful a glue as the protective instinct she called out in me, and my love for her when she was at her best. I've always thought that if we had been nearer in age I couldn't have stayed close to her, but there was never any filial competitiveness between Laura and me. On my side it was all parent; on hers, all child.

"So who're you going to be? Daisy Mae, no doubt," I said, ruffling her silky hair.

"Uh-uh. Moonbeam McSwine. She gets to show off everything she's got. And you've got to admit I've got plenty."

She pulled her Peter Max T-shirt tight over her breasts and hips. She was right. In the last year she had bloomed physically into the woman she would be, and that woman lacked nothing. I felt again the unease I had felt when I looked at her earlier that day, at graduation. It wasn't, after all, a child I would be tending in Atlanta.

"Let's get one thing straight," I said. "There's not going to be any funny stuff about sex. The first time there is I'm calling Papa. I might put up with the other stuff more than once, but the first strike is out when it comes to sex. I'm going to have to be at work late a lot of the time, and I'll be going out with my own friends, and you're going to be on your honor. I need to know I can trust you not to go wild with boys."

"Are you a virgin, Merritt?" she said sweetly, crinkling her eyes at me.

"What I am is twenty-two years old," I said coldly, angry to the core of me. The backseat of the pot-smogged Chevrolet and the damp, hot hands of the man whose name I had nearly forgotten floated into my mind and were gone again. "It's none of your business whether I am or not. I know how to handle myself. Nothing you've ever done has shown me you can do that."

"Bet you're on the pill," she singsonged. "Bet you're not taking any chances on getting PG. Wouldn't it be simpler just to get some for me? Then you wouldn't have to worry about me getting knocked up."

I was up and halfway down the stairs toward the living room, where my father still sat in front of the TV, before I heard her first shriek of fright. It was so desperate that I stopped and turned around to look at her. She clung rigidly to the banister, and her face and knuckles and lips were bleached white.

"I won't ever say anything like that again," she whispered.

"You won't if you're coming with me," I said grimly.

She dropped her head onto her chest and let the curtain of hair hide her eyes. But I saw the silver snail's tracks of tears on her chin anyway. I reached over and wiped them away with the tips of my fingers.

"Why do you do that?" I said gently. "Why do you always push things with me?"

She flipped the hair off her face and looked squarely at me. There was nothing childish in the topaz eyes.

"I have to know I can't run you off," she said. "I have to know you'll stay with me no matter what I do. I have to know you won't leave me."

"You must know that by now. The only exception is the sex business. I *will* send you away over that if I have to. But you must know that I'll stay with you otherwise. Haven't I always?"

After a silence she said, "*Are* you on the pill?"

"*Laura*—"

"I need to know," she said fiercely. "I need to know you won't get pregnant and have some awful baby you'll have to take care of!"

"I'm not on the pill and I'm not going to get pregnant," I said in annoyance. "But if I did, I wouldn't stop taking care of you. You could help me take care of the baby—"

"No! No baby."

"That's what I just said," I said, and led her back to bed and tucked her in. She was asleep before I closed her door. But it was dawn before I finally slept.

She was as good as her word, or almost. Through most of the sprawl and scrabble of the seventies, Laura lived with me in the pretty little carriage house I found behind a big brick Buckhead estate and managed, with more success than not, to stay out of harm's way. She never did get into the creamy little clique of sorority girls at Westminster whose fathers were the cadet corps of the city's leadership; she went to few of the house parties and debutante balls at the Piedmont Driving Club or the Cherokee Club, and she did no volunteer work for hospitals and hotlines. She wore no starched shirtwaists and wrap skirts and kilts, either, and her grades were just enough to keep her in school. But she grew fully into the voluptuous beauty that her preteens had portended, and she had many suitors from the big houses on Habersham and West Wesley Roads. She ignored them and became thick with a small clique of taciturn, bearded, bell-bottomed, pot-smoking renegades, the ones on art and theater and dance scholarships, the ones who hung out in the burgeoning Virginia-Highlands and Little Five Points sections after school, talking endlessly about creativity and their stake in it, about their art, about their work. I was never quite sure what most of them worked at, but work they did. Or at least, they did not seem to play. They were the most detached, uncommunicative group of young people I ever saw, except among themselves. They might have existed in any decade; in any decade they would have been the ones who painted the flats and fiddled with the lights and drowned themselves in booming, jittering music, their ears stoppered with plugs and their faces empty and inward. They acted and rehearsed and danced and plucked or tooted at instruments; they stayed late and alone in stark, white-lit painting and sculpture laboratories, on empty stages. In my time we would have called them beats, LSU being a good ten years behind the rest of the country in its argot. I think they called themselves freaks. The decade washed over them carrying the flotsam and jetsam of revolt: Kent State and terrorists and protests and pornography and drugs and gas shortages and streakers and Richard Nixon's disgrace and fall and disco and *Roots* and NOW. And they scarcely noticed. They worked. I did not know whether to be glad or sorry.

Laura did indeed make the cast of *L'il Abner*, and every-

thing else that Westminster mounted on its sleek new proscenium thrust stage. She was electric on a stage. She was beautiful and more than that; she was compelling far past her
years. She had an eccentric, focused talent that would have
been notable in one ten years older. She went about with the
pack of darkling young who were her constant companions,
her family, and, I suspected, her safety net. If she had a
boyfriend I never knew it. If the group had sex, casual or otherwise, among themselves, I never knew that either. When
Laura wasn't in a play she was in rehearsals, writing scripts
and screenplays, at the movies with the group, or talking
about all of it in one coffee shop or basement rec room or
black-painted, spotlit bedroom or another. I might have
wished a more balanced life for her, better grades, more college and matrimonial prospects, but in truth, I was mainly
relieved that she was happy in her amniotic bubble of obsession, and thankful that she felt safe there. I knew she did feel
safe. Laura safe was Laura grooving on an even keel. I seldom
went over to Westminster for anything but a conference on
her grades or to see her perform.

"She should go on to a good drama school," one of her
advisors told me when she was a sophomore. "She has a real
gift. I think she could be one of the ones who makes it on TV
or Broadway. Maybe even movies. Providing she's tough
enough to stick out the lean times, of course, and that's something neither I nor she can know yet. What's your feeling
about that?"

"I don't know either," I said. "I expect if she had some
support, some help, somebody with her all the time, she could
stick it."

"This she'd have to do alone," he said. "And she'd have
to do it in New York or L.A. She can't get what she needs
here. She's talking about the Actor's Workshop in New York.
I think she could get in. Could you and her father swing that,
do you think?"

"We could swing the money," I said slowly, thinking of
the never-ceasing largesse of Cap'n Andy that kept Laura off
her boat and out of her salt-blond hair. "I don't know about
her going away by herself, though. She's never been alone—"

"Could you handle New York by yourself if you went to Actor's Workshop?" I asked her toward the end of her junior year. "I mean, with just a roommate? You know I can't pick up and leave the agency and go with you."

"Sure I could," she said. "I could come home whenever I wanted to. You could come up. Would you let me go, that's the question."

"You'll be eighteen then," I said. "It will be your decision, not mine. If you think you can handle it, it's entirely your business."

She frowned. "But I want you to tell me it's all right to go."

"I can't tell you that," I said. "You need to know that inside yourself."

"No, you tell me," she said stubbornly.

"I'm your sister, Laura, not your mother," I said crisply. It seemed to me, suddenly, that we both needed to hear me say that.

"Well, I know that," Laura said, and flung away trailing the fringes of her tattered blue jeans over her bare feet. But at the door she stopped and looked back at me. There were fine white rings around her eyes; I had not seen them there for a long time. I would, I knew, do a lot of thinking about New York. I hoped she would, too.

In the end, it was academic, because my father died the next winter. He had a heart attack somewhere at sea off Baja, California, and was dead by the time the rescue helicopter came scissoring in. I was shocked and stricken, but somehow dimly, as if he had existed on another plane than Laura and me, and perhaps by then he did. A death unseen, I have learned, is a death unrealized. I watched my mother die, touched her new coldness. It is not she who comes to trouble, tentatively, my dreams, to seek validation. It is, even now, my father.

Laura was cool and flip, whether protectively or not I could not tell.

"Yo, ho ho," she said. "We'll get enough money for Actor's Workshop, won't we?"

We didn't. He left the Baton Rouge house and his meager

estate to Cap'n Andy, and she promptly sold the house, withdrew her support to Laura, and bought a bigger boat. By the time her lawyers got around to telling us that we were essentially on our own, she was casting her net in the rich waters off Sardinia. I found it was hardly difficult at all to bury the pain of that, but Laura was frantic.

"What am I going to do?" she sobbed. "My grades aren't good enough for a scholarship. Can you send me? Do you make enough?"

"I just can't, Pie," I said, in anguish at her pain, but somehow relieved, too. The thought of Laura in New York alone had been a stone in my heart for a long time. "I could probably send you to Georgia, or Georgia State, but I'm not making the kind of money for anything else. I don't even know if I can swing the next two years at Westminster."

"Then get another job," she shouted, her face suddenly contorted with rage and grief. "Work nights! Borrow it! Or I'll run away, I swear I will; I'll go to New York or Hollywood on my own! Bootsie Cohn is going after graduation; I'll go with her! I'll be a hooker if I have to! I hate him! I hate her! I hate you!"

Her words were a knife in my heart, but I was angry with her, too. I loved her and the need to protect her ran deep, but I had had her in the fullest sense of the word since her babyhood, and I was suddenly weary of the roller coaster that was life with Laura.

"Then by all means hit the road," I said coldly. "Maybe you could send me a buck or two along the way. You could probably pay me back for what I've spent on you in twenty or thirty years."

She slammed out of the house, and did not come home for three days. After learning from Westminster that she had been in school all three days, and calling around until I reached the mother of the emaciated redhead to whose house she had gone, I did not try to contact her further. She'll come home when her clothes get dirty, I thought. She'll come home when she needs some money. I went to work, came home, cooked my dinners, and settled down with my checkbook and records to see how we were going to be able to live. I will at least have some peace and privacy for a little while, I thought. But I did not enjoy it. Her absence clamored in the house. Even gone, Laura pulled at me like the moon the tide. She still does.

She did come home, eventually, but that was the real beginning of her long, careening odyssey away from me. She was either sullen or rebellious, spent more and more time with her flock of gifted starlings, and began to get into trouble. She skipped school, flew into rages when she was there, smoked cigarettes in the restrooms and on the grounds, smelled of a sweeter, slyer smoke when she finally came in. The conferences concerning her behavior began. I was soon averaging one a week. Luckily, my boss was a laid-back ex–flower child who did not care when his staff got their work done, so long as they did. I did a lot of mine at home, at night, trying not to watch the clock as I waited for my sister to come home, trying to think that things would soon right themselves. I suppose I always knew that I was a timid disciplinarian, that I feared her pain more than her capacity for self-destruction. I had always been able to redeem Laura with love.

The night she came in frankly drunk, with magenta suck marks on her neck and shoulders and her now-blond hair in her eyes and her skirt conspicuously backward, I lowered the boom on her. My heart quailed, but I hardened it.

"Maybe I can't pay for Saint Ida's," I said, "but I can manage one or two boarding schools you would like a whole lot less. There's one in the mountains where you work in the kitchen and the pigsty to help pay your tuition. I don't think it's got a proscenium thrust to its name. Stop this crap or you're up there, I promise you. I called them today. And if you don't think I mean it, try me. I told you I wasn't going to put up with any slutty stuff, and that includes drinking."

I hoped she would mistake the tremor in my voice for anger.

"You can't make me," she slurred. "You're not my fucking mother."

"No? I fucking well thought I was, the way you've been behaving," I threw back at her furiously. "Decide now, toots, I'm not going to tell you again."

"How're you gonna stop me?" she said truculently, but I thought I saw hesitation on her face. Even like this, slack-faced and with her mouth pulped and smeared, she was still one of the prettiest things I had ever seen. Fear and anger and love warred inside me.

"I'm going to stop paying your tuition at Westminster," I said. "And you can kiss your allowance good-bye. I'm going to tell the mothers of all your little playmates not to let you in their houses. And I'm going to call the cops the first night you aren't in this house. You're underage, and they'll pick you up within the hour. I don't think you'd like juvie any more than you would Saint Ida's or Lottie Brewster Academy."

She stared at me for a long time, and then dropped her eyes and ran, stumbling, to her room and slammed her door. She did not do it again.

For a long time after that she seemed fairly content, if never quite the winged thing she had been. She finished Westminster with barely passing grades and a string of triumphs on the stage, and started at Georgia State, with resignation if little enthusiasm, in the fall of her eighteenth year. There was a good, if not remarkable, drama department there, and considerable lagniappe in the person of a charismatic young professor who eventually directed her in some truly luminous, innovative plays. Her awesome focus kicked back in and her strange, canted gift throve. She won raves in the local newspapers and more when the troupe toured around the South. She was invited to try out for several local professional productions and the cast of one national touring company, and garnered high praise there, too. She had, apparently, no time for anything but the theater; for that entire first year I do not think she went out with a young man. I praised her, went to all her performances, stayed up to have cocoa and cookies with her when she came late from rehearsals and performances. Often we would talk and laugh until nearly dawn. My own work did not seem to suffer, nor did hers. I was, after all, still only twenty-eight, and she was eighteen. The gap between us seemed far smaller than it had when she was a child. She had, as she had once promised, grown up fast. For the first time I felt that the bond between us was more that of best friends, of true sisters, than that of parent and child. My own star was rising steadily at my agency, with a creative directorship in view, and I had several pleasant, if not flammable, relationships with attractive young men. And I had my sustaining friendship with Crisscross. She had her theater and her future. Things were, for a time, really good between us. Looking back, I can see that it was the best time by far.

And then I met Pom Fowler, and it was as if the year of peace and affection had never been. From the beginning, she hated him. She had not liked most of my other men friends, but there had been none of the spitting animosity that Pom called out. More than that, he seemed somehow to actually frighten her.

"He looks like that stupid little asshole on the top of wedding cakes," she said scornfully, her voice shaking. "He's ugly and stupid and he smells like a hospital, and goes on and on about the poor people till you want to barf. Shit, why can't he pay that kind of attention to you? To us? We're poor, too! He doesn't even act like I'm in the room. And those snotty-nosed little brats . . . how can you oooh and ahhh over them like that? They're horrible children! They hate you, anybody could see that."

I knew that she had grasped the seriousness of Pom's and my relationship, even though I was careful to downplay it and he, having been warned, tried his best to do so, too. He succeeded only in seeming to ignore her; even I could see that. Only the two little boys made much over Laura, and they could not keep away from her. Something in her face and manner drew them like magnets. They were at her heels constantly when Pom brought them over. But she was so sharp with them that he did not do it often. We stayed mostly at his house, where she would not go. She did not tell me why until nearly a year after she met Pom.

"You think I get a big thrill out of watching those brats act like you're going to poison them and waiting for you and him to go upstairs to hump and leave me with them?" she hissed then, on a day when I had asked her, once again, to spend Sunday with us and the boys at the house in Garden Hills.

"You're being terribly unfair," I said to her. "They're just little boys who've lost their mother, and now they're afraid they're going to lose their father, too. They're much better about me than they were. You can see that. It's going to be fine eventually, I promise. Why can't you see that Pom likes you and wants to be friends?"

"Wrong! He doesn't want to be my friend, he wants me to be *gone!* He doesn't give a shit about anything but getting you to take care of his precious little house apes so he can go make millions healing the fucking sick! But he's too big a coward to tell me to butt out himself; he wants you to do it. You think I can't tell, but I can."

She was so upset that there was a choking whistling sound in her chest, and her white face was splotched with red welts. I put my arms around her and drew her down on the sofa beside me so I could look into her face.

"He doesn't have a cowardly bone in his body," I said. "He's the bravest man I've ever known and the best. He's been beaten and hosed in the civil rights marches; he was in Africa in the Peace Corps. He's spent the last two years working eighteen hours a day in a clinic that treats people for free, down in the worst of the housing projects where all the rioting is, and the drugs and the crime and everything. He wants to spend his life doing that; he's going to establish his own free clinic when he can. He doesn't care anything about money; he'll probably never have a dime to call his own. And he doesn't want you to butt out. He wants you to butt in. He wants you to come and live with us for as long as you like . . . if we should get married, that is."

She stared at me for a long time, and then she said, softly and bitterly, "If you do that you will never see me again. If you move in there and play wifey to that man and mother to those retarded kids, I'll be gone before you've unpacked your suitcases. If you'd rather take care of another bitch's little bastards than your own sister, go right ahead and see how long I hang around here."

I looked at her in shock and incredulity. Her jealousy and terror were so complete and devouring that I could not seem to breathe the air in which they reverberated. I don't know,

now, why I was so utterly dumbfounded by her words, but I was.

Finally I whispered, "What has gotten into you? You're nineteen years old! You're a junior in college, with a wonderful career ahead of you; you've been planning to go to New York when you graduate for a long time now. You don't need me to take care of you any longer. For goodness sake, Laura! You're my sister, not my child. You don't need me!"

"You promised," she said, the tears beginning.

Pom and I were married in the little Mikell Chapel of Saint Philip's Cathedral the following June, with only his parents and brother and sister-in-law and the boys and Crisscross present. Laura was not there. She had left a week before to go with the vulpine, redheaded Bootsie Cohn to California where, she said, Bootsie had been promised a part in a movie being shot in the Sonoma wine country. The second unit director, who was Bootsie's boyfriend, had promised he could get Laura a job in the production company.

"Give my regards to Dr. Kildare and tell him to go fuck himself," the note that I found on the kitchen table the next morning said. "Tell him not to worry, he won't see me again. Neither will you. I'm taking your Mastercard. Maybe I'll even pay you back one day, but don't hold your breath."

It was signed Laura Louise Mason.

And, except for a very few times when she came through town on some theater movie business or another, I did not touch the sweet white flesh of my sister Laura again for a long, long time, though I sometimes glimpsed a bit of it, briefly, on film.

There was never a day between that one and this that I have not missed her.

On the hot afternoon in the early summer of 1995, when I went down through the parched grass to the Chattahoochee River behind our house to set the latest *Rattus ratti* free, I still missed her as sharply as ever. I could almost see the child she had been skipping ahead of me on the path in the heat shimmer; I could almost see the angry, beautiful nineteen-year-old she had been when she left.

"I miss my girls," I whispered to the big black rats I was

bearing to freedom in the wire trap. "I miss Laura. I miss Glynn."

My sister. My daughter. My sister, Laura, my daughter, Glynn, the thought of whom still, after sixteen years, gave me a small, fresh shock of joy and surprise. My daughter, my good, good girl . . .

The rats, who had been quiet, looked at me with their whiskered Chinese faces and black, glinting little eyes, and began again to scrabble and squeak in their prison.

"Chill out," I said, shaking the cages slightly. "You're almost home free."

2

Pom was obsessed with the rats. The first thing he did when he got up in the morning and came home at night was to check for bodies. When the first poison failed to give satisfaction, the exterminators brought out different traps, matte black and high-tech, and placed them about, baited with poisoned birdseed. Birdseed was, they said knowingly, the rat chow of choice. Ours were not interested, but Mommee was: The first night the traps were set out we heard a muffled thump and a howl and found Mommee shrieking in the upstairs hall, her hand stuck in one of the traps. After that we set them out of sight, but the rats did not bite. Instead they gnawed electrical cords and burrowed through two inches of carpet and flooring to get into a closet where I had stored and forgotten a waxed wheel of cheddar from Vermont. We found their neat little oblong droppings in different places every morning. The few who did take the bait inevitably died, reeking, in the walls.

The rats came, the exterminators said, from the river and the grass and weeds around it. Another big development was going up just upstream from us, and when the trees were felled and the ground cleared the rats came downstream looking for more hospitable housing. Pom had suffered the squadrons of invading raccoons with fairly good grace, because they had not yet managed to get into the house, but the rats maddened him.

"Somebody damned well should have told us about that development before we closed on this house," he raged. "But oh, no; everybody swore that all the rest of the river land belonged to a little old lady who would never sell. I wouldn't have bought this house if I'd thought we were going to be covered up with subdivisions and rats."

"Well, little old ladies will go and die," I said, giving his untidy hair a ruffle. "Apparently her children didn't share her ecological ideals."

"We might as well have stayed in Garden Hills," he grumbled.

I wish we had, I thought, but did not say.

Pom bought the house on the river five years before, when a fellow physician at Buckhead Hospital retired and moved to Captiva. He went with his friend out to see his house on the river and called the real estate agent that night. He drove me and the children out to see it the next day, as a surprise. The four of us stood in the pale lemon sunshine of a Georgia autumn and looked at the big stone pile fitted into the edge of the river forest and fronted with green winter rye as smooth as a goofy golf course. Behind it the hardwoods flamed and the river ran swift and silent between its overgrown banks. There were no other houses in sight. Plantings were lush and perfectly tended, chrysanthemums burned in the neatly mulched borders and in big Chinese urns on the terrace, and a small oblong attached to the Realtor's sign said "heated pool." The house was intimidating to me; it seemed enormous in the emptiness and the river silence. It was well designed, obviously the work of an architect and not a builder drunk on châteaux and faux Tudor; it fit its site nicely, and there was not a Palladian window in it. I thought it was handsome, and the boys and Glynn frankly gaped in awe. But it did not then and does not now look like home.

"Do you like it?" Pom grinned.

"For what? To live in?" said seventeen-year-old Jeff.

"Where are all the neighbors?" said eleven-year-old Glynn.

"There's a pool! Cool! The guys will all want to come home with me," said Chip, who was twenty and in his sophomore year at Wake Forest. His fraternity was so far the dominant institution in his life.

"Pom, I could never keep this thing clean," I said. I don't know why I said it. I had Ina three mornings a week now, and I knew that she had more time. In truth, I loved the shabby, bursting Cape Cod in Garden Hills where we had raised his sons and our daughter. I loved my neighbors and the aging, jointly owned pool and playground and the overwhelming sense of community that emanated from the neighborhood like sweet breath. I did not want to move. We had never even seriously talked about moving.

It was obvious that Pom loved the house. We needed the room, he said; the boys already needed a place to entertain their friends and Glynn soon would. Westminster was just over the hill; I wouldn't spend hours car pooling anymore. There was luxury shopping and some good new restaurants over in nearby Vinings. He was sick of the fumes and clamor of the city; he wanted us to have the peace of the river and the woods while we were still young enough to enjoy them. He had always missed the unspoiled outdoors of his boyhood. He could have the hunting dogs he had long wanted; Glynn could have her pony at last. I could garden to my heart's content. I could have a splendid custom office for the freelance writing I planned to do, now that the children were older. And it undeniably lent the clinics an air of respectability and substance to have their director living in a house like this. It would be good for business and even better for entertaining, and he was going to have to do increasingly more of that.

"It's not going to hurt Glynn's prospects to live here, either," he said, smiling at her and then at me.

"Prospects for what?" Glynn and I said together.

"Oh . . . the Peachtree Debutante Club and the Junior League and all that stuff, an appropriate marriage," he said, flipping the back of Glynn's smooth, ash-blond Dorothy Hamill cut. "I know you don't care about that stuff now, Punkin, but you will."

"No, I won't," she said with her lips, but there was no

sound behind it. I don't think Pom noticed. I looked at him in amazement. I did not know he cared about that stuff, either. I didn't know he used terms like "appropriate marriage." I didn't know he wanted a house like this. When had all this happened?

We closed on the house the following week and moved in just after Thanksgiving. Our first Christmas there looked like Lord and Taylor's Fifth Avenue window. The tree that stood in the two-story foyer was fifteen feet tall. Anything else would have looked like a toy. The children and I crept about the huge new spaces, getting lost and looking involuntarily over our shoulders and out into the dark winter woods, where nothing or anything might be watching us. Pom worked as late and long as he ever had, but he never failed to take a turn around his castle when he got in at night. The rest of us came to appreciate much about it; Pom fell deeper and deeper in love. He hated the encroaching armies of shoddy, expensive subdivisions that swarmed around it as a cultivated Roman might hate the battering Visigoths, and I think the rats came to be a symbol of all that threatened his new kingdom. He would not rest until he ousted them.

For my part, I was glad to have the prospect of neighbors, even the kind who would live with Palladian windows and fake crenellations, and their vanguards, the rats, never appalled and disgusted me as they did Pom. I even began, secretly and with not a little shame, to root for them in the ongoing war that they could not win.

Finally Pom settled on a fleet of small wire humane traps baited with unpoisoned birdseed, that he scattered all over the house except in Mommee's regular orbit. They worked well. We caught rats in droves. He fastened ropes to the traps and simply took them and their writhing cargo down to the river and lowered them. When the traps stopped bobbing and bucking, he hauled them up and dumped out his drowned victims and brought the traps back and set them out again that night. But these dawn executions cut into his working time, and he soon turned the task over to me. I protested, but he held firm.

"Come on, Merritt, surely you can lower a rat trap in the river," he said. "It only takes a minute or two. Just dump 'em in the weeds afterwards. I don't want to have to do it at midnight. You can take the dogs for a run while you're at it. I really don't ask you to do much of anything extra."

He didn't. Mommee was the only exception, and sanctioned time away from her was hardly an imposition. Shamed, I agreed to take rat duty. The very first day I did it the solution struck me. By now, I felt a special bond with the rats. I thought that the good souls who made up the Underground Railroad might have felt something of the same affection for the fleeing slaves who passed through their venues. It did occur to me, early on, that the rats I freed might be simply circling back into the house, but that did not bother me as much as the thought of more poison or neck-breaking traps. It wasn't as if we didn't have room for them.

On this day the dogs larruped ahead of me, running in crazy circles in the tall grass and broom sedge that bordered the path, their noses scouring the earth and their fringed tails waving. The sun bounced off their sleek coats. The drone of insects and the buzzing of cicadas and the soft purling of the river as it ran over the small rapids off our bank were the only sounds. Even the rats fell silent. It was very hot and still and seemed no time at all.

I reached the bank of the river and knelt and opened the traps. The two rats blinked and wriggled their snouts for a moment, but they did not move.

"Haul ass, bubbas," I whispered, and shook the cages, and they streaked for freedom in the weeds, as fast in their clumsiness as small alligators. I looked after them until the underbrush had closed around them, and then I dumped the traps into the river and pulled them out so that they would be wet when I went back and stretched out on the bank in the shade and closed my eyes. I heard the dogs come bounding past me, heard the twin *choonks* as they went into the river, but I did not open my eyes. I lay still, listening to the cicadas. The heat pressed down on me like a fist. It struck me that I had never heard July flies at the beginning of June before.

It had been a strange winter and spring. Christmas Day had seen an afternoon temperature of seventy-eight, and by February first the daffodils and crocuses were in full bloom. By March everything was lush and green, and then a series of late ice storms blasted much of the green black. April, usually as wet and green as the bottom of a lake, was so dry that grass seared and new blooms withered. May, usually balmy and perfect, was cold again. And now, in early June, there had been a string of days so heat-stifled and stale that it might be late August. But no summer storms swept in from the west to relieve us.

Nationally things were no better. Everything seemed out of kilter. A spring and summer of record-breaking heat was forecast for the West, while in the East neither the National Weather Service nor the *Farmers' Almanac* nor the weather wackos foresaw an end to the blistering drought. Some said it was El Niño, some the widening hole in the ozone layer, some a Muslim conspiracy to bring the industrial West to its knees. Everybody had a theory. A renegade climatologist in Mono Lake, California, was predicting catastrophic earthquakes all over the country before fall. Since he was a pupil of the gentleman who had predicted the disaster on the New Madrid fault years before, which had not occurred, the media did not give him much credibility, but accorded him endless ink nonetheless. Even those of us who had tired of the litany of doom the strange, unsettled weather called forth felt a slight, ceaseless visceral unease. The hairs on my arms and at the base of my scalp crawled often, for no reason at all.

"Don't you feel it?" I had said to Pom at breakfast just the weekend before, holding up my goose-bumped arms for his inspection.

"Nope. But you're a walking barometer. Why don't you go swimming? You haven't used the pool in ages."

"Mommee always wants to go in when I do," I said. "I'm afraid she'll get in over her head and I won't be able to get her out."

"Let her swim with you, it might calm her," he said, making notes on an edge of the newspaper. I saw that he was adding up a column of figures. "Take Ina in with you. You could surely handle her together."

"Can you see Ina in a bathing suit, towing Mommee around our pool?" I said, beginning to laugh. Ina was built like an interior lineman, wore faultlessly tailored blazers and slacks and Doc Martens, and was active in NOW. She referred to herself as a personal household assistant. I didn't care what she called herself as long as she stayed; she was worth every cent of the scalp-crawling salary we paid her. She could have tossed Mommee across the room if she had wanted to, but she did not like dealing with her. Mommee needed, she insisted, her own attendant, a practical nurse or some other substantial companion. I agreed with her, but Pom did not.

"I will not have a stranger changing my mother's diapers," he said, and that was that. Diaper duty fell to me. I didn't really mind. Disposables were not difficult to deal with, and Mommee was usually docile with me. It was implicit in the contract, after all.

"You let Ina get away with murder," he said, not looking up. "For what we pay her she ought to do a water ballet every afternoon, if you want her to."

"Yeah, right," I said. He kissed me on the top of my head and went off to the clinic, still staring at the figures on the scrap of newsprint.

Now I lay on my back with my arm over my eyes, seeing wheeling black spots against dark red and feeling sweat gather at my hairline and thinking about earthquakes. I thought about Laura, too. The familiar dull worry began, deep inside me; the old pain bloomed softly along its pathway of scar tissue. Irritation followed. It was just like Laura to locate herself squarely on top of the San Andreas fault.

Laura lived just outside Palm Springs now, in what looked to be a kind of latter-day Anasazi dwelling carved out of the base of the great jagged mountains that swept abruptly into the desert sky. It looked, in the photographs she had sent when she moved there, strange and ancient and enchanting. It was a condo, and was, she wrote, so expensive that she was sure Sonny shit whenever he wrote out her alimony check. Sonny was her ex-husband, a minor filmmaker and major coke addict. He was her third ex. The other two had been in "the industry," as Laura called it, but in more major positions than Sonny.

Laura seemed to be marrying in the same descending order that her career followed. She was a photographer's stylist now, and in her spare time made what she called earth adornments, jewelry made from desert stones and horn and shell, and wrote New Age poetry. In her photos she was still, at thirty-eight, as blindingly beautiful to me as she had been at eighteen, but it was the tragedy of her life that the camera did not find her so.

"The camera doesn't love me," she had written disconsolately after her first film, a slight thing about three Southern sorority girls during the civil rights era, bombed spectacularly. "I simply don't photograph. I had a little surgery; David thought it might be something to do with my chin and nose, but that wasn't it. It comes from the inside, David says. Whatever I have on the stage doesn't get through the lens."

David was her first husband, the director of the failed sorority movie. He was on a fast track then, young and promising and hip, and he left his second trophy wife to marry Laura. Both of them were hot, so the buzz went. The little movie's failure did not even slow David's trajectory; his is an awesome name in Hollywood now. But it shod Laura with lead. There had been a few other small movies, because she was obviously a gifted actress, and a good bit of television, but nothing stuck. She had done highly lauded stage work in L.A., and still did some, mainly with touring companies, and a few commercials, but there again the fickle camera refused to connect with her. Now, in addition to the stylist's job and the jewelry and poetry, she did dinner theaters around the state, and a very occasional low-budget movie, and worked sometimes as script supervisor or makeup or wardrobe stylist, and was thinking of becoming an agent. After all, she wrote, she knew virtually everybody who was anybody in the industry, and David and Marcus, the middle-level studio executive who followed David, owed her. Her contacts were faultless.

"And you have to admit I can still hack it in the looks department," she said in the latest of her letters. I did have to admit it. Despite the periodic dark times she went through, she looked stunning, vivid, and bursting with health and vitality. But I could not read her sherry eyes. They shone with such an opaque glitter that light seemed to bounce back from them.

"Coke," Pom said matter-of-factly when I showed him the photo.

"No. She promised not," I said.

"I know it when I see it, Merritt," he said. "I see it all day."

"I don't believe it. She couldn't hold down all the jobs she does if she was on coke."

"Sure she could, for a good while. It's a powerful stimulant. You can run on it twenty-four hours a day. If she's just started back, she could go for months yet. We'll know when the telegrams for money start coming, won't we?"

Pom and I had bailed Laura out of two bad times, when she lost jobs and husbands and condos at the same time. He had always thought drugs were involved. I had put them down to her innate fragility and her inability still to handle being alone for long periods. She was self-destructive then, erratic and inconstant and somehow insatiable. But I had not believed she would turn to drugs or alcohol. She had always been so careful about what she ate and drank, had exercised so meticulously, had had a daunting regimen of self-care and anointing. And it had been years, literally, since the last telegram.

Now, though, I lay in the thick heat of Georgia and thought of my little sister in her magical cave, astride the place where two great tectonic plates met, self-destructing, if my husband was right, all over the high desert.

"I should go get her," I said to Pom when we had that conversation about her. "Just go out there and snatch her back. She doesn't do this when there's somebody around to bolster her. I could steady her. She could make good money in local theater and television. She could help with Mommee, maybe, until she gets her own place. And you know Glynn adores her."

It was true; the few times that Laura had visited us, flitting through town like a migrating butterfly, Glynn had been fascinated with her. And she had seemed to adore Glynn, spending endless hours with her, dressing up and showing my shy child her exotic case full of stage makeup, rearranging Glynn's thick, tawny hair. Glynn's first word had been 'Aura. She still called Laura that sometimes. Laura actually courted Glynn, almost flirting with her, watching me to see how I reacted. I didn't care then. I was glad for the attraction between them. I still thought something might bring Laura home one day.

I still did not see the danger in her.

"Not on your life," Pom said, when I spoke of bringing Laura back to Atlanta. "She made her bed. Or beds. Let her lie in them. I'm not having an addict in the house with Glynn."

I did not think he really considered Laura an addict. He had always seemed to like her, to be fascinated with her even in the face of her rejection of him. He was impatient with her inability to order her life, but he had not demurred when the requests for money came in. He simply did not want his own orderly life disarrayed, I thought, especially with Mommee worsening. And he was, of course, accustomed to command. All doctors are.

Nevertheless, the remark about Laura's being an addict stung.

"No addicts in the house with your daughter, nossir," I muttered after he had left for work. "Just a madwoman."

But I was not ready to say this to him. The intimation that his mother might be mad gave him real pain. Sooner or later, I thought, he would work through his denial, and then he himself would see what needed to be done. Action would follow swiftly. It always did when Pom saw the need for it.

The sun moved to the west and broke free of the shading trees. I drifted, sweating and flinching away from the hum of midges and gnats. Their sound, and that of the chuckling of the river, seemed to swell and fade in my ears like the tide. Finally it stopped. I dozed, and did not wake until a shower of droplets hit me. I sat up, blinking stupidly. The dogs were milling about me, shaking themselves. River water was flying everywhere. It felt wonderful, like liquid ice on my sweating skin. The powerful smell of wet dog ran up my nose almost like the scent of skunk, burning not unpleasantly.

All of a sudden I was so hot that I could not bear my clothes, could hardly bear my own skin. I stood up and shucked off my shorts and T-shirt and panties and bra, and hit the water in a flat, clumsy racing dive. I knew that it was deep here off this bank, dark and murky in its depths, undercutting the bank. I had lain here for hours at a time before, watching

for the huge, lazy catfish that hung suspended there sometimes, seemingly trapped in the still, particulate layers of sunlit water before the thick darkness started. The river closed
over me with a shock of coldness that stopped my breath for a
moment. Our cold May still lived here, in the water.

I opened my eyes underwater. It was like looking through
heavy scrim. The water tasted of mud and fish, an oddly clean
taste. I could see the layers of sunlight above me, and in them,
the steadily pumping legs of the dogs. They had joined me in
the water.

I gave a lazy kick and my head broke the surface. The sun
was warm on it and on my shoulders, though the cold still
claimed the lower part of me. It was a wonderful feeling, both
exhilarating and silkily indolent. I was a good swimmer, and
my long bones seemed to float me effortlessly. I had won meets
in high school, and been a lifeguard two years running at our
community pool during my summer vacations from college. I
loved the water. It is like a second element to me.

I turned over and did a fast, easy crawl out into the
middle, where the current was stronger, and then turned
over and churned back to the bank in a back stroke. The
dogs were trailing along behind me, their sleek, wet skulls
beautiful, their healthy teeth shining in their twin grins.
But they were beginning to breathe heavily, and I did not
want them to go far from shore. For a time the three of us
paddled mindlessly in the pool of sunlight near the bank,
lost in pure sensory pleasure. Once or twice I porpoise-dove
down into the darkness and came up trailing bubbles, for
the sheer joy of it.

"I'm forever blowing bubbles," I sang to the dogs.

Samson looked over my shoulder and stiffened, treading
water. He gave a low, breathy *woof*. I turned.

One of the rats was swimming toward us, his wet head
barely breaking the surface. He swam steadily and strongly,
looking directly at me with his glittering eyes. I trod water,
too, watching him in disbelief. I had never heard that rats
swam unless they had to. Certainly not straight toward people and dogs. Could he be rabid? A waterborne rabid rat.
Under the spurt of alarm, I thought of President Jimmy

Carter and the swimming rabbit that the press had made so much of. The banzai bunny, I thought they had called it.

"Shoo!" I shouted, splashing water at the rat. "Go on back!"

The dogs headed purposefully for the swimming rat, ears flattened, eyes intently focused.

"Get out of here before you get retrieved," I shouted, and splashed again, and the rat turned and made smoothly for the bank. He scurried up it and torqued off into the undergrowth. The dogs, bored and tired, abandoned the chase and dropped down on the bank and regarded me alertly, panting. Still I did not come out of the water. It simply felt too good.

"We could start our own theme park, make some bucks," I told Samson and Delilah around a mouthful of brown-tasting river water. "Forget the dolphins. Welcome to Rat World. Come swim with the rats."

This struck me as so funny that I began to laugh aloud, and swallowed water, and floundered out and up the bank and flopped naked in the sun beside them, laughing and coughing. I don't remember ever feeling quite the same kind of suspended well being as I did that afternoon. Only when the big bronze bell that we kept in the kitchen sounded did I remember where I was, and that we were going out to Pom's fundraiser in less than two hours and I had just ruined my hair. And that Mommee was in some sort of uproar again. That was what the bell meant. Ina rang it whenever Mommee had a spell and I was not at hand. Mommee would not calm down, these days, for anyone but Pom or me. Usually that meant me.

"Shit," I said drearily, and climbed to my feet and dragged my dry clothes on over my wet body and started for the house. "This has got to stop."

I had only recently come to feel this. Or rather, I suppose that I had felt it for some time and had not let the feeling form itself into a thought, much less one I would voice to Pom. But Mommee's slide into senility had accelerated rapidly this summer, as if controlled somehow by the strange weather, and few days recently had gone by without alarms and tears and craziness, and such increasing disorientation that I dared not, now, leave her alone at all. Once she had wandered out onto the verandah while I was taking a shower and headed for the river, stumping along at a good clip in her flowered duster, her gilt-blond wig riding high and goofily on her head. Ina had caught her more than halfway to the water. Another time she had turned on all the stove burners and pulled out empty saucepans and set them on the burners. Finally the stink of burning metal brought me at a run; I had thought she was asleep in her room. She usually was, at that time of day. The very next day she had taken my gardening shears and gone out into the back garden and cut the heads off every single one of the antique roses I had coaxed lovingly into showy profusion there. I found her strewing the petals from my murdered Love, Honor, and Cherishes on the grass, humming and mumbling. When I cried out in horror she began to wail and made for the river again. I don't think I was very gentle with her when I caught her and marched her back to her room.

Since then I was beginning to have distinctly mutinous thoughts about Mommee. I was beginning to frame eloquent arguments for live-in help with her or even a good nursing home; I went about muttering them under my breath often, tasting the validity of them. I did not know what it was going to take to sway Pom, but I knew, now, that I needed to try. Even when I cringed with guilt, even when I knew that it was not her fault, that she would not have chosen dementia, I knew it. No one in the house with Mommee had any sort of life. Glynn had taken to staying at school late to work on her painting or in her locked room reading and listening to music when she was at home. She had stopped having her friends over after school almost a year ago. She was as agreeable and industrious as ever, but there was something haunted and strained about her face this summer. It seemed thinner, finer-boned, sharp-edged, almost as if her lovely skull had shrunk. She no longer laughed.

This frightened me thoroughly. She had had such a near brush with anorexia when she was thirteen that I had taken her to our family doctor, and, on his advice, to a therapist who specialized in eating disorders. Because she was so young, and a gymnast to boot, he had been hesitant to say that she had clinical anorexia, but her thinness was truly alarming to me.

After six months in therapy she began to eat more and gained some of the weight back, but her delicate exuberance did not really return, and she became a child of silence, secretive and obedient and as severely, chastely loving as an effigy on a medieval tomb.

I had told my fears about her to Pom only a week before, when her classes at Westminster were over and she had not yet left for summer camp. She would not do that until early July. She had spent a great deal of time since school ended with this friend or that, spending nights at their homes. And the new thinness, if it really was that, hurt my heart. It was hard to tell about the thinness. Glynn wore long cotton granny skirts and bulky, loose tops all that spring. But so did all her friends.

"If she's started that again, I don't know what we'll do," I said to Pom. "She's sixteen. She's too old for me to control her meals. She never eats them here anymore, anyway. Darling, it just can't be good for her to have Mommee here. She never brings anybody home anymore. She never gets any of our attention. She doesn't come up to talk to me before bed like she used to."

"She's growing up," Pom said. "It's natural that she's spending time out with her friends. It's natural for her to have secrets, to stay in her room by herself. It's what teenagers do. Don't you remember those years when we thought Chip and Jeff would never come out again? Besides, she doesn't look thin to me. She's tall and slender just like you. She's beautiful. We're lucky. Pretty soon it'll be boys she's out with, and not girls, and then you really will have something to worry about. And you know Mommee adores her, Merritt. Lighten up. She's a good kid."

"That's what worries me," I said. "She *is* a good kid. She's the best kid I've ever seen. She's too good. It's the good-little-girl thing; it's the classic pattern for anorexia. And Mommee may have adored her once, but she doesn't even know who she is half the time now. She had a screaming fit when Glynn went into her room the other day. Pom, listen. We can't go on like this. I've got to have some help with Mommee. It's Glynn I'm worried about now. If you won't consider a nursing home, at least let me get someone in—"

He was silent for a long time and then he looked at me, and there was real pain in his blue eyes.

"What's changed?" he said. "Why is it that you could handle all this last year, or last month, and now you can't? You have Ina three days a week, and you can have her full time any time you want her. The boys are long gone. Glynn will be at camp most of the summer, and she's going to visit that friend of hers in Highlands for the rest of it. What do you want to do that you can't do now? Mommee's just a frail, sick little old lady. How much longer can she live? I just need you right now. It won't be too long before she's gone and you'll have all the time in the world."

I had no reply. Put that way he was right. It did not seem that Mommee could last much longer; the fury of the dementia seemed to be eating her alive. And it had been I who had suggested she come to us when she was unable to stay in her house any longer. His pain at the thought of a nursing home had been too much for me to bear. But she had not been so bad then, and Glynn had seemed so much better . . .

I answered him now, though, stamping along the path toward the house and the clamoring of the bell. I did not speak the words aloud, but they were full and whole in my mind.

What do I want to do? Who knows what I want to do? Maybe I want to go back to work and own my own agency and win Clios. Maybe I want to take off with Crisscross and go to Cancún. Maybe I want to raise Siamese cats, or buy a llama. Or go sit on a mountaintop in India and find myself. I want to take one quiet pee that Mommee doesn't shriek for me. I want to come into the house with a load of groceries and not have Ina stalk around after me telling me what the old lady did wrong that day. I want to walk into my own guest bathroom and not smell shitty adult diapers. I want my daughter to come home after school and bring her friends like she used to do. I want her to stop drifting around like a ghost; I want her to stop studying and get into some adolescent mischief. I want to hear her laugh. Of course she's a good, responsible child, but she's also a lovely young woman and my best friend when she's not under siege, and I want her back. I want you to come home and make love to me before dinner like you used to, without having Mommee scrabbling and kicking at the door. Do you even realize that you hardly ever eat dinner with us anymore? Do you think I just love these intimate, stimulating little dinners alone with Mommee? You try wiping stringbean purée off her chin after every bite. When you say, "We take care of our own," you mean me, Bubba.

The bell accelerated its angry summons and stopped, and I broke into a lope and hit the searing-hot flagstones of the verandah and leaped like a gazelle over them into the dim, cool kitchen. It was empty, but I could hear voices from the living room, Mommee's the high, thin wail of a scolded child, Ina's the exaggerated crispness of an exasperated adult. The air of the empty kitchen still rang with the percussion of the bell.

Halfway into town, stuck in the malodorous traffic that seemed forever clotted on the old ferry roads around the river, Pom noticed my hair.

"What did you do to it?" he said, studying me through his wire-rimmed sunglasses. "You don't look like yourself. It's nice, though. Exotic."

"Tondelayo, that's me," I said.

What I had done to it, after taking the scissors away from Mommee before she decimated the other drapes in her room and getting her into a bath and coaxing one of her tranquilizers down her and waiting until she nodded off, was to pull the wild tangle of air-dried frizz straight back behind my ears and slick it down with so much gel that it looked shellacked. Then I coiled it swiftly into a high bun and gelled that, too. I skinned into a white linen halter and long black wrap skirt with a slit in it, cinched a red patent belt around my waist, added red high-heeled sandals that I had worn once and vowed never to wear again, and slashed bloodred lipstick over my mouth. Hearing the crunch of Pom's Cherokee on the driveway and the light, waspish tap of its horn, I grabbed long gold earrings and a massive gold bangle bracelet he had given me last Christmas and flew down the stairs without my bag, any makeup but the lipstick, or a wrap. On my way through the kitchen I grabbed his blue blazer, which was hanging from the pot rack still swathed in dry cleaner's wrap, and the striped tie he had requested. On my teetering way down the verandah steps I impulsively snatched a huge red hibiscus blossom from the bush beside the walk and stuck it into my hair behind my ear. I knew the gel would hold it like superglue. Cookie, the pretty coffee-skinned nurse from the clinic whom Pom had inveigled into staying with Mommee because her regular sitter's car wouldn't start, grinned at me and said, "Uh-*huh!*" as we passed.

"Uh-huh yourself," I grinned back. I liked the tough, flirtatious Cookie. "Call me if she gets out of hand. We're at the Driving Club."

"That'll be the day, honey," she said. "I took a knife away from a two-hundred-pound crackhead today. You mama-in-law gon' look like Mother Teresa after that."

"You wish. See you before midnight. Got your jammies?"

She held up a bulging tote and I laughed and got into the Cherokee and laid the blazer and tie on the backseat and Pom gunned out of the driveway, spurting gravel. As usual, he was late to his own party.

As we turned into the driveway of the Driving Club he looked over to study me again.

"I feel like I've run off with another woman," he said.

"And how does that feel? Does it do things for you?"

"It could. It definitely could. You look Eurasian, or something. Like that woman in the William Holden movie. Is it true what they say about Oriental women?"

"There's only one way to find out," I said, and leered.

Just before we stopped the car under the portico, I pulled down the sun visor mirror and looked at myself. I had hardly even glanced at my reflection before I left the house. A strange, carved face looked back at me. The gel had lacquered my streaked brown hair to a shining tortoise shell color, and without the softening bangs that I had always considered necessary for an angular face my sharp cheek and brow bones and tilted nose stood out as in bas relief. Without makeup the coppery freckles ran together over my cheeks and the bridge of my nose, making me look as though I had been long in the sun, or did indeed have the golden blood of the East in my veins. The red lipstick and the hibiscus blossom looked barbaric. I smiled theatrically. My teeth flashed stark white in my face.

When I got out of the car I felt the reckless blood of that alien half-caste warm my face and chest. For a moment I wanted to prowl, to stalk like a jungle cat, to growl low in my throat. I took an experimental prowling step and the high red heels wobbled so that I stumbled.

"You okay, Mrs. Fowler?" said Clem, who parked cars. He reached out to steady me.

"I thought you said you'd never wear those shoes again," Pom said.

"I said a lot of things," I sighed, abandoning Tondelayo and tripping cautiously into the Driving Club on Pom's arm.

This was perhaps the ninth or tenth clinic gala we had attended. Both of us could predict the course of the evening down to the air kisses on the way in and the slightly tipsy mouth ones on the way out. Compared to some of the other fund-raisers in town, this one was simple, even modest. Pom did not think the huge flowered and gilded and costumed balls and galas that benefited most of the city's good causes were seemly for a charity clinic, and he had the aging sixties' radical's contempt for privileged pleasure and play in the name of underprivileged pain. So he would allow seated dinners for perhaps a hundred couples at this club or that, or a private home, with simple floral centerpieces and candles and perhaps a combo for dancing afterward, but that was all. In the beginning he had not even allowed that, insisting that the fundraiser be catered drinks and a few peanuts and pretzels at the clinic. I had finally disabused him of that.

"You're asking some of the richest and most influential people in Atlanta and the South to part with a very considerable amount of money," I said. "You've got to give them more than bad scotch and peanuts down in the projects. What's next, pork rinds at Juvenile Hall? You can show them what the clinic is all about another way; have slides at the party or tours beforehand, or buses with drinks and hors d'oeuvres on board, or something. I don't mean you've got to give the auxiliary free

rein; I agree, you'd end up with a bacchanalia or worse if Betty
Burton had her way. But at least a good club or a pretty home,
and live music, and really good food."

He had considered my words, and when the aforementioned Betty Burton, who was that year's auxiliary president,
told him in exasperation that several of last year's attending
wives had told her that they had been accosted by homeless
persons on their way into the clinic and they would never go
down into that part of town again, he capitulated.

"Okay," he said. "All right. All those spoiled ex-debs
ought to have to work down there, or better yet, spend a week
or two in the shelters. But have at it. Just don't let Betty and
her merry band do anything silly. The first Night in the
Seraglio or *Gone With the Wind* hoo haw will be the last."

And because Pom was popular with his peers and considered something of an urban saint by the Atlanta news media,
the clinic dinner parties were a great success. Only a hundred
couples came, admittedly, but they were, as Betty burbled, the
select hundred couples in the city. I have always thought that
the clinic dinners were popular because the gilded hundred
were weary in the extreme of Nights in the Seraglio, and
grateful to sit down and listen to the music they had been
young to, and chat with the friends they had grown up with,
and drink good liquor and eat good food and go home early.

I don't like balls and banquets, but I always enjoyed this
one because so many of the doctors and their wives who came
were old friends, and this was often the only time in the year
that I saw them. There is a kind of emotional shorthand that
binds doctor's wives, and it is a sweet and easy thing to have
friends with similar context. Many of the men had been close
to Pom ever since internship and residency, and one, Phil
Fredericks, had been his roommate at Hopkins. Phil was with
him at the clinic now, and Jenny, his funny, volatile wife, was
one of my few close friends. I did see Jenny, for tennis and
auxiliary work and sometimes for what we called escape days,
when we took off and spent afternoons at the movies or
antiquing or hiking in the North Georgia hills an hour's drive
away. Or at least, I used to see Jenny.

I saw her now, waving from a round table half full of

couples close to one of the tall windows that overlooked the twilight green of the Piedmont Park woods.

"I saved a place for y'all," she said. "Hey, Pom. Lord, Merritt, what have you done to yourself? Have you been to Canyon Ranch, or what? You look fabulous."

"No Canyon Ranch. This is what's called the last-resort look," I said, hugging her lightly and smiling around the table. It was largely women now, most of whom I knew, two of whom I did not. The men had sucked Pom into their circle and swept him out onto the terrace, where a small knot of men I did not know stood holding drinks and munching hors d'oeuvres from the tray a waiter was passing. From the rapt attention that Pom's group of doctors was according them, I knew they were visiting Big Bucks. I saw tall, skeletal Bill Ramsey talking, rocking back and forth with his hands in his pockets, and then there was a burst of laughter and I knew that Bill had told one of his scurrilous jokes in his exaggerated Savannah drawl. One of the Big Bucks said something and everyone laughed again, and Pom slapped him on the back. I stared. I could not remember ever in my life seeing Pom slap anyone on the back.

"*Big* bucks," I muttered to Jenny.

"The biggest. Must be dead ripe, too. I don't think I ever saw Pom whack anybody on the back before. What's gotten into him?"

"I really don't know," I said. "Sunspots or El Niño or something."

"Well, anyway, what have you been doing? I've missed the tennis and the escape days. Is it Pom's mother?"

"She's not doing so well," I said. "She's a little addled these days. I've been staying pretty close to home."

"What I hear is that she's absolutely wacko and ought to be in a nursing home," Jenny said. "And that you've been looking after her full-time. Lordy, wasn't it enough that you raised those two boys after Lilly took off? And then with Glynn and all . . . Pom is a darling and a saint, but he's just like all doctors, blind to what's ailing his family. You ought to go on strike."

I sighed. I knew that Phil would have told her; there was

practically nothing about Pom that Phil did not know or could not intuit, and he told Jenny everything. And if Jenny knew about Mommee, every other doctor's wife at the table knew. Miz Talking Fredericks, Pom called her. But perhaps I could head her off before the two women I did not know heard every last detail about the saga of Mommee.

"I don't mean to say he's not a saint; we all know he is," Jenny said hurriedly, seeing that she had made me uncomfortable. "I just happen to think that you're a saint, too."

"Not me," I said. "That's Pom's department. One saint to a family."

"Pommy always was a saint," one of the strange women said, and Jenny and I looked at her. I smiled inquiringly. Had I met her before? There was something about the dark eyes, and the tiny, pearly teeth. A child's teeth . . .

"I'm sorry, I thought you knew Sweetie," Jenny said. "Sweetie Cokesbury. You know, she's Leonard's wife. Or bride, I should say. They're just back from St. Maarten; they honeymooned on that enormous boat of Leonard's, or should I say ship?"

"Oh, of course," I said. "I'm sorry. We *have* met. I think it was a while ago, though—"

"It was," said the woman. Her voice fluted like a tiny wind instrument. "It was way back when Pommy was still in private practice. I had just lost my darling husband, and Pommy took pity on me and asked me to a lovely party you all gave at the River Club. I always tell Pommy that he saved my life that night, because that's where I first met Lennie, and one thing led to another, and . . . here I am. I don't wonder you don't remember. I was considerably slimmer then. I swear, after eating my way through the Caribbean, I'm the one that ought to go to Canyon Ranch. Lennie's always trying to put meat on my bones, as he calls it. Can't stand skinny women. I bet you can eat like a hog and not gain an ounce! Back when Pommy and I were growing up I was a little bitty thing, too."

I remembered then. Sweetie Carroll she had been when we met, tiny and dark and so cloyingly flirtatious that I was amazed that the men at the party did not think her a caricature of a Southern belle as I did, but they had not seemed to.

Most of them hung on Sweetie's every honeyed word. Now she was as solid and round as a butterball and tanned to a deep bronze, and so blond that her pouffed hair seemed spun of gilt. She wore a black dress so low-cut that her ponderous, sun-speckled breasts seemed in danger of bobbing out of it, and her ears and throat and fingers flashed with diamonds and emeralds. Leonard Cokesbury was one of the richest men in the Southeast. He had inherited a fortune in Coca-Cola stock.

"I remember," I said. "I'm sorry. I forgot my glasses along with everything else, we were running so late. You and Pom are from the same hometown, aren't you?"

"Childhood sweethearts since we were three," she said, laughing a tinkling laugh. I thought of crystal shattering. "Our daddies were in the timber business together. I was in and out of Mommee's house so often she used to say I was her only daughter. I tell you, the trouble Pommy and I got into, you just wouldn't believe. There wasn't a day that passed, hardly, that we weren't together. I could tell you some tales about that husband of yours that would curl that pretty hair of yours! He gave me my first little kiss, and took me to my first prom, and I used to go up to dances at Woodbury Forest. Mommee used to say she already had my weddin' gown picked out. But then he went on up there to Baltimore and got involved in all that civil rights stuff, and he changed, he surely did. And now look at him. A real entrepreneur, as well as a saint. Who would have thought it? I'm so proud of Pommy, I surely am. And proud of you, too, Merritt. I hear what a saint you are in your own right. It's so good for Pommy, after that Lilly person. I thought Mommee was going to die when he brought her home the first time."

I simply stared at her. Her words were like mercury spilling out of a broken thermometer; there seemed no way of stopping them, of picking them up. Pommy? Mommee? I had never heard anyone call Pom's mother that but Pom and then us, his family. This ridiculous woman seemed to know as much about my family, especially my husband, as I did. I smiled stiffly as the words tumbled and skittered on. Beside me I heard Jenny snicker softly.

"Well," Sweetie went on, "I just wanted to tell you that all Pommy's old friends were so happy for him when he found you, and proud, and all that. Taking those poor little boys to raise after that woman ran off, and giving up your own career, and your sister on your hands all your life and then her going off like that, and of course poor little Mommee, and then I understand your daughter hasn't been at all well . . ."

She looked at me with eyes as avian and voracious as a starling's. Her smile widened; the sharp little teeth gleamed.

"My daughter's just fine," I said, smiling back. My mouth felt stretched.

"I'm so glad! As I said, you are truly to be admired, you surely are. You all come see us real soon. I'm having a glorious time doing over that big old white elephant. Tell Pom I've put in an old-fashioned rock garden just like his grandmother Parsons used to have at Sea Island. He's really just got to see it."

"I'll tell him," I said.

She waggled her fingers at us and tottered off to join the circle of men on the veranda. I could see the peeling, brown, bald head of Leonard Cokesbury in the crowd. From behind she looked like a little black cube topped with cotton candy, but she had beautiful legs, tanned and shapely. Her skirt was very short.

We were silent for a moment and then tall, raw-boned Dot Crenshaw across the table said, "We'll watch until she goes to the ladies' room and then we'll rush her. Jenny can tackle her, I'll stick her head in the john, and you can flush it, Merritt. God, what an awful woman!"

"But rich," Jenny and I and Pam Crocker next to Jenny said together, and we all laughed.

Later, after dinner, I went to the ladies' room to see what I could do about my naked, sweating face. The heat on the terrace, where we had had coffee, was stifling, even at ten o'clock. I washed my face and was standing there dripping and blinded, groping for my towel, when the door whooshed open and I heard Sweetie Cokesbury's piccolo voice again.

"Sweetie, hello," she bubbled. "You have the right idea; it's simply sweltering, isn't it? Let me hand you that . . . "

She passed me the towel and I mopped my face and looked at her. She was gleaming and enameled; there was not a gilt hair out of place. I wondered what she had sprayed herself with to preserve her surface in the heat.

She dabbed at my skirt with a paper towel.

"Here, you've splattered," she said. "Listen, I really meant what I said, you know. Not many women I know would have had the gumption to stick it out, to hold things together after everything else you've been through, when that silly business at the clinic came up. When was it? A long time. I remember Bush had just been elected . . . "

I looked at her in the mirror. She was smiling brilliantly at me.

"What business was that?" I said.

"Oh, that little nonsense about the Negro doctor. Or was she Indian? None of us were sure. And none of us believed it, of course. It was just that Pommy always did adore the Negroes—"

The door swished open again and Jenny came in.

"Pom's looking for you," she said, and stopped. I think now she must have seen something on my face, though at the time it felt perfectly still and blank.

"I have to run, too," Sweetie said. "I just wanted you to know you have a real fan on Habersham Road."

She bustled out, leaving a trail of Opium behind her.

"What was that all about?" Jenny said, looking after her.

"Did Pom ever have an affair with a black woman doctor?" I said.

"What? No! Of course not! Did that bitch tell you he did? She's lying . . . "

Jenny's voice rose in incredulity and anger. She caught herself and lowered it, and took my hands and looked into my face. Her hands felt scalding hot. Mine must be ice-cold, I thought stupidly.

"Do you *know* that he didn't, Jenny?" I said.

"Of course I know it," she said, almost hissing in her effort to keep her voice low. "Don't you think Phil would know if he had? Even if nobody else on earth knew, Phil would, and he would tell me. He's never said a word about any affair with any black doctor. God, I suppose she meant Bella Strong. She's that Jamaican doctor they had on staff for a year or two, before she went to Africa, you remember. That's just ludicrous. Bella had a fiancé on the faculty at Morehouse;

she married him and they both went to Biafra or somewhere—"

"She didn't mention a name," I said. I felt as though I were speaking through a mouthful of Kleenex. My mouth was desperately dry.

"Somebody should throttle her," Jenny spat. "She's been after Pom for years, I thought you knew that. Phil said she used to follow him around like a puppy before he went off to prep school, and I think he did ask her to a dance or two up there, mainly because his mother made him. When he married what's-her-name, in Baltimore, she practically went into mourning. To hear Phil tell it, the whole stupid little town did. When that broke up, her husband conveniently kicked off—I wouldn't be surprised if she didn't put rat poison in his juleps—and she high-tailed it up here to grab up ol' Pom before somebody else did. But it was too late. He'd already met you. She hung around for several years trying to get into our crowd, but nobody invited her anywhere, and finally Lennie married her. Well, hell, Lennie'll marry anybody. You can just imagine how much she thinks of you, can't you? Of *course* she's lying. Can't you see what she's trying to do to you? I'm going to tell Phil the minute we get in the car. I don't care how much money Lennie Cokesbury has; the clinic ought not touch a penny of it. And they won't, either, if Phil has anything to do with it. God, but Pom's going to be furious—"

"Tell Phil not to mention it to Pom," I said. I knew it would do no good to ask her not to tell Phil. "I mean that, Jen. It's . . . I just can't stand the thought of people talking about us that way. I've never once in twenty-six years thought of Pom and anybody else—"

"Well, that's because there hasn't *been* anybody else," she said. "I'll tell Phil not to tell Pom, but somebody ought to put the fear of God into that lying bitch. I'd love to do it myself."

I turned to the mirror and began dabbing lipstick on my mouth. My hand was shaking so that the lipstick ran wildly up my cheek. I began to scrub at it with a tissue.

She reached over and put her hand on mine, and I stopped scrubbing and looked at her in the mirror, and let my hand drop. I felt hot and then cold, all gone inside; I ached all over as if I were getting the flu.

"You do believe me, don't you?" Jenny said.

"Of course I do," I croaked. I cleared my throat and said it again, more strongly: "Of course I do."

"If you have any doubt at all, ask him. Ask him, Merritt. You know he won't lie to you."

"Maybe I will," I said. She was right. Pom would not lie to me. He never had.

"Do it," Jenny said.

But I did not think I would. Partly it was because I did not believe Sweetie Cokesbury's words; Pom? An affair? Simply impossible. I would have known.

Partly it was because it did not matter. No matter what my mind believed, something deep inside me must forever look at Pom now as a man who had or had not had an extramarital affair. There was an option, no matter how incredible, where none had existed. We were in new territory, a place with a different geography. It was as if I stood on a shore and saw, not the horizon that I had always seen, but a new shoreline, another country. I did not believe Sweetie, but still I could see that other shore. Possibility rejected still exists.

From that it was only a small step.

With anybody else, then? All those nights and weekends away at the clinic, all that time . . . if not this Jamaican Bella, then someone else?

I tossed away the Kleenex and followed Jenny out of the ladies' room. I believed her with all my heart, but something in my guts hurt; my very womb ached.

Pom and Phil were waiting for us in the doorway of the dining room. Pom came up and put his arm around me and buried his nose in the wilted hibiscus.

"Tondelayo wait up for big man?" he said.

"Big man going out on toot?" I said, my heart sinking.

"Big man going to take Big Bucks bwanas out for—Oh, hell, you can guess where the Charlotte contingent wants to go. I'll try to palm it off on Phil after a little while. You take the car and go on. I'll get a ride. Don't wait up; I was only kidding. We'll probably be a while."

"I wish you wouldn't," I said, and he looked at me. I had never said it before.

"I have to, honey. These guys are almost sewed up. There's nothing on the agenda for a long time after this. And Cookie's there, so you should be able to sleep without having to check on Mommee."

"I know," I said. "I just miss you sometimes."

"Me, too," he said, tightening his grip on my shoulders. "I changed my mind: do wait up."

"Maybe I will," I said, smiling, and he smiled back and started across the dining room after Phil. Halfway across he looked back and then dropped to one knee and flung one arm out and laid the other hand across his heart.

"But soft," he shouted, "what light from yonder window breaks? It is the East, and Merritt is the sun!"

And I laughed, my heart turning over beneath the white halter. Just before we were married we went to see a rerun of Zeffirelli's *Romeo and Juliet*, that consummately beautiful film in which the luminous nakedness of the two young principals ignited such a controversy. I had been so moved by it that I had wept mutely when it was over, and was unable to speak for a time after we left the theater for the sobbing that kept bubbling up in my throat. Pom, trying uneasily to comfort me, stumbled in his haste and clumsiness and went down on one knee. Looking up at me, he laid his hand over his heart and said those words, and I stopped crying and laughed, and then wept again at the flood of love that welled up in me, to see him there on the asphalt of the parking lot, telling me in those ineffable old words that he loved me.

I had not thought of the incident for a long time until tonight. Now, the same tide of love surged through me. This time I laughed and did not cry.

"Have fun, you incredible fool," I called back to him. When the Cherokee came round, I rolled down the window on my side, and found the late-night jazz program from Clark College. Don Shirley curled out into the warm night: *Orpheus in the Underworld*; I had had the album at school. I hardly thought of the ugly words Sweetie Cokesbury had spoken in the ladies' room during the entire soft, mimosa-smelling drive home to the river.

Hardly.

3

Mommee thought my daughter, Glynn, was the angel of death. When she had first come to stay with us Mommee was still able to watch television, or at least, to sit fairly quietly and watch whatever it was that she saw on the screen. Only later did she become so agitated and distractible that she could not sit still, but got up to shuffle and roam and mutter after a few minutes before the set.

One winter evening about a month into her time with us we sat, Mommee and I, before the set in the downstairs library, watching an early movie. It was an old one called *Devotion*, with Paul Heinreid and Ida Lupino, about the Brontë family, and in it death was depicted as a sinister figure on horseback, wearing a dark, swirling cape. The caped rider came closer and closer to its victim on the misted moor until, at the end, it swept her up in the cape and vanished. I had seen it as a child and it had frightened me half to death, but I did not think Mommee would take in enough of it to alarm her, and indeed, she did not appear to, clapping her hands and crowing with laughter when the cape made its final, fatal swirl.

But an hour later Glynn came home from a swim meet in her long, black, red-lined cape, a pretty but troublesome fad that her crowd affected that year, with her wet hair streaming down her back, and burst into the library swirling her cape dramatically, and Mommee began to scream.

"Death! Death!" she shrilled, pointing at Glynn, and became so hysterical that I had to take her upstairs and give her a Xanax and brush her hair until she fell asleep. When I came back down Glynn was sitting at the kitchen table staring out at the dark winter woods, fiddling with a half a bagel. The cape lay across a chair.

"The caped crusader strikes again," she said mildly, not moving her eyes from the darkness. But I saw that her finger-nails were digging into the bagel, and I went over and dropped a kiss on top of her damp, chlorine-smelling head.

"Sorry, Tink," I said, using her father's old nickname for her. When she was a child she flitted about with such restless grace that he called her Tinkerbell, after the fairy in *Peter Pan*. She disliked it now, so we seldom used it, but I sometimes forgot.

"I never should have let her watch that thing. It was the cape; you know she isn't afraid of you. She'll have forgotten in the morning."

"No, she won't," Glynn said matter-of-factly, and put the bagel down and went up to her room.

And Mommee hadn't. Glynn put the cape away at the back of her closet, but often, after that, Mommee would look at her and begin to wail, "Death! Death!" Since she didn't always do it, I concluded that the image simply flickered into her mind at random intervals when she saw Glynn, borne on God knows what faulty synapse. But Glynn thought she did it, sometimes, on purpose.

"She'll look and look at me, and get that funny sort of sly look on her face, and then she'll start yelling," she said once, after a death-screaming spell. This time it was Pom who took his mother upstairs to calm her. When he came back down it was Glynn's bedtime, too late for him to help her with her science project as he had promised. She was fourteen then, going on fifteen.

"That's ridiculous," Pom said sharply. "Mommee isn't devious. She's old and she has Alzheimer's. We've explained that to you."

Glynn said nothing, but went upstairs to her bedroom and closed the door.

"She may be right, you know," I said, when the sporadic spells continued. "It does seem to happen most often when you're home and we're all together. Look at the payoff. Mommee gets you all to herself, or me, or both of us, and Glynn is left by herself feeling like a pariah, or worse. It isn't her fault; she gave the cape to Jessica, even though she loved it, and I didn't even suggest it. She did it on her own. But she's the one who has to sit down here by herself while we hover over Mommee. Even if Mommee isn't doing it deliberately, it must feel like punishment to Glynn. Between the clinic and Mommee and the howling about death, she hardly ever sees you anymore, and it was going so well."

"I'll talk to her," he said, and perhaps he did. Glynn never spoke of it.

Ever since Glynn's flirtation with anorexia, Pom had, at the therapist's suggestion, been making a real effort to spend more time with her, and, after a year, Glynn was very gradually adding a layer of becoming flesh to her elegant, long bones, and regaining color on the cheekbones that were a medieval refinement of mine. But since Mommee's arrival and the onset of the death business, she had begun to draw away from us again, and spent more and more time in her room with the door closed. Glynn did not act out or give us trouble overtly. She never had, from her serene babyhood on. She simply withdrew into silence. She began staying away from Mommee. The cape was, must have been, long forgotten, but her face had lodged in Mommee's roiling mind as that of a death's head, and thus it stayed.

When I got up the morning after Pom's party it was later than usual, and Pom had long since gone to the clinic. A note beside the coffeemaker said, "BB Bwanas impressed with T&A but I've seen better right here. Be home early." Mommee was still asleep, and the guest room where Cookie had slept was empty and tidy. Cookie's note, taped to Mommee's closed door, said, "I gave her a pill because she had a real fit last night when Glynn came in and it was 3 A.M. before I got her settled. She should sleep till midmorning."

Glynn was home, then. I had not expected her to return from the house party at her friend Jessica's family vacation home at Big Canoe until tomorrow afternoon, Sunday. I wondered if anything was wrong. I pushed open her closed door slightly and saw the slight mound of her sheeted body sleeping deeply in the gloom. "Morning, pretty," I whispered. I closed her door and tiptoed into Mommee's room and looked down at her. She, too, was sleeping soundly. Her breath came light and regularly from between slightly parted lips.

In the morning gloom she looked young and very pretty, almost like a child; she had lost weight since the onset of the illness and seemed actually to have shrunk in her bones. The diffused light gave her face a nacreous cast, like the inside of a wet seashell, and she slept with her fists curled under her chin, childlike. She wore a long white cotton nightgown with a ruffle around the neck. Cookie had brushed the thin gilt-white hair before she left, and it floated over her forehead like a newly shampooed toddler's. Pity and affection squeezed my heart. This was not a Mommee anyone often saw, transmuted into the tenderly loved small girl she must have been long ago.

I brushed the hair off her forehead with one finger.

"You didn't choose to be like this, did you? Sometimes we forget," I whispered.

When I went back down the hall I heard the shower in Glynn's bathroom running, and I went in and sat down on her bed.

"You're home early," I shouted into the bathroom.

"Be out in a minute," she called back.

She came out wrapped in Pom's huge, white terry robe, which she had appropriated. It hung down to her ankles and drooped over her slender hands. Her hair was wrapped in a white terry turban. Lord, but she was lovely; the oval face under the towel looked, scrubbed clean and almost translucent, like that of a very young novice in a fifteenth-century convent. Siena, I thought, or Assisi. I could almost see the delicately veined, pearly lids dropped over her eyes and the long fingers clasped in prayer. She had not yet acquired her light summer tan and looked, damp and shining with body lotion, like she had been carved out of alabaster. She had my height and coltish slenderness and tawny hair, though hers hung thick and smooth, and Pom's blue eyes, mine and my father's chiseled cheekbones and Mommee's tender mouth. Her coloring, or lack of it, was entirely her own. Her paleness could be mistaken for plainness, until you looked at her features one by one. Then she was extraordinary. But she was without real impact yet; that, I thought, would come later, when everything had coalesced into maturity. I hoped that day was still a long way away.

"Hi. What're you doing home early?" I said.

"Oh . . . nothing, really. We all left last night. It wasn't just me."

"Why, sweetie? What happened? Is something the matter?"

"I don't guess so, really. It just seemed like a good thing to do. Mr. and Mrs. Constable sort of had a fight, and it upset Jess so much that we all decided to just come on back. Marcia took her to her house."

Once, I knew, Jessica would have come home with Glynn for succor. Poor Jess. Poor Glynn.

"What was the fight about? Feel like talking about it?" I said casually. More and more often these days she did not bring her problems and hurts to me, but took them to Jessica. I knew, from Laura's childhood, and later Chip and Jeff's, that this was a normal stage of growing up and away from us, but it still hurt. This child was so vulnerable, so without armor. . . . But Jessica was across the river in the arms of another friend, and my daughter had come home to a house empty except for an old woman who howled of death. And there had been more trouble from that quarter. Who did she have left to talk with but me? I hoped desperately that she still felt that she could.

"I don't think so," she said noncommittally, and then she whirled to face me. Her face was miserable.

"Mr. and Mrs. Constable are getting a divorce," she said, her voice treble and childish. I had not heard that voice in a long time; it was the voice of small Glynn, when she was frightened and angry.

"Oh, sweetie. How do you know?"

"Because they had this awful yelling match last night,

after dinner, when they thought we were all asleep. I think they were both drunk. They drank an awful lot of wine with dinner, and after. You couldn't help but hear what they were saying, and it was just awful, just gross. Poor Jess finally ran out there screaming for them to stop, and then her mother cried and Jess cried and everybody else cried, too, and her father slammed out of the house and went down to the boathouse. Her mother took off after him. And Jess just got hysterical. So we left. We took her mother's Blazer. He's been going around with some woman at his office. I think Mrs. Constable just found out last night, and I know Jess did. I hated it, Mom!"

"Oh, love, I'm so sorry," I said, putting my arms around her and drawing her close. She lay slackly against me for a moment, and then stiffened and pulled away.

"And when I came in—" she said.

"I know. Mommee. Cookie left a note. What was it, the death thing again?"

"Yeah. Mom, sometimes I think . . . I just wish she wasn't here! I wish Daddy was home more! What's the *matter* with everybody?"

It was a wail of pain and impotence. I felt tears sting my eyes.

"I think you're just running head-on into adulthood," I said, wishing she was still within arm's reach. I wanted, suddenly, to march into Mommee's room and shake her and shout, "You leave my little girl alone! You've had your life! You stay out of hers!"

"You come on home and stay home," I wanted to yell at Pom.

"Well, then, adulthood sucks and I don't want anything to do with it," she said, her voice wobbling on the edge of tears.

"I don't blame you. It ain't what it's cracked up to be," I said, trying to keep my voice light. "But I don't think you've got a lot of choice in the matter. Don't worry, baby. You don't have to take on the whole world yet. That's what we're around for. By the time you do, you'll be able to handle it. You're a strong person and a very good and dear one. You'll know the right thing to do and you'll do it."

"So are you, and so do you, but things aren't all that red-hot good for you, are they?" she muttered, not looking at me. "I mean, you've still got Mommee on your neck. And Aunt Laura. And me and all my hang-ups, and you had the boys . . . I mean, what kind of life is it for you? It doesn't look to me like being strong and good matters diddly-squat."

"I have you, and that's the shiningest thing in my life," I said. "And I have your dad, and that's the next shiningest. I have everything I want." I hated it when the pain of the world bore in on my vulnerable child, though I knew very well that it must.

"Do you have Daddy, really? Do we really have him? Are you sure, do you promise? I know Jess thought she had her dad, too . . . "

So that was it. More than pain at her friend's grief, more than the betraying craziness of her grandmother, she was feeling the cold wind of loss and emptiness herself, where none had ever existed before. Well, I knew about that, didn't I? Thanks to Sweetie Cokesbury, I had felt, for a moment, the breath of that awful, empty wind.

I got up and went to her and put my arms around her.

"I'm sure of that. I promise that. Your daddy isn't going to leave us, ever. Not of his own will. We're at the very center of his heart, you and me. Don't you ever doubt that."

"Sometimes you can't tell," she whispered against my shoulder, but I could feel her body relax slightly. I could also feel her ribs, sharp and separate, even under the thick, swaddling terry cloth. I went very still, resisting the impulse to feel all over her body with my hands. It would, I knew, be a terrible violation.

"He won't always have to work so hard," I said. "Mommee won't be with us much longer. She just can't be. Things will get better. I'm heartbroken for Jess, but that's not going to happen to your father and me."

"I thought for a minute she was going to die," Glynn whispered.

"Whatever happens, she won't do that," I said. "She'll have you and all her other friends, and maybe what you heard wasn't as bad as it sounded—"

"It was."

I was silent. It probably had been. Then I said, "Tell you what. Since we've got a free Saturday, why don't we go over to Lenox Square and Phipps Plaza and buy you a whole raft of new summer clothes and then treat ourselves to lunch some-where fancy? Your choice. Spare no expense."

After a moment she smiled reluctantly, and I felt a great stab of love at the way her face bloomed into life.

"Anywhere I want? The Brasserie? The Tavern?"

"You call it."

"A black spandex miniskirt?"

"Oh, Lord, Glynn . . . we'll see."

"*Yessss!*" my daughter exulted and slapped me a high five, and disappeared into her walk-in closet, restored, for the moment, into childhood and safety.

"You know we have to talk about it. You know we do," I said.

"I know," Glynn said, staring into the banana split she'd ordered for dessert. She had managed the hamburger and some of the french fries, but I knew that the sweet mess pooling in the glass boat before her was making her physically sick.

"And you don't have to eat that," I said, smiling so that she would not catch the fear under my words. "I don't insist that you eat stevedore's meals. I just want you to eat some-thing substantial consistently."

"I know. I'm going to do better with it. I was going to start up at Big Canoe, and I did . . . I ate real well until we . . . you know, came home. After that I just couldn't."

"You know I'm not trying to bully you or spy on you, don't you? I wouldn't do that," I said. "I wasn't peeking at you. I saw you in the mirror beside the door when I was leaving, when you were trying on the bikini. It scared me. Glynn, if you could really once see yourself with other eyes and not the eyes of this illness—"

"I know it must be pretty gross. Everybody up at Big Canoe said I looked like a skeleton when I put on my bathing suit. I thought I looked great. I know it's like last time, and I know I promised I'd tell you if it started again. But you all have been so upset about Mommee, and I thought I could handle it this time. And I was, except for last night—"

"When did it start, baby?" I said.

She looked around the leather banquette. In the dimness of the Tavern, the shopping bags holding her new clothes gleamed with gilt letters and logos like the plunder of an emir, and she looked, in their midst, like a young princess with her smooth hair and her loose, silky, new ivory tunic. But I knew that under the tunic her young bones thrust like spears. I had indeed seen her nearly naked in the betraying dressing-room mirror and lost my breath in terror. In the unforgiving, greenish fluorescent wash she looked worse than she ever had, literally starved. Somehow bruised, maimed. How could I not have seen?

"I'm not sure," she said, pushing aside the melting dessert. "It hasn't been all that long. I really haven't lost all that much weight. I've been overdoing the swimming, maybe—"

"Are you running again?"

During her first bout with anorexia she had run constantly, for miles along the river or on the track at school. Since it was winter then, she ran in sweatclothes, and we did not notice the increasing thinness. I did worry sometimes that she was overdoing it; she must have run five or six miles a day, and more on weekends. But Pom was pleased.

"She's got a runner's build, and it's a good habit to get into," he said. "She'll be active all her life. I'm glad she's not a couch potato. I can't stand fat women."

When the illness surfaced both her therapist and internist forbade the running and limited her to swimming, and she agreed. But I know that she missed it.

"Some," she said, turning her head away. "A little, after swim practice. I know. I promised. I'll stop that, too."

I reached over and took both her hands and tugged them, and she looked back with tears standing in her eyes. They swam like liquid blue light in the gloom.

"You can't stop by yourself, Glynn," I said. "That's what this is all about. You remember what Dr. Flint said, that anorexia is about control and the control gets to be such an obsession that it starts to control you? This is not a calamity;

you remember Dr. Flint saying that it would probably crop up a few more times till you got a handle on it, and that the important thing was to catch it early. So I really do have to know how long it's been going on. We can help you, but we have to know that."

"Mama, not we, please! You, I'll tell you, but please don't let Daddy know yet—"

"Okay, all right," I said. "Not yet. Tell me. I'm not going to fuss at you."

"I guess maybe a year or so—"

"A *year!*"

"It didn't get . . . it didn't start to go so fast until lately."

"Is it something at school? Is it us, your daddy and me? Or Mommee—"

Mommee. Of course it was Mommee. Mommee, demanding, deposing, dethroning, unstoppable. Uncontrollable. I should have seen that, too; Pom should have.

"It *is* Mommee, isn't it? Oh, honey, you should have said something. We could have talked about it—"

"Yeah, but what could you have done about it?" Glynn said. "You can't change her and she can't help it and nobody can stop it. I know all that. I can't blame her, but Mama, she sucks all the *air* out of the house! She takes up all the *space* in it! She gets every bit of everybody's attention all the time! And I work and work and swim and swim and paint and paint and my grades get better and better and I get *zero*. Zip. Or a little pat on the head, and 'Way to go, old Tink,' and then Mommee hollers again. . . . And I feel so guilty because it bothers me and I *know* she can't help it! I feel guilty all the time about the way I feel about Mommee."

She whispered the last, and the tears overflowed and ran down her cheeks to her chin. She did not move her hands to wipe them away but finally her face contorted and she jerked her hand from mine and scrubbed her face with it and gave a great, rattling sniff.

"I didn't mean to cry," she gulped.

My own eyes filled. I found a Kleenex and handed it to her.

"I think you have every right to cry," I said. "We haven't

been very considerate of you, have we? You must know that we are both prouder of you than of anything we've ever done ourselves, or ever will do. I think maybe it's that you've been *such* a great kid that we take you for granted while we try to cope with Mommee. That's going to stop, I promise you. The first thing we're going to do in the morning is have a family conference about this the way we used to do. Daddy said he'd be home all day."

"No!" Her head came up and her eyes widened. She clenched her teeth so hard that white ridges stood out in her jaws.

"I won't talk to Daddy about it! You promised! I won't! I can't! I know *you're* proud of me, but he'll have an absolute *shit* fit about the weight thing! You *know* how he feels about that; you *know* he doesn't like Dr. Flint! You *know* he thought the whole thing was silly and trivial last time, and that I ought to be doing some really important work rather than all that therapy and stuff about food—"

"Glynnie, where on earth did you get that idea? Daddy was *terribly* concerned about you! He was willing to do anything in the world to get you better; he will be again—"

"I heard him," she said softly. "I heard him talking to you about it over and over again! There's a place in the upstairs laundry room where the vent pipe or something acts like an echo chamber and you can hear whatever anybody is saying down in the den; I've known about it since I was little. I used to listen all the time. I heard him say that I was impossibly sheltered and naive, and that he treated eight-year-olds at the clinic who could take better care of themselves than I could, and that I ought to volunteer down there and do some real work and see some real misery and forget about starving myself to death."

She fell silent and I simply stared at her. My poor, good, frightened child, crouched in the dark beside a clothes dryer, straining to hear how she measured up to Pom and me, to hear how her life was working out, to hear what catastrophe would be coming next, so she could begin to figure how she might control it.

"Daddy wasn't criticizing you," I said, not bothering to

deny that Pom had said all those things, for he had. "He was just frustrated and frightened because nothing seemed to be working, and he didn't know what to do next. It was during that time when you and Dr. Flint were trying to get used to each other, you remember, and nothing much was happening, and you were still losing weight."

"I heard him say once that he hated fat women," she whispered.

"Oh, honey! He didn't mean little girls!"

Her silence spun out and then she said, "I'm being a real jerk, aren't I?"

"Not for a second. You need to talk about what's bothering you. We'll get started back with Dr. Flint before you leave for camp, and I promise I won't mention this to Daddy until you've seen her. Glynnie, he adores you. I wish I could convince you of that."

"I wish he would," she said in a low voice.

Then she laughed and looked up. "Maybe I should get a pet. A dog. I'd love a big old dog—"

"Well, there's Samson and Delilah."

"But they can't come in the house. I wish I had a dog that would stay with me in my room. I always think about a big dog in my bed with me. But if we got one you'd end up having to take care of it when I went off to camp and then to college, along with everything and everybody else."

"We could have a cat," I said. "Maybe even a couple of kittens. They could keep each other company, and they aren't nearly the trouble dogs are."

She shook her head.

"Jess brought Muffin over here the last time she came. She'd just picked her up from the vet's. Mommee screamed so she had to take Muffin home."

And they hadn't come back, Jess or Muffin either, Glynn did not say so.

"Well, we can easily keep a cat away from Mommee. It can live in your room, or they can. If you'll see Dr. Flint and really, really try with the eating I promise we'll go to the Humane Society and pick you out two wonderful kittens when you get back. And Mommee be blowed."

She smiled, unwillingly at first, and then genuinely.

"Okay."

"So. Better now?"

"Yeah."

"I love you, Glynn."

"Me too you, Mom," my child said.

Pom wasn't home that afternoon after all. When we got home, laden like panoplied elephants with Glynn's booty, Ina told us that he had been called back to the clinic to see a child running a horrendous fever with what sounded, Pom had said, like meningitis. The young doctor on duty had called him to ascertain the diagnosis. He didn't know when he would be done.

"Oh, Ina, I'm sorry," I said. "You've stayed two hours past your time already, while we were gobbling our way through Phipps Plaza. Come on, I'll run you home. I know the bus schedule is awful on weekends."

"I don't mind," she said. "I think you ought to stay here. Miz Fowler's awfully antsy today. Looks like she got some kind of motor goin' cain't nobody turn off. I wanted to give her one of them pills but Doc he say no, she had one last night. I don't think Glynn ought to stay with her by herself."

I sighed. "Well, then, Glynn will run you up to the bus stop. Thanks, Ina. I don't say it enough, but I don't know what we'd do without you."

"Me neither," she said, showing her gold tooth in a smile. "And you need two more of me."

"Where is Mommee now?"

"She up there takin' all her clothes out of her closet and pilin' 'em on the floor," Ina said. "I figure let her, it might take some of the starch out of her, and I can put 'em back Monday. Don't you go botherin' with that."

"I won't."

When they had gone I went upstairs and into Mommee's room. Ina was right; the floor and the chairs and her bed and her chaise and her writing desk were all piled with teetering stacks of clothes. She had even piled clothes in her bathtub.

She scuttled busily among the stacks, counting them and petting them and bending over to sniff them as if they were beds of flowers. She hummed to herself and kept up the ceaseless flow of *sotto voce* conversation she had these days with God knew who.

"What are you doing?" I said, smiling at her from the doorway.

"Getting ready to go to Europe."

"Really? What fun. Who else is going?"

"Papa and Teddy and Big Pom and Lolly and Jasmine," she said in a playful singsong. "But not Mama. Mama has to stay home."

Her adored Papa was, of course, long dead, as were her brother Teddy and her husband, Big Pom. Lolly and Jasmine had been favorite dolls.

"Well, you're certainly taking a lot of clothes. Are you going to be gone long?"

"Till the end of time," she said, and turned back to her task.

"You ready for your juice now?"

"No. I wouldn't say no to an old-fashioned, though."

She smiled slyly, and looked sideways at me.

"We'll both have one before supper," I said. To hell with Pom's edict that liquor and her pills did not mix. She'd had no pills today, and the drink would make her sleepy.

"Pom too?"

"Pom's at the clinic," I said. "But maybe he'll be home by then."

"I want Pom."

"Me, too," I said, and closed her door softly and stood listening for a moment as the humming and murmuring began again. Then I put my head into Glynn's room.

She was not there, but all the new clothes were laid carefully about her room, with the accessories that she planned to wear with them. I smiled. I felt somehow safe and soothed when Glynn showed interest in such normal teenage things as pretty new clothes. The careful groupings of clothes and shoes and bags and necklaces spoke of many good times ahead, lighthearted days and nights through which my lovely child would drift like a butterfly, float like a swan. I went downstairs with a lighter heart than I had had the entire day. She was in the kitchen drinking a cola and hanging up the telephone. It was not, I was happy to see, a Diet Coke.

"Is it okay if I go over to Vinings with Marcia and Jess?" she said. "There's a movie we want to see. I'll be home way before supper. Marcia's driving."

"Sure. Just call if you're going to be late."

"I will. Thanks, Mom. For the day and the clothes and everything."

"It was entirely my pleasure," I said.

She grabbed up her summer straw hobo bag and went out to wait for Marcia and the apparently restored Jessica by the mailbox. I got the portable intercom speaker that let me check on Mommee and went out onto the terrace by the still blue pool and stretched out on a chaise. I had a sheaf of bills with me, intending to go over them, but instead I laid them on the flagstones and put my head back and shaded my face with my arm and listened to the drone of the too early cicadas and the sulky wallow and slap of the river at its banks. The heat today was thick and wet and heavy, and unlike yesterday there was no wind. I meant to move into the shade of the umbrella table and tackle the bills, but instead I fell heavily asleep and dreamed a boring, long dream about taking a shower. It seemed endless, and did indeed last, I figured later, over two hours.

I heard the screams before I smelled the smoke.

I came floundering up out of my sweaty sleep, trying for a moment to work the screams into the dream of showering, but they would not fit, and even as I sat on the edge of the chaise shaking my head, I knew in a deeper part of me that they belonged outside me, upstairs in my house. I was halfway up the stairs before I realized that they were not Mommee's screams, but Glynn's. My heart dropped like a stone and I took a great gulp of air, and thick, sour smoke cut into my lungs. I could see it then, lying in white, roiling strata in the upstairs hallway, billowing from Glynn's room. I stumbled, caught the banister, and hauled myself the rest of the way up, shouting my daughter's name: "Glynn! Glynn!" At that moment the smoke detector came on.

"Mama!" came Glynn's voice, muffled and high with fear. At the same time I heard the thin, henlike squawk that meant Mommee was alarmed, and she shot out of Glynn's room and scuttled, head down, into her own room at the end of the hall. The door slammed shut behind her.

I followed the smoke and Glynn's cries into and through her room and into her bathroom. It was so thick with smoke I could hardly see, but I made out her figure bending over the bathtub, flapping at the smoky white mess piled there with a towel. She had stopped screaming, but she was choking and coughing.

"Get out of here!" I screamed at her and began to cough, too. The thick smoke smelled and tasted of fabric.

I grabbed her by the shoulders and pulled her out of the bathroom and dashed back in and groped for her shower handle. I turned it and water sprayed down onto the burning cloth. It hissed and spat; the smoke turned gray and the smell became that of charred, wet cloth. I slammed the bathroom door and ran, eyes streaming, lungs bursting, out into the hallway. Glynn leaned against the wall, face in hands, sobbing.

"Go downstairs and wait on the patio," I shouted. "And call the fire department from the kitchen on your way! I'll get Mommee."

"Let her burn," my daughter shrilled in fury. "Let the old witch burn! Do you know what that is in there? That's my new clothes! All of them! She put them in the bathtub and lit them with the fireplace starter! I came upstairs just as she was doing it!"

"Go!" I screamed, and she went.

It seemed to me that the smoke was already clearing, but I dashed to Mommee's room. The door was locked. I pounded on it.

"Come out of there, Mommee," I shouted. "The house is on fire! You've got to go downstairs!"

"I want Pom," came the fretful wail. "I want Pom!"

"Well, he's not here! Mommee, open this door *now*! You'll burn to death if you don't!"

"I'm going to tell Pom you yelled at me!"

"Get out here right now or there'll be no more TV for a month!"

She opened the door a fraction and peeped around it, grinning.

"I made a big fire," she said.

I grabbed her shoulders roughly and pulled her, whining and wriggling, down the stairs and outside onto the patio, where Glynn was talking urgently on the cellular phone.

"Watch her," I said. "I think it's going out, but I have to check. Are they on the way?"

"Yeah, they got the alarm before I called."

I started into the house again and Mommee started for the river. Glynn sprang after her and jerked her back.

"You sit down and shut up," she said coldly. "You're lucky you aren't ashes along with us and the whole house. I mean it. Don't you move."

Mommee began to wail. Glynn sat her smartly down on the chaise and stood behind her, holding her down by her shoulders. Glynn's face was mottled white and red with outrage, and tears still ran down her face.

The first fire truck came wailing in then.

The fire was out when they got upstairs, but they doused the bathroom and Glynn's bedroom with water from their hoses anyway. The hoses were big as boa constrictors; the mess they left was incredible. The clothes were a sopping char, and the walls and mirrors of Glynn's pretty bathroom were velvety with half-inch-thick soot. The bedroom was not too bad, smoke-wise, but the carpet and curtains and upholstered pieces were sodden. I thanked the firemen and they left and I stood in the doorway, mindless with relief and with anger at Mommee. Shock made my arms and legs weak.

Mommee streaked by me and into the bathroom, with Glynn in pounding pursuit. The old woman stumbled on a wet bath mat and I caught her just as she was about to tumble into the bathtub with her handiwork.

"Look at the fire! Look at the fire!" she crowed with glee, reaching down to pat the blackened mess. Wet soot came away and smeared her arms and hands and streaked her face and matted her hair. She peered sideways at me. She looked like a crazy toddler caught in its mischief—her eyes gleamed and her color was high—and she babbled and laughed and clapped her hands.

"I'm sorry, she got away from me," Glynn gasped. Turning to Mommee, who was wriggling in my grasp, she shouted: "You like it? Is it fun? You like what you did to my new clothes?"

"Fun!" Mommee shrieked. "I had fun!"

"You old bitch! I *hate* you!" Glynn screamed into Mommee's face and burst into tears again, then turned and ran downstairs.

Mommee began to cry too, grizzling and whining like a child. She looked up at me out of the corner of her eye, and dropped her lashes, and turned the crying up a notch. She could always get around Pom this way.

"Come on," I said angrily. "You can damned well stay in your room while I try to clean this mess up. And you can cry till this time tomorrow, as far as I'm concerned. Pom isn't here to soothe your butt now."

I dragged her, kicking and yelling, out of Glynn's bathroom and down the hall and locked her in her room. She began to kick the door and howl in earnest. I knew that she would go on doing both until hoarseness made her stop. I did not care. I went downstairs, found Glynn in the kitchen sobbing, and hugged her hard.

"We'll replace the clothes, of course," I said. "And I promise you we'll do something about Mommee. This is way, way too much."

"Daddy won't let us," she hiccuped.

"Don't bet on it," I said. "Why don't you call Marcia or Jess and see if you can spend the night over there tonight? I'm going to have to dry your room out before I can clean it."

"Can I? I don't think I can go up there again right now."

"Of course you can. Go on and call and I'll take a swipe or two at the bathroom. It may not be as bad as it looks."

"I could help."

"You can help later. This time's on me."

I got some sponges and detergent and buckets and a mop and went back upstairs. Mommee howled on and on; the kicks showed no signs of abating. I ignored them and took a deep breath and went into Glynn's bathroom.

It was as bad as it looked and worse. I knew that we would have to have professional cleaners, the sort that dealt with fire and water damage. The oily smoke and soot clung to everything, invaded every crevice in the tile. I mopped up a little of the standing water and wiped off a few surfaces, but managed only to smear myself with soot and my shorts and shirt with thick black goo. Wiping off the mirror, I looked in. I looked like an aborigine, black-faced and white-eyed, with wild coppery hair.

I was sitting mindlessly on the floor with my back against the bathtub when Pom came thudding up the stairs, taking them two at a time.

"God in heaven, what happened?" he shouted. "The alarm people called the clinic and said there was a fire; is anyone hurt? What's the matter with Mommee? Are you all right? Was Glynn here?"

"A, there was indeed a fire," I said. "Mommee put Glynn's new clothes in the bathtub and lit them. B, what's the matter with her is that I locked her in her room before she killed herself or set another fire. She's fine, just pissed. C, yes. I'm okay. D, yes, Glynn was here. She found Mommee doing it. I think she's out on the patio. I wish you'd go talk to her. She's terribly upset."

He stared at me for a moment and then went, not downstairs to Glynn, but down the hall to Mommee's room. I heard him speaking softly and coaxingly at her door. The crying and kicking stopped. In a moment he was back in Glynn's bathroom, saying, "Where did you put the key to her room? She's scared to death."

I looked at him in silence, and then said, "It's on the marble-top table. I can't believe you're doing this."

"Doing what?"

"Going down there and petting that old woman after she destroyed all Glynn's new clothes and bathroom and most of her bedroom and could have burned down this house and killed all three of us. I can't believe that, Pom."

"Well, you and Glynn are obviously all right and the fire's out. She's obviously not all right. I never heard her so agitated."

He turned and went out of the bathroom. I laid my head on my forearm on the edge of the bathtub and closed my eyes. We had to deal with the matter of Mommee now, but the thought of the evening ahead tired me so that I wanted to go to sleep right there, my head on cold, filthy enamel, the sour smell of destruction in my nostrils.

He stayed in her room a long time. I had made up the downstairs guest room for Glynn and had a sandwich supper on the table when I heard Mommee's door open. Glynn had decided to stay home; Jess's house, she said, was still an emotional uproar, and Marcia's grandparents were visiting. She had washed her face and combed her hair and changed her clothes and seemed restored to a sort of distant calm, though she said very little. When she heard Mommee's shuffling steps on the stairs, and Pom's low, soothing voice, she stiffened.

Pom came into the breakfast room, his mother clinging to his arm and shuffling like a frail, crippled centenarian. If I had not seen her streaking for the river like a wild thing that afternoon, I would have thought something had happened to her, a stroke, perhaps, or a bad fall. She looked up at Glynn and me under lowered lashes, and her lips trembled. So did the hand that clutched Pom's arm. Glynn looked at me and rolled her eyes, and I felt a fresh spasm of anger at Mommee. Ordinarily her punished-child routine occasioned only amusement in me, but tonight it did not amuse me at all. There had to be some sort of accountability for what had happened; we must not let her think she could win approbation and cosseting with destruction.

"Mommee has told me that she's sorry about what happened, and that she didn't mean to do any harm to Glynn's clothes," Pom said. "She didn't know what the fireplace starter was. Now I think it would be a good idea if you two told her you were sorry, and then we'll all have some supper and watch TV and put the whole thing behind us. Maybe Glynn could run up and get us some Rain Forest Crunch for later."

He stopped and looked at Glynn and me, waiting for our apologies. I simply stared at him. Glynn's face began to redden across her cheekbones, as if she had been slapped.

"Sorry for *what?*" she burst out. "I'm not the one that set fire to those clothes! I'm not the one who almost burned the damned house down! I'm not about to apologize!"

Pom's face reddened too.

"For screaming at your grandmother, for one thing," he said. "For calling her names. She's not too out of it to remember things like that. She was heartbroken. You know she didn't know what she was doing! You know we never, never yell at Mommee! It would be like yelling at a baby!"

"I won't apologize," Glynn said tightly. "She damned well did know what she was doing. I've seen her playing with the fire starter before. I won't apologize and I wish she was out of here! Then maybe the rest of us could have some kind of normal life—"

Mommee began to wail again. She turned her face into Pom's shirt and pressed it there, clinging to him, sobbing.

"You will apologize or you will not go to camp or anywhere else this summer, young lady!" Pom shouted. "I will not allow abuse of someone helpless in my house! I don't know what's gotten into you; I don't even know who you are!"

"You're right, you don't!" Glynn cried. "Here's a news flash; I'm your daughter. Remember me? The kid who's been hanging around your house for sixteen years waiting for you to—"

"*Go to your room!*" Pom roared. "*We'll talk about your behavior tomorrow! And don't you come out until I say you can!*"

"I don't have a room! That old witch ruined it!" Glynn cried and turned and ran into the guest room and slammed the door. I heard it lock behind her.

My head buzzed with horror and anger and for a moment I could not speak. I tried to control my voice, but it came out ragged and without breath behind it.

"Have you lost your mind?" I whispered at Pom. "Can you hear yourself? Did you hear how you talked to your daughter? It wasn't her fault, Pom. Maybe Mommee can't help it, but neither can Glynn and neither can I, and this crap cannot go on any longer! Pom, your mother almost burned down our house! She almost killed your wife and daughter, along with herself! *Something has got to be done about her!*"

Mommee's wails escalated, and she began to gasp for breath and choke and cough.

"*Shut the hell up right now, Merritt!*" Pom shouted. I did. I could not have spoken if my life had depended on it. Who was this dark, roaring man? What had happened to us?

"I will talk to you when I get her quiet," he said tightly but in a lower voice. "Maybe by then you will have gotten control of yourself."

He turned and helped his mother back up the stairs. She leaned heavily on him. Just as heavily I sat down at the table. I felt as if the whole world had exploded in my face, and the pieces were still falling to earth around me like lethal rain. I had to get up, I had to go and see to Glynn; I had to make him understand. . . . But I could not move.

I was still sitting there when he came back down, this time alone.

"I gave her a shot. She's asleep," he said. "I don't understand what's going on around here, Merritt. I don't know why things are falling apart all of a sudden. Why can't you cope with one sick little old lady anymore? Why has Glynn turned into such a spoiled, helpless brat?"

I knew that I would be terribly angry with him again later, but right then I was merely endlessly tired. I could not imagine where I was going to find the breath and strength to make him see.

But I knew that I must, so I inhaled deeply and said, as calmly as I could, "You aren't here most of the time. You don't see. You can't possibly know. I've coped as long and well as I could; so has Glynn. She's a very long way from being a spoiled, helpless brat, Pom. You should have seen her today, she was so funny and normal, and so proud of her new clothes—"

He leaned forward, as if to better understand me.

"Why shouldn't she be normal, Merritt? She's sixteen years old. She's had everything on earth that could be given to her; she's had the best life we could make for her. She never learned to abuse sick old people from us—"

I knew then that I would not remind him of the anorexia, nor tell him of its recurrence. In this mood it would surely become another weapon for him.

"She has never in her life abused Mommee, if you insist on calling it that. But she has a limit, and this business with Mommee has stretched her far thinner than you can possibly know. Even I didn't realize—"

"Both of you should have to work in the clinic all day," he said in exasperation. "It would make what you think you have to do look like a garden party. Why weren't you watching Mommee? Where the hell did she get the fireplace lighter? Why wasn't someone with her? Merritt, we made a deal a *long* time ago. It was your idea, as I recall. You were all for it. You'd look after the kids and the house so I could do this work. You said yourself that it was the most important thing you could imagine. You said you loved taking care of the kids and seeing that things ran smoothly for all of us. And you did it so well and you still had plenty of time to yourself, even when the boys were at their most troubled, even when Glynn was a baby and a toddler. You did almost anything you wanted to; you never had to stop your freelance work. What changed? Why can't you look after the people who need you, all of a sudden?"

"The people who need me don't need only me now," I said, trying not to shout or weep at the words. They seemed so unfair that I could not imagine how he could even think them, much less say them. But I knew that he meant them. His face was wrinkled with the need, the desire, to understand.

"Your daughter needs you, too," I said. "She's played second fiddle to the halt and the lame at that clinic for a long time now. And then here comes Mommee. Every time Glynn expresses need of you you give her a lecture about people with real trouble, about doing real work. Pom, the reason we made the deal in the first place was so that your children, and later our child, would never have to live the way the people in the clinic live. That was the most important thing in the world to you then; that they have better lives than that. So that's the way I raised them, and now you criticize Glynn precisely because she's *not* like them. She's *not* spoiled and trivial; she's as good and responsible a child as I know. But she needs you, too. And she doesn't often get much of you. As for Mommee, she needs more than me *or* you now. If you were with her all day you'd see that she's gone beyond anybody's care but professional people's. With the best will in the world, I can't keep her safe now, or us safe *from* her. I cannot be with her every second out of the day, nor can Ina. Where was I? I fell asleep outside on the chaise while she was occupied up in her room and Glynn was out. With the intercom beside me. I couldn't give her a pill because you said not to, and I had just had a long emergency session with Glynn. I was exhausted. I'm sorry. Where did she get the fireplace starter? I do not know. I've taken all the matches in the house away, and I thought I'd locked up all the fireplace starters. Glynn's right, Mommee does know what they are. She's started several small paper fires with them. Yesterday she cut up one of the drapes in her room with garden shears because I'd hidden all the other scissors, and that was with Ina in the house with her. The deal isn't valid anymore, Pom, because things have just changed too much. Can't you see that?"

"I'm trying. But it all boils down to the fact that Mommee is not responsible for what has happened to her, and I will not have her punished for helplessness."

"So instead you'll punish Glynn for it. And me."

"I've never punished you."

"Somehow what *I* need seems to have gotten left out of the equation," I said.

"Well, then, what is it that you need, Merritt?" he said with the exaggerated calm that you would use with a child in mid-tantrum.

"I need . . . some air and light and some attention," I said, surprising myself. "I need for you to think about what I need before I tell you. I need you to be with me, just *me*, every now and then. I need full-time, professional, live-in help with Mommee, a nurse or an attendant of some kind. Either that or she is going to have to go to a nursing home."

"She's *not* going to a nursing home. She's not going to be left in the care of total strangers. We've discussed that. It's not an option."

"Pom, your mother is out of her mind. She is not who she used to be. She does not know what she is doing, maybe, but what she is doing is destructive in the extreme. You wouldn't allow this sort of . . . drudgery . . . to fall on anybody in your clinic. Why are we so much less important to you?"

"People don't treat their family members that way."

"I didn't think they made servants and captives of them, either."

He got up and took a sandwich from the platter and went out of the kitchen. At the door he looked back.

"I'm going to catch up on some paperwork," he said. "And I want you to try to calm down. We'll talk again in the morning. Glynn can sit in on it, too. I'm willing to listen to what both of you have to say, but you're going to have to respect my point of view, too. Meanwhile, we're just spinning our wheels. I'll probably be up late. You turn in. It's been a hard day. Mommee will sleep through. We'll get somebody in to clean up Monday."

I did not reply, and then I called after him, "I'm going to tell Glynn she can come out of her room now. She hasn't had any supper."

"Yeah, all right," he called back. "But I don't want her going out anywhere. She's still grounded until we talk this thing out."

"Where would she go?" I said into the empty air of the kitchen. He did not, of course, hear me.

I went to the downstairs guest room door and knocked softly.

"Come out, the storm's over," I said. "I've got a sandwich and some milk for you. We'll all talk this out in the morning. The fire just got your dad upset—"

"Thanks, Mama, but I really don't want anything," she called back. I could hear the TV going. "I'd like to watch TV for a while and then go to sleep. I'll be fine in the morning."

"Don't just stay in there and brood. Come watch TV with me. Daddy's going to be working till late. And Mommee's out for the count."

"I'm not brooding. I really am tired. And *Dune* is on again, and you know you hate that. I'll see you in the morning."

"Night, then. Sleep tight."

"Night, Mama."

*   *   *

I fell asleep before Pom came to bed. When I woke, it was morning and he was sitting on the foot of the bed in shorts and a faded T-shirt, toweling his hair. I knew he had been out running along the river. He was drinking coffee and held out a cup to me.

"I'm sorry if I was a pompous ass last night," he said. "I shouldn't have lost my temper, but we had a bad thing at the clinic; I think we're going to lose a kid. And then the fire—"

"I'm sorry about the child," I said. "Is it the meningitis case?"

"Yeah. Listen, I think I'll make some pancakes. I'll take some in to Glynn. I should probably apologize to her, too. I guess I was pretty heavy with her last night—"

"Yeah, you were," I said.

He went out of the room, and I heard him rooting around in the pots and pans drawer and knew he was looking for the skillet he liked to use for pancakes. Presently I heard the spatter and sizzle of the batter. I finished my coffee, and stretched, and got up to dress. I was just padding downstairs barefoot when I met him on the stairs coming up. His face was still and empty, and the white ring that I had not seen in a long time was around his blue eyes. My breath caught in my throat.

"What?"

He cleared his own throat, and then he said, "She's run away. Glynn. I went to her room and there was no answer and I went in, and she was gone and the bed didn't look slept in, and there was this note—"

I took it out of his hand. My own hand trembled so that the note fluttered crazily.

"Going out to Aunt Laura's for a while," it said in Glynn's round backhand. "She said I could come. I can't stay here anymore and things will be better for everybody without me. Don't worry. I have my birthday money and Aunt Laura charged the ticket to her American Express card. I'd say I'm sorry but I'm not."

I put my hand up to my mouth. I could not make any words come out. How had she done it? How did she know what to do? But in my mind I could see my child dialing Palm Springs; hear the low, anguished conversation; watch her creep silently up the stairs to her ruined bedroom to get some clothes and her small stash of money; see the lights of the Buckhead cab as it waited up on the road.

"What in God's name got into her?" Pom exploded. "How could she do such a stupid thing? Of all the irresponsible, childish—"

"Hush," I said, and went into the kitchen and dialed Laura in Palm Springs.

The phone rang and rang, and then Laura picked up.

"I thought it would be you," she said almost gaily. "Yeah, she's coming. I'm picking her up at Ontario a little after ten. Don't fuss, Merritt; I'm really looking forward to having her, and apparently you all have one too many children around the house at present. Cut her some slack. She's old enough to visit her aunt if she wants to. We're going to take off and just drive; I've got this incredible rebuilt Mustang convertible, a sixty-five, a classic, and we're going to take it on an inaugural journey. I thought up the coast, to L.A. and Malibu and maybe even up to San Francisco. Top down, radio on. Sunshine all the way. I know people we can stay with along the way; she won't need any money. And besides, I've got plenty now. My new barracuda of a lawyer just parted Sonny with a wad. This is going to be my victory tour—"

"Laura," I interrupted, "You put her on a plane back home the minute you can get a reservation. I mean that. I can't have her tearing up and down the California coast in a convertible—"

"With a loose woman?" she laughed. "Why is that worse than a crazy woman who sets her clothes on fire? Or someone who locks her in her room when she protests? Jesus, what a circus. Lighten up, Sis. Haven't you ever heard of the age of consent?"

"Laura, for God's sake—"

Pom tore the phone away from me and yelled into it: "Laura, don't screw around with something you don't understand. Get her back here. I'll pay you back. But do it."

Her low, liquid laugh spilled out into the room, like a little baroque quartet.

"Fuck you, Pom," she said, and hung up.

He turned to me, his face near purple, the blue eyes burning like embers in a dying fire.

"I always knew she was going to do something dangerous, to herself or somebody else," he said. "If I could get my hands on her I'd strangle her. She ought to be committed; she should have been put away years ago—"

"So what are you going to do?" I said through lips numb and stiff with shock and fear.

"Keep calling until Glynn gets there and tell her to get herself on back here or she's going to be in the kind of trouble she never knew existed. For starters," he said, "she'll be lucky if I don't slam her in a convent."

I turned without a word and ran up the stairs.

"Where are you going?" he shouted after me.

"I'm going to go get her," I said over my shoulder.

"Don't be a goddamned fool, Merritt," he yelled. "You can't do that! Who'll look after Mommee? I can't take any time off from the clinic—"

"Fuck the clinic," I said furiously, "and fuck you if you don't like it."

From behind her closed door Mommee began to howl dismally.

"Fuck you, too," I said to her and slammed my door.

Three hours later I was on a plane west, feeling virtually nothing but the giddy, not unpleasant sensation that I had leaped off the very edge of the world and was falling free in clean, blue space.

4

Laura met me at the Los Angeles airport at two o'clock that afternoon. Glynn was not with her. Our meeting felt strange and disconnected from reality, like something you would see in a film. I knew that I was tired from the long trip and the near sleepless night before; in Atlanta it would be late afternoon now. And I had not managed to eat much of my plastic-encased airline lunch. But it was more than that; more, even, than the simple incredibility of what I had just done. It was Laura. She was the Laura I had always known, and yet she was not.

It had been six years since I had seen her, though we had talked a few times on the phone before this morning, and I wrote once in a while and received a scribbled reply now and then. It stood to reason that she would have changed. She had been through three hectic marriages and three hard-fought divorces, and I knew her career was not flourishing. If she had been a real success in films we would have known. I did not hear much about the plays she was in, and the TV commercials that were the bones of her income were apparently local and regional ones. And the stylist's job, and the jewelry and poetry and talk of becoming an agent all spoke eloquently, though not of success. Of course she would not be the Laura who had breezed through Atlanta those six years past, on her way to the Caribbean to do a film starring Mel Gibson. "Susan Sarandon gets him, but I get the best sex scenes." She was thirty-two then, at the very apogee of her looks and talent, fully bloomed and ripe, seeming to shine. She was still happily married to her third husband, whose career had not yet vanished up his nose, and her own career seemed poised at last to career skyward.

She was thirty-eight now. The Mel Gibson movie had not, after all, gotten off the ground, and the marriage had crashed into it. I don't know what I was expecting.

She was leaning against a pillar just beyond the arrival area, wearing blue jeans and a white T-shirt and cowboy boots. For a moment I was not sure it was her, though the posture and the tilt of the head were all Laura. She was deeply tanned, something I had never seen before, and her hair was a yellowish platinum, sleeked straight back behind her ears. Her teeth flashed white in her dark face when she smiled at me, and for a moment she was purely a creature of celluloid, none of my own and nothing to me. But then the sherry eyes crinkled, and she moved toward me with the old hip-shot Laura prowl, and I knew her once again.

We hugged, and she gave me a little sucking air kiss on either side of my face. She smelled of Opium, as she always did, and of something else; was it whiskey? Had she been drinking? Laura had never drunk much after her last disastrous foray into alcohol and pills, and that was years ago. I did not think she used anything now, despite Pom's words about cocaine. But I did not know what the smell might be. Medicine of some sort, maybe. When I pulled back from her, still holding her hands, to look at her, I saw that her face was much thinner, and sharper of cheekbone and brow, and there were delicate taupe shadows under the extraordinary eyes. She wore no makeup that I could see, and her lips were slightly chafed. Around her eyes was a faint webbing of tiny white lines. And she was definitely thinner. I could see sharp ridges of hipbones through the tight, white-faded blue jeans, and even the bones in her hands were sharper, more fragile.

"Wow," I said. "Look at you. You are a bona fide glamour puss."

"God, Met, glamour puss? Who's writing your material? It's for a film I just finished; I'm letting it grow out now. Well. You look good yourself. Not at all like a middle-aged lady who just ran away from home."

She used her old toddler's nickname for me; she had not been able, at first, to manage Merritt.

"I didn't run away, as you well know. Where's Glynn? Is she okay?"

"Oh, yeah, she's fine. Aghast at what she's done and scared shitless that you're going to snatch her home to Daddy and he's going to kill her, but basically she's fine. We thought it would be better if I came by myself, to sort of see how the ground lay. Neither of us wanted her to get spanked in the middle of LAX."

"Nobody has ever spanked Glynn in her entire life," I said. "Did she say we had?"

"No. Lighten up. She just acts like you do. Come on, I'm parked at the curb and they're going to tow me for sure. You have luggage?"

"Just this," I hefted my carry-on.

"Not planning to linger, are you?"

"No. This is not a social call. You know I just came to take her home. We're not going to argue about that, Laura."

She held up a propitiating hand, and walked ahead of me down the concourse toward the baggage claim. I followed her, the duffle slapping against my leg. Fatigue and strangeness hovered around me like a miasma. I felt as though I was walking and walking, and not getting anywhere. But presently we were through the thronged claim area and out into the strange bronze sunlight of early afternoon. We did not speak until then.

A red Mustang convertible, top down, was pulled up to the curb in the no parking zone, and an airport cop was just walking around behind it to get the tag number. It was an old model, but it gleamed as if it had just come, newly molten, from the factory.

"Oh, Lord," Laura said huskily. The southern accent she

had lost in high school drama class crept back. "I guess that's nonnegotiable, huh?"

"Afraid so," the cop said, staring at her. Even in the Los Angeles airport, where half the women who walked through were blond and wore the jeans–T-shirt uniform and were probably Somebody, Laura stood out. The indefinable, old electric charge smote the air around her. I saw the cop register the fact that here indeed *was* Somebody and hesitate very slightly. I knew then he was lost. Laura did, too.

"You see, officer, my big sister has come all the way from Atlanta to see me for the first time ever, and my radiator started acting funny in the desert, and I just got the car and I don't know anything about it yet, and I wanted to surprise her, and I was running *so* late . . ." Laura let her voice trail off and crinkled her nose. She grinned, managing somehow to make the grin both repentant and imploring. He grinned, too, slightly.

"Well, seeing as how it's your big sister—"

"That's very decent of you," Laura said, and made that sound as if it were an invitation into her bed.

I tossed my bag into the backseat and Laura climbed into the driver's. As she started the ignition the cop appeared at her side.

"I wondered if you'd mind," he said, handing her in a blank ticket pad. "I've got this kid—"

"Of *course*."

Laura took the ticket pad and scribbled on it with his proffered ballpoint and handed it back with a flourish. He examined it, and broke into a broad grin.

"This'll kill him," he said. "*Batman* was his all-time favorite. Seen it four times."

"Hope he likes it," Laura said, and gunned the car, and we were out of the shade of the overhang, into the strange pewter air.

"You didn't," I said, laughing helplessly.

"Why not? He saved me a fine," she said. "Some people do think we look alike."

Not anymore, I thought, and felt a rush of sadness for her, and the old, fierce, protective love.

"You've got her beat a country mile," I said, and she

smiled, and it was the old, sweet, enchanting Laura smile, without salt or shadows in it.

"I'm glad you're here, for whatever reason," she said. "I was afraid you were going to be furious with me."

"I should be, I guess. At you and Glynn. But right now I'm madder at Pom and maddest at Mommee, and neither one of them can help it, really."

"He can't help screaming at Glynn and grounding her for the rest of her life? And yelling at you? The old lady can't help setting Glynn's clothes on fire and then squalling for her sonnyboy?"

"She has Alzheimer's, Laura. She doesn't know what she's doing most of the time. And he . . . well, command is sort of what he does. It's what a doctor is all about; it's got to be that way or he can't function. Pom runs a charity clinic down in the projects. Can you imagine what that would be like if he couldn't control it? Sometimes he forgets where he is; it's hard to turn a lifetime of habit on and off. And he's crazy about his mother, and this illness just devastates him. I think it frightens him, too. To get outside help, or put her in a home . . . that means that he can't take care of her, that it can't be fixed. He just can't handle that yet."

"Poor baby," Laura said. I was too tired to keep the discussion going, and did not answer. She was silent for a while, too.

She wove the car in and out of the heavy traffic on what the signs said was the San Diego Freeway. It could have been any large artery in any commercial-industrial area of any large city in the world. The air was noxious, foul and tasting of metal and sulfur and asphalt and gasoline. It stung my nose and eyes and throat. I felt tears start, and a scum of stinging stickiness film my face and arms. The heat was monstrous. Every few minutes we would come to a halt in a frozen river of traffic and the air would eddy and sway, cobralike, above the glacier of cars, and horns would begin to shriek. Before we had gone five miles I surrendered.

"Could we put the top up?" I said. "Maybe you're used to breathing this stuff, but it's stripping my throat out."

"Yeah, Atlanta has such pure air," she grinned, and I smiled reluctantly, because Atlanta's air is frequently just as

awful a stew of assorted fumes and stinks, only with the addition of killer humidity.

She pressed a button and the top rose and glided silently
into its groove. She raised the windows and turned on the air
conditioner and the immediacy of the devouring air shrank
back, leaving us sealed in a capsule of quiet and stale cool,
rushing air. The Mustang's windows were tinted gray-green
and gave the landscape outside the sinister air of a futuristic
movie set on some alien, metallic planet where a thin no-
color ether took the place of air. The strangeness I had
brought with me bloomed into fullness, and I gave myself up
to it.

"Nothing feels real," I said, lying my head back against
the headrest.

"Nothing is," she said. "That's our secret. You're going to
do just fine out here."

She pushed a tape into the deck and the pure, somehow
lonely voices of the Fifth Dimension spun out into the car:
"When the moon is in the seventh house/And Jupiter aligns
with Mars/Then peace will guide the planets/and love will
steer the stars./This is the dawning of the Age of Aquarius . . . "

She turned her head to me and smiled.

"This was one of the first albums you ever bought me,
remember? When you were in college and I was feeling kind of
down? It's always seemed the most comforting song to me; it
promises so much . . . "

I remembered. She had played the record over and over,
shut away in her room, until it had become inoperable, and I
had had to buy her another.

"Do you need comforting, Pie?" I said, like her reverting
to an old nickname.

"Who doesn't? But no, not really. I just like the song,
that's all."

Her tone said the discussion was over, and we fell silent
once more. She turned onto the Santa Monica Freeway, and I
watched as names I had heard all my life sailed by on off-ramp
signs: Century City, Twentieth Century Fox Studios, La Brea,
Venice. I acknowledged them in my mind, but felt no curiosity about them as I usually did such signs in other new places.

Here in this hurtling gray-greenness, everything was strange and consequently nothing was.

She made another turn and said, "I think we'll try the San Bernardino Freeway. It's a little longer, but you'll have a better shot at the mountains this way. Sometimes this stuff lifts outside L.A. proper."

"What mountains? Will we pass the Hollywood sign?"

"No, that's back there behind us, in the Hollywood Hills. I've seen it about twice. We'll see the San Gabriels and later the San Bernardinos. I hope. Right near Palm Springs the mountains come right down to the road; they're really something. It's beautiful country. I hate it when I have to leave."

I put my head back and closed my eyes. Pom's face swam into the space behind them, furious and anguished. I felt a stab of pity and love, and then, once more, the cold, constricting anger that had set me on this journey. Only this morning, it was. It felt like days, weeks. Pom's face faded. I must have slept.

When I opened my eyes again the seemingly endless string of flat, sun-blasted little towns and strip shopping centers had given way to long stretches of pastel desert broken by strange, spiny, sentinel cacti and scrubby copses of small, silvery gray, wind-ruffled trees. The metallic sky had turned deep blue, and to our left a tidal wave of sharp, deep-shadowed mountains rose. They were so clearly defined that I could see small folds and crevices, carved cliffs and rock faces, the lighter scars of tracks and roads. They were stained the colors of earth and air: rose, brick, taupe, dust-gray, slate, deepwater blue. Beautiful; they were as alien and beautiful to me as the face of the moon.

"Are those the San Gabriels?" I said. "Where are we?"

"No. The San Bernardinos. We're just past Ontario, coming up on Redlands. Home before long," said Laura. She stretched both arms straight out and rotated her head on her neck.

"I'll bet you could use a drink and something to eat," she said. "I left Glynn making miso soup. She only said yuck six times."

"How can she be making miso soup? I don't even know what it is, much less Glynn. You may be sorry."

"Nah. It'll be good for you and her, too. Full of vitamins," Laura said. "Listen, Met, it may be none of my business, but she worries me. She's a neat kid . . . Lord, what a beauty; I had no idea . . . but she's not really a kid. She doesn't giggle, she doesn't squeal, she doesn't preen and look at herself in mirrors, she doesn't even have any hot rollers or makeup with her. What's going on with her? What's wrong at your house?"

"There's nothing going on with her," I said stiffly. "She's never giggled and squealed and all that silly teenage stuff; I think we're going to be spared that. She *is* a good kid; the best. She writes and paints, and she's good at music and great at science, and her grades are tops, and she's a terrific swimmer; she wins meets . . . and there's nothing wrong at our house. Thank you for asking, though."

"Don't mention it," she said dryly. "Nothing the matter, huh? That's why she runs away from home and you come tearing out here right behind her? There damned well is something wrong, and if you don't know it, she's in even worse trouble than I think she is."

"Look, it's just this stuff with Mommee," I snapped. "That's going to be settled when we get home, believe me. It's not easy to be sixteen in a house with an addled old lady—"

"It's more than that," Laura said. "No, I will not shut up, so spare me that familiar scowl. She may be your daughter, but she's my niece, and she came to me for help. Have you looked at her lately, really? God, Met, she's so serious, and pale, and so damned *thin*! And she seems apprehensive, even scared, all the time; she whispers like she's listening for something. What does she do for fun, clean out her closets? Or no, I remember, there's nothing now to clean out, is there? She told me about her new clothes. Christ. Why do you put up with that old harpy? No wonder Glynn ran away. I bet Pom's sainted boys split long ago, didn't they?"

"The boys are twenty-two and twenty-five," I said. Anger thickened my voice. She had always known just which buttons to push. "Chip is working in New York for a brokerage house, and Jeff is in med school at Hopkins. They're gone because it was time for them to go out into the world; nothing drove them away. Mommee wasn't even with us when they left. She was with Pom's brother and his wife then."

"What did *they* do, leave her on a hospital doorstep and skip the country? So now you have her. And I mean you, because I bet Pom doesn't spend more than five minutes a day with her. Brings old Mommee home and leaves you with the whole thing, you and Glynn."

"It was my choice, Laura," I said evenly, determined not to fall back into the old pattern of attack and defend, thrust and parry. I could not stop myself from adding, "Everybody can't run away."

My voice sounded smug even to me. But she only shrugged.

"Why not? Where is it written? So you're going to cart my niece home tomorrow, huh?"

"That's right."

She gave me a long, oblique look from the sherry eyes.

"Let her stay," she said. "Let me show her some of my world. I know a zillion people in the industry; we could see studios, and screenings, and go to lunch at famous places, and I could introduce her to some really famous people. It's fantasy land, maybe, but it's mine, and what kid wouldn't love it? She might even turn into a *real* kid."

"Even if I wanted to, Laura, I can't," I said. "Pom is really angry at both of us. He'll get over it, but if I push him much right now he's going to ground her for the rest of her life. I don't want him to really punish her."

"Bullshit," Laura said. "It's you he'll punish. Listen, has she ever had a boyfriend? Has she gotten her period yet?"

"She's a late bloomer. I was. Lots of her friends are."

She was silent for a long while, and then she said, "Anorexia can kill you, Met."

"Do you really think we haven't been treating her . . . eating disorder?" I cried. "She's been to doctors and in therapy since she was fourteen. It's much better."

"Couldn't be much worse," Laura said. "Why not try something different? Aunt Laura's Sure Cure. I advise a long motor trip in sunny California, with the top down and good food and new clothes and exotic locations and glamorous people—"

"I can't let her run all over California by herself, Laura. Be reasonable." My heart was thumping with annoyance and something else I did not want to examine.

She was silent again, and then she said, "She'd be with me. What you mean is, you can't let her run all over California with a crackhead actress. I haven't done a line or had a drink in years, if you're keeping score. Besides, you could come, too. See my world. I'd love that, Met. I'd love to show you what draws me, what makes me real. I've always wanted to; I've always thought that if you could just see it, you'd understand . . . you might see who your daughter is, too, or who she could be. You might even see what you are. You might like what you see."

"Oh, Laura! I have family—"

"I thought *we* were family," she said softly. She kept her eyes on the road and the mountains. They were darkening, casting long blue shadow fingers over the earth. Reaching for us in the red car.

She looked over at me then.

"Aren't we three here just as much family as your four back there?" she said.

"Pie, please understand—"

"Oh, I do," she said. She did not speak again.

I was silent, too.

We swept over a rise and down into the vast, mountain-ringed bowl of a valley. Its flat bottom was steeped in shadow like tea, but light still limned the peaks of the mountains, and the sky over them was going silvery. On our left and right stretched huge fields of what looked at first to be strange, stylized, prehistoric birds, all in frenetic motion. They ran in orderly rows that reached to the base of the mountains. I drew in my breath, and then saw that they were propellerlike windmills, all running in place before an unseen wind.

I exhaled in pure delight. Laura looked over at me and smiled.

"I know," she said. "They never fail to knock me out, no matter how many times I pass them. They're driven by convection, the hot air rising from the bottom of this valley where the mountains hold it in. It's like someone has literally planted the wind."

I smiled at the lovely little turn of phrase, forgetting completely that I was angry with her.

"What are they for? What do they do?"

"Power. They can light this desert up for a hundred miles. Back when the big quake up at Big Bear Lake took out all the power these guys went right on working."

"Quake . . . Lord, that's right," I said, remembering the strange weather and the talk of storms and sinister atmospheric phenomena and the renegade climatologist on TV. "Y'all are supposed to have the big one any minute now. No way am I going to let Glynn stay out here with that hanging over you—"

"Jesus, Met, we have them all the time, little ones, and none of them ever turn into the really big one. Northridge *was* the Big One; everybody says so. We barely felt Big Bear, and it wasn't far. If you're thinking about that wacko scientist, you might remember how the New Madrid business turned out. You're just reaching, now."

And I took another deep breath and let it out, and was quiet, because that's just what I was doing.

You can see Palm Springs a long way away. It is a great swathe of green, a dense emerald prayer rug, flung down in all the tawny, wild-animal colors of the desert. I found it hard, when it came into view, to look away. Palms, jacarandas, hibiscus, lantana, and a great many other exotic flora for which I had no name yet, formed bowers and islands in the almost continuous velvet carpet that, Laura said, was a network of golf courses without parallel in the United States. These were spotted with flashes of silver and blue: ponds, water holes, lakes, and the swimming pools of hundreds of hotels and villas, all catching the last of the sun. In the shadow of the mountains, and up in their steep foothills, lights were beginning to bloom. It looked like a Fabergé village or a particularly glittering Disney theme park.

"Where are the people?" I said. There seemed to be no cars moving on the arrow-straight toy roads that bisected the green.

"At cocktails. Or getting ready for cocktails. Or in some cases getting over the ones they had at lunch," Laura said. "This is the hour of the dressing drink."

"What do you do if you don't drink?"

"Oh . . . eat. Make love. Garden, if you are so undistinguished as not to have a gardener. Bicycle or run; it's too hot to do it any other time, except early morning. Ride the tram."

She gestured ahead, and following her hand I made out a miniature railway snaking up a mountainside, with a tiny tram toiling slowly up it, toward the pink-gold light just receding from the peaks. I thought that what you saw from the top at this hour must be incredible.

"That looks like fun," I said. "Have you ever been up to it?"

"Believe it or not, I haven't. It's sort of like New Yorkers and the Staten Island Ferry. But we could go tomorrow. Glynn wants to."

"The plane I want leaves at noon," I said. "I don't think we could make it if we did the tram."

"There's another one at six."

I did not answer her. The teasing, singsong note I remembered from her childhood was back in her voice. It made me want to shake her and hug her close at the same time. I did not need for Laura to revert to childhood; I had enough on my hands with one agitated child.

Laura swung off the freeway and onto a narrower road. It ran for a time through low, sculptured buildings where fairy lights bloomed on outdoor patios and cobbled streets twisted off into the blue shadows of other buildings. There were people here; strolling in and out of shops, sitting on terraces sipping drinks, jostling and crowding in the canyonlike streets. The buildings were adobe, I supposed, and bleached by the fading light; they reminded me more of Casablanca or Tangier than the American West. Then we were through the cluster and Laura nosed the car up an even narrower road that seemed to climb straight into the roots of the mountains.

Buildings here were low and many-leveled, climbing with the earth. Lights starred some of them. At the end of the road, where the mountains jutted straight up into a rock cliff, lay the carved white cluster of Merlin's caves that I remembered from her photographs. They were beautiful, but seemed somehow inimical to life. Where would you put your garbage cans in this place? Where would you hang your wet bathing suits, air your rugs? Where would you park your car? When we swung around behind, I saw where: a long, low, white, stable-like building with twisted log supports housed a scattering of Mercedeses and Jaguars and BMWs. There were one or two more Mustang convertibles like Laura's, gleaming in the dusk. Some of the spaces were empty, but Laura stopped and stared at one that was not. The dusty back end of what appeared to be a late seventies Pontiac protruded from it.

"Shit. Somebody's company has got my space," she said. "Everybody knows not to do that; now I'm going to have to call around and catch whoever it is, and they're going to give me all that crap about not knowing their guests were parked there and . . . oh, it's Stu! Oh, good! Or at least I hope it's good. Damn him, he knows I'm going to have to park in the driveway now. It embarrasses him for people to see that wreck he drives—"

"Who is Stu? I'm surprised Glynn let him in. She knows better," I said uneasily, thinking that I was not exactly thrilled to have Glynn left alone with one of Laura's men friends. My mind swiftly built Stu from the air: lithe as a panther, snake-hipped, ponytailed and earringed, teeth bleached the white of bones and flashing in a tanned face, jeans riding low, and shirt unbuttoned to show the gold chain nestled in the thatch of chest hair. The gold chain holding the key to Laura's condo.

She caught my tone and laughed.

"Stu is my agent. Stuart Feinstein. He has a key. No, he's not going to ravish Glynn. He's far more likely to be feeding her something healthy and horrible and regaling her with lifestyles of the rich and famous. He's a darling, an angel, my best friend; he's never given up on me. And he's HIV positive and I think he's got active AIDS, though he won't say so, and that's breaking my heart. He seems awfully frail lately. I think I'm the only client he still does much for. He truly believes I'm an extraordinary actress, and that's more than I can say for most people around here these days, including, sometimes, me."

"AIDS—"

"She's not going to catch it from him, Met. Not unless

she's sleeping with him, and I doubt that. He's gay as a goose.
You're not going to catch it, either. Doesn't Pom see HIV at
that famous clinic?"

"Of course he does, all the time," I snapped. I was not
accustomed to having my sister treat me like a child.

"And I do, too. I volunteer at Jerusalem House back
home; it's this wonderful place where people with active
AIDS go and live out whatever time they have left. Their
families won't have them. The volunteers are incredible; they
do literally everything that needs doing. The residents are
pretty great too, come to that."

"Terrific," she said, climbing out of the car and stretching. "What do you do there?"

"Well, I help out with public relations. In fact, I'm going
to take that over full-time when we've got Mommee settled, I
think. I'd love to put what I know to work for them."

"PR. Whoopdedoo," Laura said, and went into the gated
back entrance of her condo without looking back. Picking up
my tote I followed her. I felt like a Junior Leaguer discussing
her provisional work. In fact, I had not wanted to join the
League, and was pleased that Glynn did not, either. But still,
that's how Laura made me feel. I tried to run lightly and
authoritatively up the little curved staircase, needing to regain
my big-sisterhood again. Out here in this vast, glittering
desert, without my familiar context, I had the uneasy feeling
that I was not at all the woman who had boarded the Delta jet
in Atlanta that afternoon. But if not her, then who?

She opened the door and vanished into it, and I stood for
a moment simply breathing in the alien sounds and smells,
and thinking what I would say to my daughter. Somehow, in
all the long afternoon and evening, I had never sensed what
would be right. I could not feel my way into the meeting
ahead. But then, I had never had a daughter who had run two
thousand miles away from home, either. I had no precedent
for this.

". . . and so I said, well, darling, somebody's got to tell
you, and I might as well be the one, because I really don't give
a happy rat's ass, see, and the plain truth is, you look like a
bratwurst in that dress."

The voice was a tiny, breathy, beelike drone, and might have come from a petulant child, except that there was a sort of corrupted warmth in it that no child could possess. Over it I heard my daughter's laugh. It was what I thought of as her real laugh, the one she used when she was flat-out tickled and delighted: a belly laugh, a charming, froggy croak.

The other voice laughed, too, and said, "Yes, well there are distinct advantages to dying. You don't care what you say to who. I'll bet nobody ever said anything even remotely like that to her in her life. And you know what? She went back and changed the dress."

"Really? Was it better?" Glynn said.

"Oh, tons. This time she only looked like a meatloaf."

I stood still, feeling as if I were eavesdropping on children at play.

"Are you really dying?" Glynn said.

"I really am. Not for a while yet, I don't think, but yep, I'm definitely buying the farm," the bee voice said.

"Is it awful?"

"Sometimes. Sometimes it's pretty awful indeed. And then sometimes it's almost hypnotic, a nice, dreamy, underwater feeling. I kind of like those times."

"Which do you feel most of the time?"

"You know, most of the time I really don't think much about it," he said. "HIV people learn to live right square in the moment. Like babies."

He must have seen Laura then, because he cried, "Hello, dollbaby! Look what I found messing about in your miso. Can I keep her? She's quite the prettiest thing I've seen until you walked in."

"Stuart, you faithless hound," Laura said, and there was the sound of her air kiss and an answering smack of lips on flesh. "This is my niece, Glynn. She's running away from home."

"Well, I know that," he said. "In fact, I know just about everything there is to know about this dollbaby, including the fact that her mama is coming to get her and is in fact here, if that long, tall shadow I see on the floor there is to be believed."

I felt myself flushing and walked into the kitchen.

A tiny man looked at me. He was damply pale and bald as an egg and looked very old. Then I saw that he was not old, but very ill. Illness seeped out of his pores and dragged at the flesh below his eyes so that the whites showed; illness had eaten away at the meat of him until only his bones were left, fragile and somehow very formal and lovely under the translucent, greenish skin. He had deep-shadowed dark eyes and the remnants of a dark beard, spotty and dry now. His smile was one of singular sweetness and mischief. I felt myself smiling back.

"The shadow says hello," I said. I looked past him. Glynn, still flushed with laughter, stood stiffly against the refrigerator, backed up against it. Her eyes were wide and her silky hair, fresh-washed, hung in them. She wore her Guess jeans and one of her voluminous, knee-length sweatshirts and her Doc Martens. She should have looked ridiculous, but instead she looked beautiful, and so frightened and vulnerable that I felt tears well into my eyes. I loved her and was glad to see her and was even gladder that it had turned out to be as simple as that.

"Hi, baby," I said, and she began to cry and ran across the floor and buried her head in my neck. The sweet-smelling top of it came up past my ears now. We had known early on that she would be tall.

Laura drew the little man out of the kitchen and I rocked Glynn gently while I held her, and then said, "Such a lot of tears for such a skinny kid. Don't waste 'em on your ma; save them for when you need them. I'm not going to holler at you. Didn't you know I wasn't?"

"Is Daddy terribly mad at me?" she said, her voice muffled with tears and the cloth of my blazer.

"Terribly. But I imagine he'll be over it by the time we get home. In fact, I'm sure of it. He's even madder at me, if that's any comfort. But what he really is, baby, is scared. He's scared because his mother is sick and crazy and he can't help her, and he's scared because he yelled at his only daughter, whom he loves more than anything in the world, and she was so hurt she ran all the way across the country by herself, and he thinks maybe he can't get her back, and he's scared because

I took off right behind her. Think about that: the three main women in his world and one is crazy and the other two are on the lam. How would you feel?"

I felt her laugh a little and thought that the tears were over. She raised her stained face to me.

"I feel like such a dork," she said. "I wasn't trying to hurt him or scare him, or you either. I just . . . it just seemed like after what he said nothing would ever be the same, and I didn't think I could stand that. And it wasn't fair, Mama, it wasn't fair—"

"Oh, Glynnie," I said, sighing at how far she had to go, and how little my words could help her. "Almost nothing is, really. There's what people feel about each other and what they do to each other, but hardly any of it is a matter of fair. I want you to grow up expecting all sorts of wonderful things, but I mustn't let you grow up expecting fair."

"You think he'll forgive me, then?"

"He already has. He got up this morning and went downstairs to make pancakes especially for you. He was taking them in to you when he found your note."

"Oh, poor Daddy—" her eyes welled up again.

"Let's not go too far with this," I said. "Daddy acted like an ass and he knows he did. He needs you to forgive him as much as you need him to forgive you. He may not have gotten around to realizing it yet, but he will before you see him again. And I promise you, the Mommee stuff is going to stop."

She sighed deeply. "Will you forgive me?"

She brushed the drifting, wheat-colored hair out of her mouth. Her blue eyes were still shuttered with the thick, gold-tipped lashes that were Laura's lashes, too. She was not yet ready to look me full in the face.

"For what?" I said, brushing the hair back and looping it behind her ear.

"I must have scared you to death. You never would have taken off out here otherwise."

"You did. You did indeed scare me to death, and I do indeed forgive you. Now wash your face and come on in the living room. I want to meet this strange man who had you yodeling like Mammy Yokum."

"Mammy who?"

"Go on and wash. Scram," I said. "We'll talk some more about this after I've called Daddy and told him when our plane gets in."

She hesitated for a moment.

"Mom . . ."

I knew she was truly over the spell of tears and nerves. "Mom" was back. "Mama" was for the bad times.

"Hmmmm?"

"Oh . . . nothing."

She vanished into a door that I presumed led to a bathroom and I went into the living room to meet Stuart Feinstein.

He and Laura sat close together on a large, white sofa before a fireplace. A small fire of some strange, sweet-smelling wood snickered behind a beautiful, old, wrought-iron screen, and a bottle of white wine and four glasses stood on a coffee table of weathered gray wood. Besides a tall white lamp, large pillows, and a pair of black canvas butterfly chairs, the room was empty of furniture. Bookcases lined three walls but were bare, and whiter spaces on rough adobe walls spoke of paintings that had once hung there. One wall was uncurtained glass, and the view out over the night-blue bowl that held Palm Springs was breath-stopping. I could see why Laura had fought so hard to keep the condominium. It would be like living in the sky, like a god.

"Join us. We're celebrating," Laura said, and Stuart Feinstein waved his glass. It was nearly empty. Laura did not appear to be drinking.

"Celebrating what? Surely not a runaway teenager and a grim old bat of a mother in hot pursuit."

"Well, of course, that. But there's something else. I've just finished a movie—I promised Glynn not to tell you until we got here—and this angel of a man has gotten me an interview with the *Hollywood Weekly*. That may not mean anything to you, but it means shit-all in the industry. It might even mean I can kiss that goddamn concho jewelry good-bye."

She reached over and hugged Stuart Feinstein hard and gave him a smack on the mouth, like a child. He hugged her back with one arm, the other hand balancing the sloshing wineglass.

"How about it, huh? Can the old man still deliver or what? Huh?" he crowed. Also like a child. In the light of the big, white lamp I could see that he was not only ill, but, as I had first thought, rather old, or at least far from young. They looked poignantly like two children, I thought suddenly, huddled together on the big, white sofa as if for comfort against the limitless night outside. The image brushed at my mind like a black bird.

"A movie! Oh, Pie, that's really wonderful! Tell!"

I poured myself a glass of wine and sank cross-legged to the floor in front of the fire. A small sheepskin rug cushioned my bony buttocks against the quarry tile floor. A picture flashed through my mind that I had not seen there in many years: a dorm room at college, before I moved back home, crowded with Noxema-dotted girls in nightshirts, sitting on the floor and the beds, laughing and talking, talking, talking. Some of that same laughter bubbled somewhere in my chest. I felt, for just a wing-flutter of a moment, very young again.

"Well, it's not the lead, but it's a career maker," Laura said. Her voice sang. "The movie is about this guy, he's a real sonofabitch, coming up in the industry, from a gofer to a studio head, and about the people he does in on the way. Kind of like *The Player*, only darker, denser. It's a real character piece; not so much action, but these intense, devouring relationships. Caleb Pringle did it. You know, *Bad Blues* and *Burn*? The character stuff is his signature . . ."

She stopped and looked at me, waiting for me to recognize Caleb Pringle and register my delight and wonderment. I did not have the foggiest notion who he was. I had never heard of *Bad Blues* and *Burn*.

"I'm sorry, Pie, I haven't seen a movie since Mommee came. I'm hopelessly behind. Tell me about this Caleb Pringle. He sounds like he ought to be manufacturing cashmere sweaters in New Hampshire, or something. *After* you tell me about your part."

"I play one of the women he seduces and leaves behind in the gutter, as it were. An older woman, an actress hoping to make a comeback, still very beautiful, but lost, fragile, doomed. He's just starting out when he meets her, and she still has terrific connections, so he uses her for that and then dumps her. Remind you a little of *Sunset Boulevard*? Believe me, it's better. I commit suicide, or my character does. Liquor and pills on the deck of his empty, locked beach house, only ambient sound and this strange, white sunlight. There's this seagull who sits on the railing and stares at me while I'm dying—it sounds dumb, but it's very powerful. Pring says it's best-supporting stuff. He says nobody but I could have done it. This interview—God, Met, it's going to help so *much!* The guy who's doing it is a shit, but everybody reads him first, and I can handle him."

"He's latent," Stuart said. "Makes him mean."

"Oh, you're telling! You said you'd wait," wailed Glynn, coming into the room. She had brushed her hair back and tied it high, so that the bare symmetry of her facial bones showed, and her skin was flushed with scrubbing and excitement. We all smiled at her. It was impossible not to. Where did I get this lovely being? I thought. I thought I would kill the first thing that hurt her.

"You can tell her who plays the jerk," Laura said.

Glynn turned to me, her face suffused with rapture.

"Rocky MacPherson," she breathed, as if she were saying "'Ave Maria.'"

"Rocky MacPherson? Isn't he that kid who keeps busting up thousand-dollar hotel rooms? See, I do keep up."

"He's an incredible actor," Glynn cried. "He's all . . . all spirit; he just burns on film. Caleb Pringle uses him in almost all his movies."

"He's also about fourteen, isn't he? It's a real stretch from busting up the Biedermeyer to studio head. He *must* be good."

"He is, as a matter of fact," Laura said lazily. "Very focused and *very* sensuous. He's almost stopped with the hotels. Pring has brought him a long way. And as for studio heads, I don't know many over thirty anymore. I found our love scenes very . . . believable."

"Oh, God!" Glynn cried, her eyes closed in ecstasy.

"Like to meet him?" Laura said casually.

"Oh, my God! Oh, my God! Don't tease about something like that . . ." my rapt daughter whispered, and I looked at her in faint alarm. Was this the child who had said only last week that she planned to have her children by sperm bank because she couldn't stand the thought of any of the stupid boys she knew touching her?

"I'm not teasing," Laura said. "Stu says they're screening *The Right Time* sometime this week. Rocky's sure to be there. I can easily make a call or two and find out where and when. Pring was supposed to let me know, but Stu says he's out of town courting some money guys for a new movie. The production office will still be open. They'll give us some passes. That is, they would if your mother would let you stay for a few days."

She dropped her eyes and fiddled with the silver bracelet that circled her thin wrist. I wanted, as I had wanted so many times in the past, to shake her until her perfect white teeth rattled.

"Mother . . . Mom . . ."

I took a deep breath. I was certainly not going to allow Pom to punish her for this flight. On the other hand, I could not let her be rewarded for it, either. Glynn was a responsible child, but I had a horror of her coming to think that running away was an answer. There had been too many flights, literal or figurative, in my life to allow her that notion. I knew the prices paid all around for them. But my heart hurt me, just the same. Damn Laura. Damn Pom. Damn Mommee.

"Not this time, Glynn," I said firmly. "This isn't a pleasure trip, remember? We've got to go home tomorrow. Your father is already fit to be tied, and there's nobody with Mommee. Show him you can be grown up about things this time and I wouldn't be surprised if he didn't let you come back and visit Aunt Laura before school starts."

"But Rocky MacPherson—"

"Rocky MacPherson is the very last reason on the face of this earth I would let you stay in California, Glynn. I don't want to hear any more about him, or this. Aunt Laura spoke before she thought."

I gave Laura a long, level stare and she gave me her three-cornered kitten's smile in return. Stuart Feinstein studied the contents of his glass with interest.

"I think I'll go to bed. I'm very tired. Excuse me, please," Glynn said, her voice shaking, and walked with absurd and touching dignity out of the room. I heard her steps climbing stairs somewhere off to the right. All of a sudden I felt old, as old as Mommee, as old as the world. Old and dull and inflexible and . . . all right, mean. And tired within an inch of death.

"Good work, Laura," I said.

"I didn't mean any harm," my sister said. "You ought to lighten up on her, Met. You could lose her if you keep treating her like a prisoner."

"Do tell me where you acquired your child-rearing expertise," I said, suddenly furious with her.

"Not, apparently, the same place you acquired yours."

The old sullen petulance was in her voice.

"I managed to keep you fed and clothed and out of jail for a lot of years," I said.

We stared at each other.

"It's late. I've got to be getting back," Stuart Feinstein said, rising painfully. He seemed for a moment to totter. Laura broke the stare and turned to him, putting her arms around him.

"No way am I letting you drive all the way back tonight," she said. "Met and I will save our fight for tomorrow; it's nothing new. It's been going on for thirty-odd years now. We know the rules. You can have the couch. I'll even give you the mink throw. I'll make you cinnamon toast for breakfast and you can go back after that. Please, old Pooper. I just can't worry about you passing out on the road tonight."

"I'll take you up on it, if you dollbabies will stop fighting," he said, giving us the sweet smile. "You're too precious and pretty to fight. Merritt, did anyone ever tell you you looked like Kay Kendall? She was an English actress, very classy. Used to be married to Rex Harrison. An offbeat beauty with such a nose, and a smile that could melt your fillings. You've got both of them. You're far too pretty a dollbaby to fight with this bad child."

"I'll stop if she will," I said, managing to smile at him.

Even ravaged with illness, his charm was enormous. "I need to sleep more than I need to fight. Where am I sleeping, Laura? Not, I hope, in the room with Camille up there."

"No. I'll sleep on the other bed in her room. You take mine. It's the first door at the top of the stairs. I need to get up early, anyway, and you need to sleep a little. If you're set on the noon plane you can zonk in till about eight."

"Thanks," I said. "I guess I'd better call Pom and get it over with. I'm surprised he hasn't called four hundred times by now. Is there a phone upstairs?"

"There is, but why don't you wait until morning? It's one A.M. in Atlanta now. And he may have called; I turned off the answering machine and the phone bell. Glynn was spooked bad enough as it was."

"Oh, shit, Laura," I said. "Now he's going to think that we've all three run away or been ax murdered or something. But you're right. I forgot the time difference. He's got early pediatric clinic in the morning. He'll be asleep by now. Wake me when you get up. I need to get that over with."

"I will," she said. "You go on up. I want to talk to Stu a little while longer."

The last thing I heard as I climbed her deep-carpeted stairs into darkness was my sister's melted-butter voice saying, "Now, tell me everything you know about Pring. Don't leave anything out."

I didn't call Pom the next morning for the simple reason that Amy Crittenden called me first. Laura came and shook me awake at six A.M.

"Grendel's Mother is on the telephone for you," she said.

"Who?"

"The snottiest woman I ever heard in my life. She says she's Pom's secretary, but I doubt it. He'd have fired her years ago."

"Oh, God. Amy," I sighed, and reached for the phone on Laura's bedside table.

"Hello, Amy," I said as cheerfully as I could. "I'm sorry you had to call. I was going to call in a little while."

"Well, I wish you had thought to do it last night, Merritt," she said in her long-suffering tone. I wondered if Pom really heard her anymore. Laura was right; he'd have had to fire her.

"Sorry. It was so late there when we got in that I thought I'd let Pom sleep," I said. "What's up?"

"You could have called any time. Doctor hasn't slept in twenty-four hours. Neither one of us has. His mother was terribly agitated, and your housekeeper declined to come in on her day off. Doctor was so distraught that he called me. I was glad to come, of course. He absolutely must have his sleep; we have pediatrics this morning, I expect you know. He asked me to call you and find out if everything is all right. You simply cannot imagine how worried he has been, what with his daughter running off like that, and then you, and his poor mother—"

"Yes, I'll bet he was," I said, idiot laughter tugging suddenly at my mouth.

"Well, Doctor has some messages for you," she went on briskly, after waiting a space for the apology that did not come.

"I'll bet he does. Shoot, Amy," I said, gulping back the laughter.

"The first is that he has you and Glynn booked on Delta's noon flight out of Los Angeles today. The tickets are waiting for you at the counter. The second is that you're to come straight to the clinic on your way from the airport. We had to bring his mother with us this morning; he simply could not spare me another day, and of course it was out of the question that he stay home with her. She has been terribly disruptive; we have had to lock her in the children's playroom, I'm afraid. Two of the nurses are with her, but she is upsetting the children no end, and of course we cannot spare the nurses indefinitely."

"Where on earth is Ina?" I said, the picture of Mommee commandeering rocking horses and dolls from tearful toddlers threatening to undo me completely.

"I think Doctor had some words with her when she refused to come in," Amy said repressively. "I believe he discharged her."

"Shit! He can't do that!" I shouted. "Sorry, Amy. It's not your fault. But Ina is my right hand; I can't manage that old . . . Mrs. Fowler without her. You tell Pom—"

"He is going to be tied up most of the day," Amy said. I could have sworn there was satisfaction in her voice. "He is most adamant about your coming to pick Mrs. Fowler up, though. Oh, and one more thing—"

I drew a long breath.

"And that is?"

"He has made Glynn an appointment with a new therapist tomorrow at two P.M. Dr. Ferguson; we think very highly of him. He specializes in families. He will want to see you, too."

I did not speak. A red mist of rage seemed to start on the horizon and roll toward me. I watched it with fascination.

"Are you still there, Merritt?" Amy said. "We must insist that you pick up Mrs. Fowler as soon as it is possible. She is utterly out of control. Yesterday she got away from me and got into the swimming pool and I had to go in after her clothed. My foundation garment was ruined."

A great yelp of laughter escaped me. I simply could not help it. The red mist dissipated.

"You give Doctor a message for me, Amy," I said, choking on laughter. "You tell Doctor that Mrs. Doctor and Daughter Doctor are not coming home on the noon plane today. It will be two or three days, at least. I will let him know when we decide. And we will not be here after an hour or so."

"Where may I tell him you are going?" Amy said. She sounded as if she were trying to speak with her jaws wired shut.

"You may tell him," I said, "that we are going to the movies."

5

In the middle of my first night in California I woke feeling that I was on a boat and lay awake trying to think why that might be. After a moment of profound disorientation, in which the light of a whiter moon than any I knew at home flooded a room I could not put a name to, I remembered where I was and why, and sat up. The green glow from Laura's digital bedside clock said four ten a.m. I sat listening, holding my breath, but heard no sound that would account for the boat notion. The house was silent and still, and presently I got up and pulled on my robe and went into the adjacent bathroom. The top floor of the condominium was chilly, and the air that poured in through the window I had opened was dry and sharp and smelled of the desert. I thought of my child sleeping in a narrow twin bed across the hall from me, in Laura's guest room, and wondered if her sleep was troubled, and if she, too, dreamed of boats. I had a sudden, nearly irresistible urge to tiptoe across and open the door and look at her, but hesitated to wake her. She needed respite from the tension of the night before, and so did I. Tomorrow, I thought. We can sort it all out tomorrow. Or rather, later today.

I had turned on the cold water tap and was bending to splash my face when the cold tile floor beneath my bare feet rolled greasily, as if it were the deck of a boat. It rolled again, more strongly. I clutched the sides of the washbasin, thinking that I had not, after all, dreamed the motion. But what could it be? The floor seemed to undulate, and I felt queasy and queer. Was I going to faint, had an illness of some sort overtaken me? It was not until I noticed that the glass accessories on the countertop were tinkling and the towels were swaying on their bars that I thought: earthquake. By the time the terror hit, the motion had stopped.

I cannot remember a simpler and deeper fear. It had never occurred to me that the real terror of an earthquake is not, in its first instant, the threat of injury or death, but the simple betrayal of one's primal covenant with the earth. With that connection gone, anything at all is possible; no horror imaginable is beyond possibility. It is the old, cold, howling terror of the abyss, that black and limitless space that underlies all the armaments and rituals of the human condition. We all sense it is there, in the deepest and most unexamined core of us, but there are few things that call it out past the careful layers of civilization. The convulsing of the earth is one.

I froze to the washbasin, holding my breath, and then turned and fled from the bathroom straight downstairs, where a light burned. I would remember that flight with shame for the rest of my life. When the earth began to retch, I ran, not to my child, but to the light. The fact that there was no light and no stirring in Laura and Glynn's bedroom assuaged the guilt only slightly. I like to think that if I had heard evidence of alarm from my daughter I would have gone there instantly, but now I will never know for sure. It was the first chink in the surface of my selfhood, the first of my intimations that Merritt Fowler might not be Merritt at all, but someone unknown to me.

Downstairs a single lamp burned, and Stuart Feinstein sat on the sofa wrapped in a beautiful, dark fur throw, sipping from a glass of amber liquid. His face was so gray and ravaged that at first I thought the same fear that had frozen me had gripped him, but then he saw me and gave me the sweet child's smile, and the grayness receded somewhat. It was not fear, I saw, but illness and despair.

"Did our little twitch wake you, dollbaby?" he said.

"Twitch! My God! It felt like . . . I thought for a minute I was on a boat! The floor rolled—"

"About a three point eight or a four," he said. "A mere shiver. We get one like that about twice a week, maybe more this summer. We have ever since I came out here. I don't even get out of bed anymore unless I hear wood splintering. I used to lie there and listen to the Waterford crashing, until I got smart and packed it all up. This was nothing, I promise. Come here and have a snort with me."

I went over and sat on the opposite end of the sofa. He tossed the end of the throw over me and passed me his glass, and I drank. It was scotch, very good scotch. Even I could tell that. My usual drink is vodka in whatever is tart or sweet, and then not often.

"Thanks," I said, passing the glass back to him. "I needed that, as they say."

"Thank you," he said, and when I looked at him inquiringly, he said, "For not being afraid to drink after me. Or for not showing it if you were. Is this your first earthquake?"

"I work with AIDS patients at home," I said. "I'm not afraid. And yes, it is my first earthquake. Now that I *am* afraid of."

"Don't be. Like I said, we get them all the time. We're close to the San Andreas here, and it grumbles constantly. But it's already had its big one; we're not scheduled for another thirty years. San Francisco, now, that's another story. The Hayward is ripe."

"How do you know? How can you be sure of all that?"

"I can't, of course," he said, running his hand over the rich, shining folds of the mink. "But the odds are good. That's about all anybody can hope for, isn't it?"

I could see blue veins through the dry, crepey skin of his hands, and fancied that I could see the bird's bones themselves. Stuart Feinstein was a man who would know about odds. Somehow the thought, or perhaps the whiskey, made me relax.

"I'll go back to bed and let you get some sleep in a minute," I said. "But first, tell me about this movie Laura is in.

Tell me about this Caleb Pringle. There's something there, isn't there? They're something to each other, or were . . . ?"

He took a deep swallow and made a face and put the glass down on the coffee table.

"The movie's good. Her part is good, and she's very good in it. She's a real actress, you know; this part could be the one that gets these schmucks out here to see that in her, and not just her tits and ass. There's a lot riding on it. She's almost past the age where she can play babes; she'll have to do it on the acting from here on out. Pringle sees that in her, and he can get it out. I'll give him that. Yeah, there's something between them; I think that's why he put himself on the line with the studio over this part of hers. He almost doubled her pages. From what I hear, it paid off. I don't hear much anymore. I'm a has-been. I was that before the disease was obvious. I was never all that much of an agent; she was the best thing I ever had or ever will, now, and I called in an awful lot of chips to get Pringle to let her test for this one. Once he did, she did the rest. The chemistry was there between them from the first. You could see the lightning hit. They were together all through the filming, hot and heavy. I was welcome on the set because of that, and that only. No, don't protest, dollbaby, I know I'm done in the industry. I don't care, really, except for her. I'm sick of it; it eats you alive. Makes you little. I'd have pulled out of it long ago except for her. The last thing I could do for her was to get her this interview with Billy Poythress. It was the last chip I had. The production office wouldn't even tell me when the screening is, but she can find out when she's up there. Poythress will know. After today there's nothing much I can do for her except hold her hand and pray."

"Does this Pringle care for her? Is he good to her?"

He made an impatient gesture.

"He was while they were shooting last winter. He couldn't do enough for her. Everybody knew about them. The media was all over it. As for now, I don't know. He hasn't been around. He's off chasing down money for a new film. I heard he was in Europe for a while; he may still be there. If he is, he hasn't let her know. I don't think she's heard from him in a month or so, but she wouldn't tell me that. Tells me what she has from the beginning: It's the real thing for her, the rest of her life, and so forth, and so forth. Says he feels the same. But I've got a bad feeling about it. She doesn't look good to me. She's thin, she acts like she's somewhere else most of the time. Sleeps too much. Sometimes her eyes are red like she's been crying. Like I said, she's not going to tell me. Doesn't want to worry a sick man. Like she could help it."

"So what kind of person is he? Would he dump her; does he do that?"

"He's an asshole jerk, is what I think. He's a phony. Wears tennis sweaters and a baseball cap, drives an old woody, got freckles and a gap in his teeth and a big, crooked grin. His name isn't Caleb Pringle; it's Sherman Goetz, but I don't care about that. Nobody out here uses their real name. Yeah, he'd dump her. He sure does do that. He does it after every film. It's his schtick, ditching his last film's squeeze when shooting's over, just like copping ideas is his schtick. He calls it derivative filmmaking, says it's an art unto itself, to take a film that's already been done and do it better. Some other folks call it stealing. But he's good at it. He has the touch. He makes big bucks. I just want to make sure that he does right by her in this movie, no matter what he does to her personally. After it comes out she's not going to need him."

"I don't like the sound of this stuff."

"Neither do I, dollbaby. That's why this interview is so important. It's her ticket to ride. You make her promise to dress up pretty and be polite to Poythress. You look after your little sister for me."

"You're not going with her?"

"No. I think I'll stay here and kick back a little. Lie in the sun by her pool, sleep in, have some friends over. We worked it out last night. She's going to stay at my place above Sunset. You really ought to go. It's a great location. Right near all the things she'll want to show Glynn. The Sunset Marquis, where the interview will be, is right down below. And you'd have a terrific view. All of Hollywood at your feet, as it were. And I wouldn't exactly be an asset to her at this stage."

"Stuart, I just have to get Glynn home. But I really wish

we could stay, just to get to know you better," I said. "I wish there was some way I could thank you for being so good to my sister."

"You can go up there with her. You can give her moral support and have a good time yourself, is what you can do, dollbaby. She says you haven't had much of one lately. You or that pretty child of yours, either. Go. Enjoy. Giggle. Drink things with flowers in them. Eat only things that will make you fat. Ask for autographs. Drive that little red car too fast. Wear things that let your pretty tchotchkes hang out. That's what you can do. What's two more days out of your young life?"

"They are long days, believe me. But I think you're the best thing that's happened to Laura since she came out here," I said, getting up and kissing him on the cheek. "I wish you'd stick around to take care of her."

Then I winced, remembering why he could not. He smiled.

"I wish I could," he said. "Somebody is always going to have to do it. But now there's you. God looks after fools and actresses."

"But I can't do it indefinitely," I said.

"Why not?" he said. "Haven't you almost always, one way or another?"

"Oh, Mom, look! Oh, it's just so *cool!*"

Glynn stood on Stuart Feinstein's tiny balcony, staring out at the valley that cradled Los Angeles. I went out and stood beside her. The valley looked to me like two dirty cupped hands holding a city captive; the gray-yellow smog that lay thickly over it seemed the foul breath of the captor. It was not cool to me or beautiful; the sense of alienation I had felt at the airport the day before was back full force. But she was right in a way. It was a stunning vista. It had the impact of a slap.

We had left Palm Springs at seven, and Laura had kept the car at a steady eighty miles per hour through the desert, until the clutter of small towns and shopping centers began.

We had gotten into L.A. well before ten, and wound our way through the stalled traffic on back streets, up into the hills to Sunset and across it. Stuart Feinstein's building rode the crest of one of the canyon ridges directly above Sunset, and we pulled into his parking lot just at ten. After Amy's call at six, there did not seem to be any point in going back to bed, so I woke Laura and Glynn. Over bagels and coffee I told them we were going to Los Angeles after all. They were both jubilant; last night's conflict melted with the cold desert dew. The careening drive was brushed with a magical giddiness.

We were flushed from wind and sun—Laura had kept the top down all the way this time—and from laughter. The minute she had pulled out of her own driveway a great gust of liberation and silliness had swept us all, and we had laughed and shouted and sung songs out of our respective girlhoods all the way to the L.A. suburbs. I had not felt anything like it since college. Once or twice then my sorority sisters and I had driven in someone's convertible over to the Gulf Coast for spring break, crowded and sunburned and giddy and drunk on wind and speed and possibility, singing endlessly, laughing, laughing. This trip felt like that. In the hurtling Mustang, my blowing hair stinging my face and desert grit peppering my bare arms, I was someone else entirely than the angry, worried woman who had driven this road not twenty-four hours before. I had no sense, for that space of time, that Glynn and Laura were daughter and sister to me. We were, for those few hours, all young and all free and all waiting to see who we would be when the car finally stopped. I don't think I will ever forget that windborne flight through the California desert.

Back inside, Glynn and I prowled the small apartment while Laura closeted herself in the bathroom with Stuart's cellular phone. She had turned back into Laura when we opened the door to the apartment, kicking off her shoes and padding restlessly about, humming, picking up bric-a-brac and putting them down, straightening pillows, riffling through the opened mail in a shallow copper bowl on the coffee table. Finally she said she needed to make a call or two and then we'd change clothes and go prowl around Sunset a little.

"I don't have much to change into," Glynn said hesitantly.

"I don't have anything, to speak of," I said. "Do you have to dress for Sunset Boulevard?"

"Not the way you mean," Laura said, looking me over lazily. I was wearing the knit pantsuit I had worn yesterday, the one I usually travel in. "But not the way you are, either. Glynn's fine in her jeans and tee, but you are definitely from Away. Waiters will snub you. Street people will howl with laughter. Let me see what Stuart's got. He's about your size now, with all the weight he's lost. You can bet he'll have the right stuff."

"I can't wear Stuart's clothes, Laura," I said. "That's a terrible presumption. I'll see if I can find something on Sunset, maybe. You can bear the shame of being seen with me that long."

"Nonsense," she said, and went into the bedroom and began pulling open drawers and tossing clothes onto the huge, canopied bed. It was ornate and theatrical, by far the most imposing piece in the apartment. Somehow it made me want to avert my eyes. I hoped Glynn and I would not have to sleep in it, but I saw no other bed.

"Anything on Sunset will cost you an arm and a leg," Laura went on. "I wear his clothes all the time. He probably wears mine, too, when he's at my place. He'll be flattered."

She brought me out a couple of pairs of blue jeans, faded almost to white and beautifully pressed, and an armful of T-shirts, and went to make her phone calls. Glynn and I explored, the clothes slung over my arm. The apartment was small and low-ceilinged, and almost bare of furniture. Indentations on the thick, gray carpet spoke of furniture recently removed, and lighter places on the walls of vanished paintings, as they had in Laura's place. This place was much less opulent, much more utilitarian, than her condo, but it had the same air of transience, of waiting. The air was stale and close, and the few pieces of furniture left were lightly skinned with dust. Plants and a large ficus in a corner drooped, and in the tiny kitchen dishes sat in a rubber drainer on the counter, washed but not put away. They were yellow melamine, patterned with ivy. I could not imagine a Hollywood agent eating off them. I could not imagine a Hollywood agent living so meanly as this, especially in an aerie above Xanadu. Automatically I picked up the dishes and put them away in the cupboard over the sink, and filled a plastic pitcher with water for the plants.

"You're at it again," Glynn said, grinning at me from the doorway.

"At what?"

"Taking care of people. Of things."

"Well, the plants are in dire straits, and Stuart was dear to let us stay here. I thought I might as well—"

"It's a nice thing to do. You're a nice lady. I wasn't criticizing you."

Laura came into the kitchen, a tiny white frown furrowing her forehead.

"Nobody in this asshole place answers their phone anymore," she said. "Billy Poythress's oh-so-*excruciatingly* British secretary said he was tied up with the East Coast but would see me this afternoon at two at the Sunset Marquis for lunch as planned, unless, of course, his plans changed, and then she'd let me know. That is, if I could be reached at this *numbah*. I said I would be out all morning and would just have to take a chance. She said she quite understood. Bitch. I'd say he was screwing her, but I don't think he does women. Maybe she gives good—"

"*Laura.*"

"Sorry. Go on and get dressed. I could use a cup of coffee and all Stu has got is instant."

"Did you get the production office?" Glynn said as I went into the bedroom. Something in her voice told me she enjoyed saying the words.

"Nobody's answering there, either," Laura said. "Which doesn't surprise me. If the receptionist isn't around, and she almost never is, nobody else will answer. Too demeaning for filmmakers."

In Stuart Feinstein's bedroom, cell-like except for the towering Egyptian barge of a bed, I took off my pantsuit and panty hose and pulled on a pair of the blue jeans. They were so tight that I could scarcely zip them, but the other pair was tighter still, so I put them back on and riffled through the T-shirts.

They, too, fit so snugly that I could see every rib on my torso. I chose the largest, a white one that had faded Day-Glo fried eggs and bacon strips on it and said "Eat your breakfast." I looked at myself in the large mirror on the bathroom door and laughed. I looked like a punk adolescent boy in the alien clothes, angular and slouching and high-rumped. It was not, somehow, a bad look. I would never have worn the clothes in Atlanta, but seeing that I had no other choice, I was not going to worry about it here. Nobody knew me. Impulsively I took off the barrette that held my hair back and shook it out, bending at the waist. When I straightened up it flew about my head in a mass of tangles and ringlets and snarls that looked, in this place, not so wrong either. I went out and stood still for inspection by Laura and Glynn.

"Jesus, that's perfect, except for the shoes," Laura said, and Glynn said in surprise, "You don't look in the least like you. Not in the least. It's terrific. I *think*. You sure don't look like anybody's mom. Dad would die."

Then she dropped her eyes. I knew how she felt. I had forgotten Pom for the moment, too. I felt the familiar flush of guilt start, and pushed it back. I would call home that evening, I thought. No matter how angry I was at him, he could not be having an easy time.

Laura went back into the bedroom and returned with a pair of beautiful boots, pointed of toe and with a slight, undercut heel. They were worn but carefully tended, and looked expensive.

"Put them on," she said. "They may be a little big but you can stuff the toes. You can't go out in those Hush Puppies."

"They're not Hush Puppies, they're Ferragamos," I said indignantly, but I took them off and put on the boots. They were only a little loose. I went to the mirror and looked. Laura was right. The boots were perfect. I could not help swaggering just a little when we left the apartment. It was a feeling that seemed to start in my hip joints.

"These boots were made for walkin'," Glynn sang, and I hugged her and we all laughed and went down into the fever dream that is Sunset Boulevard.

An hour later we were sitting at an outdoor cafe, drinking

iced lattes against the sultry heat and watching the passing parade. Sunset Boulevard never fails you. Anywhere else it might seem freakish, almost grotesque, a Fellini street, but here the streams of strolling denizens looked charming, stylish, festive, funny, each in his own costume like people in a Mardi Gras parade. Everyone seemed either very old or young; I saw no one who appeared to be my age, and certainly no one who appeared to be my age as I was at home in Atlanta. Women were thin and striking and either wore chic black or chic jeans or so little of anything that they should have been on beaches. Men wore virtually the same thing, except the ones in outright costumes. There was enough spiky hair and pierced body parts and leather to break the monotony, and a careful scattering of Gap Prep, as Laura called it, but these last were, she said, almost surely visitors from the Valley. The rest belonged. We sat with our jeaned legs stretched out, sipping the lattes and watching, eyes shielded by sunglasses. I stared through mine at my daughter and watched heads turn as people passed her. She eclipsed all the passing young women, with a beauty built of chiseled bones and taut, polished bare skin and the wheat sheaf of hair. Why did she look so different than she did at home? I wondered. She wore almost exactly what she would wear there on any given day. But a flame, a new kind of blood, seemed to shimmer under her skin. Here, in this thick, metallic sunlight, Glynn shone like a tall candle.

A skeletal man on Rollerblades wearing a house dress and ankle socks and carrying a Vuitton tote whirred by and gave us a smile and a nod.

"Pretty ladies," he singsonged.

"Thanks," we all yelled after him, and laughed again.

"Don't mention it," floated back on the little hot wind he left in his wake. In a moment he was lost in the slowly roiling crowd.

"I love this place," Glynn said dreamily. "Everybody is so happy."

"Everybody is stoned on something," Laura said, smiling at her, "but I know what you mean. Sunset always makes me feel like something funny and fine is about to happen."

For no reason at all I thought of Stuart Feinstein, back in Palm Springs, huddled like an old, ossified baby in his nest of dark mink. Some of the silly shine went off the morning. I doubted whether, despite his proximity to Sunset Boulevard, anything funny and fine was left for him.

"I wish we could do something especially nice for Stuart," I said. "I can't get him out of my mind. He seems so vulnerable. Is there anything that you know of that he needs, Laura?"

"Oh, Met," she said, and smiled an exasperated smile. "Don't start trying to fix things up for Stuart, for God's sake. He doesn't need anything you could give him. You happen to have a cure for AIDS on you?"

"I just thought . . . his apartment is so bare. There's almost nothing in it. I thought maybe we could find some pretty pottery dishes, or a print or something—"

"He doesn't buy things that will last anymore," she said. "It depresses him to shop for things that will outlast him. He had some really nice things, or at least Bobby did, his lover who died a few months ago. They lived very well indeed. But Bobby's family from Iowa or some awful place came and took all his things away while Stuart was out of town, even the paintings and china and silver and crystal. There was some gorgeous Waterford. The only thing they left was the bed. Left it sitting there like a slap in Stuart's face when he got back. He hasn't seemed to want to make much of an effort about anything since then."

"Does he have, you know, enough money? He said he didn't handle clients anymore, except you. Does he have enough for food and medicine and all?"

"He has enough. I give him some every month. I know he's okay that way."

I looked at her. In the brassy sunlight she looked bleached and a little shrunken, even though she was still so beautiful that it was hard to look away from her. My careening, wind-scattered little sister caring for someone else?

"He doesn't seem the type to take it, somehow," I said.

"He doesn't know it comes from me. I deposit it to his account every month on the condition that it stays anonymous. He thinks Bobby did it just before he died. It gives him a lot of comfort to think that, that Bobby died thinking about his welfare. If the truth be known, Bobby was a little shit who never once thought about any welfare but his own. His only gift to Stu was HIV."

"It's a wonderful thing to do, Pie," I said, meaning it.

"It was part of the settlement with old No-Nose," she said, stretching lazily. "He thinks the extra was for massages for me. Fought it tooth and nail. But we got it. He'd shit sunflowers if he knew it went to Stu. He always hated him. Listen, gang, we've got time to do some serious shopping. Y'all game? I want something drop-dead-fuck-you to wear to this interview. This guy's got prettier clothes than I do."

The Sunset Marquis Hotel lay halfway down North Alta Loma, on a hill so steep that you practically had to cling to walls to walk down it. I thought that climbing it to Sunset must be sheer torture for leg muscles. Stuart Feinstein's cowboy boots were wobbling on my feet after two hours of shopping, and Glynn tottered in new high wedgies. Laura, in stiletto-heeled sandals and a new black mini so tight that she had to take tiny, Chinese-empress steps, could navigate scarcely any better than we two. The three of us clung together, arm in arm, wavering and laughing and looking, I imagined, like those old cartoon posters with the characters leaning far back, front foot far forward, that read, "Keep on Truckin'." We were out of breath and dripping sweat when we reached the little hotel.

Inside it was cool and shadowy, with a tiny lounge on the left, full of people looking as if they were closing enormous deals, and a little restaurant on the right full of very young men and women who all looked like Glynn. Rock stars, I thought; Laura had said this place was a hangout for traveling rock bands. Glynn gave them all long, devouring looks. They all looked back at her. One half-raised a hand as if to greet her, then dropped it. He leaned over and said something to the others at his table, and they all turned and studied Glynn. Even in the artificial dusk, I saw her neck and cheeks redden, and she turned away. We went into the chic little ladies' lounge and combed our hair and washed our hands and put on fresh lipstick, and then headed for the dazzle of light at the back, where the hotel opened into a tree-and-flower shaded patio around a brilliant blue pool. Laura stopped beside the maître d's desk, and I took a deep breath, and heard Glynn take a similar one. Then we were following a young waiter in white shorts and shirt around the pool to a round table in a corner, shaded with wisteria and some other red-flowered vine I could not identify. Every other table was crowded with people, most of them men in jackets and no ties, and there was a constant low chiming of telephones. Almost every table seemed to harbor someone talking on a phone. The drink of choice, I noticed, was mineral water with lime. So much for the legends of Babylonian excess I had cherished since girlhood.

"Mr. Poythress is running a little late, and says please order drinks or anything else you want and he'll be right along," the young waiter said.

"What a pity," Laura drawled, giving him a slantwise smile from under the brim of a huge, new, black straw hat. In it she looked enchanting, mysterious, completely feminine, something out of the forties, out of the time of Gene Tierney and Veronica Lake. The young man smiled back, dazzled. He looked over at Glynn and smiled even wider. She, too, had a hat, a slouchy canvas affair with a flower the blue of her eyes tucked under its brim. With the sunglasses and the tight blue jeans and wedgies she looked somehow androgynous, like a pretty medieval boy. I felt rather than saw eyes all over the patio swing toward our table and stop. Glynn and Laura made a riveting pair. I settled my sunglasses more firmly over my eyes, hoping I did not look too much like their duenna.

"Enjoy," said the waiter, and hustled off to get our Calistoga water.

"You might know the bastard would be late," Laura said. "He's probably watching from the men's room window, going to let us sit here just long enough to be insulted but not long enough to be righteously indignant about it."

From another table a voice called, "Laura!" and we turned. A thin, brown young man in the inevitable sunglasses and baseball cap got up from a table full of similarly dressed young men and women and came toward us, smiling and holding out his arms. He bent over Laura and kissed the air on either side of her face, and then stepped back and studied her, head to one side. He seemed not much older than Glynn.

"You look absolutely fabulous, lovey," he said. "Are you in town for the screening? I heard you were in Palm—"

"Corky, love," Laura said. "How good to see you. No, I'm really just up for an interview. I'm meeting Billy Poythress, if he ever gets here. Corky, this is my big sister, Merritt Fowler, and my niece, Glynn. This, you two, is Corky Tucker, who wrote *The Right Time* and is going to make us all rich and famous."

"From your lips to God's ear," he said. "It's nice to meet you both. I can see now where Laura gets it."

His smile slid with equal approval over Glynn and me, and I smiled back. "Hello," I said. Glynn said nothing, but smiled, a small, three-cornered smile with her mouth closed. I had never seen that smile before. Mona Lisa now . . .

"Will you sit for a minute?" Laura said. "Catch me up on the buzz about the film. I've been out of town, and I'm dying to hear—"

"Just for a second," he said, slipping into the fourth chair. "Billy Poythress scares the shit out of me. I doubt that I know anything you don't, though. Tomorrow night's going to be a complete surprise to all of us. Caleb isn't talking about it, but I hear some big changes have been made. Margolies insisted after he saw the rough cut. Nobody knows what they are. I wouldn't even speculate, knowing Margolies. A chorus line and a collie dog, probably. Maybe a black tap dancer. But you know all that, of course. Caleb's undoubtedly told you. You're the one who should be spilling the buzz—"

"Pring is back then," Laura said carelessly. "No, I've not seen him yet. I've been at home, back in Atlanta, just got in this morning. I brought Merritt and Glynn back with me for the screening, but I haven't had time to call Pring. Is he at home, do you know?"

I stared at her. Atlanta? She did not look at me.

"I hear he's holed up out at Margolies's place in Malibu, pitching the new film. It's about Joan of Arc, or some saint. God knows. Margolies probably remembers Ingrid Bergman in the original. The skinny is that he'll let go the money only if he likes this version of *Right Time* and if Caleb can find the right saint for the new one. He's talking about a nationwide talent search, the old *GWTW* business—"

"My God, Joan of Arc," Laura said, and laughed indulgently. "Maybe they can get the collie to play Joan. Burn a saintly dog. That ought to part Margolies with some dough. What does he think of *Right Time*, have you heard?"

"I don't think he's seen it since he asked for the changes," Corky Tucker said. "Tomorrow night's the night for all of us. I heard that somebody from the production met him at a party in Malibu and he smiled, though."

I laughed, thinking he was making a joke, but Laura looked over at me and said, "Whole films, whole careers, have risen and fallen on Margolies's smile," she said. "Listen, Corks, do you think you could get three tickets for tomorrow night for me? I'm not going to be any place Pring can call me, and I really do want these two to see the film. I think they think I do porno flicks, or something."

"Sure, I'll have three left at the box office for you. It's at the metroplex in Century City, you know, where we screened *Burn*. I hear Margolies will be there with most of the Vega brass. Probably won't be able to hear for all the folding money rustling. Maybe he'll put all the Fowler-Mason women in the Joan thing. You three are turning heads all over this patio, you know that?"

"Go on with you, you big old tease," Laura said in a mock belle's drawl. "You're just trying to turn our poor heads. Thanks for the tickets, Corky. We'll see you tomorrow night."

"Six o'clock. Everybody's going on to Spago after. Say hi to Caleb for me if you see him before then."

"I will," Laura said, and he went back to his table. Everybody at it waved at Laura. Laura waved back, smiling widely. She still did not look at me. I felt the strangeness and unease rise like mercury in a hot thermometer.

"What's this business about being in Atlanta?" I said.

"I'll tell you later," Laura said. "Here comes Poythress."

Over the years since I left the agency I have formed the habit of talking silently to Crisscross. I tell her things that I

somehow never tell other people; when something particularly absurd or embarrassing or appalling occurs I tell her. When
I am happiest or saddest or silliest I sometimes tell her, too. I
tell her these things in person, of course, when we do meet,
but I talk with Crisscross far more often than I see her. When I
saw Billy Poythress approaching us around the pool I tuned
her in.

"Lord, CC, he looks just like Porky Pig," I radioed across
the miles home. "His cheeks hang down and jiggle and he has
a round little butt and little plump bow legs, and that snouty
nose. He should have an apple in his mouth. And you should
see what he's got on!"

Billy Poythress did indeed look like Porky Pig, but a corrupted, faintly malevolent Porky. There was something
dried-out and unhealthy about him, even though he literally
shone. His cheeks and forehead glistened with sweat or
lotion, his little eyes glittered in folds of flesh, and he wore a
lilac and purple satin baseball jacket and cap that gave back
light like sunlit lava. Clay-red hair curled from under the
cap. His teeth flashed white in a wide smile, and rings on the
hands he held out to us as he trotted across the pool apron
glittered, too. Heads at every table swiveled to follow him.
Hands lifted in salute. Voices called after him. He acknowledged them all with little nods, but he kept his eyes on us.
The eyes on the patio found us and lingered, to see who was,
this day, Billy Poythress's anointed.

He stopped and looked at us, hands clasped under his
chin.

"I couldn't even guess," he said in a lilting falsetto. "You
three have utterly confounded me!"

"I'm Laura Mason," Laura said, uncoiling herself from her
chair and extending her hand to him. He mopped his brow in
mock relief, even though he was, I was sure, well aware which
of us was Laura.

"As good a guess as any," he said, and I felt the hair rise
on the back of my neck. It was a purely visceral reaction.
Nothing good was going to come to Laura from this posturing
little man.

She introduced us and he kissed us on our cheeks and

patted our hands and said that he should be doing an interview with all three Fowler-Mason girls, and then he settled himself into his seat and looked around the patio. At a slight lift of his plump hand the waiter scurried over, nearly tripping in his haste.

"You're not Clint; where is Clint?" Billy Poythress said. There was a slight petulance in his voice. Sulky Porky.

"Clint tore his rotator cuff playing volleyball yesterday and had to have surgery," the young waiter said. "My name is Charles. The maître d' asked me to take special care of you."

"Oh, screw his rotator cuff," Billy said. "What a bother. He knows exactly what I want when. I hate having to go over it all again."

"I'll get it right, I promise," said the waiter, smiling winningly. I felt a curl of anger at Billy Poythress. What a spoiled brat.

"Well, then, I'll have a split of chilled D'Iberville water, no ice, one wedge of lemon, *not* lime. You have it; Clint keeps it on ice for me. And then I'll have a wedge of papaya with the tuna carpaccio and the gazpacho verde with plain croutons, *not* the garlic, and a plate of polenta with parmesan. You don't have to shake your head at me; I *know* it's not on the menu. Clint always tells the kitchen when I first come in. Make *sure* the parmesan is Reggiano. And I'll finish with the lemon crème brûlée and decaf espresso. Lime there, *not* lemon. Oh, dear. How rude. I've gone bumbling ahead of you ladies. Please . . . "

And he gestured for us to order. The young waiter, scribbling furiously, cast us a wild look.

"Caesar salad and iced decaf," I said, picking the simplest thing I could find on the menu.

"That sounds good," Laura said, and smiled at the waiter.

"Same for me," Glynn said. He smiled so broadly that I thought his peach-fuzz cheeks were going to split. He dashed away.

He was back in an instant.

"No papaya today, but there's some pretty passion fruit," he said anxiously. "And the polenta's gone, but the cook has some nice potato and rosemary risotto, a fresh batch. And just between you and me the crème brûlée has seen better days. . . . "

His voice trailed off and I looked at Billy Poythress. His face had swelled and gone deep red, and his eyes were lost in slitted folds of flesh, but his smile remained fixed.

"Get Tony for me," he said, gesturing at the maître d'.

"Sir, I can—"

"*Get Tony!*"

The boy turned and fled. Billy Poythress turned to us, face still vermilion with temper, smile still fixed, and said, "This is insupportable. I eat lunch or dinner here two and three times a week. I *always* mention this place in my columns. I absolutely *rave* about the food, even though there's better at half a dozen places on Sunset alone. I put this place on the map with anybody who counts the day it opened; half the people come here because I do. I will not put up with this sort of treatment."

The maître d' arrived, lean and saturnine in a dark suit, bending slightly and correctly from the waist over Billy Poythress.

"There is some dissatisfaction?" he said in a flat, precise voice. It occurred to me that this was far from the first time he had stood here like this.

"I ordered papaya and polenta, and that's what I want," Billy said tightly. "You've never run out before. This waiter, this Charles person, is totally incompetent, and I want him fired. On top of everything else he was extremely rude to me. *Extremely* rude."

His voice had risen to a treble shout, and I felt rather than saw heads turn all over the patio. I looked down into my Calistoga water. I felt my face begin to burn. Across the table from me I felt Glynn flinch. Laura sat very still.

"No, he wasn't," she said then, sweetly, and smiled up at the maître d'. "I thought he was perfectly polite and charming, and most attentive. It's scarcely his fault if the kitchen is out of something. I'm afraid Mr. Poythress is upset at me, and spoke before he thought. I apologize to both of you."

And she smiled her enchanting triangular smile, the one that mesmerized cops and directors and older sisters alike, and sat silently, looking obliquely up at Billy Poythress under the brim of the hat.

He flushed an even deeper magenta, but dropped his eyes.

"My apologies, too, Tony," he muttered. "The young lady has better manners than I do. I will expect some adjustment on the bill, however."

"The house will be happy to have all of you as its guests," the maître d' said stiffly, and turned and walked away. We four sat in silence, and then Billy Poythress said, "You are an example to us all, Laura Mason. At least I saved you a hefty check; I make it a policy never to pick up a tab. Now. Let's finish our drinks and then we'll have our little interview. Let me tell you about this place; did you know that Van Heflin drowned in the pool here?"

I glanced involuntarily at the azure pool and turned away. So did Glynn. I knew that whenever after we thought of the Sunset Marquis, we would both see the body bobbing in the bright water, facedown, like a dark, drowned bird. What a terrible man this Hollywood columnist was. I thought that Laura would pay dearly for her courage.

Our food came and we picked at it in silence, listening as Billy Poythress, good temper restored, regaled us with industry gossip, most of it scurrilous and some of it, I thought, actionable. Then he told us about his boyhood in St. Louis and how he had come West to be a journalist, but found that he was "too sensitive, too vulnerable," for that hard-edged profession, and so had drifted into what he called the people game.

"Everyone wants to know everything about everybody with any celebrity, and I have contacts that no one else has," he said. "I give enjoyment to a great many people every week. It makes them happy and it makes me happy. It's an ideal way to make a nice little living."

Better than nice, I thought. I would wager that Billy Poythress had not paid for a meal in twenty years.

We finished our coffee and he pushed away his cup and took out a little leather notebook. I saw the tiny Hermès logo stamped inconspicuously on it.

"Now," he said. "I'm going to do something a little different with you, Laura Mason. From what I hear—and I hear *everything*—this role of yours in Caleb's new movie is soon going to be the talk of the industry, so I thought we'd talk today about you and Caleb instead. Simply *everybody* will be wild to know about that. He hasn't had anybody on the side since way before *Jazz*; there was some buzz that he was leaning toward little boys. But you've put an end to that. So do tell me all, my dear. I promise to give you as many inches as you give me dish."

We were all silent. I did not dare look at Laura. Every instinct told me to simply grab her and hustle her out of there, but this was, after all, her territory and her career, and I had to trust that she knew best how to navigate in it. But the sense of danger was almost palpable.

"Stuart told me this would be about my part in *Right Time*," she said finally. Her voice was low and level and pleasant.

"Well, we all know that Stuart isn't exactly at his best these days, don't we?" Billy said, smiling. Smiling. "I really don't think you're very well served there, dear, but you know best about that. No, I told him quite plainly that I wanted to know about your little *affaire d'amour*. He said he didn't think you would have any problem with that. After all, it's been getting beaucoup ink ever since filming started."

"I don't know if I can do that," Laura said presently, and looked over at me. Her face was strained and set. I knew what this interview meant to her. Nevertheless, "Don't," I said back to her with my eyes. "Don't."

"Well, it's your call," Billy Poythress said, putting his notebook back in the pocket of the bizarre jacket and lifting his hand for the waiter.

"Wait," Laura said. "Let's talk some more about this."

"Good," he said, settling back.

"You'll want to be private for this, so Glynn and I will walk around on Sunset for a while," I said. "Why don't you meet us at that bookstore you like when you're done?"

She nodded, not looking at me. I stood, and Glynn did, too.

"It was nice meeting you, Mr. Poythress," I said tightly. Glynn mumbled something I did not catch.

"You too, pretty ones," he said, beaming. "Enjoy your day."

When we finally reached the crest of Sunset, breathing hard, Glynn said, her voice subdued, "He's awful, isn't he?"

"Yes," I said, but said nothing more about Billy Poythress. What, after all, was there to say? What he was burned in the air like the afterimage of a great blast.

We had a pleasant stroll in the cooling afternoon, and bought a couple more odds and ends to flesh out Glynn's Hollywood wardrobe. I had thought to find something I could wear tomorrow night to the screening and Spago, but did not, after all, have the heart to look. I did not think I wanted to go. I would let Laura take Glynn. Billy Poythress had been all I wanted to know about Hollywood.

We did not speak of him again until Laura joined us at the bookstore, and then only briefly.

"Did it go okay?" I said. She was distracted and pale.

"I don't know," she said. "God, what an asshole. It may have been all right. There's no way to tell until I can talk to Pring. I'm going to go back to the apartment and try to call him. Then we'll go get some early supper. We've had a long day."

"Good idea," I said. "We'll get a Coke or something and walk on up, give you a little time."

"Thanks," she said briefly, and walked out of the store. Her head and shoulders were erect, but there was no lithe spring in her step, none of the old Laura prowl. My heart hurt for that.

When we finally got back to the apartment the shadows were long across Sunset below us, and the hills behind us were blue. A few lights had come on far across the valley and twinkled like fallen stars. In the spreading stain of twilight the view really was beautiful, soft and somehow tender. Nighttime must be the real time, here.

Laura was not about, but I heard the shower running. Presently she came out, wrapped in a white terry robe that must have been the departed Bobby's, her face scrubbed shiny, blond hair dark and wet down her back. Her eyes were very red. I knew that she had been crying.

"Any luck?" I said casually, avoiding looking into her face.

"No. I can't reach him. He's probably still out at Margolies's and that number wouldn't be listed. He's probably called here, but I forgot to turn on the answering machine. Stu doesn't use it anymore. Let me get dressed and we'll go get something to eat. I think I'll take you to Orso's. Best pasta in the world."

And it was good. We sat at a candlelit corner table in a little walled patio, under the branches of a huge, low-spreading tree, and ate sublime pasta and drank red wine and looked as Laura pointed out this industry notable and that one, and laughed when she told stories about them only slightly less scurrilous than Billy Poythress's had been. We did not mention him, and she did not mention Caleb Pringle again, but both men were as surely present at the table as if they sat across from us. We finished early and left, and it was scarcely ten when we went to bed.

Glynn fell asleep almost instantly, but I lay awake for a long time in the outrageous bed of Stuart Feinstein's, which turned out to be a waterbed and sloshed disconcertingly whenever one of us moved. There would be no question of feeling an earthquake in this bed, I thought, but tonight, unlike the last one, the idea brought me no alarm. The damage tonight was inside Laura and not the earth.

Sometime deep in the night I thought I heard her crying softly on the living-room couch, but when I slid out of bed to go to her the sound stopped, and I stood for a while at the closed door and then got back into the waterbed beside Glynn. The last thing I remembered as I slid into thin, restless sleep was that I had not, after all, called Pom.

6

I called him first thing the next morning, though. Somehow his weight and presence were palpable to me even all these miles away. I had what felt uncomfortably like a child's simple need to check in with him, to see if I was doing okay far away from home all by myself. I disliked the feeling so much that I almost did not call, but then I thought, it's not that I'm asking permission to be here. I already know he doesn't want me to be here. It's that I'm telling him where we are and when we'll be home. Anyone has a right to know where his child is, even if he's angry at the one who took her there. An adult would make this call.

So I did. I called the clinic. A voice I did not know said that Dr. Fowler was in a meeting across town and not expected back until late afternoon. No, he hadn't said where. No, Miss Crittenden would not be in, either; she was taking a few days of her vacation time.

"I'm a temp," she said cheerfully. "They called me in on short notice. I don't know where Miss Crittenden went. Maybe one of the nurses knows; shall I ask?"

"No, if you'd just take a message for Dr. Fowler," I said. "Tell him his wife called from Los Angeles and said that she and his daughter plan to come home tomorrow on the midday

Delta flight. Please ask him to call me at this number around eight your time. We'll be away after that."

I gave her Stuart Feinstein's number.

"Oh, yes, Mrs. Fowler," burbled the temp. "I saw both your pictures on the doctor's desk just a few minutes ago. So pretty, both of you. I'll be sure to give him your message."

"You don't happen to know if Dr. Fowler's mother is in the office, do you?" I said.

"His mother? No, I don't believe so. I can find out for you, though—"

"Never mind," I said. "You'd know if she was."

After I hung up I dialed the house. Could it be possible that poor Amy Crittenden was baby-sitting Mommee for Pom? But no one answered, and presently I heard my own voice, the one Pom calls my playing-grownup voice, say, "You've reached the Fowler residence. We can't come to the phone right now, but if you'll leave a message we'll return your call as soon as possible. If you're trying to reach Dr. Fowler, call the clinic at 555–3004, or his answering service at 555–0006. Thank you."

"Don't mention it," I muttered, faintly troubled. Could something really have happened to Mommee, some accident or illness? Guilt poked its head into my mind, and I booted it out. Pom was a doctor, after all. What better hands for her to be in if calamity had struck? I would only have called him anyway.

But the guilt skulked behind me as I went out into the living room, where laughter and the smell of coffee beckoned me. Glynn and Laura must have woken early, I thought, but looking at my watch I saw that instead I had slept late. It was nearly ten.

They were out on the balcony. Below them Sunset swam in a white-bronze haze, and the tall buildings of downtown were barely visible. The mountains behind us were totally invisible. You could feel the heat's promise and taste the air already. It was dry, but as enervating to me as Atlanta's thick summer humidity. I thought of clean, sharp sea air, of pines and Canadian cold fronts. Pom and Glynn and I had planned to take an August vacation at a cottage we sometimes rented on Penobscot Bay. I felt a sudden shiver of fierce longing for it.

Laura looked up when she heard me. If she had been crying the night before there was no evidence of it now. Her face was loose and lazy, softly beautiful as it had been when she was very young, all the hard dry lines gone, and her eyes seemed brimful of liquid light. She was licking jam off her fingers, her legs propped up on the iron railing. A grease-spotted white paper bag lay on the little wrought iron table beside her, and the buttery remains of croissants were scattered about. A carafe of coffee sat beside it, and pots of jams and jellies. A half-smoked cigarette lay in an ashtray on the arm of her chair. Across from her Glynn sat cross-legged on a rickety aluminum chaise, wolfing the last of a croissant. Both of them grinned up at me.

"Morning, Glory," Laura said in a lazy, sated voice. "Hi, Mom," Glynn said. There was a sort of stifled hilarity in her voice, as if I had caught them doing something forbidden. Then it spilled over into a giggle.

I smiled.

"You two look like the cats just finishing up the canary," I said, and poked at the paper sack. "Are there any of those left? Don't tell me you've scarfed them all up."

"All gone," Laura hummed, giggling, too. "Vanished down the gullets of three voracious Mason women. Or do I mean rapacious? I know I mean Mason-Fowler women . . . "

I looked more closely at her. She sounded almost like she had when she had come in tipsy, when she was at Georgia State. But I smelled nothing, and besides, I knew that if she had resumed drinking it would not be in the morning, and not around Glynn.

It dawned on me then, and I looked more closely at the cigarette. It was clumsy and homemade, not a commercial brand.

"You're smoking pot," I said in disbelief. "And Glynn, you are, too. Laura, what in the name of God has gotten into you? You know Glynn doesn't smoke that stuff—"

"Neither do I, normally, but it's the drug of choice for nausea, and boy was I nauseated this morning," Laura said, stretching mightily.

"You should have heard her hurling," Glynn said. "It was gross. I'm surprised it didn't wake you. It did me."

I gave her a later-for-you-young-lady look and said, "Why were you sick? Surely there's something else that works as well as this. If you really are sick, you shouldn't be smoking this stuff."

"I get sick before I see myself on film," she said. "I always have. It's some kind of stage fright, I guess. And there's nothing better than pot. Nothing has ever stopped the heaving but that. I've tried everything. I can't barf in the middle of the screening tonight, obviously. Lighten up, Met. I don't do it except then."

"Well, Glynn doesn't do it, period," I said, furious at her. Things were going along so well among the three of us and now this. It was as if she simply could not go for long without provoking me back into the authoritarian role. She had always done it.

"I just had a couple of puffs, Mom," Glynn said. "Just to see what it was like. It didn't do anything for me except make me hungry. I ate three croissants and nearly a whole pot of jam."

"Yeah, she really did," Laura said. "You know, pot could be just the ticket for what ails her. You can bet it would fatten her up better than all those shrinks you've been carting her to. Cost a lot less, too."

"Let's get one thing straight, Laura," I said tightly. "You will not give Glynn pot. You will not give her crack, or whatever it is that you all stick up your noses out here. You will not give her liquor. You will not do anything that will put her at risk in any way. I want her to get to know her aunt, and I want her to have a good time while we're here, but I will not tolerate this kind of crap. Your lifestyle is your business only until you let it spill over onto her. Then it's mine. I've got a good mind to take her home this afternoon. We can still get the four o'clock flight."

"*Mommm*," Glynn wailed. "I'm sorry. I just didn't think. I didn't even like it—"

"It's a shame you have to punish her because you're pissed at me," Laura said, looking off into the smog. Then she ground out the cigarette. "But you're ever the vigilant mother lioness, aren't you, Met? I almost forgot you were for a while."

I knew what she was trying to do, but it angered me anyway.

"I don't have to be," I said. "How I am out here is entirely up to you. It seems to me you're the one who called the lioness out."

She smiled. It was her old, sweet, open smile.

"You're right. I did. And I'm sorry. I could have gone in the john and smoked this. It was inappropriate and I won't do it again, I promise. I'm really uptight about this screening tonight, it means so damned much, but that's no excuse. If you'll stay, I'll be so exemplary you won't know me."

"If you take me home for smoking pot Dad will never trust me again," Glynn whispered, and I knew that she was right. Everything he thought about Laura, and about my hasty flight West and our staying over, would be vindicated. It never occurred to me not to tell him, and I knew that it would never occur to Glynn, either.

"I know I sound stuffy and old-fashioned, harping at you about pot," I said, knowing that I did. "I hate always being the heavy. But you both know I can't condone that."

"We both do," Laura said. "It won't come up again."

"Then let's put it behind us," I said. "What's on for today?"

Glynn jumped up and hugged me, and said, "I'm going down to the strip and look for some tights and shoes to go with my silk tunic. Laura said they could be an early birthday present from her. I can't go to a Hollywood screening in Doc Martens. You don't have to worry, Mom; you can sit right here and see me the whole time. It's just to those boutiques down there."

I sighed and let her go. I was not going to be the crow in this flock of songbirds anymore.

"What about you? You want to shop, or prowl, or anything?" Laura said. She did not move from her chair. I did not think she wanted to go out, but I did not know what she did want.

"I think I'd just like a lazy morning," she said. "Keep me company. I'll make a fresh pot of coffee and some toast for you. At least there's bread and jam left. We haven't really talked since you got here."

We drank the coffee and sat for a while in companionable silence. The slight, constant pain of missing Laura was stilled, and the solace of seeing my daughter behaving like an ordinary teenager, flitting off after clothes and bubbling with the excitement of a real Hollywood screening, was soporific. The pot incident shrank into the category of adolescent hijinks. On this sunny balcony not yet baking in the heat, the air of festivity and holiday was very strong, and the sense of sheer youngness, of the head-spinning innocence and camaraderie of college, was even stronger. How long since I had spent even a few days in the sole company of women with whom I shared deep bonds? Not, surely, since school and the days just after, when Crisscross and I spent long weekend days together, laughing, talking, *being*. Except for the scratchy prickle of Pom and the faraway, half-forgotten furor of home, lodged far back in my mind like a faint tickle in the throat, I was nearly perfectly steeped in well being.

"Tell me about this Caleb Pringle," I dared say into the suspended sunny morning. I could not have said it before.

There was a silence, and then Laura sighed. It was a long sigh.

"He's the director of *The Right Time*. He's probably the hottest director in the industry right now. Everything he touches turns to money, which is all the studios understand, and most of it turns to awards. He's really good, really creative in a strange, dark, almost delicate kind of way. There's always a touch of decadence in his films, what he calls a sweet corruption, but there's this surprising innocence to them, too, even the most violent. And some of them, like *Burn*, were really violent. He has a mind like I've never seen and a vision like I've never encountered and—"

"And you're in love with him," I said. I would have known from her tone even if Stuart Feinstein had not told me. I did not mean infatuation, either. I had seen Laura through several of those. This was different.

"Yes." She swung her eyes from the undulating skyline and fixed them on me. Tears shimmered in them, but there was a strange, sweet smile on her face, one I did not associate with Laura. It was tender and it was somehow humble. For some reason that frightened me rather badly. I remembered Stuart's words.

"So are congratulations in order?" I asked, trying to keep my tone warm yet casual.

"I . . . don't know. Yes. I think so. Oh, Met, I *do* think so; we've been just so close, just so . . . awfully close. . . . We were together constantly during the shooting of *Right Time*, and just after, when we came back and he started editing. We laughed all the time, at everything. I know the sort of reputation he has, but he said things—we did things—you can't do and say things like that unless you're really in love with someone. You just can't. I know. I've said and done practically everything there is to say and do to a man, and had them said and done to me, and this wasn't like that. There was nothing on earth held back between us. I can tell when I'm being fed a line. This wasn't that. He was always talking about next year, or years from now, and he'd said he wanted me to come up to his place in the mountains. He doesn't take *anybody* there; everybody knows that. Everybody knows about that place, and the way he goes off up there by himself. But he said he wanted me to see it—"

"Where in the mountains?" I asked. I did not care, but I wanted the happiness to stay in her voice and on her face for a little longer.

"Up in the Santa Cruz mountains below San Francisco. It was just the wreck of a big old hunting lodge when he bought it; but he's completely done it over. It's all national park land now, but you can have a place on it if it was there before the park was, and this was. Some very rich San Francisco guy built it in the early twenties. It's *really* isolated, I hear, and very beautiful; that's redwood country up there, and the land is so wild and rough that you can hardly walk it, much less get roads through it. There's a little private road into his property, but except for that and an old fire tower where his hermit caretaker lives, there's nothing else. He used to tell me about it, about how much he loved it, and how important it was to him, and what he did up there, and what we'd do. . . . I might almost have thought this was just, you know, a fling or something, until he asked me up there. But then I knew it was what I thought it was—"

"Why are you talking about it in the past tense, then?" I said gently.

"I wasn't, really," she said, and smiled again. This time it was a strained smile that did not reach her eyes, and I damned myself for speaking. But I wanted to know more about this man, about his capacity to hurt Laura. What I already knew did not endear him to me.

"You were. Look, Pie, if he really loves you and means all this, nobody in the world is going to be happier for you than me. But if there's even the remotest chance that he could hurt you—"

"Pring would not hurt me," she said. But she did not look at me.

"Then why hasn't he called you? Why didn't he let you know about the screening?"

"Oh, Met, he just gets so totally involved when he's got a new movie in this stage, with everything up in the air and all the ends flying loose—it's like he's all swallowed up, hypnotized, or something. Stu said he was in the middle of courting this Margolies for money; you know, you heard what Corky said. Or he could be up at the mountain place. There's not a phone up there except in the caretaker's place."

"A hermit with a phone?" I smiled, hoping to divert her. The anxiety in her voice was too painful to hear. I was very sorry I had brought up Caleb Pringle.

"Well, he's not really a hermit. He's a writer and I think he does something about earthquakes, too; he's got all this equipment and stuff up there, Pring says. It's just that he almost never goes down into any of the towns. But Pring has to have some way to tell him when he's coming up and what he wants done, and all that. I don't think he'd go up there and use the phone in the tower. He doesn't much like this guy, or rather, he thinks he's nuts, or something. Obsessed, he says. But he keeps him on because he does a pretty good job and he doesn't pay him anything. Pring lets him live in the tower in exchange for keeping the place up. The guy has some money, I think."

"Terrific. A rich hermit with a phone. Just who you want peeping in the windows in the middle of a mountain idyll."

"He doesn't come around the place. Pring says it's like

being alone in the middle of a primeval wilderness up there. Oh, Met, nothing ever sounded so wonderful to me as that—"

"Well, I hope you spend years and years up there, baby," I said, reaching over and kissing the top of her head. The strange platinum hair, flying free today, felt like the pelt of an animal, glossy and strong and a little rough. She smelled, as she always did, of her signature Opium.

"You'll love him when you meet him," Laura said into my shoulder. "He should be at the screening. He always is. I'm so glad you and Glynn are coming."

"Moral support?"

"No. More like prizes to show off. Let him see what an impeccable gene pool I come out of."

"I'd rather think he was going to carry you off to the mountains than count your teeth and breed you," I said, laughing.

She stiffened, then relaxed.

"Well, come to that, we *would* have absolutely gorgeous children, Met. Someday, I mean. Although I have to say my clock is definitely ticking."

I pulled back and looked into her face.

"You're not serious."

"No. It was just a thought. He's crazy about kids, though. And he's wonderful with them. There's this little kid in *Right Time*; you'll see tonight. When we started shooting nobody would have given you any odds at all on getting a decent performance out of the little cretin. But after Pring got ahold of him he changed completely. It's a remarkable performance. In front of Pring's camera he's just magic."

"Well, I look forward to the little cretin and everything else," I said. "Now. What shall I wear that won't embarrass you out of your wits? Not, I suspect, the faithful pantsuit and the Hush Puppies?"

She rolled her eyes at me and got up, stretching.

"God forbid. Follow me. I know just the thing."

Just before we left for the screening I called Pom again. I got answering machines both at home and the clinic. The morning's worry crept back, stronger this time.

"For God's sake, don't spoil this night stewing about Pom and that old woman," Laura said. "If there'd been anything wrong he'd have called you here. You gave him the number, didn't you?"

I nodded. The phone had not rung all afternoon. I was particularly aware of that because every now and then Laura would look at it as if willing it to speak. Damn Caleb Pringle, I had thought. If he had any feeling for her at all he'd call her. Nowhere is that far away from a telephone.

"Pom's punishing you, is what it is," Laura said, tilting her head at the bedroom mirror. We were all three in Stuart's bedroom, finishing dressing. Once again I thought of college: date nights, proms, fraternity parties. The strident, embattled seventies seemed to have skimmed LSU without leaving any stigmata at all.

"Pom doesn't punish people," I said. "He wouldn't even think to do it."

"How do you know? Have you ever run away from home before?"

There was a combative note in her voice, and I did not answer her. I knew that she was nervous about the evening; more than nervous. The shimmer that always hung about her when she was keyed up was nearly visible, and she had been pacing and smoking all afternoon. Not, I was grateful to see, the homemade marijuana cigarettes, but far too many unfiltered, stubby ones. They smelled powerfully, and when I asked her what they were she said, "Players. I know. They're awful for you. Pring got me started on them. I really don't smoke much, but I'm giving myself permission today."

I studied her in the mirror, smiling a little because she simply looked so wonderful. She had brushed the platinum hair straight back and plaited it so that a fat, glossy braid hung down her brown back, and she wore the short black minidress she had worn the day before. It bared her arms and back and much of her breasts, and the only other adornment besides her golden skin was the very high-heeled black sandals. She wore no stockings and, I could see through the fabric of the dress, no bra. She wore no lipstick, either, but had made her tawny eyes up heavily. A faint scattering of the family freckles showed on her scrubbed cheekbones. She looked so much like the young Brigitte Bardot, all sensuality and insouciant innocence, that I could not help staring. I never tired of looking at her, this beautiful chameleon who was my sister. She could be, literally, whoever she chose at any given moment. I wondered if very beautiful people ever simply got tired of the beauty, ever found it a barrier between them and life. I had heard actresses and models bemoan their beauty as burdensome on assorted talk shows, but I had always put that down to cloyingly false modesty. You had to wonder, though. When you looked like Laura, did people expect far more of you or far less? I thought it was a question I might ask her soon.

"Well," she said, turning to inspect Glynn and me. "The Mason women can hold their heads high tonight. Lord, but we're something, aren't we?"

Abruptly, my introspection fled before a gust of the giddy laughter that had bubbled in my chest for the two days I had been in California. She was right. We really were something. I had sleeked my hair back and gelled it the way I had done the night of Pom's party, and she had found a huge, tawny artificial tiger lily in a drawer, and stuck that over one of my ears.

"Don't even ask where he got it," she said.

She had done my makeup: bronze cheek blusher, matte gold eyeshadow, thick strokes of inky liquid eyeliner and mascara, some sort of pink-gold powder on my cheekbones, only a hint of coppery gloss on my mouth. The effect was startling, bold and rakish. Only my own freckles, unmasked by foundation, softened the theatricality. I never would have allowed it to be done to me at home, but I was far from home in more than miles this night. I wore the faded jeans, the boots, and the jacket to a tuxedo she found in the back of Stuart's closet.

"What under it?" I said, when she hauled it out.

"Nothing," she said matter-of-factly, and in the end that was what I wore. The jacket was a single button shawl collar, and fit tightly enough so that it did not gap open. But you could see my freckled chest all the way down to my diaphragm.

"I can't wear it like this," I gasped, looking into Stuart's mirror. "I'm all knobs and bones and freckles. What boobs I have have vanished like the morning dew."

"If you had any you couldn't wear it, but it looks wonderful, very chic and go-to-hell. Come on, Met. I dare you. What do you care? You don't know anybody who'll be there tonight."

"I know my daughter, who in one moment is going to groan, '*Motherrrrr,*'" I said, looking at Glynn. She was grinning in pure delight.

"No, I'm not," she said. "You look great. Totally cool."

"Oh, well, then of course I'll wear it," I said. "That's the ultimate accolade. Not at all what somebody's middle-aged wife and mother has come to expect."

I spoke lightly, but I was absurdly pleased.

"You can be those and other things too," Laura said. "Out here, you're the other things. It's about time."

Flying on the crest of the laughter, I did not stop to examine that. I looked at Glynn and said, "Speaking of other things, who is this waif? Kate Moss?"

"Better than that," Laura said, studying Glynn fondly. "Way, way better than that."

Glynn wore the silky tunic that had escaped the fire simply because she had been wearing it. She wore it over tight leggings the color of burlap, and on her narrow feet were soft suede ankle boots in a slightly darker shade. She had folded the tops over to make a wide cuff, and Laura had brought out a wide, aged brown leather belt from Stuart's closet and looped it loosely around her waist, so that it just rode the top of her hipbones, and bloused the tunic over it. Glynn's hair fell straight to her shoulders from a central part, like a pour of molten vermeil, and she wore no makeup at all except a faint stroke of the coppery blush, to further hollow her cheekbones. She looked younger by far than her sixteen years, and more than ever, to me, like a creature of centuries-old alabaster and dim golden light from high, arched stone windows. It was such an otherworldly effect that for a heartbeat it gave me a small, terrifying *frisson*, as if I had looked upon my daughter in her coffin. But at the same time she seemed literally to burn with life. I shook my head and the image faded.

"I feel like I'm Cinderella, going to the ball with two total strangers that I'm supposed to know," I said. "Come on and let's get out in the air and light, otherwise we're all three just going to vanish into thin air."

"Beam us up, Scotty," Glynn laughed, and we went out into the twilight that was spilling down the canyons onto Sunset Boulevard.

We were late to the screening, because the traffic on Santa Monica and La Cienega was at a virtual standstill.

"It doesn't matter; nobody gets to these things on time," Laura said. For the moment, it was pleasant simply to sit in the stopped Mustang, the top down, the late sun gleaming off the red lacquer, and see, from behind our dark glasses, eyes in all the other cars turn to us. Again I felt the simple urge to preen and flirt and toss my hair that I had felt in those long-ago college convertibles, streaking toward the sea. I knew I would not feel this way again; it would not be possible back in Atlanta, no matter what open-top car I sat in. Atlanta knew me for what I really was. This feeling was born of strangeness, mine and my context, or lack of it. I did not care. This moment was sweet.

By the time we had parked the car in a labyrinthine underground parking lot and made our way up in an elevator to a middle floor in a white building identical to the ones in the cluster around it, it was nearing six-thirty.

"It's all offices," Glynn had said in disappointment. "It looks just like downtown Atlanta. I can't imagine Rocky MacPherson in a place like this. Do you suppose we passed his car?"

"No, I imagine Rocky came in a limo if he came at all," Laura said. "He alternates between those and his Harley. If he's to be believed, the last time he rode in a car he was coming home from his christening. They look like offices because they are; the money stuff gets done here. The glamour stuff is done either on location or at a studio. This is a movie theater owned by a chain that does sound mixing; production companies rent it or one like it when they need to screen something. There'll be music and dialogue, but it'll still be considered a rough cut. Never mind, everybody who is anybody connected with this movie will be here. This is the first time anybody's seen this version but Pring."

We got off the elevator and were in a vast, low-lit lobby furnished in large steel and tweed pieces, with a few towering plants and a terrazo floor and a wall of windows curtained now against the fierce glare from the west. The lobby was empty except for a catering crew setting up a bar against one wall. A ticket booth held a young woman reading a magazine. From behind double swinging doors came a blat of sound that became music.

"Shit, we're late," Laura said, taking our tickets from the bored young woman, she took a deep, shuddering breath and we went inside, and stood for a moment, blinking in the darkness. The movie had not started, but there was sound coming from speakers on the walls, a hard-driving, atonal rock beat, and blank white film flashed by. There seemed to be no seats at all left.

"I see two down front," Laura whispered. "You and Glynn go on down and take them. There's a row here in back empty. I'll meet you in the lobby when it's over."

"No, you sit with Glynn and tell her what's what," I said. "I won't know anything about anything. I'll see you after."

They went down the aisle. Heads turned to follow them. I saw Laura nod and smile at people she knew, and watched my daughter glide behind her with the airborne gait she used when she was acutely self-conscious and trying to hide it. Pride rose in my throat, bringing with it a slight prickle of tears. My daughter and my sister. My beautiful girls. They were the focus of every eye in the theater. I heard a slight buzz of conversation follow them, saw them slip into two seats down front, and found my way to a back row where no one else sat. Sliding into the low, cushioned seat I let my breath out gratefully, and realized how nervous I had been about seeing my sister's performance in her presence. This was much better. In this anonymous darkness I could suspend my knowing of her, give myself totally to the movie and the woman she would become.

Looking back, I can remember scarcely any of *The Right Time*. It was as Laura had said, dark both in content and technique. While I was watching it I was mesmerized; I could tell that the acting was excellent, and the cinematography and lighting and sets were arresting. The sly aura of corruption was overpowering, yet affecting. I had the odd sense that it was every contemporary film I had seen, and yet was none of them; Stuart Feinstein had said Caleb Pringle's trademark was the derivative made new by art, and I recognized both the derivativeness and the art. I knew from the outset that it would win awards, and there was certainly enough sex and violence, both beautiful, to assure its box office appeal, but later I could not have described it to anyone. Partly, I suppose, it was because I was so focused on waiting for Laura to appear that I missed much of the film's context. Partly, but not all. Somehow *The Right Time* did not speak to me.

About fifteen minutes into the film a small group of men slipped into the seats next to mine. I nodded and they did, too, and we all fastened our attention on the screen. I did not notice them particularly, except to note almost subliminally that the man next to me wore a dark suit and a tie and had tiny, pointed highly polished shoes on small feet that almost dangled above the floor and that he smelled powerfully of something I could have sworn was Old Spice. Every boy in my high school class had worn it for dates and proms. But that could hardly be true out here, in this time, and so I tuned out the scent and lost myself in the images on the screen. Surely, any moment now, Laura would appear. . . .

Twenty minutes into the film I saw Laura walk up the aisle past me and out the doors. Light from the lobby flared and then faded. I turned around and looked after her; was she ill again? Had the morning's nausea overtaken her? She had not looked ill; had seemed, in my brief glimpse of her, simply Laura, in her black and her expanse of bare tanned skin, vivid and arresting. She did not look at me or anyone else. I did not want to get up and rush after her and saw that Glynn still sat in her down-front seat, eyes glued to the screen. If anything had been wrong, surely Glynn would have known. There was a slight murmuring, like a wind in trees, in the theater, but it did not seem to have anything to do with Laura's leaving. No heads turned when she passed. I settled down again to watch.

The man on the end of the row made a short, low sound when Laura passed us, and in a few moments he too got up and went out. I sat for a few minutes more, increasingly rest-less, and then the little man beside me left too. He did not speak to the two other men who had come in with him, only nodded, unsmiling, to me and went up the aisle in the sprad-dling waddle of a penguin. The two remaining men looked at each other, but said nothing.

It was only then that it occurred to me that Laura was not in this movie.

Shock and a swift, punishing grief kept me in my seat for a moment, motionless, and then anger jerked me out of it. This was why Caleb Pringle had not called her, then. He knew her part had been cut, of course he did; he would have to have known. It was he who directed the new version. He knew, and he did not tell her. Instead he let her see for herself, in a the-ater surrounded by everyone who had worked on the film, who knew what her part had been and what she and Caleb Pringle had been to each other. He knew and let her talk about both the part and the relationship to that poisonous little slug, Billy Poythress. Or, if he had not known precisely that, he should have anticipated such interviews. It was, after all, Caleb Pringle who had told her that her part was, to quote Laura, "best-supporting" stuff. I was so angry that I shook all over, so angry that my knees trembled on my way up the theater aisle.

I looked around for her, blinking against the pitiless fluo-rescence, but the lobby was empty except for a white-coated waiter leaning against the wall behind the buffet table, smok-ing a cigarette. Even the young woman in the ticket booth was gone. When I approached the waiter he stubbed out his cigarette and stood at attention.

"I'm afraid the bar isn't open yet," he said, showing his perfect white teeth in an opossumlike smile. Everybody in Los Angeles, I thought irrationally, had perfect white teeth. Maybe the Chamber of Commerce passed bleaching kits out to newcomers, or the Welcome Wagon.

"I don't want a drink," I said. "I'm looking for a young woman in a black dress, with blond hair in a braid. She came out a few minutes ago."

"Yeah," he said, rolling his eyes in appreciation. "She sure did. Went into the ladies' room so fast I thought she was sick or something. Then some guy went in there, right after her. Some real squealing been going on ever since. Nothing to me; I don't care. You see everything out here. But if that's where you're headed you might want to knock first."

I glared at him and went swiftly toward the room marked "Ladies," but paused at the door. I could hear the sounds of sobbing clearly, Laura's sobbing, and a man's voice speaking lowly, urgently, as if soothing her. It must have been the man in the seat down the row from me; obviously a friend from the production then, someone who would know what the amputation of her part would mean to her. I went back into the lobby and sank down on a steel and chrome bench. Her friend was probably in better position than I to comfort her, but I could not make myself go back into the theater. I had never heard Laura cry that I had not moved to comfort her. To sit still and know that this time I could not was agony.

I was still sitting there, wondering what on earth I could say to her, what she would do now, when Glynn came into the lobby, like me, blinking in the light.

"Where's Aunt Laura?" she said. "She left and didn't come back; did you see her go by? Mom, I don't think she's in the movie. I think something happened to her part—"

"I think so, too," I said. "It's awful. It's monstrous. Somebody should have told her. She's in the rest room now, crying her eyes out, but there's a man in there with her, comforting her. He was sitting in my row, so he's got to be a friend. I think he's the best one to be with her right now. We'll stick around till she comes out and then we'll take her home. She's not going to want to go on to any cast party."

I thought then of Glynn's whole-souled anticipation of this evening, of going to a famous restaurant with movie stars, of meeting this Rocky MacPherson who loomed so large in her small pantheon of heroes.

"I'm so sorry, Tink," I said. "I know how you were looking forward to tonight. But you can see that something like Spago would just kill her—"

"I know," Glynn said. "No sweat. I heard somebody say Rocky's not here, anyway. Poor Aunt 'Aura. This is not a good place, is it? Hollywood?"

"No," I said, getting up and giving her shoulders a hug. Their sharpness, beneath the silky flow of her tunic, jolted me anew. I had almost forgotten the anorexia.

"Thanks for understanding," I said. "You're a neat kid. As if I didn't know that."

We went back to the bench and she sat for a moment, worrying her fingernail with her teeth. Then she said, "He should have told her. How can she be in love with somebody who could let this happen to her? If she was that close to him, why couldn't she see what a jerk he is?"

"The old saw about love being blind is true, I guess," I said. "Most people will bend over backward not to see the bad in somebody they love."

"Then how on earth do they keep from being hurt all the time," she said, pain sharp in her voice.

"They don't. People do get hurt, most by the people they love. Otherwise they wouldn't care. It's a price you pay for the love. Most of us think it's worth it. Most of us don't get hurt this bad either; people who really love you just don't sell you out."

"But you can't really know—"

"No. You can't really know."

"So. Love means hurting. Or it could. Wow. What a wonderful thing love must be," Glynn said, anger and misery in her scornful voice. I did not answer her. How could you explain it to someone who had not yet known it? But Glynn loved; she loved me; I knew that she did. She loved Pom.

And she had felt the pain of that love. I knew that she had not yet drawn the parallel, perhaps would not. You start young to bury that knowledge deep. The hurt in my heart for my sister spread out to encompass my daughter. Damn you, too, Pom, I thought. She's too young to equate love with rejection and punishment. You should not have yelled at her; you should not have punished her. Not when none of it was her fault. You truly should not have done that. You're going to have to make that up to her. I can't let that go.

The young man behind the bar came over to us carrying glasses.

"The bar just opened," he said. "You two look like you could use a little something. It's just white wine," he added, taking in Glynn's youth. "Or I could bring some Perrier or something."

"No, wine's fine," I said. "Thank you. This is nice of you."

"My pleasure," he said, smiling at Glynn. She kept her head down and did not smile, but she sipped at her wine.

"Thank you," she mumbled. My good girl.

We had almost finished our drinks, sitting in silence, when the door to the ladies' room opened and Laura came out. I leaped up and ran forward. A tall man in blue jeans and a tweed sports coat over a T-shirt walked beside her, arm around her. His head was bent to hers. His hair was dark and curled over his ears, and his face was snub-nosed and freckled and attractive in a boyish, unfinished sort of way. He seemed very young. He looked up at me and I saw that he had hazel eyes with laugh lines fanning out from them, and a network of tiny, dry creases about his mouth and on his forehead. Not so young, then, just seeming that way . . .

I knew instantly that this was Caleb Pringle. I could feel my teeth clench. My eyes moved, almost reluctantly, to Laura's face, and I realized that I had been avoiding looking at her. Her face was red and swollen, and still damp from tears and undoubtedly a scrubbing with paper towels, but she was smiling, a misty, full smile. Her head nestled into the hollow where his neck met his shoulder.

"Oh, poor Met," she said tremulously. "Waiting to pick up the pieces. Oh, I'm so sorry you had to be here for this. It's all right, Met, I promise it is. I understand now. It was Margolies who made Pring cut the part; he cut two others, too. He wanted the emphasis to be all on Lorna's part. She's his new patootie. I should have known that. Pring couldn't argue with him on the cuts, not and save the picture. Not and get Margolies's backing for the new one. Margolies made it clear that if he didn't like *Right Time* he wasn't going to put any money into *Arc*, and oh, Met, Pring's got to make *Arc*. It's going to be by far the best thing he's done, and there's already a script, and several parts cast, and Pring will lose the actors if he has to go back to the drawing board on money, and there's this absolutely wonderful part in it for me, better than *Right Time*, better than anything I've ever done, the lead, really . . . "

She stopped for lack of breath, and laughed. It was a carol, a lark's song. I smiled, in spite of myself.

"This is Caleb Pringle," she said. "I forgot you didn't know him."

Caleb Pringle smiled. The pleasant, ordinary face bloomed into something extraordinary.

"This is my big sister, Merritt Fowler, Pring," Laura said. "Of whom you've heard more than you probably ever wanted to know. To whom I owe everything. Be nice to her. I think she's probably mad at you."

"As well she should be," Caleb Pringle said. His voice was wonderful, deep and smooth as dark honey. "I could kick myself for not making sure she got my message about the part. I called from Margolies's place several times but by that time he was so paranoid about the way *Right Time* was going that I think he was bugging my phone calls. I couldn't get Laura, so I called Stuart and told him to tell her, but apparently he forgot. I should have made sure—I know HIV gets to the brain eventually—but I didn't. And believe me, I am terribly sorry, both for Laura and this big sister I have, indeed, heard so much about. I apologize to you both. I feel like a worm about *Right Time*, but it's over and I can't do anything about it, and *Arc* is going to be a very important picture for a lot of us. I hope . . . I think . . . it's going to mean a lot more to Laura than *Right Time* ever could have."

He stopped and looked at me, still smiling. I did not know how to respond. I was not ready to let go of my anger over Laura's humiliation tonight; I did not want it tossed aside lightly. But I wanted to be happy for her if indeed this new opportunity meant so much more, and I realized that I knew less than nothing about her world and Caleb Pringle's. It felt important to me to be fair. If he really had tried to get a message to her.

I saw Stuart Feinstein's wrecked face and heard his voice: "I called in a lot of chips for her on this one." And "There's nothing more I can do for her but hold her hand and pray."

Not the words of a man who would forget a phone message of such import. Not a man to let a cherished friend be ambushed by pain.

But I knew that HIV did indeed, in many cases, affect memory and reasoning. I did not know what to say. And then I looked at Laura's radiant, ravaged face, and did know.

"As long as you take care of my little sister you don't owe me any apologies at all," I said.

"I'm certainly going to try," Caleb Pringle said. He leaned over and kissed Laura on the top of her head.

"Laura told me everything about you except what a stunning woman you are," Caleb said. "If there are any more of you at home I could cast a whole movie around the Mason women."

I smiled politely, not wanting to be complimented just now. It would be very easy for my tremulous liking for this man to slump back into anger.

"There are, and here she comes," Laura said, just as Glynn got up from the bench and walked toward us.

"This is my niece, Glynn Fowler," Laura said. "Isn't she something? Look at that face; wouldn't a camera love those bones, though?"

Caleb Pringle didn't speak, only looked at Glynn. He stood very still, and his face did not change expression. He did not move. He did not speak. Then he said, "I imagine it would, yes. Hello, Glynn. I'm Caleb Pringle, the director of this debacle, and I want to assure you, as I have your mother, that I meant no harm to your Aunt Laura, and that I have found a way, I think, to make it up to her. I hope that you will forgive me. I'd like very much to be in your good graces."

Glynn did not blush or drop her eyes or stammer. She looked at Caleb Pringle for a long moment, an adult's whole, measuring look, and then said, "I love Aunt Laura very much. I hope you will be good to her."

She said it in a soft, grave little voice, a near whisper, and he smiled. It was a smile of quick, pure delight. It had been an extraordinary thing for a very young girl to say, and I was flooded with pride in her.

"I'll try not to disappoint you," he said. "And for a start, will you three be my guests at dinner tonight? It's at Spago, and the food is really very good. I expect you've heard of it. I want Laura to show the flag, and I'd love to show you two off.

Most leading ladies' relatives are fat and wear aqua polyester pantsuits."

Glynn giggled, a soft little snort.

"Mom has one of those," she said, grinning. "She almost wore it tonight."

"I do not, and I did not," I said.

"Well, she would have lifted the taboo on aqua polyester pantsuits forever, but I like her just like she is," Caleb said. "You, too. You look just like a new young star on her way to Spago. The paparazzi will fall all over you. Will you come?"

Glynn looked at me, her face luminous with hope, and I looked at Laura.

Okay? I asked with my eyes.

Oh, yes, hers said.

"We accept with pleasure," I said, and he nodded and said, "I'll have my car brought around. We can pick up yours later. I'll tell you a little about the movie on the way over. Oh, by the way, weren't you sitting down the row from us, Merritt? Next to Margolies?"

"*That* was Margolies?"

"Aka the penguin. They tried to get him for *Batman*. How did he seem to be liking the movie?"

"I don't know," I said. "He left before I did, just after you."

He was silent a long moment. Then he said, casually, "Was he smiling, do you know?"

"No," I said. "I don't believe he was."

"Shit," Caleb Pringle said softly, almost savagely. And then, "Well, he will. Come along. Your carriage awaits without."

The carriage was a stretch limo of such length and dazzling, sepulchral whiteness that I was embarrassed to get into it. Laura, however, slipped in without even looking at it, and I heard Glynn give a little gasp of joy. This would be incendiary stuff with her small crowd at home. The driver, a diminutive Hispanic in correct livery, nodded and bowed and smiled us into the car.

"Lord, but this is chopping tall cotton," I said, looking around me at the limo's interior. It had a bar and more electronic gadgetry, including a tiny television set, than I had ever seen, and there were fresh flowers in a bud vase. Peruvian lilies, I thought. Telephones sprouted all over.

Caleb Pringle laughed.

"The studio hired it," he said, and pressed a button. The privacy shield rose noiselessly. "I'd much rather drive my old Woody, but Margolies is in love with these things. They must cost Vega as much as *Ishtar* did. I've always thought these things were like riding in a coffin on wheels. Jesus here, however, is a jewel. He thinks I'm working for Ryan O'Neill, who seems to be his idol. I think it's because I once told him I was working for Orion, because now every time he drops me off he says, 'Tell Orion O'Neill Jesus say 'allo.' Oh, well. The first time I shot in Mexico, my Spanish was so bad I told everyone I was making a gorilla. I was a sensation there for a while."

We burst into laughter and Caleb Pringle popped open a bottle of champagne that rested in a silver bucket and poured it, and passed it around. We all took a glass.

"To *Arc*," he said. "Because this is where it starts."

He raised his glass and looked at Laura, and she smiled dazzlingly and raised hers.

"To *Arc*," she said. "And everything else."

We drank. "Mmmm," Glynn said, her nose buried in foam. "It's like drinking perfume."

"The old monk who invented it said it was like drinking stars," Caleb said, smiling at her, and she said, "Oh, it is! That's much better!"

He told us a little about *Arc* as we ghosted through the spangled night toward the restaurant. The people and cars on the street looked as unreal, as phantasmagorical, as images in a fever dream. The limo's glass was tinted, but I thought that they would have seemed ephemeral, anyway. I had the notion that legions of Los Angeles's homeless were watching our rococo progression and felt myself redden in the sheltering dimness, even as I knew it was an absurd thought. There were no homeless in Beverly Hills. At least, I did not think so.

Arc, Caleb said, would be a story about power and

passion and innocence and the loss of it, and would proceed on the thesis that Saint Joan had not, after all, been burned at the stake in 1431, but had recanted and lived, and had a passionate affair with the French monarch who was supposed to have abandoned her to her fate, and had, as he said, "changed history another way entirely. I'm not going to tell you just how, because that's the kernel of the movie and Laura will tell you that I never talk about that, but it's delicious just the same, and powerful. I want that delicate and battering sense of passion corrupted, of innocence transmuted into power of another sort, of obsession, of purity given over to the service of . . . the world, I guess you could say. Can't you just imagine all that religious frenzy, that virginal rapture, put to the use of the body? It could blow a world apart. It will, in *Arc*. The focus will be on the mature Joan, the lover of the monarch; the young Joan will be only a prelude, for contrast. Joan the woman will carry the load. And what a woman: tormented, passionate, guilty, hungry, sated, rapturous, humble, exalted—it will be an unforgettable role."

"Who will play the Dauphin?" I said. The concept made me recoil, but it undeniably had power as well as perversity. I could see why Laura was so enraptured by the prospect of playing the adult Joan. It would have everything for an actress.

"I don't know. I haven't cast that yet, either," Caleb Pringle said. "And it won't be the Dauphin. It'll be the Dauphine."

"Oh, my God," breathed Laura into the silence. "Of course. How perfect. Saint Joan would never have been seduced by a man, but a woman? A woman with sleekness and subtlety and a great worldliness—"

"A woman like that would be a monster if she did that to a young saint," I said.

"Ah, but Joan was not a saint," Caleb Pringle said. "Not until after her death was she canonized, and of course in *Arc* she will not die, but you're right. The Dauphine will be a monster. The exact opposite of what the French call a *monstre sacre*, a sacred monster. My Dauphine will be a profane monster. A profane, monstrous, enchanting ghoul, stronger than Medea or Lilith. All evil. Totally depraved. An eater of flesh.

Irresistible. It will play wonderfully off all that vast, untouchable innocence."

"It will be a masterpiece," Laura said. Her voice was hushed.

"It sounds like the worst of Roman Polanski," I said sourly. The whole *Arc* thing made me unreasonably angry and disgusted. Just like, I told myself, somebody's relative in an aqua polyester pantsuit.

"Well, I've heard that before," he said mildly. "Glynn? What do you think?"

"I think," Glynn said, "that I see what you mean. All that . . . *untouchedness* . . . spoiled with hands. Like snow when feet have trampled it. It's still snow, only is it, really?"

He clapped his hands lightly.

"Exactly. *Exactly.* Innocence corrupted is still innocence, only soiled. Or is it? The conundrum at the heart of the matter. Are you sure you don't write screenplays on the side?"

She laughed, embarrassed, and dropped her eyes. I stared from one of them to the other. Where had she gotten that? What could there possibly have been in her short experience to enable her to grasp it?

Then she said, "Will Rocky, you know, MacPherson? Will he be at the restaurant, do you know?" and she sounded so much like the teenager I knew that I smiled in the dark in sheer relief.

"I believe Rocky is in the slammer in Carmel as we speak," Caleb said. "He seems to have taken a dislike to his room at the Pebble Beach Lodge and trashed it. This time I'm not going to bail him. Let him sit there and miss the screening and all the petting and the ink. I'll send somebody down there to get him out tomorrow. Maybe. Or maybe I won't. He's been told what would happen if he did it again."

"Oh, nuts," Glynn said, and then buried her face in her hands.

"Don't be upset," Caleb said, putting a hand on her shoulder. "I'll get him out in the morning if it will please you."

"I'm not upset," she said from between her fingers. "I'm embarrassed. *Nobody* says nuts, absolutely *nobody.*"

He laughed for a long time, a young, free sound, and she

laughed too, behind her long fingers; her old, froggy belly laugh. Then we had some more champagne, and Laura fixed her makeup, and Caleb thumbed the dial and soft rock poured into the car, and we were there.

At first glance Spago looks like a diner made of double-wide trailers set side by side. At second glance it doesn't matter what it looks like. One glance at the army of shoving, shouting, sweating photographers mobbing the entrance and you know you are in one of those rare places on the earth where powerful forces converge.

"Who are they waiting for?" Glynn whispered in awe.

"Anybody famous who happens to come in," Caleb said. "And anyone who looks like they ought to be famous. You. Your mother. Your Aunt Laura."

"Yeah, right," Glynn said, but when Jesus helped us from the car the paparazzi did indeed rush at us, frantically, shooting rapidly into our faces, mine and Glynn's as well as Laura's and Caleb's. The little Hispanic darted at them making fierce shooing sounds, and they parted just enough for us to run into the restaurant.

"Wow," Glynn said, lifting a luminous face to mine. "Did you see that, Mom? *Did* you?"

"I did," I said. "Ridiculous. Don't let it go to your head. You're flown enough with yourself tonight."

"*No!* I want to be more flown! I want to be flown all the way to the moon!" she caroled, and did a little pirouette in the restaurant's foyer. Her hair fanned out in a surge of silk, and her eyes closed in rapture. Caleb stood and watched her, unsmiling once more.

"Glynn," I said warningly. Enough was enough.

Caleb Pringle scanned the crowd inside. I looked, too. It seemed to me that every beautiful woman in Los Angeles was in Spago tonight, and every older man, and all of them were rich. Everyone could have been Someone, but I could not tell who all those someones were.

"Are all these women in movies?" I whispered to Laura. "If so, who are they? I never saw so many beautiful women and so many gorgeous clothes, but I don't know who anybody is. Am I supposed to?"

Caleb overheard me and laughed.

"No, you're not, mostly. Who they are is women who go to Spago."

"What do you mean?"

"I mean, that's what they do. They get invited to Spago and then they spend the rest of the week, day and night, getting ready to go. And after they've gone they kick back and wait until they're invited again, and the whole thing starts over."

I looked at him in disbelief.

"You're kidding."

"Only a little. Look, there's somebody I want you to meet. Let's go over, and then we'll find the rest of the gang. I think they put us in a private room."

We followed him through the thronged room, and again, as I had in the movie theater, I felt rather than saw eyes follow us, heard a small, windlike sigh ruffle the surface of the room. Ahead of me Laura pulled her shoulders back and tucked her buttocks in and fell into her prowl. My own shoulders went back and my spine straightened automatically. Next to Laura, Glynn was floating again.

Laura stopped suddenly. She looked up at Caleb.

"That's Margolies over there," she said, and her voice was low and angry. "That's who you want us to meet, isn't it? No way, Pring, absolutely no way in hell am I going to go over there and make nice on the bastard who cut me out of that movie. No way. Nada. What are you trying to do to me?"

"I'm trying to save you a little face, my beautiful ass. That's what I'm trying to do," Caleb Pringle said lazily, but there was something urgent in his voice. "Listen, Margolies doesn't have any idea who you are; the cut wasn't personal. It was for his Jacuzzi-brained honey, I told you that. He wouldn't recognize your face if it got up off the cutting room floor and bit him. As far as he knows, you're somebody he's meeting for the first time, somebody he knows I want for *Arc*. He'll be charming and polite and think you're entirely as fetching as you are, and how smart I am to put you in the picture, and that'll be that. And nobody else in here knows you've been cut from Margolies's new picture, because nobody at all does, but they soon will. And what will they remember? They'll remember that you sat at Margolies's table the night of the screening and he slobbered over you and everybody smiled and giggled and yukked, and you were with me, and I'm doing another hot picture with Margolies, and they'll go around telling the whole industry that they were here the night he hired you for *Arc*. The fact that you weren't in *Right Time* after all will be forgotten because *Arc* is going to be newer and ten times hotter than that. *Capice?*"

"I do. Yes," Laura said. "Thank you, Pring. I shouldn't have doubted you."

"No, you shouldn't," he said, and tugged her braid, and we moved toward the corner booth where the little man who had sat beside me at the screening shoveled in pasta, head down over his plate. He was, oddly, alone. I would have thought studio heads traveled with retinues.

He looked up when we stopped beside him and smiled. It reminded me of the smile on the face of Bruce, the mechanical shark they used in *Jaws*. The eyes above the smile were chips of basalt, old and cold and long dead. I thought that I had far rather meet Bruce in the water than this man.

"Caleb," he said, and his voice was smooth and thick, a flowery oil. "Dear boy. We meet again. Yes. Sit down and introduce me to these pretty things with you. Yes."

Caleb handed us into the empty seats in the booth, putting Laura across from Margolies so, I thought, he could better look at her. He motioned me in beside her. He put Glynn next to the little man, and nodded to a waiter, who produced a chair as swiftly as if he had woven it out of air and set it at the end of the booth. Caleb Pringle draped his long frame over it.

"Leonard, this is Laura Mason, about whom I have told you an enormous amount," he said. "I want her very badly for *Arc*, and I know that after you have looked at her for a few minutes you are going to let me have her with abiding joy. And this is her beautiful big sister, Merritt Fowler, from Atlanta, and the stunning child beside you is her daughter and

Laura's niece, Glynn Fowler. Maybe we should put them all in *Arc*. What do you think?"

Leonard Margolies nodded sleepily at us, and the shark's smile widened. "Yes. Lovely, both of them. Yes, we should probably do that, my boy. If indeed there is going, as you seem to think, to be an *Arc*. Yes."

I wondered if the repeated "yes" meant anything, or was just a habit peculiar to Leonard Margolies. It was disconcerting, like hearing a toad hiss. Or a penguin. Or, of course, a shark.

"Oh, there must be an *Arc*, Leonard. It will be the jewel in your crown, as it were," said Caleb evenly. "Especially with Laura here on board. I take it from your comment, or lack of same, that you think *Right Time* might use a little touching up."

"Well, my boy, yes. A tad of cosmetic dentistry, shall we say. Yes. We will, of course, discuss that in the morning. I'm staying in town just to talk to you about it. See what I do for you? Come to my office about seven. We'll order in."

Caleb laughed. I did not think there was much humor in it.

"It will be," he said, grinning around the table at us all, "in the nature of the condemned man's last meal. Never mind. Let's order something wonderful to eat and drink, and be very merry, for tomorrow, et cetera."

Leonard Margolies raised a limp white hand and two waiters collided with each other trying to reach him first.

"Bring us something bubbly and *so* expensive for these pretties here," he said. "Yes. Lots of it. We'll order for them after we've toasted them; I want to think about what they should eat. Yes. I assume," he said, looking at Laura and me and then at Glynn, "that you belles drink something besides bourbon and branch water."

We smiled and nodded and he said, "Good. Good," and looked at Glynn again.

In the low light of the restaurant she had the afternoon's unearthly shine back, the shine that made me think of alabaster and medieval effigies. Excitement flamed along her cheekbones, but shyness paled the rest of her face to pearl-white. Her eyelashes lay along her cheeks, and I knew that she was struggling with shyness, struggling not to seem what she was: a sixteen-year-old sitting beside one of the world's legendary studio heads in one of the world's legendary restaurants. My heart squeezed in empathy. If I was tongue-tied here, how much worse for her. Too much; we had heaped too much on her tonight.

Abruptly Margolies leaned over and whispered into her ear, and she started and turned to look at him, the satiny hair swinging out, and then she began to laugh. It was the belly laugh. Margolies smiled conspiratorially at her, his eyes alive now, and heads turned toward us, and faces smiled. I had seen the effect of Glynn's infectious croak before.

"What on earth did you say to her, Leonard?" Caleb grinned.

"That will be our secret, won't it . . . is it Glynn? Yes. Glynn. We shall never tell, shall we?"

"Never," Glynn said. The shyness was gone. She looked at him as one might a favored uncle. Forever after, she never told me what he said.

Margolies studied her openly, turning his head this way and that, smiling a faint smile. It was a gentler smile, but I thought the shark ghosted just below the surface. I was suddenly glad we would be going home the next day.

"Tell me, Glynn, do you want to be an actress like your pretty aunt?" Margolies said. It was more than a casual question; he sounded genuinely interested. I thought that this sudden, real charm was not the least of his power.

"No," she said. "I don't think so. I don't think I have, you know, the looks and everything for it. I think I might like to write or paint, though. Or maybe do something with music."

"Ah, then, the creative urge is there," he said.

"As well as a rather startling perception," Caleb Pringle said. "She caught the absolute essence of *Arc* before I'd even worked it out for myself."

Margolies looked at her some more.

"You like *Arc*, my little Glynn? Yes?"

"I don't think anyone is going to *like Arc*, exactly," she said shyly. "But I think everybody is going to be, you know, different after they see it."

He did not reply, but nodded several times.

We sat quietly for a bit, a silence that puzzled me but did not seem strained. Into it, Caleb Pringle said presently, "Well, if she doesn't want to be in the movies like her aunt she could always save France."

Leonard Margolies looked at him and then at Glynn again. The smile deepened.

"She could indeed," he said. "Yes. She could indeed do that."

Glynn looked puzzled and started to say something, but Laura made a small motion toward her and smiled, and she fell silent. There was a kind of suppressed glee in Laura's face that I could not read, and a sleepy sort of triumph in Caleb Pringle's. But no one said anything else.

The champagne came and was uncorked, and Leonard Margolies tasted it and said, "Yes," and the waiter poured it all around. Margolies lifted his glass.

"To Miss Laura Mason and her pretty sister and niece. To a wonderful visit with us. May the magic of Hollywood never fade."

We drank.

"Now. What can I do to make your trip memorable?" Leonard Margolies said, putting his glass down. "What have you seen? What would you like to see? Have you seen a real studio, had a Hollywood tour? I like to think Vega is one of the great ones. I would be most happy to show you around it. Yes."

"I can't think of anything any more special, than to see Vega in the presence of the man who built it," Laura said. Her cheeks were flaming, and her eyes glittered. She had drunk her champagne rather faster than I liked to see. Laura never could hold her liquor.

"Oh," Glynn cried in delight. "Could we? Mom? Could we do that? Oh, Jess and Marcia would just *die*!"

"Glynn, you know we're going home at noon tomorrow—"

"But if we went early? Maybe we could do it real early?" her voice broke in something near despair.

"Mr. Margolies has an early breakfast meeting. You heard him. No, darling, he's been kind enough to us as it is."

"Wouldn't it be fun if we gave her a test?" Caleb said, as if I had not spoken. "It only takes a few minutes. Glynn, would you like to have a real screen test? We could send you home with a tape of it, so you could make *sure* Marcia and Jess die. Leonard, we could do that, couldn't we? We can meet afterward—"

"We could do that, yes. The meeting can wait," Leonard Margolies said. He sat back, hands together like a Buddha, smiling. Shark, penguin, and toad had fled, leaving an indulgent uncle.

"*Mom*—"

"Why not, Merritt?" Caleb said. "We could have you on the plane in plenty of time. I'll send Jesus with the car for you and he can wait, and take you to the airport afterward. Send you both off like royalty. It would be something to tell the gang, wouldn't it?"

He was looking at Glynn.

"Oh, really, Caleb, I don't think—" I began.

"It would give me great pleasure," Leonard Margolies said. "Yes."

"Oh, come on, Met. There's no earthly reason not to do it," Laura said. "How many young girls in the world will ever be able to say that Leonard Margolies personally gave them a screen test? Let her have something wonderful of her very own."

And of course, there was no reason not to do it. It seemed to disaccommodate no one, and we would make our plane home with time to spare. And Laura was right; after that, there was not apt to be anything special for Glynn for a long time. Why not let her have this luminous moment without spoiling it? I did not know where my reluctance was coming from.

"Well . . . all right. It sounds like fun and we both appreciate it very much," I said. "I can't imagine why you're being so nice to a couple of visiting Georgia relatives, but we accept with great pleasure."

Glynn's face abruptly went stark white and she closed her eyes.

"Thank you, Mom," she said, in such a breathless small voice that we all looked at her. She looked as if she was about to faint.

I had seen the look before; it meant Glynn was stressed to the very limits of her being, every circuit overloaded. This was simply one liter too much joy in her cup. The next step would be nausea and vomiting, perhaps unstoppable tears. The embarrassment that followed these scenes was killing for her. She had not had one in a very long time; her world until this trip had been orderly in the extreme. I knew that she could not eat her dinner now, not in this place, not with these people. I put my hand on hers and said, "I think Glynn and I will skip dinner, after all, and go back to the apartment. We've both had too long a day, and she has an early morning call tomorrow—isn't that how you say it? I'll just ask the waiter to call us a cab; you all go on with your dinner, please."

Glynn did not protest. She looked at me gratefully. No one else protested, either; her white face was eloquent.

"You do that, my nice, pretty girl," Margolies said as fondly as if to a favorite niece. "Get your beauty sleep and be fresh for your big scene. Caleb, the car, I think."

"Of course. I'll send you both home in the limo and it can come back for Laura and me," he said. "I'll drop her at her car when we've finished dinner. I should have paced this better. Of course she's worn out."

When we got up to leave, Leonard Margolies kissed both our hands. Holding Glynn's, he said, "You mustn't take all this frou frou too seriously, my dear. It's very good make-believe, but that's just what it is. Make-believe."

Thank you for that, I said silently.

"I won't," Glynn said. "Thank you, Mr. Margolies. I'm looking forward to tomorrow."

He smiled.

"No more than I," he said. "Yes."

Caleb waited with us in the foyer until Jesus arrived with the limo, and then hurried us down the steps, his long body blocking Glynn from the milling paparazzi and the exploding flashbulbs. He handed us into the car and said, "Until tomorrow, then. You made a big hit with a very tough customer tonight, both of you. Rest on your laurels. Jesus will pick you up at six, if that's okay, and we'll shoot at eight. Jesus, take care of these ladies. They're *very* good friends of Orion O'Neill."

We rode home in the tomblike quiet of the ridiculous limo in silence, simply too full of the last seventy-two hours to speak. When we reached Stuart Feinstein's aerie above Sunset Boulevard, Jesus handed us as tenderly out of the limo as if we had been Fabergé eggs.

He started to drive away, and then put his head out the window and chirped, "You tell Orion O'Neill Jesus say 'allo!"

7

The production studio where the test would be done was in Culver City, just off the San Diego Freeway South, near the airport. The limo picked us up at six. Our driver this morning was not Jesus, but a dark, impassive man who might have been a Pakistani, or from another Middle Eastern nation. He did not speak except to confirm our destination, and we did not, either. Much of the shine was gone from the limo when Jesus was not at the wheel.

Despite the lateness of the hour when we went to bed, neither Glynn nor I slept well. Overexcitement did that to her, I knew, and her restless tossing set the waterbed to rolling like a frail craft in a nasty sea. I clung to my side of the mattress and tried for oblivion; I knew that the next day would be hard for us. The excitement of the test and the proximity to the world of casual glamour and unreality that Caleb Pringle commanded, the rush to make the noon plane, and the meeting, at last, with Pom all lay ahead, stuffed into this one day like sausage into a casing. Add to all that the shuffling specter of Mommee and jet lag, and the mere thought of the next twenty-four hours stunned me with fatigue and a lassitude that seemed to settle in my very bones like some Victorian malaise. There was no way to know what it did to Glynn. Like a young bride on the eve of her wedding, she could not see past the altar of the screen test.

We were up before five, padding blindly around the kitchen for juice and toast and coffee, bumping into each other in Stuart's tiny coral and aqua bathroom. I pulled on the much-derided blue pantsuit and hastily packed my few things, tossing the jeans and T-shirt I had worn into Stuart's washing machine and hanging up his tux jacket. Laura had said she would come back to the apartment and wash and dry the things we had borrowed, and his linens. Glynn had been living out of her duffel, so she had little to pack. She would be made up at the studio, Caleb had said, so she needed no make-up, and I, weary of the last two day's ersatz Merritt, wore none, either. By the time the heat-grayed morning came sliding in from the east we were sitting on the little balcony, watching Sunset Boulevard come wearily alive and sipping coffee. Humidity was thick in the air and the heat was already shimmering off the hazy towers of Century City and downtown. It was going to be a smoggy, broiling day. I thought of Atlanta, and the heat and thickness we had left behind us, and sighed. The vision of the Penobscot Bay cottage superimposed itself over the scene below. Cool, sharp, resinous, clean, clear—that was what I needed. Clarity. I was starved for starkness and clarity.

"Do you think they made it up last night?" Glynn said in the rusty voice of early morning.

"Who?"

"Oh, Mom. Aunt Laura and Caleb. You know she didn't come in. The sofa bed wasn't out. She had to have spent the night with him."

"I thought they already had pretty much made it up," I said. I did not trouble to pretend that I thought Laura had spent the night anywhere but with Caleb Pringle. Of course she had. I had seen her face last night at Spago when she looked at him. Laura was in love with him. Spending the night was what she did when she was in love, or thought herself to be.

I thought that it was not much of an example to set for an unworldly sixteen-year-old niece, but Glynn had seemed, on this trip, far older than sixteen much of the time. There was a perceptiveness, an adult insight and tolerance in her that we did not see in Atlanta. But then we did not see much of anything about Glynn there except her carefully guarded, post-Mommee demeanor. How much richness were we missing in our daughter, I wondered wearily. Well, that would stop, too. Mommee would be gone, and Glynn would have room and air to become whoever she might. In the sun of her father's undivided attention, we just might see the last of the starving child who haunted the house by the river. Already, out here, she was eating far more. I hated the thought of the looming confrontation, but resolved that it would come soon. I did not want to lose this budding wholeness of Glynn's.

"What do you think of him?" Glynn said.

"Caleb? Well, he's certainly attractive, and he's being lovely to us. And he seems to be very fond of your Aunt Laura. I don't really know what I think yet. I don't know any other film directors to compare him to. What do you think?"

"I think he's wonderful. He's funny and not at all stuck-up, and he doesn't make me feel like a silly kid. He treats me like someone he enjoys listening to and being around. I hope Aunt Laura marries him. I'd love to have him for an uncle," Glynn said.

I could not see Caleb Pringle as anyone's uncle, nor, come to that, anyone's husband, though I knew he had been married twice before. I did not think he was or ever could be a creature of the thousand lilliputian tendrils with which marriage and children bound you. But then, neither could I see Laura trussed with them. We were, Glynn and I, far away from home and out of our milieu altogether. Without my context, I found it hard to catch the sense of the people I met. I had never stopped to think how much I depended on simple familiarity.

"I wouldn't count on that," I said. "I think they'd have an alternative relationship at best."

"You mean like just a long affair or living together all their lives but never marrying?"

"Something like that," I said. "This place just doesn't seem set up for plain old garden-variety marriages."

"Well, that would be okay, too," my child said placidly. "As long as I got to see him every now and then."

"Don't you go getting a crush on Caleb Pringle," I said. "The percentage in that is less than zero."

"I don't get crushes anymore," she said loftily. The limo came then, saving me from wondering when she ever had. I had seen little evidence of them, except the occasional almost obligatory infatuation with untouchable celebrities like this troublesome Rocky MacPherson about whom I had heard so much. Pom had said once, almost wistfully, that it looked as though he was never going to have to run off some obnoxious, lovesick little punk.

We got to the studio about six-thirty. It was a large, sprawling, one-story brick and aluminum building that looked vaguely like a warehouse, sitting in the middle of an asphalt parking lot that, I thought, would be worse than Death Valley at midday. There was a high wire fence around the whole complex, topped with barbed wire, and a heavy steel gate with a guardhouse. It managed to be both forbidding and banal, far removed from the fabled Hollywood studios that had lived always in my mind.

There were few cars in the lot. The limo's driver lowered the silky, whispering window and said a few words to the guard, who consulted a clipboard and nodded. The driver followed his pointing finger around to the back of the building, which was even barer and less attractive than the front, and pulled up to a plain steel door next to a loading ramp. Glynn looked up at me and rolled her eyes.

"So much for *A Star Is Born*," I said, ruffling her silky hair. She had washed it and blown it dry, and it seemed to drift around her face, never quite settling. She wore the same tunic she had worn last night, and the leggings and boots. Caleb Pringle had asked specifically for them.

"I wasn't expecting all that old silent-movie stuff," she said. "I know they don't do that anymore. It would have been fun, though, wouldn't it?"

The driver opened the door and we went inside. A young woman who seemed hardly older than Glynn was waiting for us. She wore blue jeans and a sweatshirt and enormous, clunking Birkenstock sandals over thick ragg socks, and had a head of glorious, improbable, Dolly Parton hair. Over her tiny mouse's face it looked so incongruous that Glynn and I both grinned.

"It's one of the wigs Laura wore in *Right Time*," she grinned back. "I've always wanted to try it on. I don't think the effect is quite the same. I'm Molly Shumaker, Caleb's gofer. He and Laura are waiting for you on the set."

On the set. Waiting for you on the set. The words ran down my spine like little spiders, and I felt Glynn, beside me, shiver. I could just begin, dimly, to understand the magic in those words, feel the glue that held my sister out here, when the Eastern stage was so much more obviously her metier.

"After you, Miss Fowler," I said, and Glynn gave me her I'm-having-second-thoughts-about-this smile.

"I'm not sure this was such a hot idea," she said in a tiny voice.

"Well, it's too late to back out now," I said. "Besides, you'd lose your home-court advantage over Marcie and Jess."

"Right. Let's do it, then," she said, and squared her thin shoulders, and marched ahead of me behind Molly Shumaker.

We followed her through a labyrinth of dark halls with closed doors on either side, past a dimly lit canteen, through an empty, cavernous sound stage where cameras stood like sleeping dinosaurs and cables snaked across the floor, and into a second huge room. It was brightly lit from banks of ceiling lights and standing floor lamps, and in front of a large white screen at the far end a group of people fiddled with equipment and drank coffee. Among them were Laura and Caleb Pringle. They were obviously talking and laughing with the crew, but the room was so large that we could not hear them. We went toward them, and I realized that both Glynn and I were walking on tiptoe. Leonard Margolies was nowhere to be seen.

Laura turned and saw us, and came running over and gave us twin hugs. She smelled of soap and lotion and wore a gray leotard and tights with red running shorts over them, and running shoes. They were obviously her own, and I thought that she must have left some of her clothes at Caleb Pringle's house. He was in running clothes, too, sweatpants and a T-shirt that said *The Right Time*. The baseball cap on his still-damp dark hair said the same thing. He smiled, and stood waiting for us.

"Isn't this *exciting?*" squealed Laura. "Isn't it a *beautiful* day? Did you sleep at *all?* I wish you weren't going home today; there's so much else I want you to see . . . "

She sounded so much like she had when she was a teenager and things were, for a moment, right in her world that I smiled. I had not seen her this exuberant in a long time, not since before she left for Hollywood. The tautness was completely gone from her face; the thin angles were smoothed, and her skin shone with soap and health and something else entirely, which I knew was sheer happiness. I had seen that before, too, if only rarely.

"Yes to all the above except going home. No more discussion about that," I said. "I don't have to ask if you slept well. No, don't answer that."

She hugged herself with glee and did a little dance step.

"Can't you see the answer?" she sang. "Oh, Met, he's back one hundred and ten percent; last night was just—incredible! How could I ever have doubted him? Oh, it's going to work out, it is . . . "

I shivered. "Listen, Pie, don't rush it too much," I said. "Please. Hold just a little back till you're sure . . . "

Beside me Glynn said nothing, only studied her aunt gravely.

"I am sure," Laura laughed. "You're just being a big sister. Be my friend for a change! Be happy with me!"

"I am," I said, smiling. But I wasn't; not really. There was something about her that reminded me of an out-of-control toddler rushing toward a cliff. Laura, being Laura once again.

Caleb came over.

"Listen, you guys, let's get this show on the road so there'll be time to make a tape for the purpose of gloating," he said. "This is what we're going to do. John Metter there behind the camera will shoot it; he's the best I know, and shot *Burn* and *Right Time* for me. We're editing the final cut of *Right Time* so he was here anyway. You'll have the *crème de la crème*, Glynn;

he wins big-time awards, Oscars. We're going to do a very short scene from *Arc*—one where the young Joan sees for the first time the shape of things to come, you might say. It's just a few lines, and you'll just read them off the TelePrompTer—very simply. Don't try to act. Just think about the words and say them. We'll do it in front of this backdrop, because I want the focus to be on you. John will come in close at the end; don't mind him. Just think about the words. It'll be just you, but I need another female voice to read a few lines off-camera, and a woman's arm and hand. I've asked Laura to do the honors there. Let her get a head start on feeling her way into Joan. I'll be in back of the camera with John and I'll give you a few simple instructions, nothing you'll mind. Don't be nervous. It'll be fun. You look perfect, by the way; I don't think we're going to do much to you, but our makeup person is waiting to fluff you up a little. Molly will take you back there. Any questions?"

"I . . . no. I guess not," Glynn mumbled through dry lips, and I thought with dread that she was going to freeze, and then she would castigate herself mercilessly for months. This had not been a good idea after all; my instinct had been right about that. She didn't need anymore self-doubt.

"I don't know about this, Caleb," I began, but he held up a finger and smiled at me and said, "Trust me. I won't scare her. It's really simple. Piece of cake. That little bit of shyness and tentativeness is just what I want."

I fell silent. Caleb nodded at Molly, and she touched Glynn's arm and the two girls went out of the room. I looked from Laura to Glynn.

"I'm really worried about it," I said. "She's been having a go-round with an eating disorder and her sense of self-worth is in the basement right now, and then there's been a difficult time with her father and grandmother . . . if this doesn't turn out, she's going to be more than embarrassed."

"Laura told me a little about things at home," Caleb Pringle said. "Don't worry about her, Merritt. Even if she's awful—and I don't think for a minute she will be—we can make her look fabulous. This guy is a wizard. And she's a very beautiful girl. I have an idea that the camera is going to love her. That's everything."

"I told you how good he was with kids," Laura said, putting her arm around me. "He wouldn't do anything to hurt her. I wouldn't let him. I'll take care of her. It won't take long. You'll be glad you let her do it; the tape is going to be a treasure."

I raised my hands and then dropped them. I was trying hard not to hover over Glynn; the therapist had been adamant about that.

"Good," Caleb said. "Laura and I thought it would be easier for Glynn if you waited in the canteen while we're shooting. I've always found that parents on the set spook young actors. You can stay if you like, of course, but it'll be more effective if you see the finished product on the monitor."

"Whatever's best for her," I said helplessly.

"This is, I think," he said. "By the way, Leonard sends his regrets; he had an unexpected morning meeting with somebody from back East. He'd like to give you the full studio tour and dinner if you could possibly stay over, or if not, maybe you'll come back soon. He's really taken with both of you. Laura too. Leonard doesn't get taken too often."

"Thank him for us," I said. "Maybe we can come back sometime."

Molly came back with Glynn. I stared at my daughter. Nothing seemed to have changed about her, and yet everything had; I could not tell what the makeup artist had done, beyond hang a heavy, rough-cast metal cross on a primitive chain about her neck, but her face had been altered. Her eyes seemed larger, her cheekbones even more prominent, and there were tender shadows in places I had never seen shadows before. Her skin literally shone; it seemed as translucent as alabaster over the bones of her face, although there did not seem to be any makeup or powder on it. Someone had drawn her hair back so that from the front it looked cropped at the nape, and the hair at her hairline had been feathered into silky bangs that brushed her eyebrows. She looked young and frightened and somehow stricken and almost completely medieval in the tunic and tights and the big cross. I could see now why Caleb Pringle had wanted her to wear them. Her wrists looked impossibly thin, and there were red marks around them that manacles might have left. My heart lurched with pity and fear for her; I had never seen anyone look so vulnerable.

She grinned at me then, and crossed her eyes, and the tortured child fled and she was Glynn again, and it was all right.

"Don't you know enough to genuflect in the presence of a saint?" she said.

"If you're going to develop temperament before they even shoot this thing, I'm snatching you out of here," I said, laughing.

She made a pantomime of gagging, putting her forefinger into her open mouth, and Caleb Pringle laughed, too.

"The whole course of history might have changed if little Joan had had the wit to do that to the Dauphin," he said. "You ready? Molly, Mrs. Fowler is going to wait and see the final on the monitor. Take her and give her some coffee and a sweet roll, will you? I'll send for you when we're done."

The last thing I saw before the door closed behind me and Molly Shumaker was Caleb Pringle bending intently over my daughter, who sat with her face raised to him and her eyes closed. In the white light flooding down on her she looked again unearthly and ephemeral, doomed. But he said something to her and she smiled. I let the door swing shut.

"I don't know why I'm so nervous," I said to Molly.

"You're great," she said over her shoulder. "You ought to see some of the mothers we get. The poor kid who was in *Right Time*; God! We got to the point where we were seriously thinking about drugging his mother's coffee. She was a terror."

The time seemed to drag torturously, though in actuality it was only a little over an hour when Laura came for us.

"How did it go?" I said, following her back through the maze of corridors.

She gave me her three-cornered kitten's smile over her shoulder, the one she had always worn when she knew a secret or had been into something forbidden.

"You'll see," she said.

They were waiting for us in a tiny studio with padded swivel seats and a large, incomprehensible control board and banks of television monitors mounted overhead. There was a large central screen, and Caleb Pringle was sliding a tape into a slot on the board below it. He turned and gave me an enigmatic nod. Glynn sat in the back row of seats, hunched over, her fists knotted, one atop the other. She had been crying, and would not look at me.

"What is it, sweetie pie?" I said, sinking into the seat beside her and glaring up at Laura. Laura—why did I listen to her? I always ended up coming to some sort of grief when I let her persuade me to do something my instincts cried out against. Why had I thought that would change?

Glynn did not reply. She shook her head. She still would not look at me.

"It was pretty intense," Laura said. "I had no idea she could tap into that so soon. It took me months to learn to do it. These are just release tears, aren't they, Punkin?"

She ruffled the bangs on Glynn's forehead. From the machine, Caleb Pringle said, "This is quite . . . extraordinary. See it before you decide to report us to the child abuse squad."

I sank back against my cushion, squeezing Glynn's cold hand, and waited. I had every intention of giving my sister and her lover as fierce a tongue-lashing as I could muster. But I would, in fairness, wait until I had seen the test.

The screen flickered with light and numbers rolled past and a voice I did not know said, "Test for Glynn Fowler, *Arc*, June 1995. Take three." There was a bit more flickering, and then there was Glynn, sitting on a wooden stool against a stark, shadowy backdrop. She sat with her knees together and her hands loosely clasped on her lap, and her head dropped onto her chest. Light fell on her from above, as from an opening in a ceiling; otherwise the set was very dark. The camera came in on her, very slowly, until I could see only her head and shoulders and the great cross lying against her tunic. The angle of her head was heartbreaking. She did not move.

From off camera a woman's voice whispered, "Joan. Little Joan," and Glynn raised her head slowly and looked in the direction of the voice. I drew in my breath. It was not Glynn who sat there, but someone who had taken her over, moved into her body. The feeling it gave me was terrible, near nausea but not quite that. This was what possession must look like.

The voice spoke again, louder, and I recognized it as

Laura's, but her voice as I had never heard it: low, caressing, sly, somehow as evil as the hiss of a snake.

"What do your voices say now?" Laura's corrupted voice said.

Glynn dropped her eyes back to her hands. Slowly they picked up the great cross and caressed it, a soft, unconscious, washing motion. The camera moved in further, as slowly and softly as fog.

"Nothing. They say nothing," she whispered.

I had never heard such sorrow in my daughter's voice, never such bewilderment. Never such despair, but despair as quiet as a sigh, or a little wind.

She lifted her face again, and the light caught it, and the camera came on. Her face filled the screen now. Her eyes looked out as if at empty space, and they were blind. Her face was awful, beautiful, lost. I held my breath.

"They say nothing," she said again. I felt tears spring into my eyes. Glynn's hand tightened in mine, but I could not look at her.

"There is another way," Laura's low, dreadful voice said. "There is another voice that will speak, if only you will listen, and your heart will sing with it, and your body burn."

Without moving her eyes, Glynn said, "All my life it has been my passion to serve France and my Lord. Only these. But now my voices tell me nothing and my Lord is silent and my passion is cold in this cold place. If there is another voice to make my heart sing, for sweet Jesus' sake, Lady, tell me it."

Two great tears gathered in her eyes, and her lips trembled suddenly, and she looked down. The tears slid from beneath her lashes and tracked down her face. She sat silent. Laura's voice was silent, too.

Very slowly Laura's white hand came into the frame and reached over. Her finger caught a tear that trembled on Glynn's chin, and so slowly that it seemed to take whole minutes, her finger traced the tear over to Glynn's lips, and brushed the wetness across them. Glynn's lashes dropped still; they shuttered her eyes, but the slow crystal tears continued, one by one.

"You hear it now," Laura said.

The camera froze on the closeup of Glynn's face with Laura's finger on her lips, and then the screen went blank.

For a long moment no one spoke. I could not find the breath to breathe, much less to speak. The little moment was heartbreaking, terrible, and so pregnant with both innocence and evil that it did not seem to me there could be words for it. I hated it. I felt horror and terror and furious rage; how dare he make this of my daughter? How dare Laura? But even as I sat paralyzed, trying to find breath and words, I knew that the test was, as Caleb Pringle had said, extraordinary.

The lights came up and Caleb said, matter-of-factly, "I've never seen a first test like it. She is incredible. You do see that, don't you?"

"I see it. I also see that it is depraved, and evil, and if I had known it would be like this I would never on earth have—"

"But that is just how it should be," he said softly and patiently, as if he were talking to a child. "She has caught completely that awful innocence at the moment of corruption; seen the snake as it enters Eden. If she were not your daughter you would see."

I knew he was right. If I had seen this moment in a theater and not known Glynn, I would have been struck silent with its sheer power, instead of with horror and rage.

I took a deep breath and looked at Glynn. She was looking back at me with a simple, whole-souled desire to please; it was a look I saw practically every day at home.

"Well, I do see. And I'm totally impressed," I said as lightly as I could, and smiled at her. "It was a beautiful job, Tink. How on earth did you do that? Seem so frightened? Cry like that? I didn't know you'd ever felt like acting might be something you'd like to try—"

"I wasn't acting," she said earnestly. "I don't know what happened, quite. I was sitting there, scared out of my skull and sure I was going to throw up, or stammer, or something, and then I heard Aunt Laura's voice and it was so . . . I don't know how to say it, but it made me feel so . . . *bad*. It was like something exploded behind my eyes. I started to cry, and I couldn't stop, and I was scared of her; I forgot completely it was only Aunt Laura—"

"That *is* acting," Caleb Pringle said, smiling at her. "That's just what acting is. On your part and your Aunt Laura's. She called it out, maybe, but you're the one who let it go. I don't know what else you'd call it if it wasn't acting. Too bad you can't stay and be our Joan."

He spoke to her, lightly, but cut his eyes toward me.

"Don't even think it," I said.

"Mom . . ." Glynn began, her voice pleading, rising.

"Met, listen . . ." Laura began.

I got up out of my seat.

"The test is wonderful and Glynn will love having the tape, and you were kind, and that is that," I said. "There will be no talk now or ever about her doing Joan or any other movie at any time. We are going to the airport now and catch our plane, which is something we should have done a long time ago."

"Met, don't you realize what this means? There's going to be a nationwide talent search; it's the role of the century for a new actress!" Laura cried. "How can you say no? Let her do it this once; she doesn't necessarily have to have an acting career, just this one role—there'll never be another young Joan as good as what you just saw. Pring will tell you that."

"Laura, what part of no is it you don't understand?" I said. "Besides, it's Mr. Margolies's decision; how can you just assume—"

"Margolies would say yes," Caleb Pringle said mildly. "Margolies is going to go right through the roof of his Turkish bathhouse when he sees this. He thought we had our Joan last night, didn't you know? You saw how he looked at Glynn. But you have to test; sometimes the camera just kills them. That obviously isn't the case here."

"I don't care what the case here is," I said. "You can show him the test or not. But Glynn is not doing this movie. Get your things together, Tink; we've got to make tracks."

She did not argue with me, but she did not move from the seat, either. She stared at her hands. Then she looked up.

"Daddy would be so proud," she said softly.

I felt as though she had hit me in the stomach. Was that it? Something of her own, something that was, without any doubt in the world, on any level you chose to regard it, extraordinary, to show her father? Something he would have no choice but to notice? Either that, or the subtlest form of manipulation, and one of the oldest. The child's ultimate weapon: Daddy would let me.

"You know good and well Daddy would hate it," I said tightly. "Now come on. Let's go."

"Your mother's right," Caleb Pringle said to her. "It's probably no role for a sixteen-year-old. I thought all along we'd have to use an older girl for Joan, but I just wanted to see . . . I never meant to cause a family rift. Tell you what. Why don't you go in my office and call your friends back in Atlanta? Gloat unforgivably. Tell them you were offered the part in the movie but you turned it down. Rub it in six ways to Sunday."

Glynn broke into a slow smile.

"Can I, Mom?"

"Be my guest," I said. "Gloat till you drop."

She followed the cheerful Molly Shumaker out of the room, and I turned to him.

"Thanks for that," I said. "I'd have ended up as the world's heaviest heavy."

"It was my fault," he said. "I should have run this idea by you before. Frankly, I was hoping the test would convince you. But I don't push people; it never works out."

"She's just too young," I said, feeling defensive and a little foolish, a lioness who had charged what she thought to be a threat to her cub, and found it a shadow.

"It's not the kind of world we want for her or that she could handle. Some young women could, with one hand tied behind them, but not Glynn. You must see that we've got a fight with anorexia on our hands."

"Yeah, I noticed," he said. "We see a lot of it out here. Of course to a filmmaker it usually just means that the victim will film like a dream. You're right; it's a dangerous world for some youngsters. She could well be one. I sensed a pretty sound armature under there, though."

"I hope you're right," I said. "Sometimes she just seems so fragile."

Glynn came back, her slowed steps speaking of disappointment.

"You can't tell me they weren't impressed," Laura said.

"They weren't there," Glynn said softly. "They're out here. Up north somewhere. Marcia's dad wanted her to come spend some time with him, and she hates his second wife, so her mother let her ask Jess. I think it's Palo Alto or somewhere; I know it's a long way away from here. They're going to stay a month."

Poor Glynn, I thought miserably. Jess is really gone now. How on earth can she replace a best friend?

"Palo Alto," Caleb Pringle said. "Really? I have a vacation place not thirty miles from there. Up in the Santa Cruz mountains, in a place called Big Basin. It's really something, if I do say so myself. Up there in those redwoods, it's like being right under the eye of God. And the air is so clear you can taste it, and the quiet so deep you can hear it. It saves what's left of my sanity. Listen, why don't you all drive up there and spend a little time? Glynn can see her friends and wave the tape in their faces, and you and Laura can kick back and relax, and I'll come up in a few days and we can hike and sightsee and spend some quality time together. Eat; we'll eat till we drop. I'm a great cook. I've got to recharge before we start *Arc* or I'll fall apart in midfilm, and Laura could use some rest before she goes into it, and I'd love to show all of you that part of the country. God, but it's beautiful."

"Mom," Glynn cried. "Please say yes! I could go stay with Marcie and Jess; her dad has a pool, and they belong to this marina club thing, and Marcie says there are some of the coolest guys there, and there are two whole weeks before I have to leave for camp—"

"No," I said.

"Met," Laura whispered, a soft, anguished sound.

"We can't, Laura. How many times can I say it? Don't tease about it."

"Well, some other time," Caleb Pringle said pleasantly. "It'll be there when you come back."

"Met," Laura said carefully and precisely, "I've got something in my bra poking me in back. Come see if you can find it for me, will you?"

"If you're wearing a bra I'm wearing a wet suit," I said, but

I followed her out of the studio toward the ladies' room. Better the session I knew was awaiting me be conducted in private.

She held the door for me and I went in and turned to face her. She leaned against it, head down, hands clasped over her breast, and then lifted her face to me. I was expecting one of her finer histrionic performances, but I saw instantly that this was to be no performance. Her face was white except for hectic red splotches on her cheekbones, and her mouth trembled uncontrollably, so that for a moment she could not speak. Tears were running down her face.

"Oh, baby," I began, but she held up her hand and I stopped. I watched as she struggled to control her lips, and then she said, as carefully as she could through her ragged breath, "Met. Please. Please just listen to me until I'm finished. Can you do that?"

"Laura, tell me what's the matter. . . ."

She looked at me mutely and I fell silent.

She nodded and took a deep breath and went on.

"You cannot possibly know what it would mean to me for you all to go up to the lodge with me. It's the rest of my life, Met; it's no less than that. Last night . . . last night was the springboard, but the lodge would cement everything; the lodge would give me time . . . the lodge would mean that I could spend another whole movie with him, and by that time I know that we would be together for good. I *know* that, Met. He's never asked me up there before, and I can't just say, well, my sister and niece have to go home but I'll come, because it wasn't just me that he asked."

"But why not?" I said, honestly baffled. "Why can't you? It isn't Glynn and me he's in love with, God forbid—"

"You have to be there because Glynn has to be there," she cried softly, chafing her hands in distress.

"Why on earth does Glynn have to be there? I don't understand any of this, Laura," I said.

"Oh, God, Met, can't you see how much he wants her for Joan? He's hoping that you all will stay around long enough for him to show Margolies the test and convince you to let her do the picture; I know how he thinks. He said as much. I know he wants me to get you to stay. Listen, Met, without

Glynn there may well not be any *Arc* at all, because Margolies was going to pull the plug on it this morning when they had breakfast; Pring was sure of that. He hated the new stuff Pring did on *Right Time*. And then he saw Glynn. . . . Met, it's my only real guarantee, that film. I have to do it; I have to be with Pring through it. I have to know that that's going to happen. He'll marry me after *Arc*; I know he will, if not before. But *Arc* has to happen and it's Glynn that Margolies is going to want. . . . "

I went over and put my hands on her shoulder and looked into her face.

"Baby, you must listen to me now," I said. "I am not going to let Glynn come out here and do that movie. That is not ever, ever going to happen. If there was any other way I could help this . . . relationship . . . happen, I would do it, if you want it this badly. But Glynn will not do Joan and I will not let Caleb Pringle think I'm going to change my mind, because I'm not. And I'm not going to let Glynn think that, either. Or Mr. Margolies. It's horribly, awfully dishonest; it's playing games with people's lives, my daughter's chief among them. Surely you must see that."

"I didn't mean you had to change your mind about it," she murmured. "But what's so wrong with letting him think he just might have a chance? Just for this tiny little bit of time, Glynn would never have to know. In fact you'd never even have to mention it again; your going up there would be all he wanted. You could still tell him no after a day or two. Glynn wants to go stay with her friends, anyway—she wouldn't even be around him. That way we could have a day or two together, you and I and Pring, *then* I could say well, I'll stay a little while after Met and Glynn leave, and it would be a natural thing to do, and we'd be alone, and I could . . . it would work out. If not the movie, then Met, please, please, let me have the time at the lodge."

She looked at me and saw the refusal in my face and put hers into her hands and began to cry. Her shoulders heaved and her hands shook, but the sobs were silent and terrible. I put my arms around her and held her against me. How many times, I thought dully, her pain seeping into the very core of

me, had we stood like this? She impaled on her pain; I trying
to absorb it.

"I don't understand why the lodge is so important to you,"
I said against her hair. "Can't you stay in L.A. and see him?
What is it that's so special about the lodge?"

"Because it's the place where he's happiest, the place he
loves most in the world. I want him to think of me in it; I
want him to see me there and remember how it was, how
good, how well I fit. And I have something I have to tell him,
and I want it to be there; otherwise I don't know . . . "

A coldness settled around my heart.

"What is it you have to tell him, Laura?" I said.

She shook her head against me, and then she looked up
at me and it came out.

"I'm pregnant," she said, beginning to cry again. "It's his.
I want this child, but I want him. I want him and me and the
baby to be together, a real family, and I'm afraid. . . . I have to
have some kind of insurance when I tell him. I know he loves
kids, but I don't know just how one will fit into his life now,
and I'm scared. I cannot lose him, Met; it would kill me; I
would die. That month that he didn't call . . . I was already
dead and in hell. I can tell him up there, in his place. Especially if he thinks there still might be a chance for *Arc*. Can you
possibly, possibly see?"

I stared at her more in grief and an old, sucking despair
than shock. The pregnancy was not a shock. I had always been
surprised and grateful that it had not happened before. Or perhaps it had.

"Oh, Pie," I said, my own tears beginning. "What on
earth is going to happen to you?"

"That's up to you," she whispered. "That's entirely up to
you. Can't you trade just one week of your life for the rest of
mine? I'd be off your hands then. . . . Oh, dear God, I need this
so much. I want this so much."

I held her and rocked her, staring over her head at the
blank steel door of the studio washroom, not seeing it. I want.
I need. Only you, Met. Only you, Mom. Only you, Merritt.
Help me. Fix it. Take care of me. . . .

Suddenly and violently I was sick of it, sick with the

weight of all those cries, all those years. I was tired beyond thinking, tired beyond even the effort to speak. To speak, to explain, to say, once again, no. No, it isn't good for you, no it isn't good for Glynn, no.

I thought of Caleb Pringle's words: "Up there in those redwoods it's like being right under the eye of God . . . and the silence is so deep you can hear it."

A week, I thought. A week in that healing silence and solitude. Days alone with my sister, days in which to make her see that a man who needed to be tricked was no man to hang a life on, to entrust a child's life to. Days in which to find another answer.

And I thought of what we were headed back to, Glynn and I.

"Yes," I said faintly. "All right. We'll go. We'll go and we'll figure out something about the baby, you and I. But first we'll sit down and look at the trees and just be very, very quiet, and we'll do that for a long time."

The sobs began again, and she hugged me so hard that I lost my breath.

"You'll never do anything else for me as important as this," she hiccuped. "I will love you for the rest of my life. I will love you beyond that."

"Fix your face and come on back," I said, wrapped close in this new shroud of tiredness and the stupid-simple peace that comes after a decision, any decision, is made.

"I have to go and call Pom. We have to call Marcie's folks in Palo Alto and see if it's all right for Glynn to visit."

She nodded and I left. Through the door she called after me, "Don't let him beat up on you, Met. Don't let him punish you for this. When was the last time you had some time just for yourself? Don't let him talk you out of that."

I did not reply. I walked steadily back through the still-dim corridors toward the studio, thinking what I might possibly say to my husband. Nothing came. Probably, I thought, it was because I had never, since I married him, made a decision that did not have his best interests, or Glynn's, at the core of it. I did not know how to explain my own need. And, I realized with amazement, I did not care. Pom had coped this far.

He could cope for another week. I did not expect that he would embrace the decision, but perhaps he would begin to see that sometime over the past week one of the primary rules by which we operated our lives had changed, had had to.

And maybe he would not. All I felt at the moment was a simple curiosity to see which it would be and a need to get beyond the phone call that was so great it almost felt like labor, like childbirth.

Amy answered Pom's private line.

"Oh, Merritt. Well, the prodigal wife at last," she chortled merrily, or with what passed, with Amy, for merriment. "Was it Doctor you wanted? I'll take a message, Doctor's in a meeting until—"

"Get him, Amy," I said. "Now."

There was a long pause, and I heard her dialing Pom, and then his voice. "Merritt," he said.

It was his voice, of course, but it sounded so flat and without affect that for a moment I thought Amy must have connected me with another office.

"Pom?" I said witlessly.

"Yes."

"I've been trying to reach you. I left a number—"

"I got it, Met. I just didn't call it."

I knew then that he was still very angry with me, and that this conversation would have no good ending. But there was something else under his voice, a frailty or injury of some sort, that I had never heard before. Alarm flooded me, and pity, and the old, helpless love that Pom in trouble always called out. Could Mommee after all . . .

"I sincerely hope that you're calling from the airport, Merritt," he said, and the pity and love receded, along with most of the alarm. If Mommee had come to serious harm he would not resort to sarcasm.

"No."

"Ah," he said, and waited.

"Pom, I wanted to tell you that we're going to spend another week in California," I said, speaking rapidly and, I hoped, firmly. "Laura's friend has offered us his lodge in the Santa Cruz mountains, south of San Francisco, and Glynn's friends Marcie and Jessica are visiting Marcie's father over in Palo Alto, and it's very close to the lodge, and I've always wanted Glynn to see the redwood country, and so much has happened that I need to be still and sort it all out—"

"A lot has happened indeed," he said. His tone was still level.

I could put it off no longer.

"Mommee . . . is Mommee all right?"

"No, Merritt, Mommee is not all right. Thank you for asking, though. Mommee is out of her mind and as of tonight she's out of the one decent place that would take her on short notice, and since you will be visiting the redwood country for another week I have no idea on God's earth what will happen to her now. That's how Mommee is."

Guilt leaped and anger flared higher. Pity was still there.

"I'm sorry," I said, meaning it. "I know she isn't easy. Do you want to tell me?"

"Would it get you home?"

"I don't think so."

"Well, then, no. I don't think I'll bother. Oh, hell, Merritt, it's just that . . . just that . . . I went to see her this morning before work and she didn't know who I was. She didn't know me, Merritt. She's been so traumatized by all this bouncing around, and all the unfamiliar people, that she's gone into this kind of crazy fugue state; nobody can reach her. And they won't keep her there—"

"Where's there?"

"Lenox Meadows. That high-rise place in Brookhaven, the one all the Buckhead old people go to. I called Bob Scully, the director, a couple of days ago and as a favor to me they took her right in, and if I do say so myself it's a nice place. It has everything, even a sunroom that's been fixed up exactly like the one at the Cloister, you know, where the birdcages are? A lot of the people there are confused, and they think they're back at Sea Island when they see it, and they settle right down. . . . Anyway, it seemed like the perfect solution. All sorts of services and frills: a hair styling salon and a pool and sauna and a nice restaurant and a private limo to shopping and the symphony and the arts center, you know . . . but it upset her so to be away from her family and her room that she just sort of flipped out, and she got into the sunroom and opened the birds' cages and let them all out, and then at dinner she threw soup at the waitress. So I've got to move her by tonight. I was counting on you to bring her home this afternoon, Merritt. Now I don't know what I'm going to do. My God, she actually thought I was going to hurt her! She didn't know me—"

"Pom, I'm sorry. But you must see that Mommee's gone beyond home care now. The sooner you can get her into a place that specializes in Alzheimer's and senility, the better off she'll be. Not we'll be, Pom, *she'll* be. You don't need me to do that. I couldn't admit her, anyway. You'd have to authorize it—"

"I don't know any places like that," he said, sounding lost and querulous.

Annoyance and the old pity warred in me; annoyance, for the moment, won.

"Pom, you've got a five-page list of places like that in your office right this minute. The social worker has it; I've seen it. Your office sends people there every day of the week; it's part of the outreach and resources program, or whatever you call it. All you've got to do is pick up a phone. You don't even have to do it; Amy would love to do it for you. You know good and well that if this Lenox Meadows place would take her immediately as a favor to you, any one of those places will. You've supported them for ages. You could have her in a nice room by the end of the workday. Amy would pick her up and take her, I'll bet, if you sent a nurse along. Or maybe the limo could take her . . ."

There was a long silence. In it I had a picture of Mommee, roaring and careening around in the back of a huge limo, tiny finches darting in an agitated cloud about her head. At the wheel was Jesus. When he decanted her tenderly from the limo he would say, "You tell Orion O'Neill Jesus say 'allo, hah?" I thought for one desperate moment I was going to burst into idiot laughter.

"I'm not going to put my mother in one of those places," Pom said, and the picture dissolved.

"Only poor people, huh?" I said in exasperation. "Pom,

Mommee is way, way past noticing where she is. She isn't
going to know a new place from her old room. She isn't going
to know you from a . . . a turnip. The reason she doesn't recognize you isn't that she's upset and traumatized or that
you've hurt her, it's that she has Alzheimer's disease and
that's what eventually happens to people who have it. You're
a doctor, you know that. You see it every day. She isn't going
to get better if you bring her back home and we try again to
look after her, and suddenly recognize you, and embrace you,
and get back to normal. It doesn't happen like that. You're
putting off the day she gets the kind of care that really can
help her, and you're condemning Glynn and me to another
season in hell in the bargain. Without Ina I couldn't manage
it five minutes. Even with Ina, I couldn't do the Mommee
thing anymore. It's killing our daughter. She's so much better
out here; you'd love seeing how well she is, and oh, Pom, so
many wonderful things have happened to her, and she's so
anxious to tell you about them, and good things are coming
up for Laura, too—"

"How nice," he said coldly, "that you're all having such a
good time."

"Pom, do you *want* your wife and daughter to be miserable? Is that it? How would that help things?" I said. My voice
was trembling. Why couldn't I get through to him? What
would it take? Whatever, I obviously was not going to be able
to do it over long distance, not when he was still torn with
anger at us and terror and pity for his mother.

But I was past helping him there.

"There's another reason, too," I said. "Laura's got sort of a
problem. I think it can be settled in a week, and I feel sure I
can help her work it out if I have some quiet time alone with
her. But she's not in very good shape right now, and I'm the
only one who can—"

"I cannot remember a time in my life since I was
acquainted with Laura that she did not have sort of a prob-
lem," Pom broke in coldly. "What is it this time, booze again?
Drugs? AIDS? What? What terrible calamity has befallen poor
Laura that only you can fix up for her, Merritt? Whatever it is,
I'm not going to have it spilling all over Glynn. I don't know

what the hell you're thinking of. I want Glynn back here today, on that noon plane. I'm still not sure I'm not going to punish her for her attitude toward Mommee; I'm damned if I'm going to finance a grand tour for her right now. If you want to stay I can't stop you, but I will not have Glynn—"

"I'll call you from the lodge and give you the number when we get there," I said over his escalating voice. It was not, now, Pom's voice. "I'll leave a message on the machine if you're not in. We will be back in about a week. I am sorry about Mommee, sorrier than I can say, but you are the only one who can help her now. Sooner or later, Pom, you've got to cast your vote with the living. You don't know how much I pray it's sooner. I've missed you, and so has Glynn. We love you."

"Yeah," he said. "I can tell how much even over the phone."

I let a beat or two go by, and then I said, not knowing until I spoke that I was going to say it, "Pom, did you have an affair with that Jamaican doctor you had on staff a few years ago? I forget her name—"

"I don't know who you are anymore," he said, and hung up.

I don't either, I said to the dead phone, and put it back into its cradle. I went out into the little studio where everyone was waiting for me, bright-faced with anticipation.

"Marcie's stepmother said for me to come ahead by all means," Glynn caroled. "And Jess and Marcie are simply having shitfits about the screen test. 'Scuse me. I'm sorry. Did Dad . . . is it, you know, okay?"

"No problem," I said. "Redwoods, here we come."

Laura looked keenly at me and started to speak and then didn't. Later, I would tell her all about it, and she would say something funny and awful and absolutely right, and put everything back into perspective, and the sly, thick sickness of the fight with Pom would melt out of my heart like rotting old ice. She could always do that. And in turn I would help her sort things out.

Meanwhile, to the north, the great trees waited, and the silence that was as deep and pure and old as the sea, and the sun burning through the morning fog to warm the thin air and touch our faces. . . .

"Let's get this show on the road," I said.

As I was hugging Caleb Pringle good-bye the earth beneath the parking lot gave a fishlike flop and a dolphin's roll. I froze, clinging to Caleb, waiting. The tremor did not come again.

"Did the earth move for you?" he smiled down at me.

"No, but I'll bet it would if we did that again," I said lightly, my heart pounding in slow, dragging beats.

He laughed and hugged me once more, hard.

"What would I have done if Laura's big sister hadn't turned out to be a babe?" he said.

"Put her in a horror movie and made a gajillion dollars," I smiled back. "See? I'm catching on."

We got to Caleb Pringle's mountain retreat long past dark, so I really did not see any of the surrounding country until the next day. But all the way through the tangle of suburban streets that stretched from San Jose to Saratoga I could feel the presence of the mountains to our west. Once we began to climb them, threading our way through the bewildering maze of small roads and trails that led up and over their crest and down into the Big Basin area, the unseen spires of the great redwoods seemed to lean so close over us in the little red car that we automatically spoke in near-whispers. Fog or low clouds augmented the darkness; it was like making our way through an endless tunnel whose walls were swirling gray. The silence was so dense and total that it seemed to have its own monolithic shape. Only the close-brushing branches of unfamiliar undergrowth broke the fog wall, and occasionally the red flash of wild watching eyes, or the ghostly shape of an animal whisking across the road in front of us. Twice we saw deer, and once a fox, and once something low and solid and scurrying that none of us could put a name to. By that time we were not speaking much. The darkness and the silence were oppressive, as was the growing sense that we were hopelessly lost in an alien moonscape where only inhuman things and towering, implacable giants tracked us.

We had met the dense June coastal fog just outside San Luis Obispo. It was scarcely past noon; we had left at nine and

made remarkably good time up Highway 1, the old coast road.
It had been Laura's plan to drive up that way, taking our time
and stopping wherever along the spectacular coast our fancy
dictated. It would be, she said, a drive we would never forget:
San Simeon, Big Sur, Carmel, Monterey. Perhaps we would
break the trip for the night at Carmel, where a friend of hers
had, she knew, an empty guest house, and then cut inland at
Santa Cruz and follow Highways 9 and 236 up into the Big
Basin area. Caleb Pringle's private road snaked off there, up
near the Santa Cruz County border.

I was as eager as a child to be on the road, sun and wind in
my face and the cold blue sea always to our left. I thought of
the magical flight through the desert and expected more of
that, but somehow it did not happen. The sea, from Santa
Monica on up, was wild and beautiful, and the low, empty hills
to our right were sharp and clear and still green with the spring
rains, and often blanketed so thickly with wildflowers that they
looked like a pointillistic landscape, but somehow they failed
to call out the wings in my heart as the desert had done. We
made the first three hours in a jittering miasma born of something I could not put a name to. Occasionally I thought I could
catch the shape of it, out of the corner of my eye, but it always
eluded me. Gradually we stopped our forced chatter and
singing and Laura found a faltering classical station on the
radio, and we sank into it, taking our demons with us. My
thoughts were as circular as a hamster's treadmill: Pregnant.
Laura is pregnant. Pregnant and in love with a man who is not
going to marry her; I don't know how I know that, but I do.
Pregnant. What are we going to do about the baby? What is
going to happen to her? How can I help her? Glynn: How can I
help her keep some of this new fire and surety and not fall into
all that phony movie stuff? I know I should get her away from
here now, but how can I take her home while Pom is . . . the
way he is? While there's still Mommee hovering over us?

Pom: What can I say to Pom? How can I get him to
change his mind about all this? How can I tell him how I've
changed? How have I changed?

What is going to happen to Pom and me?

I did not know precisely what treadmills Laura and Glynn

rode, but they were sufficient to silence them for long stretches of time. When we hit the fog and stopped for lunch, Laura called the local television station and found that the fog was solid up to San Francisco and not apt to lift for another twenty-four hours. "Let's cut over to 101 and blitz it up to San Jose and on over from there," she said. "There's no fog inland. We can make it tonight easily; it might be after dark, but Pring gave me a good map and we can ask if we need to. I don't know about you all, but I just want to *be* there."

Glynn and I cried, "Let's do it," almost in unison, and we all three laughed in something like relief. I realized then that the old trees were calling them, too, with a voice that was as strong as a beat in the blood. We finished our abalone salad in haste and got back into the car. Laura put the top up against the damp chill of the fog and we were off again. Oddly, bowling inland along the flat, empty Carmel valley behind the coast range, the giddiness and hilarity came back, and the singing began again.

But now, bumping along the minimal little mountain roads, with me trying to read Caleb's map by the dash light and Laura tight-lipped with concentration and Glynn silent as a stone in the backseat, hilarity had long since fled.

Finally, after we had inched along Highway 9 through the blackness for so long that I could not remember when we had last made a turn or seen a light, I said, "Maybe we should go back and ask somebody. If we've missed Caleb's road and we run out of gas or something, we could never walk back to civilization."

Laura turned her head to answer me and from the backseat Glynn said, "There it is."

And there it was, the upended log with the battered mailbox atop it that said "Pringle." If Glynn had not seen it I doubt if we would have; the road was merely a narrow dirt track snaking off into the thick undergrowth. It might have been an old logging road, or no road at all.

"Good girl," I said, relief flooding me. "You get the first shower."

"We can all take showers at the same time," Laura laughed, too. "There are four baths and a hot tub. This ain't Green Acres, I don't think."

For a long time the track bumped along through under-growth and fog, climbing and dropping, climbing and drop-ping. There was no break at all in the wall of green and gray on either side of us. Then we passed a clearing on the right, and I could just make out the base of some sort of rough tower, rearing itself up into the fog, with a clutter of small lean-tos and a rough veranda at its base. The shape of some sort of big vehicle emerged from the swirling whiteness and then was lost again, and it seemed to me that there was a lot of equipment of some sort littered about the tower's base. Far up in the fog a lone light burned yellow, as if it might have been cast by a lantern.

"The lair of the hermit," Laura said. "The lodge ought to be on down the trail here."

"The hall of the Mountain King," Glynn said dreamily from the backseat.

"It could be, couldn't it?" I said. "I think I like the lair of the hermit even better than I'm going to like the lodge. Can you just imagine what you'd see from the top there?"

"Can you just imagine climbing up those steps with a load of groceries or every time you had to go to the bathroom?" Laura said.

"Why would you do that?" Glynn said curiously. "I'd just pee in the woods. Who'd know?"

"I've been in the city way too long," Laura laughed. "I need to pee in the woods. We all do. We'll pee in the woods every chance we get. Give the hermit a thrill or two."

The road dropped rapidly from the crest where the tower stood, and made a sharp turn, and we saw the lodge ahead, clinging to the side of a hill so steep that it looked like a cliff. Lights blazed through the fog, and I could see that it was large and rambling and fell down the cliff as if it had spilled there, or grown. In front of it was only a sea of drifting gray-white, but I sensed, rather than saw, immense space.

"Oh, Lord," I said. "I take it back about the tower."

No one spoke when we opened the door and walked into Caleb Pringle's lodge. But I felt my breath stop in my throat and my heart rise up in the kind of joy I remember feeling on Christmas mornings, in those good years before my mother died. All around us light leaped and poured and ran as if melted down log walls and off great beams high in the cathedral ceiling and spread over the stones of a hearth as large as many motel rooms I had seen. It seemed to have many sources: the fire that roared in the hearth with a whispering bellow like a great wind; the immense copper hanging lamps; the old, smoky gold of the wood and log walls themselves; outsized leather sofas and chairs the color of maple syrup; the glowing Indian rugs that hung from the railing of a gallery that ringed the top floor, leaving the entire bottom floor one vast, open space. More jeweled rugs lay on the wide burnished boards of the floor, and the walls were hung midway up with a forest of antlers and the massive bleached skeletons of who-knew-what. One side of the big room was lined with furniture and paintings and bookcases and doors obviously leading to other rooms. The other was one sweep of small-paned glass in which all the light swarmed and pooled and danced. Curtains were drawn back so that you would see the entire panorama of whatever lay outside, but tonight, beyond the light, only fog lay there.

Then Glynn said, in a small voice, "Cool," and Laura gave a whoop of sheer delight, and I laughed aloud with the radiance and energy and sheer, joyous excess of it.

"Welcome to hard times," I said, and we flopped down into the lustrous swamp of the leather sofas and laughed and laughed and laughed.

We were still laughing when a man came out of one of the doors on the opposite wall of the room. We all stopped laughing as one and drew in a great collective breath. I pulled Glynn against me reflexively and prepared to thrust her behind me if he made so much as a move toward us. Laura made a small sound deep in her throat.

He was an apparition, a grotesque, something out of a pagan legend older than the earth of this young mountain range. He seemed, in the flickering firelight and reflected radiance of the window wall, taller than any normal being could possibly be, and darker, and as impassively inhuman as if he had been carved out of basalt. His skin was the color of old rawhide and he had thick black hair hanging over heavy brows and an enormous bush of black beard, and features so attenuated they might have been done by a medieval limner: long chin, long nose, high-ridged cheekbones, sharp brows. He looked like an El Greco painting of an American Indian, and he was literally covered in flowers.

Then he smiled, and white teeth split the black beard, and everything changed. I saw that he wore crooked wire-rimmed glasses on his nose, mended with what looked to be friction tape, and had small black coal-chips of eyes that danced with light when he smiled, and the beard was not a wild bush, after all, but a neatly trimmed felting that covered his jutting jaw like sleek fur. I smiled back, involuntarily. The white grin in all that darkness was utterly disarming.

"Hey," he said.

"You must be Caleb's hermit," I said.

"You got it," he said, and his voice had so much of the thick Mississippi River delta in it that my grin turned into a giggle. How could you not be safe in the presence of that voice? It was the very music of home.

"God, you scared us to death," Laura snapped. "Couldn't you have called out? Do you always just let yourself into Pring's house whenever you want to? For all we knew you might be a murderer or a rapist or something—"

"I'm both flattered and sorry," he said. "I didn't know when you all would be getting in, and these posies came for you by way of the pissedest FedEx driver I have ever seen, and I thought I'd bring 'em on down here and put 'em in water for you, and then I heard your car and thought, well, I'll light the fire and turn on the lights for them, welcome them, you know. I really am sorry. Caleb told me to take especially good care of you, too."

"Well . . . okay. Thanks. That was nice of you," Laura said, and walked toward him, holding out her arms for the flowers. Before she reached them she gave a short, sharp scream and backed up hastily.

"Jesus Christ, is that a *rat* on your shoulder?" she squeaked.

I looked, harder. It was. From a perch on his shoulder, leering foolishly from among the masses of larkspur and stock and baby's breath, was . . .

"*Rattus rattus!*" I yelled. "I'd know that face anywhere! Excuse me, Mr. . . . whoever you are, but did you know you had a European black rat on your shoulder?"

He reached up and felt, and the rat ran up to his neck and nestled there, peering now from directly under his ear. It was not a small rat, either; this *Rattus rattus* had, as my beloved Felicia back in Baton Rouge used to say, undoubtedly, seen the elephant and heard the owl. He was big, fat, sleek, and obviously as comfortably at home on this man's shoulder as he would have been in my woods at home.

"Goddamn, Forrest, I thought you were bedded down for the night," the man said mildly, and shrugged his shoulder, and the rat disappeared from his shoulder. Through the flowers I saw it wriggle into his shirt pocket and settle there.

"Pardon us both, ladies. Again," he said. "I'm used to him, but I know most people don't like them. It's not like they were cute little mice or ground squirrels. He'll stay put now, and I've got to get on back. I'll see he stays home from now on. I'm T. C. Bridgewater, by the way, Caleb's hermit, as this lady has already noted."

His smile widened, and I gave way to the laughter that was tickling at my mouth.

"*Rattus rattus,*" I gasped. "I feel absolutely at home. Do you know, I go swimming with them almost every day of my life? I live in a house by the river back home, and I'm supposed to take them down there and drown them, but instead I let them go, and they make for the water like Labrador retrievers, and there we all are, skinny-dipping in the Chattahoochee."

I stopped laughing and blushed. Glynn and Laura and T. C. Bridgewater were all staring at me.

"Mom, do you really? I never knew that," breathed Glynn. Laura said nothing, just stared from me to T. C. Bridgewater, who began to laugh. It was an infectious sound, deep and flat-out and young. It sounded younger than I thought he was: He looked, in the firelight, to be about Laura's age. Maybe forty.

"Swim with the rats," he said. "Forget the goddamn dolphins; go South and swim with the rats."

All of a sudden he and I both were laughing so hard that

we could not get our breath, gasping and bending at the waist, holding ourselves. Stopping and wiping our eyes and starting again. The sloped, distinctly untrustworthy head of *Rattus rattus* appeared over the flowers, nose quivering, and bobbed back down again. His pocket nest must be bouncing uncontrollably. I dissolved into a fresh gust of laughter.

When we finally stopped, Laura said sourly, "Well, now that the floor show is over, perhaps we can collect our flowers and let you and your rat be on your way, Mr. . . . Bridgewater, I think you said? We've had a long, long day."

"Of course. Are you Ms. Mason? Laura Mason? There's a package for you in the kitchen, too, and one for Miss Glynn Fowler."

"I am," Laura said. "The young, beautiful one is my niece, Glynn, and this crazy woman is my big sister, Merritt Fowler. The ratwoman of Atlanta. Thank you for the delivery and the fire and the welcome, and good night."

He handed her the flowers and nodded to all of us and said, "I brought you down a pot of chili in case you didn't stop for groceries. I can pick up whatever you need in the morning; I've got to go into town. Just bring me up a list before nine. And you know there's a phone up at my place, too. Good night and once again, we apologize, Forrest and I. If you hear a dog barking don't worry, it's my Lab, Curtis. Good watchdog . . ."

"Good *night*, Mr. Bridgewater," Laura said.

He opened the door and disappeared into the swirling fog. I heard him laughing all the way up to where, I thought, the trail turned. Then night and fog swallowed the sound.

"I hope he isn't going to be the man who came to dinner," Laura said. "God, these are gorgeous. Look, they're to all of us, from Pring. What a darling."

She smiled and buried her face in the blossoms.

"I never got any flowers before," Glynn said. "They're neat. So is the rat. And a dog . . . I'm glad there's a dog."

"Me, too. Maybe he'll come sleep with you," I said, hugging her, delight at nothing at all bubbling along my veins like champagne. The joy I had missed on the trip had lain up here all along, waiting for me.

Laura went into the kitchen and came back with two

parcels wrapped in silver paper and tied with silver stretch cord. She was still smiling, a misty, tender smile. She looked very young. She handed one of the packages to Glynn and began to open the other.

"Pring does it in style when he does it," she said.

"It's not from Caleb," Glynn said. She had ripped her package open and stood staring at the contents of the flat box. "It's from Mr. Margolies. Mom; oh, Mom, look!"

I looked into her box. The cross that she had worn that morning in the screen test lay nested in cotton, with a card that said, "For the only Joan who should ever wear it. I hope she will. Regards, Leonard Margolies."

"Mom, does he mean . . ." she lifted a radiant face to me.

"He only means that he thought you were very good," I said. "But what a nice thing to do. It looked just right with your tunic. You can wear it with that."

"Mama—"

"I'm not going to discuss this movie business anymore, now or ever, Glynn," I said, and she saw in my face that I was not. She walked over and sank down into the sofa, fingering the cross, her eyes faraway. But she did not pursue it.

Damn that man, I thought fervently. Damn him and Caleb Pringle, too. I should take her home.

I looked over at Laura. "So what did he give you, Pie?" I said.

She did not answer. She sat holding something in her hands, her face still and blank. Then she looked up.

"He thinks I'm playing the Dauphine," she said in a low, stricken voice. "He's sent me this silver crown pin from Cartier, and a note that says 'Vive la'dauphine and vive *Arc*!' He's got it all wrong; I'm sure Pring's told him I'm doing the adult Joan. Oh, I've got to set this straight right now! I can't let him think I'm playing that monster; not even for one more night."

She scrambled to her feet.

"Where are you going?" I said. "It doesn't matter, Pie; you know it's just a misunderstanding. It can wait until morning. You can call him then or call Caleb. I don't want you scrambling up that trail in this fog and dark, and climbing all the way to the top of that tower, it's not safe—"

"I'm going," she said in a tight, thin voice, and she grabbed up a leather jacket that hung on a peg beside the great front door and went out into the fog, the door banging behind her. Glynn and I sat and stared at each other, listening until her sliding, scrambling footsteps faded away completely. She still wore the soft, soleless driving moccasins she had slipped on that morning. I was afraid that she would fall on the treacherous path.

I was afraid of something else, too, but I would not let it into my mind, or put a name to it. I got up and helped Glynn bring our bags in, and stowed them into the bedrooms we chose off the main room—low-ceilinged, beamed, dark, intimate, places to nest in all the wilderness . . . and then we went into the kitchen and I heated up the chili and made coffee and cocoa for Glynn. We waited and waited, and finally we ate, sitting at the huge, scrubbed trestle table. Food, I thought mindlessly, and then a long, hot shower, and then bed.

I did not hear the front door open, and only when she stood there did I look up suddenly and notice Laura. She was misted all over with droplets of fog; they stood in her hair and on the scarred, buttery old leather of the jacket she wore. Her feet were wet with black mud and there were smears on both hands and the knee of her jeans, as if she had slipped on the path and caught herself on her palms. There was a thin scratch across her cheek, shockingly red against the pallor. I knew that a branch had whipped her face. Her eyes looked like the eyes of someone who had just been taken from deep, cold water after a long time: black-pupiled, blind.

"Laura?" I said tentatively. The fear roared alive like a brush fire.

"It wasn't a mistake," she said tonelessly. "I'm the Dauphine. I'm playing the monster in *Arc*. I'm both Pring's and Margolies's choice. They decided after they saw Glynn's test. Or so Pring said. I think he always meant me to be the monster. He doesn't make casting mistakes. Margolies's tootsie is going to be the older Joan. Interesting idea, isn't it? To have me seduce my own niece?"

Glynn looked from me to Laura, and back.

"Mama?" she said doubtfully. Her face, too, was white, and her eyes huge.

"There isn't any question of your doing this movie, so don't worry about it," I said as calmly as I could. "I want you to go get your bath and get into bed now. I need to talk to Aunt Laura. We'll sort it all out in the morning; it's a mistake and nothing more. Go on, now, Tink."

"Please don't call me that," she said, but she went. I turned back to Laura.

"Come and have some coffee, at least, and let's talk about this," I said, holding out my hands to her. "There's got to be some misunderstanding; he wouldn't put you in that part—"

"He has. He did. He just told me on the phone. He said there were extenuating circumstances, but that it was a much *meatier* part than Joan, and it could turn out to be the role of a lifetime for me, and he'd make it all okay this weekend."

"Then let's get some rest and have a lovely, mindless, utterly worthless two or three days just bumming around, and he'll do just that when he comes," I said soothingly, not believing it. My head pounded with her pain.

"I don't want any dinner," she said, still not raising her voice. "I'm tired and I want to go to bed. No, Met, I don't want to talk anymore, can't you understand that? Just . . . no more."

"At least have a glass of milk. You need to eat now, Laura—"

"Yeah," she said, smiling a truly terrible smile. "The monster's baby needs its nourishment, doesn't it? Otherwise its daddy won't love it."

And she went into her bedroom and shut the door. A moment later I heard the sound of the lock. I stood listening, but there were no more sounds. Finally I looked in on Glynn, who was fast asleep, and went into the kitchen to put our dinner things into the dishwasher.

Tomorrow, I thought. Tomorrow the sun will be shining and everything will look different, and we will find that this whole ugly, awful business is a mistake.

And when I woke the next morning, after a night of roiling, sweating dreams, so early that only the first sleepy twitters from birds I did not yet know broke the old sea silence, the sun was indeed fingering its way down through the crowns of the great trees, and the little grassy area outside my window, where we had parked, was as clear as if every blade and leaf had been traced in silver. But the red car was gone from it, and when I looked into my sister's bedroom, she was gone, too.

8

There was a note on a Post-it stuck to the refrigerator door. I had been looking for it. From the instant I found her and her car gone, I knew that she had not simply taken a drive or run an errand. There was an emptiness in the house that felt deep and permanent, as though Laura had never been here, loneliness like a scar. Somehow you know when someone close to you is gone and is not coming back. There is no lingering sense of their presence.

"Gone to L.A. to see Pring," the note, in Laura's round script, distorted here by haste and pain, said. "I've got to change his mind about this. I've got to get things straight. I can't stand it until I do. Be back with him when he comes in a few days. Caretaker will take you anywhere you want to go; I've already been up to ask him. He's going over toward Palo Alto anyway today so you can take Glynn as planned. And he'll show you around or let you borrow his Jeep anytime. Sorry, Met. Rest and relax and I'll have it all worked out when Pring and I come back."

It was signed, simply, L.

I sat down in the kitchen and held the note in my hands, looking blindly out at the morning sun filtering in pools through the great trees overhead. I knew that she would not have it all worked out when she and Caleb Pringle came back in a few days. I would have bet my house on the river back home that she would come back in shattered fragments and he would not come at all. I felt, in that moment, simply defeated. Emptied out and flattened as if I had been run over. All this way, all this time, all this chaos and anger behind me, all the small, frail bonds to Laura that had been painfully reestablished torn loose, all the anguish and damage ahead of her, all the old destructiveness reignited. What was I going to do about her? How could I pick these pieces up; what could I do with a near-mortally wounded sister and an unborn baby? I crumpled the note and threw it onto the kitchen table.

I could think of nothing and felt little but the great, smothering white fatigue, and so I made coffee and put on my jeans and found a heavy sweater in the bureau and pulled that on, and took my coffee and went out into the morning.

The clearing the lodge sat in was an old one, I thought; there were no stumps, no new-turned earth or fresh-planted grass, no sign that the redwoods that leaned over it had ever been disturbed. The back of the house faced up the mountain. There was the gravel driveway we had come in on last night, and a turnaround, and a three-car garage beyond it. All of the spaces were empty. The house itself sat on the crest of a long ridge below the major crest that spined the area; that was where, if I remembered correctly, the old fire tower and the scattered machinery had been. T. C. Bridgewater's lair.

The front of the house looked out over space. I had not seen, because of last night's fog, what might lie below the great bank of windows. Now, walking out onto the long deck off the kitchen and the window wall, I did. Trees. Shafts of pale sunlight through fog and trees. Ridge after forested ridge, dropping away toward the unseen coast, an undulating surf of green. I thought that I had never seen so much green, not even in the Georgia river bottoms in a damp spring. This place might be the very heart of all the earth's wild places; the master tree for all the others in the world might well be one of these redwoods.

I had never seen anything living so tall. My head tipped back to look and my eyes went up, and up, and up. At the tops, where open evergreen crowns let the morning sunlight through, the sky seemed infinitely far away, a pale, distant blue, like the surface of the sea seen from its bottom. Layers of fog drifted through the trees, giving them the look of something seen through stage scrim, unreal, haunted, primal. Other trees huddled under their shoulders; I recognized fir, alders, and oak. There were great tangles of rhododendron and laurel crowding the nearer trees at ground level, and huge ferns, and tiny, starlike flowers ranging from delicate pink to purple. The fog and mist hugged the ground and blew in skeins and scarves; the top of the trees were in constant slight motion. I felt no wind, but I heard it, last night's ancient soughing, the breathing of the trees, the sound of this vast sea of silence. I realized I was holding my breath only when I let it out. In all the world I had never seen anything so strangely, inhumanly beautiful. In this place, man would soon seem simply extraneous. I shivered. I did not think I would feel welcome for long in this world where the very earth spasmed and the great trees would not acknowledge my presence. In the storms of winter, I thought, it must be a profoundly hostile place to be.

But on this morning its archaic beauty was benign, and a ray of sun shifted and found me on the deck, and I sat in it and drank coffee and emptied my mind. When Glynn got up, then I would get hold of myself and see what could be done and prod myself into action. I might go after Laura or get hold of Stuart Feinstein and ask him to do it, or Glynn and I might simply ask T. C. Bridgewater to take us to the San Francisco airport, where we would get on the next available flight home. There were lots of options. I would address them soon. When Glynn got up.

It was almost an hour later when she did. By then the woods had done their work. When Glynn came shuffling barefoot out onto the deck, rubbing at her eyes and dragging her blanket, and said, "I read Aunt Laura's note. What are we going to do?" I said, not moving my eyes from the still surf of the trees, "I don't know."

She stared at me, and I realized that she did not know how to respond. I was not, in that moment, Mama, or even

Mom. Either of those women would be planning, bustling, readying for action. But here I sat with my hands folded in my lap and my eyes drowned in woods and silence.

"Mom?" she ventured, trying anyway.

"Come, sit," I said, and patted the redwood chaise beside me. I did not send her back to put on her shoes and sweater, or get up to fix her breakfast.

"Sit still and just look," I smiled at her. "Don't talk. Just let it fill you up. We'll never see anything like this again. It's worth the trip just to sit on this deck for an hour."

She looked, dutifully, but presently she began to shiver, and that brought me back a little way.

"Put some clothes on and we'll talk about it," I said. "Are you hungry?"

"Yeah," she said, sounding surprised. "I think I am."

Inside, the enchantment of the place lessened, and by the time she came back in pants and a heavy ski sweater similar to mine, I had made toast and scrambled eggs and fried bacon from the cache T. C. Bridgewater had brought. She ate a helping of everything and had a second piece of toast. It had been so long since she had eaten like that, in my presence at least, that I could only watch her in silence, not wanting to break the spell with words.

Finally she grinned at me and said, "Not even a Jewish mother could complain about that."

"You'll hear no complaints from me," I said. "What, besides toast and eggs, has gotten into you?"

"Well, I guess it's the air or something. And then Caleb said I needed to gain a few pounds, that Joan was a sturdy, blooming peasant girl, not a starved, watery waif. He said nobody would want to put the move on me with all my bones sticking out, especially not the Dauphine of France."

I flinched, hating the casual perversion of the words, angry at Caleb Pringle for dangling the role over my daughter when I had told him she would not be playing it.

"You know what we said about Joan," I said. "It's out of the question, Glynn."

"Oh, I know. But he made me see how I must look to other people. A watery waif? Yecchh. And you know, food does taste good up here. I was afraid I'd throw up, but it really tastes good."

I dropped it, thankful to whatever detoxified the thought of food for her, but still meaning to get her out of Caleb Pringle's orbit as soon as possible.

"I thought we'd leave for Palo Alto as soon as I do the dishes and you pack some things," I said. "Mr. Bridgewater is going to take us over to Marcie's dad's house. Aunt Laura asked him before she left."

"You mean I can still go?" Joy lit her face. "I thought sure we'd be going home today, or back to L.A. after Aunt Laura. Can I stay as long as we said?"

"You can stay until Aunt Laura gets back. I can't leave until I know what's going on with her. I'm sure she'll call before long, at least. We'll decide then."

"She said she'd be back with Caleb when he came—"

"I wouldn't count on Caleb," I said.

She dropped her eyes. "I know he can explain all this," she said softly. "I know he didn't mean to hurt her. He's a good person, Mom. They'll work it all out."

Dear Lord, she does have a crush on him, I thought bleakly. Maybe I'll put her on a plane in a day or two and wait here for Laura. Ina could look after Glynn.

But then I remembered that Ina did not work for us anymore. Pom and Mommee came flooding back into my head, along with all of the strife boiling around them; how could I have forgotten? The trees; somehow the green trees had sucked them from my mind along with all the other effluvia of home. I was not ready to go back to things the way they were, I thought clearly, and I did not want Glynn to go back to them, either.

"There are some women's clothes in my bureau," she said. "Really cool things. Some of them look like they'd fit me. Do you think Caleb would mind if I took some of them to Palo Alto? I'd get them cleaned. I don't really have much—"

"I'm sure he wouldn't," I said dryly. "I doubt if their owners will be back for them."

She looked at me, but vanished to her packing without speaking. I was not surprised that Caleb Pringle's house would be full of the clothes of cast-off women, but it annoyed me. If he cared for Laura he would put them away. But maybe it was not one of the things that mattered to Laura, or to a man like Caleb Pringle. And it was none of my affair. I would wear the clothes in my bureau gratefully; I had nothing with me for the chill morning breath of these mountains.

I remembered then that I had promised to call and tell Pom where we were, so I put on a red-and-black plaid wool shirt I found hanging on a peg behind the door and called out to Glynn where I was going and went out again into the chill, soft morning. The white fog was thickening and drifting higher into the trees, and by the time I reached the turn in the gravel road the sun had vanished altogether.

It was like walking through a Japanese watercolor. The edges of everything were faded and blurred, but a few details— the feathery lower branches of the redwoods, the dry-brush tips of the great ferns, here and there a stump or a boulder with its base wreathed in flowers and more fern fronds—swam into focus now and then, as sharp and clear as if they were emerging from developing fluid. The fog stilled the sound of the rustling undergrowth and the calls of the morning birds, even my footsteps in the gravel. I saw only the close-pressing walls of a shifting green tunnel, heard only the ever-present sighing of the silence. I could not see anything off to my left that resembled the tower and its outbuildings, and it seemed to me that I had walked much further than we had driven last night. Could I have missed a turn? How? I had seen no other path or road turning off this one.

But a cold emptiness crept in around my heart, the viscerally remembered feeling of the first awful lostness when one is a child. Something heavy thumped in the dense stand of wet black trunks not too far from the path, and then began crashing through undergrowth. I froze on the path, hardly breathing, unable to tell if the sound was coming closer or retreating. What had Caleb said about the wild things here? Bear? Mountain lions? Some sort of elk? Deer, foxes, porcupines, skunks, raccoons? *Rattus rattus*, of course. I was certainly not eager to meet a bear or a mountain lion alone on this fog-haunted trail from nowhere to nowhere, and not particularly eager to meet any of the others, no matter how benign. Who knew how these spectral woods changed living things? Look what they had done to me.

The crashing stopped abruptly, and I began to run, stumbling and sliding.

I heard the barking before I saw the dog. It rang out through the fog like the Hound of the Baskervilles' cry, and I stopped dead, too frightened to run. It was a hollow, terrible sound. Almost instantly the dog was out of the fog and upon me, huge and slavering and smelling rankly of wildness and wet dog. Before I could cry out it had jumped up on me with its huge paws and I stumbled and fell backward, and it bent over me, snuffling and nosing for my throat. I was just taking a deep breath to scream when I heard a man's sharp command: "Curtis! Carpe diem!" The dog stopped his business with my throat, which I realized only then had been a wet, energetic mopping of my face with a huge tongue. Carpe diem? I had surely gone mad with the sheer, inhuman strangeness of this place.

T. C. Bridgewater was suddenly beside me, looming up out of the fog like Paul Bunyan in his black beard and lank-hanging hair and checked shirt. He knelt and peered at me, one arm around the dog's neck. The dog sat leaning against him, red tongue lolling, grinning the lupine grin of a canine in perfect harmony with his world. When I sat up he gave a soft *woof*, sending a warm gust of meaty breath into my face. It was the smell of home: Alpo. I fed it to Samson and Delilah.

"Are you okay?" T. C. Bridgewater said, clumsily brushing at the dirt on my jacket and pants. "He heard you before I did and was out of there before I could catch him. Sorry if he scared you. He wouldn't hurt you. Curtis loves to have visitors."

"I can see that he does," I said, too grateful for the presence of Caleb's hermit to be angry. Fear usually does that to me, but not this fey white morning.

"I was expecting you," he said, taking my hand and pulling me to my feet. "Your sister said you needed to make some phone calls and then you'd be wanting to take your daughter over to Palo Alto a little later on. Come on up; I made another pot of coffee."

"I don't want to put you out," I said formally. My knees were stiff from the fall, and there were gravel abrasions on the heels of my hands that were beginning to sting. "I know you don't go out often. After this I promise I won't bother you."

"It's no bother. I welcome any excuse to get out and about. It's hard work, being a hermit," he said, striding ahead of me. The dog Curtis brought up the rear, panting companionably. Every now and then he nosed my thigh gently as if to tell me that he was behind me and all was well.

A formless group of shapes loomed out of the fog as we climbed the trail, and I remembered the anonymous machinery from last night, and the bulky vehicle. We stepped up to a near invisible wooden deck, low and broad, and I saw that there were deck chairs and a couple of worn chaises there, and an umbrella table, and dishes and bowls sitting under a rusty water tap. Curtis's dining room. The deck circled the base of the tower, and at one end a canvas overhang had been rigged, and a hammock and a table spilling over with books sat under it, along with a spindly-legged black steel grill and a sagging old sofa, also spilling its cargo of books. The sofa had an untidy nest of blankets on it. It was plain that T. C. Bridgewater did much of his living here. Perhaps it was his summer home. The little house atop the tower had seemed very small last night. I would, I thought, want a place in which to drink in the wildness clear of walls and a ceiling, too.

"I hate to make you do it," he said over his shoulder, "but you'll have to climb the tower to use the phone. I keep thinking I'll get one of those cellular things, but I forget . . . watch your step. It's better than a ladder, but only just."

He was right. I grasped the stout railings and began to climb the steep, long staircase behind him, feeling dizzily that I was climbing into nothing. After a moment or so I lost sight of his legs and feet in the fog. Behind me I could hear the scratch of Curtis's toenails on the weathered wood, and his panting. Even with a landing, the climb seemed endless. I wondered if Curtis often bothered.

Just as I was beginning to tire, my head and shoulders broke through the fog and I gasped. We were only a step or two from the top of the tower, and as far as I could see on every side, the fog rolled away in billows and waves, a silent silver-white sea, pricked with the ghostly tops of the redwoods. The sunlight here was fresh and strong and struck such light off the fog that I slitted my eyes involuntarily against it. It was spectacular. We were literally bathed in strange, radiant, sun-and-fog light, and the air was many degrees warmer than on the ground and smelled of pine with the sun on it.

I followed him into the single small, square room and Curtis heaved himself in behind me and flopped gratefully on the floor. The room was perhaps fifteen by fifteen feet, and all its walls were windows. A skylight opened the flat roof to the sky, and the whole thing seemed to sway slightly with the unseen, unceasing wind. It was strange to hear the voice of the wind coming from below us, but on this ridgetop there were few of the huge redwoods, and the other trees did not reach us. The tower sat in a clearing, and I remembered that its original use was that of a fire tower. I thought that from here, when the fog had lifted, you could see a fire a hundred miles away in any direction. Now we saw only the endless floor of fog and the tops of the redwoods, rising and falling on their ridges until they met the hidden sea.

I stood looking, turning around in a circle.

"I think I might never leave it," I said.

"I don't, much," he said. "So you like it?"

"Yes. Well . . . I don't know. I live in the woods at home, but they're so much tamer. Lower, and more open. I live on a river bank, but it's a gentle river. I don't know. . . . I'm so used to having hidey holes and little nooks and crannies around me, places you can go and feel snug and hidden; safe places. Up here you couldn't hide from anything, ever. It's beautiful, but I don't know if I'd ever get used to it."

"Yeah, I know," he said. "When I first came up here I was like a cat trying to make a home on a roof. I couldn't settle down and get comfortable. I put up curtains to shut everything out, and built the deck down there just so I could get down on ground level once in a while. I spent a lot of time in bed with the covers pulled up over my head. It was winter then; I thought I'd made an awful mistake. But by the time spring came I couldn't stand walls around me anymore, and got antsy

when I was shut up in rooms, and so I took down the curtains
and put in the skylight. It gets to you. You get so you can't live
with anything between you and the wildness."

He walked over to a tile counter where a coffeemaker
stood, next to a small microwave oven and a neat little convection oven. There was a miniature sink, too, and a tiny
refrigerator sat underneath the counter. It all occupied only
one of the walls, a model of compactness and planning. But it
was wildly, baroquely messy. On the other walls were waist-
high wooden counters with bookshelves under them or drawers. An open space with a chair in it made a desk. A double
bed was placed at an angle to one corner, piled high with colored pillows and draped with what looked to be a beautiful old
Chief Joseph blanket. A tall, skinny armoire stood opposite it
in the other corner. A big, black cast iron stove occupied the
middle of the room, vented out the skylight, and there were
big floor pillows and a wooden box of firewood ranged around
it. The bed looked directly at the glass door where the flames
would dance, and I thought that even on the coldest winter
night, with the Pacific gales howling and sleet and snow spitting against the windows and the skylight, that bed and
indeed this whole room must be as warm as a small animal's
burrow. The room was, somehow, an enchantment. It had the
charm of a child's playhouse, but the particular and intimate
air of someone's real home, an adult one. There were books
literally everywhere, and in front of one of the windows a big
telescope was drawn up.

"What a perfect aerie," I said, taking a cup of coffee from
him. I sat down on the edge of his bed. There was nowhere
else to sit. He had sunk cross-legged to one of the big pillows,
and Curtis lay sprawled on the other, giving occasional little
groans of contentment. He promptly went to sleep.

The coffee was hot and strong. I sipped it gratefully. The
stove was not lit, and the room still held the chill of the
thin air and the fog.

"I could light a fire," T.C. said. "But I figured you'd want
to call and then get on the road over to Palo Alto. By the time
things warmed up we'd be gone again. Wrap that blanket
around you. I'll hand the phone over to you; one advantage of

this place is that the phone reaches anywhere in it. I'll go on back down if you need privacy."

"No. I don't," I said, though I would have liked it. If Pom were in the same mood as yesterday, it would not be an easy call.

He brought me the phone and turned away to the counter where the sink was, clattering ostentatiously as he cleared away some of the mess. I dialed Pom's office. Only when Amy answered in her DAR chirrup did I realize how much I had hoped the chatty temp would be the one to answer. I sighed, not caring if Amy heard it.

"Well, well, Merritt," Amy said. "Where are we today? Hollywood? Disneyland?"

They were, I thought in annoyance, the only places Amy knew in California.

"We're up in redwood country," I said. "It's very beautiful. We're in a lodge owned by a friend of Laura's. Ah . . . is Pom in?"

"I'm afraid not. Doctor has been out of the office for the past day or two. There's a visiting team of UN doctors he's been showing around; from Zaire or somewhere. The CDC asked him to do it. It's quite an honor. They're staying over the weekend so he'll probably be tied up. I'll be glad to take a message, though."

I'll just bet you will, I thought.

"Just tell him the lodge where we're staying is in the Big Basin State Park below San Francisco. It's about thirty minutes from Palo Alto, I think, in the Santa Cruz mountains. If he needs to reach us he can call this number. It's the caretaker's phone. There's not a phone in the lodge, but we'll get the message. We should be home in a few days. I'll know for sure in a day or two, and I'll call him."

I read her out the number and heard the scratching of her pen as she wrote it down.

"You'd probably better call me," she said creamily. "Doctor is entertaining the team in the evenings. One of them used to work here; do you remember that stunning Jamaican doctor we had for a year or two a while back? She's the team chief. We were all glad to see her again. Everyone thought the world of her."

"I remember," I said. My heart began to pound. "How nice for you all. Well, if you'll tell Pom—"

"Oh, I will. Don't you worry about Doctor. We've got things well in hand now. He's feeling much better."

I hope you come down with jungle rot, I wanted to tell her, but instead I hung up smartly. I had not, I realized, asked about Mommee, and had a crazy mental image of her presiding over a Mad Hatter's tea party for the beloved black doctor and her team. I sat staring at the phone for a moment, and then turned to T. C. Bridgewater with a tight smile. He had his back to me, splashing in the sink.

"All set," I said brightly.

He turned, studying me for a moment.

"Everything okay?" he said.

"Just fine."

"Then why don't you go on back down and get whatever you need and I'll come collect you and your daughter in about half an hour. We can pick up anything else you need in Palo Alto and maybe have some lunch. The fog will be burned off by noon. It should be a good day; we've had a long string of them. You're lucky. Usually there's nonstop fog this time of year."

"Fog's pretty much all I've seen since we got here."

"This is nothing. Morning stuff. I've never seen spring weather like we've been having, not this warm and dry. It's been a strange spring all over."

I remembered the maverick climatologist who had stirred up all the earthquake madness. I had not heard a radio or seen a TV or newspaper in days; I wondered if the media was still full of him. Uneasiness stirred in my stomach like a little snake.

"Have you been hearing all the earthquake talk?" I asked. "That guy who's predicting the big one? Most people I talk to pooh-pooh it, but you have to wonder. . . . Wasn't that bad one a few years ago that collapsed the freeway bridge in San Francisco around here somewhere?"

"Loma Prieta," he said. "Yeah. Not too far. The epicenter was in a place called the Forest of Nicene Marks, about twelve miles from here. But the conventional wisdom says that the seismic gap up here was filled by that one and there won't be another in these parts for a long, long time."

Something in his voice made me look sharply at him.

"Is that what you think?"

"No. But then I'm a long way from being a real earthquake scientist. I'm more an obsessed dilettante. The big guys all say you're probably safer up here than you would be anywhere else in California."

"Somehow I don't think you believe that, either."

"Well, I do believe you're safe for the length of time you'll be here. Caleb said just a few days, didn't he? There's no indication anything's that near blowing."

"You study earthquakes, don't you?"

"Well, I do, but I'm an amateur and my equipment's not very sophisticated. Some of it I made myself. All I've got is a theory and some back-of-the-neck feelings. No seismologist worth his salt would give me the time of day. Really, don't worry about earthquakes. If I thought you all were in immediate danger I'd get you out of here."

"Then I won't," I said. "Thanks for the coffee and the phone. I'll see you in a few minutes."

He walked me to the door, and when he opened it the fog swirled in. It was still as thick as whipped cream.

"I'm going to send Curtis back with you," he said. "He knows the way as well as I do. He's good company and a good guard dog. When you get there, just send him home. Say, 'Curtis, go home. Carpe diem.' He'll come straight home. But you have to say 'carpe diem.'"

"What is this 'carpe diem' business?" I said, smiling at Curtis, who thumped his feathery tail on the floor. He was mostly Lab, I thought, a big, chunky brown dog with a thick coat that curled a little in the dampness, and sweet yellow-brown eyes. He seemed to smile at me.

"I taught him that as a kind of code," T.C. said. "He's such a big old pussycat that I was afraid he'd go off with literally anybody who whistled for him, so I taught him never to obey anybody unless they said 'carpe diem' to him. He'll obey me without it, but I'm the only one."

"But why 'carpe diem'? Is he a fan of Horace's?"

"It's kind of my slogan. A statement of philosophy, I guess. Forget the past; let tomorrow happen. Seize the day."

"Not a bad philosophy."

"It's the only way to live. Okay, you try it. Say, 'Curtis, come. Carpe diem.'"

"Curtis, come. Carpe diem," I said obediently, feeling silly. But the big dog got up lazily and padded over to me and stood beside me, looking up expectantly. I gave the silky ears a tickle and he grinned, his red tongue lolling.

"You're in business," T.C. said, and I went out into the fog, the dog padding beside me. All the way down the white-shrouded path he stayed just at my knee, bumping me softly when I strayed close to the verge, panting slightly as if he were breathing with me, telling me, "I am here and it's all right." It was ridiculously comforting, like having a trusted person with you in an unknown place.

"Curtis, you are A-okay in my book," I said, when he had delivered me to the back door of the lodge.

Glynn was waiting in the kitchen and saw him, and came running out with her arms outstretched.

"Is it Curtis?" she cried in rapture. "It must be Curtis! Oh, you wonderful, wonky old guy! *Hello*, Curtis! Oh, good boy!"

Curtis gave a soft woof of happiness and started toward her, but then sat down and looked anxiously up at me.

"Go ahead, Curtis," I said. "Carpe diem."

And he flew into Glynn's arms as if they were magnetized for large dogs. It was as pure a case of mutual love at first sight as I have ever seen. When I said, presently, "Okay, Curtis, go home now. Home. Carpe diem," he looked at me so miserably, and whined so softly and plaintively, that I relented.

"Okay, you can stay. Your daddy will think we kidnapped you, but you can stay till he comes to pick us up. Stay, Curtis. Carpe diem."

He followed Glynn into her bedroom when she went to finish packing. When I looked in on them he was curled up on her bed and she lay beside him, one arm around the great neck. She grinned up at me.

"I even knew what he would feel like in bed," she said. "He's just the big old bed-dog I always wanted."

"Don't fall hopelessly in love with him; it'll break your heart when we have to go home," I said. "We'll look at Lab puppies when we get back."

"Really, really?"

"Really, really," I said recklessly. Mommee could like it or lump it. So could Pom.

Oh, Pom . . .

The trip to Palo Alto was as carefree as a vacation drive. I suspected, from the delight T. C. Bridgewater took in showing us the giant trees and the strange fauna and flora along the way, that he didn't leave the tower often, and almost never in the presence of people. He was as excited as we were at the strange, wonderful sights and sounds and smells of the Big Basin, almost like a small boy, and when he was not tour-guiding he was regaling us with legends and stories of the Santa Cruz mountains, and told scurrilous and improbable stories about the old mountain men who had once lived here, along with the very rich men from the cities who had built the great lodges and houses and about their present owners. Glynn, in the backseat with her arm around Curtis, laughed her froggy, infectious belly laugh so often that both T.C. and I were often helpless with laughter along with her. I still don't remember if his stories were that funny, but I do remember that for the thirty or so minutes that it took us to wind down through the wet green mountains into Palo Alto, we were mostly laughing.

When we reached Marcie's father's house, a rambling old yellow Victorian on a tree-shaded street bordering the Stanford golf course, I felt that I had known this drawling, loose-jointed man all my life. Glynn was calling him T.C. and telling him about our stay in Los Angeles, and Arc, and the screen test, and how Marcie and Jessica were going to simply die when they saw her tape. She was just launching into her father's objections to our odyssey when I turned around and gave her a level look. I did not like to discourage her obvious liking for Caleb Pringle's hermit, but I did not want her to say anything to him that she would regret later, either. When Glynn's shyness broke, it was such a rare and apparently

comforting phenomenon that she talked nonstop. I had not
seen it happen often. Sometimes, afterward, she sat cringing
far into the night, embarrassed at her own loquacity. I did not
want that to happen with T.C. I wanted her to remember him
with the simple, unvarnished liking that I was feeling for him
myself. And besides, I was oddly loathe to talk about Pom. He
had no place yet in this journey. I wanted, suddenly, to keep it
all for myself. Glynn caught my look and flushed and fell
silent. But then she saw Marcie and Jess standing on the
ornate old porch, already jumping up and down and squealing,
and the flush faded, and she was out of the Jeep and running
and squealing before T.C. brought it to a stop.

In the seat behind us Curtis whined.

"Sorry, old boy," T.C. said, "it's the way they are. Genet-
ic, probably. They just can't help it. Love you and leave you.
She'll be back. Meanwhile, here's another pretty lady up here
waiting to comfort you. Take your pleasures where you find
them, my man."

I reached over and scratched Curtis's ears and he broke
into the contented panting again. I started to get out of the
Jeep and go to meet Marcie's stepmother, who had come out
onto the porch, and then stopped.

"Aren't you coming?" I said to T.C.

"What on earth for? So those somewhat overexcited
young things can go back to Atlanta and tell all their parents
that you were consorting with the caretaker just like he was
your husband? It ain't fittin', ma'am."

He grinned his sudden white grin at me and I blushed
furiously. I realized that I had been treating him like . . . well,
not like the hired caretaker of the estate where I was visiting,
who was accommodating me at the bidding of his employer.

I got out of the Jeep and started up the flower-bordered
stone walk and looked back at him. He was leaning his black
head back on the seat, eyes closed, whistling to himself, but at
that moment he opened his eyes and looked squarely at me
and lifted an imaginary hat and leered evilly. I went the rest of
the way up the path to meet my daughter's hostess, laughing.

I exchanged polite pleasantries with Marcie's stepmother,
a tanned young woman who looked as if she spent a lot of time

on sailboats or tennis courts. I smiled hello to Marcie and Jess, who were wedged into a porch swing with Glynn, listening eagerly as she talked, no doubt, of *Arc* and the screen test. And then it was time to go. I felt a sudden sharp wrench at the prospect of leaving my daughter. The fact that I would now be alone in the huge, silent old woods, in the strange, rambling house of a man I scarcely knew, without a link to any world I knew except a telephone in a fairy-tale tower occupied by a skinny Paul Bunyan of a man I did not know at all, suddenly dawned on me. I had looked forward to unlimited time and silence and solitude, but now they seemed endless, engulfing, unfriendly. I could not imagine what I would do in all that empty space for all those empty hours. I glanced back at T. C. Bridgewater, suddenly as shy and wary of his presence as if I had come upon him in a dark back street in the city. I looked at him, suddenly, with city eyes. Tall, black-bearded and browed, dark-eyed, dark-skinned—a dark man who walked more easily in the wild than on pavement, a slow-talking, Indian-faced man whose soft speech hid who knew what? A man said by others to be eccentric, who said of himself that he was obsessed. I did not know this man at all. Not at all.

As if she had caught my feeling, Glynn came over to me and hugged me suddenly and fiercely. She walked me to the Jeep, her arm still around my waist.

"Tell Dad all about everything," she said loudly. "I know you'll be talking to him every day. I'll bet he'll call tonight. Tell him about the trees and the mountains and Curtis and . . . everything. Tell him maybe I'll call him in a day or two. Will you tell him?"

"I'll tell him," I said, hugging her and feeling the edge of her bones, that were perhaps just a shade less sharp than they had been.

We drove away in silence and bounced over old cobbles toward the waterfront and an outdoor restaurant T.C. knew. He looked over at me and grinned, and said, "I think I've just been warned to keep my distance or her daddy will beat me up."

"What a silly thing to say; not at all," I said prissily, heard myself, and smiled unwillingly.

"Maybe a little," I said. "She's never seen me around any man but her father for any length of time. I think it never occurred to her that I would be, you know, up there alone with you, until this minute. That unsubtle little message was for me, not for you."

"I wouldn't think you were in the habit of making eyes at strange men," he said.

"Well, of course I'm not. I didn't mean she thought that. I just meant . . . Oh, Lord, I don't know what I meant and I don't feel like analyzing it. I'm not about to put the move on you and I don't imagine for a moment that you will on me. In fact, I plan to leave you strictly alone to pursue your earthquakes. I am going to sleep prodigiously, and read enormously, and eat disgracefully, and by the time I have filled my quota of all three Laura will be back and we'll be gone."

"And I'll be sorry," he said equably. "You're good company, you and Glynn, and I've enjoyed this morning with both of you. And Curtis is as lovesick as a puppy. Like I said, conquer and run. You're all alike. Did your sister say when she'd be back, by the way?"

"No. She said she'd let me know. I don't imagine it will be long—"

"I don't think I'd count on that."

I looked at him.

"The tone speaks louder than the words," I said. "You want to tell me what you meant by that?"

"Nothing unkind. Really. I just . . . I've seen more than a few other pretty women leave that lodge like bats out of torment early in the mornings. Mostly they don't come back. Your sister is a pretty woman and a nice one, and I don't like to think of her being one of them. And I don't want you to worry about her, and I expect you do a lot of that. I think you've got enough on your plate right now. I want you to be able just to kick back and let the woods do what they do."

It was an extraordinary little speech to make to a stranger, especially since much of it was uncannily accurate, and it annoyed me both in its familiarity and its accuracy.

"Do you dabble in dysfunctional family therapy too?" I said sourly.

"No, but I'm a member of a family that gives new luster to the word dysfunctional. I know the signs. I'm sorry. I spoke out of turn. Comes from being a hermit. Us hermits are the world's worst blabbermouths if you give us a chance. Never start a conversation with a hermit or you'll be stuck for the millennium."

"No need to apologize. But I'd be interested to know how you knew about us—or thought you did. Us Southern women are raised never to show our true feelings in public."

"Don't I know that," he said. "Well, if you really want to know, I'll tell you over a Bloody Mary and cold crab. But not until then. I'm too faint with hunger to poke around in psyches, mine or yours."

"If I show you my psyche, you've got to show me yours," I said, feeling the morning's easy familiarity slide back. I could, after all, I thought, tell this man anything. I could feel no harm anywhere in him. The very fact that he was a stranger and would remain one was both license and armor. I realized suddenly how very liberating anonymity was. It's the reason, I thought, that you can talk about things to people on airplanes that you'd never tell another soul at home. There's no context between you. Anything goes in a vacuum; the very lack of any history between you is like a shot of Demerol.

The restaurant sat hard by the south end of San Francisco Bay, next to the yacht club and marina where, Glynn had said, Marcie's father had a membership and there was a plethora of cool boys. I tried to imagine my daughter into the scene, splashing in the azure pool that was visible over a jacaranda hedge; climbing aboard one of the sleek, white sailboats bobbing at their moorings; running in a group of wet, seal-brown adolescents toward the snack bar. I could see the Glynn I had found in California, but not the one I had left home seeking. I shook my head. I wasn't much for Bloody Marys, and the one I was sipping was my second.

It seemed to me to be quite late. We had not gotten a table until after one, and we had drunk and talked, or sat in comfortable silence watching the very white sails on the very blue bay and the green mountains above them, for what felt like a long time. I had a nagging sense of something left undone, somewhere I had to be, but the sun was warm on my head and shoulders and the breeze was cool and soft on my face, and the flowering vines and tubs of blooms on the outdoor deck where we sat were hypnotic, and gradually the feeling faded. The vodka helped too, undoubtedly. By the time the crabs came, huge and rosy and served with lime wedges and a wonderful thyme-flavored sauce, I was almost totally a creature of indolence and sensation. I had shucked off my heavy shirt and sat in Stuart Feinstein's "Eat Your Breakfast" tee, feeling the sun running in my veins out to the tips of my toes and fingers. I kept wanting to yawn and stretch until all my joints popped. I did a fair amount of it.

T.C. half-sat, half-slouched across from me, his feet in huge, scuffed hiking boots, propped in an empty chair, eating lime wedges. He had taken off his jacket, too, and wore a handsome, heavy Oxford cloth shirt with the sleeves rolled halfway up his brown forearms. It was faded blue and became him. I knew that it was Brooks Brothers; Pom had dozens of them. For some reason that surprised me. A hermit in a Brooks Brothers button-down? He had removed the mended wire-rimmed glasses and replaced them with a pair of dark yellow aviator's glasses, also bent and mended, that gave his coal-chip eyes the inhuman glitter of a wild animal's. The white teeth and the black beard and hair, with red highlights glistening now in the sun, added to the impression of a predator. But his hawk's face was slack with sun and liquor and good humor, and his smile had a singular sweetness, like a sleepy child's. There was a scattering of tiny black freckles across the bridge of his nose; I had not noticed them before. Celt freckles; Pom had a few of them, too.

"Are you Scottish or Irish?" I asked, breaking the long, sun-humming silence.

"English as far back as the Domesday Book, or so I'm told. With some Yamacraw Indian thrown in, though nobody in my family will admit to it. I think it was one reason nobody made much of a fuss when I took off West. Sooner or later they probably would have paid me to stay away so nobody could see the Yamacraw in my face. Nobody else in the clan has it."

He said it so mildly that I wondered if he were joking.

"Why do you ask?" he said, leaning his head so far back that it hung over the back of the Adirondack chair, leaving his throat bare. I saw that it was pale. He was not naturally dark, then, but brown with sun and wind. Again like Pom. I was obscurely glad that his eyes were black-brown and not Pom's spotlight blue.

"My husband has those freckles and he's a Celt," I said, and then blushed hotly and was angry with myself for the blush. Lord, what a ninny, I thought fiercely. This is not prom night.

But he only said, "Ah," and went on lolling his head back, eyes closed against the slanting sun. He looked as boneless and inert as a ventriloquist's dummy that had been tossed across the chair. I sat up straighter and looked at my watch, shaking my head to clear the sweet lassitude from it. Three forty-five.

"Do you realize that we've sat here guzzling vodka and stuffing our faces for almost three hours?" I said.

He snapped his head back down.

"You need to get back?" he said, yawning.

"I thought I'd call Glynn—"

"Why?"

"Well . . . just to see that she's settled in. Let her know where I've been, in case she's tried to call—"

"I've got an answering machine," he said. "Pringle won't have a phone, but he still doesn't want to miss the four hundred calls he gets every day. He put in the machine before I even moved in. You can call her back if she's called."

"It's just that it's the first time she's been away from me for this long in a strange place, besides camp, and she knows everybody there."

"She's not going into the heart of darkness, only the heart of Palo Alto. Though they may be one and the same, at that. How old is she, anyway? Sometimes she looks twelve, and others you can see the woman she's going to be. Some woman, too."

"She's sixteen," I said curtly. Put that way, it did sound ridiculous, my fussing about my daughter.

"So why do you hover? Has she been sick? She's awfully thin, you know. Well, of course you do. Anorexia, isn't it?"

"Not anymore," I said, biting my words off short and staring at him levelly. "She's gained a good bit since she's been out here. And yes, we've had treatment and therapy for her; the best. It's working, and I wasn't aware that I hover. How do you know so much about anorexia, anyway?"

"Oldest daughter had it. It was during the time her mother and I were going through our divorce. A bad time all the way around. She was fourteen then; she didn't have any other weapons. We should have seen it before we did."

"How is she now?" I said, my annoyance vanishing. So he had walked that bad road, too. Glynn's thinness must hurt him to see. He couldn't know how much better she was.

"She's dead," he said, looking down into his glass, where melting ice turned the remnants of the Bloody Mary pink.

"Oh, my God—"

"No, no. Not from the anorexia. I think we'd mostly licked that. That's what made it so—awful. It was an automobile accident. She was with some kids driving up the Delta to a Christmas party in a town upriver, and they went straight into a semi. It was late, and the kid driving had been drinking. We should have been on top of that, too, but we were so glad she was beginning to date and go to parties that we didn't . . . we should have talked to her, of course; we should have called the kid's parents before they ever left, or something—"

He broke off and sucked the pink water through his straw, making a rattling, blatting sound. His face was shuttered and his eyes were blank. I felt tears spring to my eyes and a lump form in my throat, and reached over and put my hand over his.

"I'm so awfully sorry," I said. "I didn't mean to pry. It must be . . . terrible."

"Yes. It is."

And then he looked up and smiled.

"I've got two other kids. A girl named Katie and a boy named Tom. After me. The T.C. is for Thomas Carlyle. Family names, both of them; the old man never read a book in his life. But it used to embarrass me at school, so I started using the initials. Tom's starting to do it, too. Drives the whole family nuts. They're good kids. I'll be seeing them in the fall."

"I gather they're back home . . . where?"

"Greenville, Mississippi. Heart of the Delta. From your accent I'd say you were no stranger to that country."

"No. Louisiana for me; Baton Rouge. I went to LSU, and then to Atlanta to work, and that's where I've been ever since. I've never been out of the South except traveling. I knew you were from the Delta. There's no other accent quite like it."

"And no other place. Thank God. Yep, they're in Greenville with their mama, and likely to stay there till they're planted in the family plot. Tom's starting the university at Oxford this fall, and Katie is knee-deep in cotillions and debuts and all that retro stuff we do so well on the Delta. They're like their mother; they're absolutely certain-sure of their place, their world. I'm glad for them. They won't spend their lives wandering around looking for the place they're meant to be. But I miss them. It's all I do miss of that territory back there, those kids. I wish I could see them in my place, up there"—and he gestured toward the mountains—"but that's not going to happen, I don't think."

"They don't like it up there?"

"They don't know it up there. Annabelle won't let them come, and they can't do it on their own until they're eighteen. She thinks I deserted them for the West, and she doesn't think the life of a hermit is a proper example. She's probably right. God knows what they tell their friends I do. I see them back home when I see them. Of course, it's not really me they see there, so I guess they'll never really get to know me. But it's better than nothing."

"I don't think I like this Annabelle," I said.

"Me either, much, now," he said. "But God, I was so crazy about her when I first met her that I practically went trotting around after her baying like a hound. She was a cheerleader at Ole Miss and I was a professional fraternity boy devoting myself to drinking and screwing and making just good enough grades to stay in school and keep on doing both. Not that you could screw Miss Annabelle Pritchard of Oak Grove Plantation.

Her daddy would bite your ass off. So I married her about two hours after her graduation. It was a garden wedding at Oak Grove. I would have married her in a Buddhist ceremony to get in her pants. And I have to say, in those early years she was something. The perfect wife for a good old Delta boy living off his daddy while he decided what to do with himself. It was only when I started to change that she did. Or rather, didn't. I realize now that I asked a literal impossibility of her, but then we shouldn't have gotten married in the first place. We just should have screwed till we got it out of our system. She was on the pill from the time she was sixteen, no matter what her daddy thinks."

"You don't like your family much." It was not a question.

He laughed.

"Not worth shit. It's entirely mutual."

"Why?"

He raised the black eyebrows.

"For a proper Southern lady you sure do ask a lot of questions."

"Oh, Lord, that was rude, wasn't it? I don't know what got into me. I'd absolutely never do that at home—"

"Precisely. You're a different person out here. Like I am. Don't apologize; it's just what I hoped would happen to you. Well. My family. What to say about my family that Faulkner didn't say better? My family has always had land and money and pale skin and blond hair and bluer blood than anybody else in the entire Delta, or so the conventional wisdom goes. And not a brain in the lot of them. My grandfather owned a bank in a little town near Greenville called Pennington, and by the time he died he all but owned the town, too. My father took over both in his time, and now my brother, Cleve, is running things. I was supposed to; I was the oldest son. But I hated that damned bank like poison ivy; there was no way anybody was going to get me into the bank or the life that went with it. And tell you the truth, I don't think my father minded too much; here was this dour black cuckoo in that shiny isinglass family nest; it just wasn't seemly. Old Cleve looked the part and wanted the bank worse than hell, so when I cut out Daddy just moved him right on in there. It was the right thing to do. Cleve is the best bank president in Pennington, Mississippi, which is to say the only one."

"So what did you do? How did you get out here?"

"First I thought I wanted to be a newspaperman, so Daddy got me a job on the Greenville paper. He owned a chunk of that. I was a good writer; still am. Freelance writing is how I earn my living. But I hated the reporting part. I had to go interview the families of murder victims, of people who'd drowned in the river or gotten squashed on the highway, or of little kids who'd died of just plain being poor; black families who'd been tornadoed out of their shacks and trailer parks—I couldn't do it. I quit after a year. Then I worked in the research library at Ole Miss. I liked that pretty much, but by that time the sense that I wasn't in the right place was starting to eat at me. And things were starting to sour with Annabelle. I brought a couple of black coworkers home to dinner once or twice, and she just couldn't make the jump. I didn't like being told who I could have in my house and who I couldn't, so I started staying away a lot.

"About that time I got offered a job in a big PR firm in Jackson, and she didn't want to move, and I couldn't stay around Greenville and Pennington anymore, with my whole family nipping at my heels like hounds at a coon. . . . I don't know, I just picked up and moved to Jackson. I thought for a while I could come home on weekends and eventually persuade Annabelle to move, but you'd do better trying to get a penguin to move to the equator. She just couldn't do it. All her . . . her *self* was tied up in the town and the house and her clubs and the kids and her mama and daddy, and mine, and the plantation—and none of mine was. Then I got sent to a convention in Berkeley, and came up to those mountains with a guy I met who was a great hiker, and we got up there into the redwood country, and something in the ground just ran up out of it and through the soles of my feet and up into me, and I knew that that was it; there it was. That was my place, and that would be where I found out who I really was. So I started coming back whenever I could, and after the divorce and my daughter . . . after that, I just went up there one time and stayed. By that time Daddy had died and left me enough money to live on for a long time if I'm careful. I think he always meant me to clear out of the Delta, because he left property and stock to Cleve and my sister and cash to me. I found a place in Palo Alto and got a job in the Stanford library, just filing and sorting at first, but I didn't care; it wasn't a career I wanted. And every weekend I went up into the Santa Cruz's. And one weekend I found the fire tower and followed the trail down to the lodge, and old Caleb baby was there with a toots, and I knocked on the door and told him I'd look after his property in exchange for living in his fire tower. He asked me about money, and I thought he meant for me to pay rent, so I said I thought I could manage a little bit every month, and he laughed and said that what he'd meant was how much *I* wanted. I said I didn't want any, just the tower, and I meant it; I didn't want to be too beholden to him. So he said sure. I never did like him, but I came as close as I ever did then. And I've been here ever since."

He paused and took a breath and said, "Also, I'm clumsy except on the dance floor; I can do a mean shag. And I'm cranky and bone-lazy and absentminded and I play a good blues guitar and have one of the best collections of blues tapes in the Western world, and I read constantly and unselectively and take in stray animals and play a little tennis every now and then but no golf, and I'm a terrific cook, and I am prone to have a snort more often than not. I have no significant other, but I do, as we say in the South, entertain friends once in a while. I am clean, disloyal, not at all brave, and trustworthy to a limited degree. You, for instance, could trust me with your life, but not many other Southerners can, or do. They're right not to. I am not, as has been pointed out to me on many occasions by my family and in-laws, a responsible provider. There. Anything else you want to know you'll have to ask me yourself."

"Wow," I said, grinning a little ruefully.

"Didn't I tell you never to ask a hermit a question?"

"Do you really think of yourself like that? As a hermit?"

He frowned slightly, and the brown forehead furrowed under the flag of black hair that fell over it.

"I think of myself as someone who has to live like this,"

he said slowly. "Or maybe it's that I have to live up there. I'm not quite the same person even down here in town. I'm certainly not the same one back there in the Delta. And it's that mountain person I need to be, not those others. So . . . I guess in a way I am a hermit. I don't know what else you'd call it, and in any case it doesn't matter."

"I can sort of see what you mean," I said. "About not being the same up there. There's . . . something . . . isn't there?"

"Yeah. I thought you'd see. You're different up there, too. I'd bet the farm on that. Not the same person as you are back home. It doesn't mean you're better or worse, just different. Somebody else. You don't need or want the same things as that other person."

I did not reply. How could one person suddenly become two? I hated the thought, and said as much.

"God, how could you not be two people?" he said. "You can be fifty people, or a hundred, if you need to. Lots of people are, but they never know it. They try to bring the person they were in one place to another completely different one, and nothing fits, and they're restless and unhappy, and likely to be that way all their lives. You're lucky you felt the difference. You're at least able to realize that there is one. Whether or not you can be who you need to be up here, is another matter. But I'll tell you one thing: If you try to force the person you were back there to live up there in those woods for long, you'll end up hating them and yourself, too. If I went back home I'd turn back into the person that was of that place, and nothing about it would work. Poor Annabelle, it was that person she married. But that person couldn't stay in the Delta or in his own skin. Just could not. Up there, I'm finally me—but she hates this me. I can't go back there and she couldn't come out here with me. I'm making a real hash of this. I think I mean that you need to go with who you are wherever and whenever you find yourself. That's what I mean by carpe diem. I think."

"Carpe diem . . . "

"Yeah. Live like you need to wherever you are, every day. How could you be unhappy then?"

"How could you be with anybody else, living that way?" I said in real distress, wanting to understand.

He shrugged.

"Maybe you can't. Maybe people like that aren't meant to live with anybody else. It turned out that I couldn't. Maybe I could with somebody who was . . . of my place. But so far, nobody else has been—"

"It sounds like Joseph Campbell," I said. "You know, follow your bliss? I never really liked that idea. It seems so self-obsessed. But maybe it's the only honest way to live—"

"Yeah, well, it's why I don't talk about this to people," he said. "It does sound like New Age shit, and it's as self-absorbed as hell."

We were both silent for a while. I thought about what he had said. It would not fall into a neat pattern.

In a moment he said, in a different voice, "I'm glad it wasn't you who's Pringle's lady. At first I thought it was."

"Why on earth would you think that?" I said.

He stared at me.

"Are you kidding? You're so pretty. You must know you are; I thought when I saw you, 'Damn, it's got to be her, and she's such a classy woman, so much better than his usual ones.' When your sister said it was her I almost cheered."

I felt the hot color run up my neck and into my face.

"You must be kidding," I said. "I wish you wouldn't. I hate that kind of stuff—"

"I'm not kidding," he said, and I saw that he was not.

"But . . . Lord, you saw Laura. I mean, she's a *movie* star; she's always been the beauty, a real one. People stop her on the street and in malls—"

"And here you are, a tall, skinny lady with freckles and a mop of curly hair like Brillo and a smile that could smelt ore. Who on earth would find you pretty? Beautiful? Only about a million people like me, Miz Merritt Fowler. Don't sell yourself short. You are one terrific-looking woman, and, I think, a nice one, too. So what's eating you? Your daughter? Your airhead little sister? You got troubles back home? Fighting with your husband, are you?"

"No," I said coldly. "I am not. Why did you think I was?"

"Heard you on the phone."

"I don't remember saying anything that sounded even

remotely like I was fighting with my husband. I did not even speak with my husband. That was his secretary—"

"Look, babe, I know the tone. It's one thing I do know, the tone of a woman's hurt and anger. I'll shut up about it; it's none of my business, of course. But I do know the tone."

Abruptly the cold anger left me. I looked down at my hands. They were clasped whitely on my empty glass.

"It's not a fight," I said. "It's more of a misunderstanding. They happen in all marriages. I'll get things straightened out when I get home."

"You'll get," T.C. said. "You'll do. You'll fix. Who does all those things for you?"

Incredibly, I began to cry. I sat in the waning sun and cried silently and for a while I could not stop. He wet a napkin in his water glass and mopped my face with it, and in a little while the ridiculous tears slowed and stopped, and I looked blearily up at him. He looked back mildly concerned, but mainly serene and focused and very interested.

"Tell me," he said, and I did. I sat there, alternately sniffling and hiccuping and laughing, and I told him all of it. It seemed to take a very long time. I left out little, from my mother's death up to the present, except that I did not mention the beautiful, selfless, saintly black UN doctor who was perhaps moving even now by Pom's side through places where he and I once went as a unit. Somehow I could not manage that. To name it is to make it real, to make it yours.

When I finished, I said, "Well, that's it. The world according to Merritt Fowler. I'm sorry I cried. Hearing it out loud, it all sounds pretty trivial. I've had a charmed life, really."

He snorted. "Yeah, right. Just like I had. Listen, Merritt, don't let all that stuff ruin this for you. This right now, that up there . . . it's too good, too special to spoil. Leave that woman back home. Be here now; be all the way here. Let's see who you turn out to be up there. Let me show you the woods."

I was suddenly embarrassed and tentative. We had shown each other too much, talked too much. It was too soon.

"Show me the way to go home, instead," I said lightly. "I'm asleep in this chair. If I don't get out of here I'll be comatose."

He laughed and accepted the change of tone. He paid the check and we went back to the Jeep in the slanting light of late afternoon. We talked lightly, of light things. I was comfortable again, soothed. It had been, after all, I thought, a perfectly wonderful afternoon. On the way home we stopped for groceries. When we were back up in the mountains, just turning off onto Caleb's road by the mailbox, I said, "Tell me about the earthquakes. I know they're important to you, but I don't know how they fit."

He said nothing, and I looked over at him. His face was closed. He still did not speak, and I said, feeling myself redden again, "Sorry. I didn't mean to pry."

"No. *I'm* sorry. I was rude. You're right; the earthquakes are important. I'll tell you about them one of these days."

But he did not speak of them anymore, and I was silent until we reached the fire tower. Some of the shine had gone off the dying day. I realized that I really was tired, terribly so. I wanted only to sleep. Only that.

"Come on up and I'll see if there are any calls for you," he said, parking the Jeep. "And I'll feed you. You don't want to eat alone on your first night on your own. I make a terrific pasta and mussel thing."

"Really, T.C., I think I just want to go to bed," I said, and blushed again, and he grinned. But he did not pick up on it.

"I can't hold my eyes open," I added hastily. "It's been a fast three days."

"The air up here does it to you," he said. "Let me just run up and check the machine, and then I'll drive you on down. Curtis, stay."

He disappeared from the car and went past the tarp-covered shapes of his mysterious machinery, up the stairs of the tower. I laid my head back against the seat and thought nothing at all. Curtis, asleep on the backseat, groaned in a doggy dream and fell silent again. When T.C. got back into the Jeep I was dozing, too.

At the door of the lodge he stopped, a bag of my groceries in each arm. Twilight was falling fast down here on the ferny earth, but up in the tops of the redwoods day still rode, golden and glorious. The old silence was back.

"I'm sorry about the earthquakes," he said. "I really was rude. I'm used to sort of guarding all that from people. But you'll understand about them, I think. Let me take you on a tour of earthquake country tomorrow, and tell you about what I do up here and why I do it, and show you my toys. I haven't really done that with anybody else. Caleb thinks I've got tinker toys or something up there."

"I'd like that," I said.

"Besides, you haven't finished telling me about you. I want to hear the rest tomorrow."

I smiled. "You know all there is to know about me now," I said.

He looked at me for what felt like a long time. His face was attentive and serious; it was a considering look.

"No, I don't," he said softly. "I don't know all about you. I don't know nearly all about you."

He shifted one bag into the crook of his left arm with the other one and with the right pulled me toward him and kissed me. He had to bend far down, even with my height. It felt, after Pom's compactness, strange, exotic, like embracing another species. It was not a passionate kiss, but it was a long one, and soft, and seemed to search my mouth for some essence, find there some truth about me. I felt the long bones of my arms and legs turn to water, and the tears start again in my eyes. But it was not me who finally pulled away. Propped against my leg, Curtis groaned happily.

T.C. put my bags down on the door step and looked owlishly at me over the glasses, which had slipped down his nose.

"Put that in your pipe and smoke it, little lady," he drawled. I watched him wordlessly as he shambled off up the trail, Curtis at his side. At the hairpin bend in the trail he suddenly leaped into the air and clopped his heels together. He looked like a puppet dangling loosely in midair. When he thumped back to earth he did not look back. Curtis barked and gave a desultory prance, and fell to following T.C. sedately again, as if he had never broken stride. Then they were gone around the bend.

I began to laugh helplessly. I took the groceries in, still

laughing, and dumped them on the kitchen table, and went into my bedroom and simply fell full-length onto the bed. I did not remember my head hitting the pillow. Deep in the night we had a short fusillade of thunder and lightning, and a hard, straight rain, and it woke me enough to shuck off my clothes and crawl under the covers, and as I did, I began once more to laugh. When I awoke, many hours later, my mouth was as dry and stiff as if I had smiled all night in my sleep.

9

What woke me was a soft scratching noise at the front door. I sensed it more than heard it; all my senses were sharp and open, even before my eyes were. I got up blindly and pulled on the red-and-black checked shirt. It fell to my knees, and made a fairly proper robe. By the time I got to the door my feet were freezing, and I was awake enough to realize that I hoped my caller was T.C.

But it was Curtis who stood there, framed in fog, panting happily and wearing a red bandanna around his neck. I usually hate that when it is done to dogs at home, but up here the bandanna seemed as apt and proper as if a mountain man wore it; a useful object, utilitarian. There was a note rolled and thrust into it.

"Come in, Curtis. Carpe diem," I said, and he came inside and sat down in front of me and looked up, waiting. I took the note and scratched his ears and he went over and flopped down in front of the cold fireplace. A log fire was laid, and I touched a match to it before I unrolled the note. Curtis sighed in contentment and stretched out full-length before the snapping flames.

"It was the least I could do," I told him, and read the note.

"I'll pick you up at nine," it said. "We'll be gone most of the day, so bring a warm shirt and a poncho. There's one hanging behind the kitchen door. Tell Curtis he can stay till I get there. Hope you slept well."

Instead of a signature he had drawn one of those detestable smiley faces, only this one wore an unmistakable leer. I laughed aloud, a backwash of last night's glee flooding me.

"There's absolutely nothing as irresistible as wit," I told Curtis. "Even if it's the dumbass kind that puts bandannas on dogs and draws smiley faces. See that you remember that, dog. Stay funny and cute and you'll have lady dogs falling all over you."

Curtis thumped his tail without opening his eyes, and I went to dress warmly and get the poncho from behind the kitchen door.

Just past ten we were on the Golden Gate Bridge rattling toward Marin County and Point Reyes, where T.C. wanted to start my earthquake tour. At that time of morning the traffic was light and the fog lay out at the mouth of San Francisco Bay, piled up like whipped cream. Below us the steel-blue water heaved and rolled, and a brisk wind played the bridge like an instrument, making it sway slightly, but palpably. T.C. had unsnapped the plastic side curtains of the Jeep and the wind and cold blue air poured in on us, and I held fast to the bottom of my seat. I had thought the mountains and the red-woods would seem inimical to humans, but somehow it was here, on this consummate iron-red handwork of man, hung between two great and beautiful human habitats, that I felt the animus. I felt light-headed and uneasy, as if, should I let go, the wind would take me and eddy me out and down like a feather into that cold sea, or toss me so high into sunshot nothingness that I would never come back.

"No wonder so many people jump," I said, shutting my eyes to it for a moment. "It makes you feel like it's going to get you anyway, so why put it off?"

"I've always thought people jump because it's such a San Francisco kind of thing to do," T.C. said. "Eccentric and showy and probably very beautiful all the way down. Nothing mundane about it. No dull overdoses. No tacky guns. Laid back, kind of, but effective."

"Why do I get the feeling you don't like San Francisco a whole lot?"

"I don't *not* like it, exactly," he said slowly, looking over at the spectacular headlands where Sausalito and, beyond it, Tiburon lay gleaming in the sun like toy villages flung down by a giant's child. He wore a faded red anorak this morning, mottled with what looked to be bleach spots and ripped on one pocket. The red was wonderful with the dark skin and the beard and hair, I thought; the latter so recently washed that it still had damp comb tracks in it. I even liked the bleach spots and the tear; anything newer or better cared for would have seemed effete. I liked everything about T. C. Bridgewater this morning. Somehow he seemed to own the bridge and the wind and the vast emptiness as surely and comfortably as he owned the old Jeep. I wished suddenly that he would stop the Jeep in the middle of the bridge and kiss me again. The thought was so clear and shapely and so alien to me that I felt myself redden and hastily sought out things about him to dislike.

He's as self-absorbed as a child, I thought, and if you put him down anywhere else but those mountains he'd be as clumsy and ludicrous as an aborigine in Paris. I can just see him at the Driving Club.

It didn't work, of course; I *could* see him at the Driving Club. After all, he had been more surely born to that world than either Pom or I. And the self-absorption fit him like an animal's unconscious sense of itself.

"Shit," I said under my breath, and moved closer to the door of the Jeep.

"But?" I said aloud.

"But it just seems . . . I don't know. Extraneous. Like a stage set, or a perfect architect's model. I know people live and work here, and get married and have children and are happy and sad and die and all that, but I can't seem to picture it. It's a tinker-toy town."

"Don't let Tony Bennett hear you say that."

"Are you kidding? That poor son of a bitch probably

hates San Francisco like he does the IRS. Probably goes back-
stage and throws up every time he has to sing that song."

I laughed and he looked over at me and squeezed my
hand and said, "You look nice this morning," and we bowled
off the bridge and into Marin county, my hand tingling.

"It's probably some of the most gorgeous countryside I'll
ever see," I said chattily, as he cut over to Highway 1 toward
Muir Beach and the Golden Gate Recreational Area. "I wonder why I don't feel about it like I do the redwoods? You're
right about the city; somehow it doesn't have much to do with
the way I feel about this part of the country. I mean, I'd love
to spend some time in it, and I know I'd like a lot of the people, but somehow I just want to get back into the wild stuff."

I knew that I was babbling. I knew that he knew it. I took
a deep breath.

"T.C.," I said, "I think you'd better kiss me one more time
and get it over with so I can stop waiting to see if you're going
to do it. I'm not behaving at all like myself."

He laughed aloud and drew me to him with one arm and
kissed me long and hard, without stopping the Jeep or even
swerving it. When he let me go my mouth felt warm and
numb, and I could feel my whole body melt into relaxation.
The silly, stilted tension went out of the morning. Another
sort entirely crept in.

"Thank you," I said.

"You're very welcome," he said. "I was going to do that,
but I thought I'd wait till we were standing on firm ground, so
if you slapped me I wouldn't wreck us. If you like it I could
stop now and do it some more—"

"Drive, fool," I said. "I'm not even going to ask how you
can do that at fifty miles an hour and not even swerve."

"First thing you learn on the Delta. Whatever you're
going to do, you learn to do it in a car, because that's where we
spend half our lives. I didn't know how to kiss a woman standing still till I got to college."

"I can imagine it was a considerable handicap," I said. I
did not want to dwell on whom he kissed in college, or how,
and so I changed the subject.

"If you're going to show me earthquake country,

shouldn't you start in San Francisco?" I said. "Laura said there was still a lot of damage down around the marina, and where that bridge collapsed."

"I will if you really want to see it," he said. "But I've never thought that that stuff really belonged to the earthquake. I mean, it had more to do with people and where and how they build their structures than it did with anything the earthquake did. See, the Loma Prieta hit way up in the Santa Cruzes; only it happened so deep down that there's nothing much to see up there except some sheared-off redwoods. It's the deepest earthquake ever recorded in this part of the country. The shock waves traveled out from the epicenter and took out whatever they hit while they were still active. There are three kinds, the compressional waves that make the first big thump when the quake hits; we call them P waves because they're the primary ones. The second one is the S wave, and it comes in a rolling, side-to-side motion; it's the secondary wave. It's called a shear wave, too. The last is the surface wave. It travels slower, along the surface of the earth, and it's the largest. It finishes up what the first two don't get. In the Loma Prieta, there wasn't anything much in the way of human habitation, relatively speaking, until the waves got to Santa Cruz and then San Francisco. If there hadn't been cities there, nobody much would have noticed the quake. Do you see what I mean? The quake is its own entity. It's not San Francisco's quake or L.A.'s. Damage in a city is arbitrary, because if there was no city there wouldn't be the damage. . . . I don't think I'm making much sense. But see, it's like, the land under the marina is fill. It was literally filled with dirt and stuff to create usable land. Lots of the debris Loma Prieta uncovered turned out to be debris from the big one in 1906. That kind of land is porous and when the waves hit it, it acts just like gelatin. It's like . . . we did that, not the quake. The city did itself in, so to speak. A quake is a wild thing, and it's born in elemental wildness, in the crust of the very earth. What sits on that crust is us, not it. It's not a popular point of view, as you might imagine. I'll take you by the worst of it when we come back, if you still want to see it."

I thought of the awful images from the 1989 Loma Prieta quake, of the fires in the night and the collapsed buildings, like folded accordions, and the terrible flattened bridge. I thought of dry land turning to rolling Jell-O, of the terror that must engender.

"No," I said. "I don't think I want to see what a quake can do to a city. But I can see why it's not a popular point of view. Lord, T.C., you sound like you're in love with them—the earthquakes. Like you're rooting for them, somehow."

He looked briefly at me, and then back at the road and the heaving sea beside it.

"I guess I am," he said. "I know there's something in an earthquake that speaks to me like nothing else ever has. Maybe it's not that I'm in love with them, exactly; it's just that I need to know what all that is about."

"And you don't yet?"

"No. Not yet."

"You weren't in the Loma Prieta, then?"

"No, I was back home at my son's first big-time football game. I missed the Northridge, too. I was up in the mountains when that hit. I've never been in one, not a big one."

We drove in silence for a while, and then I said, "T.C.?"

"Yeah?"

"Are you camped up there waiting to be in an earthquake?"

"Yeah. I guess that's about it."

"And you think that's where the next big one will be? Even when everybody's saying that the . . . what, the seismic gap there was filled by the Loma Prieta?"

"That's what I think, Merritt."

"Why?"

He sighed a long, soft sigh, and said, "Because I can feel it coming. I can feel a big quake waiting to happen right through the soles of my feet. I can feel it getting stronger. I felt it the first time I went up there, when I was in Berkeley that time. That quake down in that earth talks to me like a giant that's been buried alive. I know I'm not wrong about that. What I don't know is when. Nobody knows that, not with any precision. But I know that it isn't going to be long."

I felt the hair prickle along the back of my neck.

"You said you'd get us out before it happened—"

"It's not going to be that soon. I really would know that. None of my instruments indicate that. Neither do the bottoms of my feet. I'd get you out, Merritt."

I sat looking at the empty sea and the cliffs. I felt something bleak inside me, like grief, an old, deep, tidal pull. I realized that I had been talking to him, responding to him, as if he made perfect sense. But the clear, cool top part of my mind told me that he didn't; that what he spoke was not science or even casual knowledge, but obsession. Maybe more than that.

"T.C., I don't think I can bear it if you turn out to be crazy," I said in a low voice, meaning it, and he laughed so hard that he had to slow the Jeep.

"What you need more than anything in your life is to make out with a crazy man," he said, when he finally stopped laughing. "You have not lived until you've been loved by a loony. I can promise you that, should you accept the advances I am most certainly going to make before this day is over, you will never forget the experience. I will growl; I will froth; I will snuffle. I will roar. It will ruin you for suits and the Junior League for the rest of your life."

Once again I laughed, unwillingly but helplessly. T. C. Bridgewater simply delighted me. The laugher was healing. I did not think a truly mad man could be a funny one. If he had an earthquake madness in him, well, I was unlikely to be disaccommodated by that. The rest of him was as whole and strong and as open as the earth and air of his mountains. That part drew me to it as if he had a powerful magnet deep in the center of him, and I a core of warm iron.

"Growling is okay," I said. "Froth is definitely out. Snuffling—*maybe*. Roaring—I don't know yet. We'll see."

His face grew serious in that mild, interested way that it sometimes did.

"Who is this talking?" he said.

"I don't know her," I said. "She just followed me out here. Should I keep her?"

"Oh, yeah. Yeah, you should definitely do that," he said slowly and softly, and the warm ore in my middle gave a leap.

"You'd better tell me some more about earthquakes, and

be quick about it," I said. "Why do y'all have them out here, and we don't at home?"

"You do have them back home. There've been really destructive ones in Charleston and Missouri. There's an active fault under New York City. There are faults all over the place that we don't know about and won't till they blow; Northridge was on a fault nobody knew was there. But California is the meeting place for two of the tectonic plates that make up the crust of the earth. There are seven major ones and some other, smaller ones. The ones that give California all the trouble are the Pacific plate, that's mainly under the Pacific Ocean, and the North American. That one underlies the earth out here. They kind of slide past each other, with the Pacific going northwest, and the North American vice versa, and where they bump together is the San Andreas Fault. The San Andreas is a transform fault—the plates don't destroy old material or create new. The places where the boundaries spread apart underwater and let new molten mantle rock rise are called spreading centers, and the big ocean trenches where the cold, dense oceanic plates are forced underneath the continental plates are called subduction centers. Most of the seismic activity in the world occurs within narrow areas along those plate boundaries. There's a phenomenal amount of activity in a line that runs along the western coast of North and South America, up across the Aleutian Islands, and down through the waters off Asia. It fetches up off New Zealand. It's called the Ring of Fire, because there's so much earthquake and volcano activity going on. There's nothing near to that off the East Coast. The nearest subduction center is way, way out to sea. Y'all just have to make do with hurricanes and tornadoes."

"So there's earthquake activity going on all the time, but maybe not strong enough to feel it?" I said, hating the thought. It was like suddenly finding that you had been standing on a nest of squirming small snakes all along, but never noticed until a big one bit you.

"About ten thousand a day, in California alone," he said proudly. "Only the most sophisticated equipment can pick up most of them. You start feeling them about two point seven or three. They're using a network of receivers now, for instance, that pick up signals from the army's Global Positioning System satellites and tell you where and how much the earth is moving within a fraction of an inch—and it's moving all the time. Over the ages most of the earth has moved around dramatically. You ought to read John McPhee's *Assembling California*, to see how California, and the whole earth for that matter, is made up of chunks of rock that were carried from somewhere else by earthquake action. That's over a period of millions of years, of course. Or read Kenneth Brown's *Cycles of Rock and Water at the Pacific Edge*. Fascinating; really fascinating. Somewhere in one of them is the statement that the top of Mount Everest is made from marine sandstone. That just plain fries the roots of my hair."

I looked at him. His face was rapt and his eyes were far-focused, as if they could actually see the gargantuan, millennial creep of the earth; see the ancient spasms that flung up coastal mountains and corrugated deserts, that moved future continents and countries around like building blocks. Through his dark, blind eyes I too could see, for just a moment, that vast old cyclopean tumbling. It made my breath shallow and thin and the space around my heart cold.

"It makes me feel like throwing up," I said. "If I thought about it I'd be so dizzy I couldn't walk upright on the earth again."

"Ah, well," he said. "You don't have to love it. You just have to see why I do. That's important to me, that you see that."

"I see that it's important to you," I said. "You'll just have to make do with that. Have you ever thought about teaching this stuff, or becoming a seismologist or a geologist or something? With your . . . passion for it, I think you'd make a wonderful teacher—"

"I don't want to do anything about earthquakes," he said. "I don't want to teach people about them. I just want to know about them."

"But when you do that—when you know—what then? What will you have?"

We were heading up the Olema Valley. On either side of

us sharp-boned mountains rose abruptly, a thousand feet or more. The fog that had held off so far was drifting along the road, and he slowed the Jeep to accommodate it.

"What I'll have," he said, turning again to look at it, "is a real sense of them, and if I'm lucky, a sense of where I fit in with them. A context. If I'm very, very lucky, maybe I'll know what it is they're saying to me. That would be worth anything. Why does there have to be a 'then what'? There's not going to be an end to the knowing about them; there's no 'then what' on the horizon, because there's not going to be a then, in the sense that I ever know enough about them. Does that disappoint you?"

"No, it doesn't. Knowledge for its own sake—it's a very pure concept. I think we all get too caught up in doing instead of just being, sometimes," I said, but deep down a small part of me was disappointed, and I knew that he knew it. I suppose I thought that once he satisfied his passion for them, he would take his knowledge of earthquakes and do something with it to benefit mankind. Predict, warn, mitigate . . .

I looked at him helplessly.

"It's just that all I've ever known about, really, is helping," I said. "I don't know how to let go and just . . . be. I'm sorry. I know that disappoints *you*. I think I could learn. . . ."

He reached over and pushed the blown hair off my face, very gently.

"I think you can, too. That's why we're up here. You don't disappoint me, Merritt. There's a joy to being with you for me. Watching you up here is like watching a kid learn to play for the first time in its life. One thing we're going to teach you is how to play. I don't give a shit whether you learn to love earthquakes or not. It's enough that I do."

Tears stung my eyes. When had play left my life? When Crisscross and I had stopped our weekend jaunts together? When Glynn had grown past babyhood?

When had Pom and I stopped playing? Had we ever really done it?

"I play," I said, trying for lightness. "I swim with the *Rattus ratti*, remember?"

"Oh, Merritt," he said.

"Don't," I said fiercely, blinking hard. "Don't or I'll cry, and I just goddamned well do not want to do that."

"Well, we'll start with Forrest, maybe," he said, accommodating me. "Y'all can gambol in the glades, play a little Nerf ball, maybe take a shower together. See what happens. Work right on up from there to some serious playing."

"Speaking of Forrest, where has he been?" I said. "I miss his bright eyes and sweet smile."

"Forrest takes off sometimes," T.C. said. "I don't know if there's a great sadness in him, or if he's got a lady friend somewhere, or what. I used to think it meant an earthquake was on the way. Animals, especially cats and rats, will leave an area where one is about to hit, or so the saying goes. But he's done it the whole time he's been with me, and it hasn't meant a quake yet. I thought when I found him he'd make a great canary—you know, an early warning system—but he's a dud at that."

"Where did you find him?"

"Curtis brought him to me, in his mouth, like he was holding an egg," he said. "Something killed his mama, apparently; he was just getting hair on him. Not the most attractive time in a rat's life. But Curtis was so proud of him that I just had to take him in. I fed him with an eyedropper and made him a nest out of my old socks. I think it was my socks he bonded with. Curtis has been jealous ever since. I named him Forrest because he looked so much like my father when he started to go bald. His name was Bedford Forrest, after . . . well, you know. Curtis I named after my cousin in Jackson, because he never could resist a good-looking woman, and neither can my Curtis. I like to keep the names in the family."

"Why did you leave Curtis at home?"

"Curtis once came damned close to taking a header off Point Reyes after a cormorant, and that's a four-hundred-foot drop straight into the Pacific. I had to tackle him and practically sit on him. He knows he's supposed to retrieve, but he doesn't have an ounce of sense about where to do it. Just like Cousin Curtis again. Look at those ridges over there, Merritt. See how they knock the whole landscape off-kilter? That's from past quakes. They call them shutter ridges. There are creeks here that are less than half a mile apart, but they run in opposite directions. The quakes have done that, too. And there are about fifty small ponds in this valley that have absolutely no reason to be up here because of the low rainfall, but here they are. They sit on the tops of those ridges; you can see one or two from here. Sag ponds. All from the fault."

"Are we close to the fault here?"

"I'll show you in about five minutes," T.C. said.

A few minutes later he stopped the Jeep. Just ahead of us in the road was a strip of darker asphalt, as if workmen had patched the place where a pipe of some sort had gone through it. T.C. swung down and held out a hand to me, and I scrambled out behind him. The wind had picked up here and was blowing sheets of fog out toward Tomales Bay.

"Step over the patch with one foot," T.C. said, and I did. "No, leave the other one where it is. Now. You're straddling the top of the San Andreas fault. Half of you is on the North American continent, and the other half is off the continent entirely, on the Pacific plate."

Instinctively I pulled my errant foot back onto the continent. He laughed. "You're right to be careful," he said. "In a few million years that half of you could be in Alaska, and the other half would still be here."

"It's not much of a fault, is it?" I said. "I guess I expected a huge fissure with smoke pouring out of it or something. But you'd never know it was down there if it weren't for that patch."

"I'd know," he said, studying the earth where, deep below, the great snake slept. "It's like a monster organ playing down in the earth to me. It always surprises me when nobody else hears it."

I looked at him nervously.

"Metaphorically speaking, of course," he said, and took my arm and guided me back to the Jeep.

"The fault hasn't moved here since the 1906 quake," T.C. said. "The folks who know think it's due. Earthquakes sometimes come in pairs, and some of the hoohaws think that Loma Prieta might be the first of a pair up here. Which means, I guess, that the fault right here could go anytime. But I don't think so."

"The soles of your feet are telling you it won't be here?" I said lightly.

"No. They're not telling me anything. Nothing but the singing I hear everywhere along a fault. It's in the mountains further south that my feet and the earthquake get together."

"What does that feel like?" I said seriously. I wanted to know. At that moment I cast my lot with T.C.'s obsession, or whatever it was.

"Like electricity, I guess," he said. "It runs right up your legs to the middle of you; sometimes it makes your arms and hands weak. It's like . . . sex in reverse. If you take my meaning."

"I take it," I said, and felt myself redden. This is perfect, just perfect, I thought furiously. I have been with him a little over a day and already I have cried twice and blushed about forty times. The only thing left is to swoon or get the vapors. I'm glad Glynn can't see me.

The thought of Glynn whipped my face like cold, wind-driven water. I sat up straighter and smoothed my hair with both hands. What in the name of God did I think I was doing? Bouncing along in a Jeep at the edge of the world with a mad-man who had already announced that he was going to take me to bed and howl like a wolf when he did it; batting my eyes and talking half-dirty to the same madman and loving every minute of it; asking him to kiss me, for God's sake. I am some-body's mother. She is not at all far away from me now.

I am somebody's wife. And he is more than a world away.

"You're allowed second thoughts about all this, you know," T.C. said, seeming to catch my thought. "Even third and fourths. All you have to do is call time out and things can stop right here. I would never frighten or hurt you."

"Then I guess . . . time-out," I said. I felt flat and depleted, oddly bereft, and on top of it all was a cold, seeping guilt, a stain. It seemed to reach across the continent from the house by the river to this rutted, alien road in a stunted forest of pine, live oak, and madrone: the very burrow of the snake. I missed the delight and silliness of the morning and the night before like you miss warmth and food, like you miss light in sudden darkness. The shame I felt was a very poor substitute, but it was a strong one.

"What's the matter?" he said sympathetically. "Flashback? Little blast from the past?"

"How did you know?" I said dully.

"I used to get 'em, too. Right in the middle of something transcendent—and I don't mean sex; I haven't really had any of the transcendent kind out here—I'd feel this cold, wet tentacle reaching out from home, reminding me that I was a sorry, self-indulgent hound who had run off and left his responsibilities and didn't deserve to feel so damned good. Mostly it happened out of the redwoods. What we need to do is get you back up there."

"No, I want to see all this," I said dutifully, though I didn't. I just wanted to snatch up my daughter and my sister and get on a plane home, where, even if things weren't so great, they were my things. Total unfamiliarity is only exhilarating for so long. After that it becomes like a dreadful amnesia of all the senses.

I looked over at T.C. He gave me back a half smile, waiting.

"So how did you handle it?" I said, for obviously he had settled the flashback problem long before.

"Decided I didn't want to be a sorry, guilty hound any longer. I wanted to be the new guy, the one who felt fresh joy and aliveness every morning, who went to sleep smiling, hardly able to wait for the next day. I wasn't going back, anyway; I knew that. Why keep the old sad sack around? It's like any policy; it gets very real after you practice it for a while."

"Carpe diem, huh?"

"Yeah. I wasn't kidding when I said it was the only valid way to live. For me, anyway. Probably for you, too, if the last day or two have been any example. You've bloomed like a flower. You know that's true."

"And while I've been blooming like a flower my husband has been back home working his fanny off for the sick and the poor, and my daughter's been seduced by a Jacuzzi-brained film director to do a porno flick—"

"Would any of that have changed if you'd sat around up here racked with guilt and hating the redwoods? How would it have changed? Look, Merritt, the lady you are back home is the one who deals with that stuff, and better than anybody involved deserves, as far as I'm concerned. The one who's out here . . . she's the one I'm getting to know and coming to care about a whole, whole lot. That was then, as the kids put it so inelegantly. This is now. This is here. The Merritt Fowler I kissed last night and hope to kiss again very soon is not the one who plays altar to her husband's saint and puts diapers on his mother and worries herself sick about an anorectic teenager. The one I kissed last night and hope to kiss again soon loves my woods and my dog and looks like a gypsy and laughs like a loon and eats like a longshoreman, and kisses me back like it feels fantastic. That's not to say the first one isn't valuable. It's just that the second one is so much more—complete. I think. Am I wrong?"

"No . . ."

"Then stop worrying about it. Enjoy the day and the Point and whatever you feel like enjoying. If it's not me, that's okay. The time-out still stands till you call it off."

The cold tentacle from home let go its grip abruptly and well-being flooded back. I did not have to take this any further than I wanted to. He was right. There was an enormous lot to savor about this day, to taste and explore and wriggle my toes in. It did not have to include touching him again unless I wanted to. I did not know yet whether I did or not. If I did . . . well, there was a lot of day left.

"Next thing I know you'll be handing me an apple and telling me to take a bite; what could it hurt?" I said.

"No. Next thing you know you'll be standing at the edge of the earth looking off it and, if I'm not wrong, seeing something you'll never forget. And the next thing after that is lunch. I brought it with me. I know just the place for it."

"And . . . after that?"

I could not seem to stop flirting with him. Was that the name for it? Whatever you called it, it was something that came from a part of me I had not known I had. I could not recall flirting with anyone in my life. Pom and I had been beyond that from the beginning, beyond the giddiness of discovery and into the urgent business of assuaging need almost before we knew each other. I wondered suddenly if I had ever known much more than the feel of his body and the shape of his need. I wondered if he had known more of me than the shape of my body and my ability to fill his gaps.

But it has sustained us, I said to myself. Many, many marriages have run on thinner fuel than that. It has fulfilled us. It has been what we both needed.

But not anymore.

The thought was as clear as if someone had spoken it aloud to me. And I knew it was true. If I went on with this day as it had started out, if I went on with this man, then an entirely different sustenance would be required. Forever after I would need other things.

Then find them. Go home and renegotiate. Redefine. Or simply stay here, the voice said. Isn't that what's at the bottom of all this? The thought that you might just stay? Or the thought that you might not?

We had been walking as I had been listening to the voice. Now we were back at the Jeep. T.C. opened my door and handed me up into the front seat.

"Anything after lunch is then instead of now and will be dealt with when we come to it," he said. "And you'll call the shots. Are you flirting with me, Miss Scarlett?"

And again I laughed, because he had so accurately read me.

"Why Captain Butler," I drawled, "I do believe that I am."

We drove out of the forest and onto a vast, undulating prairie. Yellow, red, and purple wildflowers blew in the steadily increasing wind like the pennants of miniature armies. The wind increased, gusting so that it rocked the Jeep and moaned around the plastic side curtains. Soon we parked and headed down a cypress-bordered footpath. The fog flew before us, revealing wind-battered dairies and huddling herds and not much else. Near the tip of the cape the wind was so strong that we struggled to walk against it. I would have fallen before it if T.C. had not kept an arm around me. The fresh, cold air was heavy with droplets, whether from the vanishing fog or spray I did not know. But I tasted salt and knew that they were born of the sea. When we broke through the cypress windbreak that guarded the path out to the tip of the cape, it was to meet the sun as it finally vanquished the fog and lit what looked like the entire western sea to sparkling foil blue. I felt the breath go out of my lungs in a gasp.

There was virtually no limit to the tossing water, or the sky that swept down to meet it, or the rushing blue air around it, or the sun riding overhead. There was land behind us and beneath our feet, but everywhere else we were drowned in a world of water and space. Steps led tortuously down to a lighthouse that rode a ledge below us, seeming to be borne up by the hollow boom of the surf far, far below. Gulls and cormorants wheeled and banked in the thermals over the water, and far down the cliff two specks soared.

"Eagles," T.C. said. "There's a nest not far down the coast, in a dead tree. I don't know why those guys always hang out over open water here; they couldn't dive into that stuff down there, and there are no fish in heavy surf, anyway. I've always thought they were playing. There are about a million nesting seabirds in the cliffs, too, and a colony of sea lions down there. When the wind's right you can hear all of it; it's bedlam. Like a tenement. Want to walk down to the lighthouse?"

"No," I said, leaning back against him, letting the wind pound me, letting it pour past my face like a tide. "No. I want to stay here. Oh, T.C. It's a glorious place, isn't it? But somehow you feel you shouldn't make yourself at home here. It's like a church; it's not a place to just hang out in."

"You couldn't, anyway," he said. "There's usually fog, and the wind today is as mild as I've felt it. A bad one would blow you over, literally. Look, Merritt. Straight out, about three hundred yards offshore. See those black shapes? There are four of them, right there where I'm pointing."

I could not see anything in the dazzle of light off the water, and then I could. As I found the shapes and tracked them, twin spouts rose from the sea.

"Whales!" I cried. "Oh, my God, T.C.! They are, aren't they? I've never seen them."

I felt him nod. His chin rested on the top of my head; he stood behind me, literally holding me up against the wind. I did not want to move.

"Grays. They're on their way back to the Bering Sea way

up north, from Baja. They go down there every winter to breed and calve in the lagoons, where it's shallow and warm. The entire population of the Pacific Gray whales does it, sixteen thousand strong. They start heading back in the spring; the whole trip is six thousand miles, and will take them three months. For some reason there's always four or six off Point Reyes into June; I've seen them several times before. Usually it's mothers with calves, like those out there. See how there are two large ones and two small? The mothers only have one calf at a time, and they suckle them like humans do. They hug the shore all the way down and back, to avoid the killer whales, and the mothers will close ranks around the calves if they spot a pod of killers, like a wagon train circling. I've seen them do it. It makes you want to cry, somehow. Brave, classy broads, aren't they?"

I stood in the circle of T.C.'s arms in the tearing wind and thought about the great mothers and their calves, braving all this, braving everything, to take their children home. . . .

The wind dried tears on my face as they came, and I did not think that he saw them. But his arms tightened around me, and he said into my hair, "I thought you'd like them."

"So brave," I whispered. "Such good mothers. Never losing sight of what's important. They make me feel ashamed of the kind of mother I've been—"

"Yeah, well, they're a lot less complicated than us, remember that. They don't have the hard choices to make. Classy broads, but strictly limited. Don't worry. You've got nothing to apologize for in the mothering department. I should have known they'd make you cry, though."

"It doesn't take much, does it?" I said. "I always seem to be weeping up here. I don't cry much back home."

"I'm not criticizing you. I'd hate it if you didn't. The first time I saw them I stood out here by myself and bawled like a baby."

Suddenly I wanted to be done with wind and tumult and water and the dangers that swam in all of them. I wanted quiet, and the sun falling in shafts through the great trees as in a cathedral, and the smell of sun-warmed pine and madrone. I wanted to hear nothing but the breath of the great silence.

"I want to go home," I said. "Can we eat lunch there as well as where you'd planned?"

"I'd planned it for around there," T.C. said, and we walked back to the Jeep hand in hand, saying nothing.

We sat locked in our separate thoughts until we were back across the Golden Gate Bridge and through the city and heading back up into the Santa Cruz Mountains. It was a comfortable silence. I steeped in the peace of the warm, sun-filled Jeep after the great shouting wind and cold of Point Reyes, listening to the soft jazz T.C. found on the old radio and, below that, the hum of the big, battered wheels on asphalt. We did not go back down Highway 1; it was as if we had both had our fill of the bellowing sea. Instead, we took 280 down the spine of the mountains, and cut over to Skyline Drive, and entered the domain of the redwoods as gratefully as if we had gained a fortress after a battle. Without meaning to I fell asleep against the window and only woke, neck cramped and mouth tasting of old salt, when I felt the motion of the Jeep stop.

"Are we there?" I said thickly.

"We're here. Or where I wanted to eat lunch, anyway. You hungry?"

"Starved. How long have I been sleeping?"

"A while. We're a good bit south of home, in a place called Mount Madonna County Park."

"What, they gave her her own mountain and park? Not bad for a material girl."

"I think they meant the other one, the one with the halo," he said. "Grab the wine and I'll take the basket. We're going to walk a little way."

We climbed into a thinning forest of redwoods and presently came upon a flight of stairs that led up into nowhere. Beyond the last stair I could see the slumped, vine-tangled shape of ruins, and a fallen chimney. A house. Here in this sunny glade among the whispering giants, its bones softened by shrouding ferns and baby evergreens and the wild white heaps of rhododendron and laurel, a house had sheltered someone and then watched them go, and fallen to the wilderness. The little pink flowers I had noticed around the base of the lodge's redwoods teemed around the steps and at the base of these great trees, and the undergrowth was dense with what T.C. said were elderberry and thimbleberry bushes. It was very quiet; the voice of the silence only murmured. The sun fell in straight, near-palpable shafts. The smell of sun-warmed evergreen was hypnotic. There was a peculiar enchantment about the stairs and the ruins, as if something very old and elemental had made it appear for us, and could make it disappear in an instant if it wished.

"I'd never have left it," I said, aware that I was nearly whispering. "I wonder who did."

"Henry Miller," T.C. said, putting the basket down on the steps and plopping down beside it. "You know, the writer. Or at least, I think he's the one. It's a summerhouse or was. I know that he had a place around Big Sur, and a lot of the artists and writers of his time hung out there with him. I've always thought this was where he came to get away from all those egos and all that talk."

I thought of the great minds and names that must have clustered around Miller, and most probably followed him up here into the redwoods. I could almost see candles and Japanese lanterns on a stone terrace, and a great fire of madrone in a stone fireplace, and hear the atonal skittering of music yet unknown in the East, and the tinkle of ice in glasses, and late-day laughter, and voices raised in argument and dalliance far into the cold, still nights.

"I wonder why he left it? I wonder who let it go like this?"

"Who knows? From what I know of writers' egos, they can't survive long in a vacuum. He probably went back down to Big Sur where the faithful could worship and adore him."

"You don't like Miller?"

"Not especially. I think he really is a dirty writer. Consciously dirty, in a way the other so-called dirty writers never were. D. H. Lawrence was never dirty to me, but the old woman who lay down in the Tottenham Road and pulled up her skirt and masturbated bothers me. It's like the sound of one hand clapping: self-aggrandizing instead of transcendent."

"You don't hold with masturbation either?"

"*Au contraire.* It's the opiate of the solitary. I just don't hold with it in the middle of the road. Me and Mrs. Patrick Campbell."

"I know what you mean," I said. "I loved the naturalness of *Lady Chatterley's Lover*, but *Tropic of Cancer* seemed awfully self-absorbed to me."

"I should have known you'd go for the lady and the gamekeeper," T.C. grinned. "Do any similarities to present circumstances present themselves? I've been practicing a Northumbrian accent, but so far it has eluded me—"

"Yeah, right," I said, grinning at him drowsily. The sun and quiet were doing their work and I was powerfully, indolently sleepy as well as hungry. "Nevertheless, I love it that this was Henry Miller's hidey hole. I like him better for knowing he needed one. Are you going to open that basket or should I just wrest it from you?"

We sat on the sun-warmed steps until the shafts of light leaned to the west and the warmth began to steal out of the air. He had made sandwiches of a delicious, chewy focaccia bread and crab and avocado, and brought grapes and chèvre that he said was made in a valley near the Big Basin. We ate them and drank the cool white wine and presently there was nothing left of any of it. I could barely hold my heavy eyes open.

"Okay. We've had lunch and it is now now," T.C. said. "I await your pleasure."

He sat opposite me, his long legs sprawled down the stairs, the leaning sun glinting off the mended glasses. He had not touched me since Point Reyes and did not move to do so now. I knew that he would honor my time-out. It made me feel safe and comfortable with him, sun- and food-stunned, boneless and caught fast in this moment. That there was a tight, fine wire of tension between us, somewhere far down, did not bother me. I had time to explore that or not, all the time in the world.

"I have to sleep," I said. "Later . . . later I'll make dinner for you, if you'll let me; I got some stuff in Palo Alto yesterday, and it doesn't seem like Laura's going to come back anytime soon to eat it. Just let me go home and take a nap and then we'll have a long dinner and then it will be now again, and who knows about that? But I need a bath, and I ought to call Glynn, and I really have got to sleep. Will you come to dinner?"

"I don't go down there," he said. "Not much; only when I have to. But I'll take you up on dinner if you'll cook it at my place. I've got the essentials for that. I'll play my blues for you, and if you're really respectful and ask me nicely I'll show you some of my equipment. Earthquake equipment, I mean; get that look of panic off your face."

"That was not panic. That was awe and wonderment. Okay for dinner, if you'll come help me tote the stuff up to your place. It's the makings for a kind of bouillabaisse."

"Done," he said, and reached down to me and pulled me up, and we walked back to the Jeep, brushing the dust and grit of Henry Miller's staircase off our rumps.

When he came to help me carry the food up, it was just past six, and I had slept hard and showered and felt cool and clean and preternaturally clear-headed. The golden haze of the past twenty-four hours was gone.

"I need to tell you now that I've decided that the time-out has got to be permanent," I said, not looking at him beside me on the path. He said nothing, merely grunted amiably, and shifted the Styrofoam cooler in his arms. Behind us Curtis capered and nosed wetly at the backs of our knees, puppyish in his relief that his person had, after all, come back.

"I mean, I thought about it hard, and it isn't fair to you or me," I went on, as if he had argued with me. "And it would be terribly unfair to Glynn, and to Pom, too. He's done nothing but good for people all his life; I can't just . . . lie out here in bed with you while he's down at the clinic until all hours, or slogging through another boring dinner to try to get some more funds—"

"I can see your point," T.C. said affably.

"I mean, think about Glynn," I continued, as if he had not spoken. "She needs a mother, not a . . . an—"

"Don't do that, Merritt," he said rather sharply. "Don't call yourself names, don't categorize yourself. You were going to say adulteress, weren't you? I'm not going to listen to that. Maybe, just maybe Glynn needs to know what a full, whole, real woman is; maybe she needs to know what joy is; but that's neither here nor there. If you say time-out, time-out it will be. I'm not going to argue with you. It's enough that you want to. And I know that you do, even if you don't."

"I didn't say I didn't want to," I said rather sullenly. "I couldn't say that after the way I've behaved, could I?"

"If you're determined to be Hester Prynne I can't stop you," he said with what sounded close to laughter under his voice. "But you haven't even earned your A yet, so why don't you let up on yourself? Speaking of Glynn, she called while you were asleep. I almost forgot."

"What did she say? Is anything wrong?"

"Absolutely nothing, unless you consider a trip to the mall for a movie and some shopping a calamity. I myself would. Relax. Her friend's father is taking them. She's having a great time. She said *cool* four separate times. There was much giggling and squealing in the background. I gather she isn't starving; her mouth was definitely full of something."

"Did she . . . did she ask about Laura? Or about me, what I was doing?"

"Nope. She was fully as concerned about her elders as any sixteen-year-old on her way to the mall would be. She did, however, ask about Curtis."

I let my breath out in a long, slow sigh.

"It sounds okay," I said. "I should be glad she's having such a good time. But I feel guilty, too; I've hardly thought about her in twenty-four hours—"

"For shame. What a terrible mother you are. You're right to deny yourself the pleasures of the flesh. But I draw the line at mortifying it. If we can't screw, at least we can eat. Are you a good cook?"

I didn't answer. I was aware, suddenly, of how prim and presumptuous my little speech had sounded.

"T.C., listen, I'm sorry if I sounded like the church lady," I said. "I can be awfully stuffy sometimes. It's just that when I woke up from my nap I needed some . . . context or something, needed to know where I fit, and where I fit is back there. If you think that means that I don't want to, you know, do that with you, you're wrong. I want that very much, but I'm not going to do it. I'll try not to be all over you for the rest of the night. And yeah, I am a good cook. Do you understand what I'm trying to say?"

He stopped on the trail and turned, and traced the line of my mouth with his free hand, looking serious and sleepy-eyed. My mouth flamed with heat, and I swallowed hard and turned my head away.

"I understand," he said softly. "It's okay. The pull of home is one of the strongest in the world. E.T., phone home. Shit. I almost forgot about this, too. A guy called you this morning before I came to pick you up, but I don't know who it was. I was downstairs, and the machine got it. The storm last night fried the machine again, so all I could make out was 'just tell her I called.'"

"What kind of voice? What kind of accent?" I said, more sharply than I meant.

"Couldn't tell for the static. I'm sorry. I really did forget. You can call when we get up to the tower. It would be your husband, wouldn't it?"

"Probably. I ought to check in; you know, I told you his mother has been very ill."

"You don't have to justify calling your husband to me, baby," he said gently.

I loved him in that moment, tenderly and without tension.

"Your wife is a damned fool, T.C.," I said, and this time he did not answer me.

When we reached the tower, he carried the cooler up for me and then whistled to Curtis.

"You need to be left alone now," he said at the door. "And I need to check the equipment. I think we'll eat outside; it's going to be a terrific night. Probably cold later on, with so little wind. The stars will be phenomenal. I'll make us a fire then, and play you some Earl Hooker. I've got one of the very few albums he ever made. Slide guitar; there's nothing like it. I've been trying to learn it, but I can't even come close. Go on, Merritt, and tend to your business. You're as jumpy as a flea on a griddle. Pity to waste good bouillabaisse on a nervous woman."

I smiled at him, my heart hammering with confusion and a kind of gathering anticipation, as though some interior engine had revved up a notch, moving me closer to an inevitable conclusion that I could not name.

"I won't be long," I said. "Mommee has probably burnt down the clinic. Fix me a drink and I'll be right down."

He and Curtis left, and I approached the telephone and sat down on the edge of his bed, looking at it. I knew, without knowing how, that this call would forever after divide time for me, but I did not know how that might happen. I did not want to pick up the receiver, to dial the house on the river—my house; why could I not think of it as that?—and wait for the fragile lines between it and this tower to solidify, to reshape reality.

"I could just forget it," I said to myself. "If T.C. had, I'd never know about this call. I don't strictly have to do this; if it had been an emergency he would have called back."

But I did have to do it, and so I pulled the phone toward me and looked out over the sweep of trees undulating away toward the sea, their tops going pink in the darkening sky now, and dialed my house, and sat back to wait, stretching my legs out before me on the bed.

The phone rang and rang, with the hollowness that always means no one is at the other end. I looked at my watch; after nine now, back home. Was he at the clinic this late? Out with the African team and their charismatic leader? Despite my nervousness, the burring phone annoyed me; I had been primed for this connection. I started to hang up, and then the phone was lifted, and a voice said, "The Doctor is in," and laughed.

It was a rich, low voice with, somehow, the dark of loamy earth and the scent of sunny grass in it: a woman's voice. I knew who it was, even though I knew also that I had never heard her speak when she was at the clinic before, much less seen her. I did not move or breathe. I could not seem to think of any words. I could not hang up, either.

"Terry?" she said finally, "I'm sorry we're running late. Pom's in the shower now. You all go on and we'll meet you in twenty minutes max."

I said nothing. I still did not breathe.

"Is that you, Ter?" she said, and very slowly and gently I put the receiver back in its cradle. For a long while I simply sat there on T. C. Bridgewater's bed, watching the pink fade from the sky and the silhouettes of the redwoods darken against it, their needles like brush strokes of India ink. I thought how easy it would be simply to crawl under the Chief Joseph blanket and slide into sleep. To sleep, and sleep, and sleep.

When I finally stood up, it was just a few minutes before full dark. The tender shaving of a new moon, almost transparent, rode above the trees and a great star bloomed above it, the first I could see. My ears rang and I could feel my pulse beating in my throat and wrists, but there was a tickle of senseless laughter at the corners of my mouth, too, and down deep and low in my stomach, the slow heating of the iron core. I took a deep breath and ran my fingers through my hair. I could see no mirror in the room, but my hair felt wild, and my cheeks, when I laid my cold hands on them, flamed as if with fever. I was suddenly conscious of the vast loneliness around me, of the amplitude of space and the relentless coming on of unbroken night, and felt a flutter of the cold, old fear I had felt on the bridge this morning. Had it really only been this morning? Suddenly I wanted light and sound and the smell and touch of T.C., just those things and nothing else. I ran down the long, steep steps in one swoop, without seeming to touch the railing. My entire body was light with the fear. It was only when I reached the boards of the veranda that I realized that I still clutched the blanket, trailing it after me.

He was drowsing on the sofa, covered with a pile of blankets and a sleeping Curtis, one hand laid against his bearded cheek, one brushing the floor beside him. He had good hands, long and brown and strong. Warm hands. I wanted to feel them on me as I wanted air to breathe. I stood, trying to get my breath, looking at him. He woke as though he felt the look. Curtis lifted his head, too.

"What's wrong?"

"Nothing. I didn't talk to him. A woman answered. I know who she is. It was probably nothing. I couldn't say a word; finally I just hung up. I feel like such a fool . . . "

I slowed and stopped.

He said nothing, only lay propped on one elbow, looking steadily at me.

"I want to rescind the time-out, T.C.," I said. "Can I do that?"

After a long moment, he said, "This is my cue to tell you that I don't take advantage of ladies whose husbands have just shit on them. But I can't do that, because I'll take you any way I can get you and be grateful for whatever changed your mind. I'm not going to have one iota of regret afterward, but if you think you are, you'd better tell me now."

"No regrets," I said. "I mean that, T.C. No regrets."

"Then," he said, sitting up and holding out his arms to me, "come here to me. Come here and let me love you. It's time somebody did it right."

And, shivering and beginning, without knowing it, to cry, I let the blanket fall to the deck and went into his arms.

Much, much later we lay in his bed upstairs with the stove throwing dancing red shadows around the room and only the incredible silver starlight pouring down on us from the sky-light, a cold, old radiance. We had not eaten the bouillabaisse; I had not, after all, cooked it. We had not listened to Earl Hooker. He had not shown me his earthquake equipment.

There is a popular song: "I want a man with a slow hand." Lying in the crook of his arm, letting my breathing slow, final-ly, to normal, I thought of that song and felt my body flush all over at the words. A slow hand. Yes. T. C. Bridgewater had, among other things, a slow hand. Our coming together had been as soft and slow and without urgency as the warm, delib-erate ripples in a tide pool. Only at the last had the urgency come crashing in, a scalding, red-black tide from the open sea that took me down with it, far, far down, so that I could only hear the sounds I was making, and that he was, as if from the bottom of an ocean. When I swam at last to the surface, he was laughing. I began to laugh, too. In all the times that I had made love with Pom, I could never remember laughing. Pom's love was like Pom: intense, focused, very, very direct. T.C.'s was utterly different, and like T.C. himself. Indolent. Inven-tive. Teasing to the point of near madness.

Slow.

I loved it. My whole body glowed with it, as if I had been scrubbed all over inside and out with hot water and warm oil. I laughed in it, cried out in it, opened all of myself to take it and give it back; tasted it on my tongue and breathed it in as deeply as if it had been pure oxygen. As soon as it was ended I begged for more and got it. By the time we had stumbled upstairs into the bed, I was so sated with it that I could not lift my head from his arm.

"Don't open the skylight," I said to T.C. when we had managed to crawl under the Chief Joseph blanket. "I'll go right out it on a breath of cold air."

"No more?" he said, running the tips of his fingers from my breasts down my stomach and into the warm pit of me.

"Please, sir, can I have some more?" I said, moving slowly against his fingers.

He rolled over me and held himself above me, looking down. His hair fell into his eyes, and his teeth flashed in the black beard. Starlight poured down over his head and shoulders, melted silver ore.

"If you want a repeat performance, you have to assure me you do C.P.R.," he said.

"I do anything," I said, reaching up to pull him down. "Anything at all. You cannot conceive of anything I don't do."

Deep into the night we lay on our backs and watched the stars through the skylight. They burned with such chill brilliance that they seemed to pulse slowly against the black velvet sky. I have never again seen stars like those. They were, in that moment, fully as alive and sentient as we were.

"What am I looking at?" I said. "What are the stars out here?"

"It's kind of hard to tell, with just a slice of sky showing. Let's see. Arcturus, going down. See, the orange one? Vega was the first one you saw at nightfall. Deneb just overhead. It's almost impossible to tell about the constellations from here. If we were outside you could probably see Perseus over in the northeast, but Pegasus is too far southeast, and the Dipper has gone down by now. You'd see them at home, though. And you'd still see the Summer Triangle. Maybe you can see a little of that here. Back home you could see the rising of the Boat and what they call the wet constellations, water carrier, fishes, and southern fish. They mean fall's coming. We can't see them out here yet."

"Same stars, then. But different sky."

"Right," he said drowsily. "You know, I think that the most awful, the loneliest thing in the world, would be to see different stars in a different sky. There'd be nothing of what you knew then. Total alienation, total newness. I wonder if the human spirit could stand it long. The bravest people in the world have always seemed to me the ones who sailed out so far that they were following different stars in a different sky. Like the ancient Bora Borans did, when they sailed all that hideous long way across the ocean in outriggers, guided by a strange star they knew only from their folklore and the old songs. God, think of it—different stars in a different sky. It makes my blood run cold. This is better; this you can bear. The same stars in a different sky, I mean."

I turned my face into his neck, hiding there, shutting out the presence of that different sky.

"Be my same stars, T.C.," I whispered, salt in my eyes and throat. "Be my same stars, because I have most surely come a terrible long way under a different sky."

"I will," he said back, into my tangled hair. I felt his tongue touch my eyelids, and knew that he tasted the salt.

"I will, always."

10

If you have been married a long time to the same person, the most profoundly disorienting thing that can happen to you is to wake beside someone else. No matter what you have done in the night with the new person, no matter how you felt about that, those first moments beside another body are an earthquake in the soul. It's because sleep is the deepest place we go besides death, I thought, lying immobile beside T.C.'s long, still body in the cold room. You come up out of the deepest place totally vulnerable. In those free-floating moments a familiar body beside you is your only anchor to life. I lay very still, listening to T.C.'s even breathing, afraid to move, afraid of what might flood over me and sweep me away. The deepest I have ever gone and the nearest I have ever been before to lost is in sleep, until last night, I thought. I was that deep and that lost last night. I don't feel like I can ever get myself back.

I was paralyzed with pure, fresh guilt, the awful and total guilt of the child certain of his irredeemability, and with the loss of anyone who could conceivably be Merritt Fowler of Atlanta, Georgia, wife of Pom, mother of Glynn. I wanted those familiar definitions back so simply and terribly that I scrambled silently out of the disheveled bed and pulled on my scattered clothes and ran on tiptoe to the door, still holding my shoes and socks. I did not look back at T.C., and when Curtis came to the door of the tower room and whined anxiously at me, I whispered through stiff lips, "I can find my own way this morning. Stay Curtis. Carpe diem." And with that I was out and gone, slipping hastily on the dew-slick steps, my feet and heart numb, racing through the cool, pearly dawn for the lodge and a shower. Hot water; hot water will bring her back, I said over and over under my breath, witlessly. I've got to get her back. But then, stopping still on the gravel path down to the lodge, I cried aloud, "Oh, T.C.!" I doubled over as if in pain, and then ran on, toward the woman I had lost somewhere in the air between Atlanta and this place. Better her than no one; better anyone than that.

There was no fog this morning, and the great trees were still at their tops, and the silence was thick. If birds sang I could not hear them. The air at ground level was much warmer than the tower room had been, and when I gained the dark, stale lodge my feet were no longer numb. I ran through the rooms flipping light switches, stopping only to put on coffee, and then tore through my airless bedroom and into the shower.

I stood there for a long time, near scalding water beating down on my body, running down my face, sluicing through my hair, scouring my mouth and nose and ears and closed eyes. I scrubbed; I washed every part of me in the French pine soap Caleb Pringle had put out. I brushed my nails and the bottoms of my feet with a little, wooden-handled brush, and opened my mouth to let the hot stream run down my throat. It felt warm and clean down to my stomach, but it stopped there. The cleansing heat did not reach the dark place in my groin where this new woman lived. I could not wash her away and wept in the water like a child because of that, my tears swirling away down the drain to meet some creek or river hidden among the redwoods. When I finally got out of the shower I was as red all over as a boiled lobster, and except for the secret cave where last night had been born, the old Merritt was back.

My busybody mind moved fast to boot out the sick, sticky guilt, and I realized only later that I was talking aloud.

"Okay. It happened and it felt fantastic and it's over. I'm not going to beat up on myself, because I loved it. There's no sense pretending I didn't. But now I'm going home. I'm going to go get Glynn and get T.C. to take us to the airport in San Francisco and we'll just wait there until we can get a plane. I'll try once more to get Laura through Stuart, and then she's on her own. I can't wait for her. I'll make T.C. understand about this, and I'm not even going to call Pom. Whatever he's got going back there with what's-her-name, he can do it someplace other than my house. If Mommee's not out of there, I'll take her someplace myself. I'll tell Amy to go fuck a duck. I'll get Ina back. Maybe Glynn and I will go to a spa or something, or take a cruise, or maybe I'll see if Crisscross can find me some freelance work, or better than that, a real job. I'll bring the dogs in the house and let the rats take over if they want to. All of that; whatever. But I'm going to do it *now*."

I sensed that if I stopped I was lost, and so I put on shorts and a clean T-shirt I found in my dresser drawer, and combed my wild, wet hair severely back and knotted it on my neck. I had not worn it this way since Los Angeles, I remembered; since then it had flown free. I looked briefly into the mirror and saw a thin, white woman with prominent copper freckles and ridged cheekbones and blank eyes, and looked hastily away. I did not look again. I drank a quick cup of coffee and slipped into sneakers and went out into the brightening morning, banging the door behind me.

It was already hot. The birds had started up, but only sporadically, and sounded muffled, as if through fog. But there was no fog. Still, the tops of the huge trees were indistinct. The day was cloudless, but it was not clear. I had scarcely gotten past the empty garage before I felt sweat start under my arms and at the edges of my hair. In the heat and scuzziness, the redwoods that had soothed and solaced and enchanted me looked flat and bleached, as if they were paper cutouts left too long in the sun. Home, it was time to go home. . . . By the time I had reached the big turn in the road, I was trotting fast.

I met him there. I stopped abruptly, simply staring at him. I had not heard him coming down the road, and I don't think he had heard me, either. His eyes widened in the darkness around them, and he stood still, too. For a long moment neither of us spoke. I could not hear any other sounds except my own quick, light breathing.

He wore faded khaki hiking shorts and a blue Oxford shirt, and he too had scrubbed himself; droplets clung to his beard and hair. His legs were long and brown and muscled; I remembered the feel of them, their strength and their warmth, and felt the red start in my neck. He stood with his hands straight down beside him, looking at me. Then, tentatively, he raised one of them toward me and said, "Merritt. I missed you. I woke up and found you gone and thought you had . . . left."

"I can't do that with you anymore, T.C.," I said, and stopped because my voice simply faded out. I stood there, staring, the separate parts of his face burning themselves into my brain, but not, somehow, adding up to a face. His eyes, his hawk's nose, his mouth . . .

With dizzying speed the eyes and nose and mouth assembled themselves and it was T.C.'s face and his body and I ran straight into his arms, throwing my own around his with more strength than I thought I had. He made a soft, choked noise into my hair, but he did not speak. I rubbed my head back and forth into the hollow of his neck; I pressed myself against him, scrubbing my body against his; I all but climbed him as I would a tree.

"Yes, I can," I cried fiercely, "and I have to, and I will, right here. Right here, T.C.! In the daylight, on this road, in this gravel, under these trees, right now, please, please—"

"God," I heard him whisper, "God. I was so scared you'd left me—"

"*Now!*" I said, and bit his bottom lip and jerked my arms loose from his and tore at the buttons of his shirt, at the fly of the shorts. "Goddamn it, T. C. Bridgewater, *now!*"

And we did it there on the hot, dusty path with our shorts caught around our ankles and the cross, startled jeers of a pair of jays overhead, and our own words and cries rising up into the still trees as if to set them whispering, swaying. Last night's dizzy plummet into heat and red darkness took me again, and I lost myself again, and felt the exact, precise moment when he lost himself, too. Just at that instant, just then, the earth moved beneath us and seemed to wheel over our heads and into the sky. By the time it had stopped rolling and shivering, we were loose and tangled and emptied out, still joined, beginning to laugh crazily.

"By God, how did you like that?" he said breathlessly. "Can I say it? Did the earth move for you?"

"Damn Hemingway for making that a cliché," I whispered, trying to get my voice to work, aware that I had ridden another earthquake like a wild horse and was not, this time, in the least afraid. I wished, even, that the earth would move again. But it did not, and gradually the birdsong came back, and the trees came into focus, and still we lay there, neither of us wanting to loosen ourself from the other.

Finally, though, I moved, and lay myself along the length of him, feeling his long body pressing itself into the earth beneath me.

"Was that a big one? It wasn't, was it?" I said.

"Nope. Same as we've been getting for a couple of weeks now. There wasn't anything unusual on my stuff this morning, except a little more recorded action. Curtis and Forrest both present and snoring. Nope, that was just a reminder. Sort of a 'that's nothing; look what I can do.' It really adds a hell of a fillip, though, doesn't it? Were you scared?"

"No," I said dreamily, resting my cheek against his damp chest. I could feel his heart slowing. "This time I wasn't scared. Maybe what people should do in earthquakes is . . . that."

"I'll call the U.S. Geological Survey right now and get them on it," he said. "Wow. Now I've only got two wishes left."

"What wish were you granted? What are the other two?"

"The one that was granted was to make love to you in an earthquake," he said. "That's a new wish. The other two are to be in a really big one and never to leave this place. But if I had to pick one, I'd pick the one I just got."

"Did it feel like you thought it would?"

"It felt like . . . yeah. What I thought it would. Actually, I've felt something like it before. It's the reason I'm up here, the reason behind everything."

"Will you tell me? Can you?"

"I'll try. I want you to understand it. It's the why of me, I guess," he said, but for a while he did not go on. I lay there, warmth from him and seemingly from the very earth beneath him seeping into my arms and legs, making them heavy and boneless and at the same time weightless. I did not think I had ever felt so totally, perfectly in harmony with the world around me, strange though it was. The frantic, fractured woman of the early morning was gone.

"I told you I'd never been in a big one, but I've been in a sort of big one," he said slowly. "Big enough to do more than rattle a few dishes. Two or three people died in Oakland when a parking deck collapsed. It was while I was at Berkeley that time; you remember, I told you about the convention, and how I came to find the tower and all? Well, the day before that there was a quake centered on the Hayward, up around Rogers Creek. I was walking across the campus when it hit. I've never felt anything even remotely like that before. It was as if . . . I came alive for the first time in my life. Really alive, in every cell and atom and follicle—there was a totality about it that just eclipsed everything else I'd ever known or dreamed of knowing. It was like, for the first time in my life, I was whole. There was a whole me there and I'd never even really known I was incomplete. I remember reading somewhere that when the Loma Prieta hit, some kids on the campus at USC Santa Cruz just spontaneously jumped up and started dancing in a circle. I did that, too. Before it stopped I was capering and whooping like a crazy man, like I was possessed. And I was. When it stopped, and I knew I wouldn't feel it anymore, I understood for the first time how ol' Ronnie Reagan must have felt in that god-awful movie when he said, 'Where's the rest of me?' I knew that after that, until I felt it again, there'd only be part of me walking around. It was then that I knew I'd have to come out here. When I got up into the Big Basin the next day I found exactly where. It's just a matter of waiting now."

He stopped and looked up at me keenly, waiting for me to speak. I could not find anything to say. Finally I said, "I wish you could find something that would . . . complete you, make you whole . . . that didn't mean death and misery to other people."

For the first time since I had known him I saw real anger in his eyes, and a quick, dark grief, and he became, for that instant, someone I did not know. I pulled away reflexively and he pressed me back again, hard.

"Don't take this away from me, Merritt," he whispered fiercely against the side of my face. "I'm going to lose the only other thing that ever did it for me."

"What was that?" I whispered back, licking the crackling of dried sweat at his temple. It tasted of him.

"You know it was last night, and just now," he said. "You know it was you. You know you aren't going to stay. And I can't go. Don't make me say that again, either."

I lay against him, sadness like a glacier around my heart. I tried for lightness.

"T.C., you're going to have to find some more accessible stars to hitch your wagon to," I said.

"Not after that day, not after last night, not after this morning. You can't go back, even when you can't go on, either. Don't settle, Merritt. Don't ever settle. Life's too short."

I was silent against him. Around us the heat shimmered, the day hummed. Presently I said, "T.C., what are we lying on?"

He moved his buttocks experimentally.

"Just offhand I'd say I'm lying on pinecones and maybe a dried squirrel turd. If you don't know by now what you're lying on, all has been for naught."

I laughed, suddenly happy. With T.C. it was always going to be the laughter that made me whole, set me free.

"No, I mean what is the earth? What kind of rock?"

"What are the stars? What is the earth? What are you doing, running your sun lines? Finding your boundaries?"

"I need to know all the way where I am, down to the core of the earth, up to the edge of the universe. I need to fix you in this firmament. I need to fix me in it."

He eased out from under me and pulled up his shorts.

"I hope some rosy-cheeked scoutmaster with an overbite hasn't got the field glasses of his entire troop trained on us," he said wryly. "They'll grow up never screwing at all. Okay.

These are almost exactly the words of a U.S. Geological Survey guy I met up here and asked the same question, almost the only person besides you who's never laughed at me about this earthquake stuff. 'The primary rock in the Big Basin area is Butano sandstone. It was formed in the lower to middle Eocene, forty-three to fifty-seven million years ago. It's light-gray to buff, very fine-to-coarse-grained arkosic sandstone in thin to very thick beds, interbedded with dark gray to brown mudstone and shale. The amount of this mudstone and shale varies from ten to forty percent. This particular formation is about three thousand meters thick and typically dips ten to thirty degrees toward the southwest. Arkosic sandstone is a feldspar-rich, coarse-grained sandstone typically derived from granite. Most of the Sierra Nevada range in California is formed of granite older than eighty million years. This rock, our rock, would have been formed when the Farallon oceanic plate was diving northwestward toward Japan. That is to say, these sediments would have eroded off an arc of volcanoes like those found today in Japan, and the Aleutians, even the Cascades. To the southwest of Big Basin, the dominant rock is the Santa Cruz mudstone, which was formed in the Miocene, five to twenty-four million years ago, and is brown and gray to light-gray, buff, and light yellow shale and mudstone with minor amounts of sandstone.' Will that do?"

"Yes," I smiled. "It's somehow very satisfying to know that. Did you memorize it?"

"I did. I asked him to write it down, and he did. It felt important to know that. It was important to him, too; I keep meaning to look him up again."

I nodded.

"T.C., can we spend the whole day naked?" I said presently.

"Aren't you the greedy little minx! Are you this greedy back home?"

Suddenly I could laugh about Atlanta and the house on the river, all of it.

"No. At home I'm . . . I guess you'd say I'm grateful."

He whooped with laughter, rolled over and over with it, choked, gulped, breathed hard, laughed some more.

"'Please, sir, can I have some more?'" T.C. mimicked

both me and Oliver Twist. "Shit, Merritt, if you don't take anything else back with you, take this fine greediness. Demand, by God. *Don't settle!*"

"Nossir."

"To answer your question, sure, we can spend the whole day naked. First we'll go swimming. I know the perfect place for a hot day. Then we'll go home and take naps. Then we'll screw. Then I'll show you my toys. Then we'll screw. Then we'll cook that bouillabaisse, or else throw it out before it poisons us. Then we'll screw. Then I'll play my tapes for you, and maybe a little slide guitar, and then we'll—"

"How doth the busy little bee improve each shining hour," I said contentedly. "Do you think we might be a trifle overextended for one day?"

"Well, we could cut out the swimming and the naps and the bouillabaisse, but not the—"

"Enough. Let's start off and see how far we get. Can we do it all naked?"

"Why not? Curtis ain't gon' tell. Forrest would if he could, but he can't. You're right. No hurry. Save some for tomorrow. We've got lots of time."

I looked up at him from where I lay on my back, mutely and with pain.

"We've already had more than lots of people ever have," he said softly, kissing the tip of my nose. "For all you know, it might be days and days before Laura comes back. Don't count, Merritt. Carpe diem."

"Carpe diem," I whispered. Above us the sun finally broke free from the entangling tops of the redwoods, and rode full into the sky.

Ever since college, there has been lodged in my mind a passage from (I think) *The Odyssey*, chronicling a time on the voyage when Odysseus and his men drifted in perfect peace and harmony through sunny blue seas, before fresh winds, through land and water so beautiful that I cannot recall any details, only a golden wash of honey-sweet sun and warm crystal water where dolphins played and time itself sang lazily in the scented wind, stopped and still. I remember from it only a sense of lazy perfection, but it is such a strong impression that since that time it has been the standard against which I measure perfect days.

"What a perfect summer day," someone will say, and I will think of that passage, and of course, the day in question pales. How could it not? Or, "This has really been a day to remember," and that time on Odysseus's journey will spring to mind, and I will think, "Not bad, for mere mortals."

The comparison had never spoiled any real days for me, but it has always been there, even though the grownup part of my mind knows full well that such days do not come to human beings.

But that day came close. It came very close. At the end of it I was able to whisper, in the pine-smelling dark of T.C.'s veranda, "Eat your hearts out, you smug Greek bastards," and mean it. Oh, it was such a day, it really was. A pinnacle day, a ball bearing on which a life turns.

When at last we picked ourselves up from the Butano sandstone and the pine needles and dust, it was close to eleven, and the heat was formidable. But it was dry heat, not the thick, wet heat of home, and instead of draining, it soothed us to sleepiness and indolence. All that day I felt heavy-lidded and sweetly weighted in my limbs, needing to reach out frequently and touch T.C. languidly on whatever part of him was nearest, to lean my head against him, to slouch against him, to feel his weight take mine.

We tied our clothing together and hung it around our necks and, wearing only our shoes, ambled down the dwindling path beyond the lodge, deeper and deeper into the redwoods, winding steadily down. Even in the deepest shadow, where moisture still clung and we walked in a green darkness, it was hot. By the time we reached T.C.'s secret swimming hole, we were both lightly sheened all over with sweat. Only the smallest and most arbitrary breezes reached here, but when they did, they felt so purely sensual and fine on my body that I found myself thinking I really must look into nudism.

I said as much to T.C., who laughed and said he didn't want anybody else but me looking at him bare-assed.

"Why not?" I said. "You have a wonderful body. I do, too.

I wonder why I never thought I did before. Right now I don't care who sees this magnificent body, and I don't know why you do, either."

"Have you ever seen an old movie called *The Enchanted Cottage?*" he said, tracing the line of my hipbone with a finger-tip. "Where those two supposedly ugly people look perfect and beautiful to each other, as long as they stay in the cottage? I think that's happened to us. Anybody else seeing us would point and laugh and holler, and then call the cops. We're a walking pair of skeletons, two long, bony middle-aged loonies flitting buck naked through the redwoods, patting each other. Don't kid yourself. Life is real and life is earnest."

"Bull. You no more believe that than I do. Life is perfect. You want to stop a minute and jump dese bones with dem bones?"

"Wait a while. We're here. Look, right through those laurels. Let's see what happens to dese dry bones in water."

It was a deep little pool of dark water, cupped in rock and thick with giant ferns, green and swaying as a tropical kelp bed, where a small silver creek fell from a ridge and paused before running on. The embracing rocks were huge and flat-tened and gray, and the tops of them lay in sun, but the lich-ened sides lay in shadow, and where they cradled the pool was far down and bearded with the ferns. Over them the great trees leaned close, so that only the peculiar shafts of thick golden light reached the forest floor and the water. The silence and stillness was so complete that only when we parted the curtaining laurels and stood on the rocks did we hear the sturdy chuckle of the creek and the little falls.

"Oh, Lord. Oh, how magical. What is this place? Does it have a name?" I breathed.

"I think it has some pedestrian name like Smith's Creek, or something. I did know, but I forgot. It's not on the park maps, I don't think; I've never seen anybody else down here. I hereby name it Merritt's Creek. You want to go in?"

I did a foolhardy thing; I scrambled down a rock, found a level place, and dove into the dark water. Only later did I think that I might have broken my neck. An older, deeper part of me knew the pool would take me gently.

"I'm in," I gasped against the breath-stealing cold. "What's keeping you?"

He dove in, a long flash of brown in a sun shaft, and when his seal-sleek black head bobbed up beside me, he gasped, "That was stupid. I don't ever want you to do anything like that again."

"You did the same thing."

"I knew it was deep and free of rocks and logs. You didn't."

"Well, somehow I did. Maybe water talks to me like the stupid fault does to you. Don't preach at me, T.C. I'm not a child."

He spat water and grinned.

"Today you are. Are we having our first fight?"

The water felt wonderful all of a sudden, the deep, aching cold gone, the lingering soft chill effervescent against my body. Looking down, I saw that he and I both were outlined with tiny, silvery bubbles.

"No," I said. "I feel too good for that. Look at the bubbles. It's like swimming in champagne, isn't it?"

I swam up against him, backing him against a submerged rock. I pressed my body against his, feeling the water take it away, pressing it back. There were subterranean currents, though from where I could not tell. The slight resistance was profoundly sensual.

"Have you ever done it in champagne?" I said against his chest.

"I'm good, but I'm not that good," he said ruefully. "Ask me again sometime when I'm not neck deep in ice water."

"You may be sure that I will."

We swam until the cold began to make our arms and legs rubbery, and then we crawled out and lay on the sun-heated rocks, breathing in the silence and the smell of the woods, feeling the sun's red weight on our eyelids. We lay there until the water's chill dried to silky coolness and that turned to heat and then to the slight stickiness of sweat.

"Lunchtime," he said finally, and we got up and stretched and looked at each other.

"Better put our clothes on," he said. "People still drive

down this road occasionally, as far as the lodge, just to see where it goes. Unless you want to shock the Kleinfelder family of Ottumwa, Iowa, out of their leisure suits."

"Nah, I'm for your eyes only. The Kleinfelders will never know what they missed."

Back at the tower the sun smote the earth where the trees had been thinned out, and I heard for the first time that old master sound of summer, the lazy hum of cicadas in the encircling forest. I closed my eyes and for an instant was home beside the river. Then I opened them and shook my head. That was for later. That was for another lifetime, or a past one.

We ate lunch on the shabby veranda, under the canvas awning T.C. had rigged up. He brought bread and Brie and some leftover grapes back when he returned from checking the answering machine, and a couple of bottles of cold white wine.

"I can count on the fingers of one hand the days that have been too hot to stay up there, but this is one of them," he said. "Today we spend right here."

Curtis had staked out a cool spot under the water spigot where the earth was splotched with dampness, and thumped his tail in welcome, but did not indulge in any unnecessary welcoming frolicking. He went back to panting his doggy grin. T.C. pointed, and I saw Forrest's shifty jet eyes glittering from a terra-cotta pot with a lush crop of thyme in it. T.C. held out his arm and snapped his fingers, but Forrest preferred the damp earth and the sheltering thyme, and only twinkled his snout slightly.

"Did you know that in New Guinea they eat your cousins, you dirty rat?" T.C. told Forrest. "God-awful big things called Capas, or something. You're lucky there are no New Guineans around. You're already seasoned with thyme."

"Do I have to keep these clothes on?" I said. "I miss the sight of your naked magnificence, and I'm hot as if it were August in Atlanta."

"Shuck right out," he said. "Just let me set up the screen here. If the Kleinfelders come by, it'll give us time to get dressed. I go around without clothes a lot in hot weather, and once a park ranger caught me naked as a jaybird, lying down here reading *The Prince of Tides*."

"What happened?"

"Nothing. He asked me how it was going and I said pretty good, and he drove on down the road. Don't ever try to wear *The Prince of Tides* as a loincloth, though."

He unfolded a tattered burlap screen that leaned against the tower base and set it up around the sofa and chairs and upended cable spool that served as a coffee table. I was out of my clothes in an instant, tossing them into one of the rump-sprung chairs. He sat back on his heels, smiling at me.

"Come here," he said, holding out his arms, and I walked over and into them. His face came just to my waist. He buried it in the space between my ribs, and took a deep breath and let it out again.

"You smell like clean water and woods dirt," he said, and I could feel his mouth against my skin when he spoke. He kissed my stomach, and my navel, and moved his lips down and down, and I felt my legs go boneless once more, and warmth bloom in the pit of my stomach.

"Care for a nooner?" I murmured.

"Don't mind if I do," he said, and got up and pulled me with him onto the deep old couch. Slow: Once again it was all slow, all delicacy and tasting and teasing, all slow-spreading like spilled honey. Then the plunging dark. When I had found my way back, T.C. was laughing and Curtis was whining and barking and nosing at us with a cold, frantic black muzzle.

T.C. reached over and patted him, and gradually he stopped his fussing, looked at us reproachfully, and went back to his spot under the spigot. He lay there with his nose on his paws, gazing at us unblinkingly.

"Curtis is as good as saltpeter in college mashed potatoes," I said ruefully. "I'd rather do it in front of a nursery school class."

"Curtis never saw people carrying on like that before. I guess he thought I was killing you, or vice versa."

"You can't tell me you've never done this with anybody else," I said. "If you try to tell me I'm the first one I'm going to pour cold wine on your not-so-private parts."

"I've never done it here," he said, not smiling. "Of course you're not the first; I've been up here a long time, and celibacy is not my thing. But every time before I've taken . . . whoever it was . . . down there. To the lodge. Impresses the hell out of them and spares me the business of waking up beside somebody I don't know and having to make small talk and all that. You're the first for up here. You'll be the only one."

"I thought you didn't like the lodge, and didn't go down there," I said. I was absurdly pleased, pleased almost to tears.

"I don't, and I don't go down there except to screw. I've never had any qualms about that. That's what the place is meant for, screwing. And it's easy to get them to leave down there. That's the other thing it was meant for. Leaving."

"Why is it different with me?" I said, running my hand over his body from his collarbone to his knees. I felt him stir again and smiled sleepily at him.

"Because I love you," he said matter-of-factly. "You know that. Don't fish. Because I love you, and I haven't any of them. And I won't, anybody else. This place is only for you, besides me."

I put my face down into his neck and shut my eyes and lay there, fitted to him from face to feet. I felt him sigh, and then only the soft rise and fall of his breathing. I blinked and let the tears that had gathered on my lower lashes run onto his chest. If he felt them, he gave no indication.

"I love you, too," I whispered. "I do love you. I don't know what that makes me. I don't know where I can go from here with that."

"You don't have to go anywhere," he said into the side of my face. "It doesn't make you anything, except Merritt who loves T.C. right here and now. Feel it all, be it all, do it all, and then leave that lady here with me. That lady can't breathe in any other air but this air. I'll take care of her; I'll keep her for you. When you go back you'll know she's always here, up here in the redwoods with me. Always with me, Merritt."

"Oh, God, why can't I just stay? Why can't I—"

"I'll make a deal with you. You can think precisely one day ahead. You can plan tomorrow right down to the nanosecond; we can do anything on earth you want; there's nothing we can get to in a day that we can't see; nothing we can't do.

But after that you have to cut it off. No planning any further ahead. No looking any further ahead. And then when tomorrow's done, we'll take another day and you can plan that one. Who knows how far we'll get? You've only been here three days. Not even that. We could have . . . who knows how long? Enough to last a lifetime, enough to love a love. But I won't waste any of it worrying about the length of it. Is that a deal?"

"It's a deal."

"Fine. Then what do you want to do tomorrow? There's a lot I'd love to show you, a lot I know you'd love to see—"

"Tomorrow . . . let's screw a whole lot tomorrow," I said. "And between times let's go get you some proper glasses frames. There must be an oculist in Palo Alto. That tape is driving me crazy."

"They're just drugstore glasses. There's a drugstore down in Boulder Creek. Anything else we need to get? You aren't going to get pregnant or anything, are you?"

"I wish I could," I said fiercely. "I wish I could. But no. I'm on the pill; I've got plenty left."

"Well, you don't need to worry that you'll catch anything from me. I'm fine that way. I've had all the tests."

"It never even occurred to me that you wouldn't have," I said.

The sun moved around to the west so that its burning fingers found us, and we moved the sofa around until the shade swallowed it. Then we set the food out on the spool-top table and ate until there were no crumbs left, not a swallow of wine. Curtis had a morsel of Brie and Forrest nibbled a grape, and then all four of us lay back in the dim heat and slept like forest creatures.

When we woke the shadows of the trees across the space that the tower occupied were longer and going blue. The heat still clung to the earth, but some of the red fever had gone out of it. I woke with sweat in the creases of my chin and elbows, my hair loose and sticking to my neck, feeling stunned and cross and gummy. I lay there thinking longingly of a shower, and only then noticed that T.C. was not beside me on the sofa. Curtis was gone, too, and Forrest's eyes no longer glittered in the thyme pot. I sat up and scrubbed my eyes with my fists and looked around.

T.C., dressed only in the khaki shorts and barefoot, knelt under the shake-roofed shed across the yard, peering intently at what I supposed to be his earthquake equipment. His toys. Curtis lay supine beside him, eyes closed. I got up, stretching and smacking my lips around the stale taste in my mouth, and wandered over to look over his shoulder. There was a small cylindrical affair fixed to a board, with paper around it and a pen clipped to a small rod over the cylinder, and beside it a larger device, or perhaps it was two of them. One was a round black object set into a terra-cotta saucer and sunk flush into the earth. Over this, a kind of tripod held a large, square sheet of metal onto which was affixed a coil of some sort. T.C. was looking at some squiggles on the paper apparently made by the pen. I had no earthly idea what any of it was, but I could tell that the cylinder that held the paper was a cardboard Quaker Oats canister. The whole affair had a kind of endearing boy's treehouse look to it, ingenious but hard to take very seriously. Beside it, T.C., with his hair hanging in his eyes and the mended wire spectacles riding on the tip of his nose, looked so like an overgrown preteen that I laughed and reached over and ruffled his hair, loving him simply and wholly.

"Can T.C. come out and play?" I said.

He looked up at me and grinned.

"Want to see my stuff? I made it myself. Works pretty good, if I do say so."

"It's going to be lost on me, but sure. Tell me about it. What's that thingummy you're looking at?"

"That's a drum recorder. First things first. This thing here"—and he touched the square sheet of metal and set it swinging slightly on its spring—"is part of a geophone. A geophone is the actual sensor that converts ground motion into a weak electric signal. Taken together, the whole business adds up to a rudimentary seismograph. See, I took a big hi-fi speaker and took the coil and magnet out, and fastened the magnet to the ground. It's fixed; it moves with the earth. Then I attached the coil to that sheet of metal, for mass, and hung it by the right kind of spring over the magnet. When the ground moves, the magnet will move with it, but the mass will stay still where it is for a second because it has some inertia. The relative motion that occurs then generates a weak electric current that can be amplified and recorded, and that shows that waves from an earthquake are being recorded. See?"

I nodded, though I didn't.

"Okay, now the drum recorder. As you can see, I made this one out of an oatmeal box. I've mounted it on a central shaft there, and I use that little motor to make the cylinder rotate every fifteen minutes. Then I hooked up that amplifier there to amplify the signal from the seismometer and connected that up to a pen-motor that converts the signal and rotates the pen. See there? It draws a line mounted on the paper. That tracks earth movement nearby. In the old days they used to darken the paper with soot from a kerosene lantern turned way up high, and the pen would scratch a line in the soot, and they'd roll the drum in thin shellac to fix the soot on the paper. The pen isn't all that much improvement, but this way I don't burn up my toys."

"Lord, hasn't it all come further than this?" I said, looking around the shed.

"Oh, sure. For one thing you can just get a PC that has an a-two board. That means analog-to-digital computer. You connect the seismometer to that. I've got one upstairs; I just ran the line out the window and down the leg of the tower and buried it underground till I got it out here. This stuff here is just because I wanted to, just because I could. I could have bought a geophone and saved myself a lot of tinkering; you can order them from several weird electronic catalogs in Texas. They use them there to look for trapped oil. Come to that, I could have just bought myself a seismograph, I guess. I haven't spent much of the old man's dough. But I got a kick out of doing it this way. Are you impressed?"

"I'm stunned. You mean you could really predict an earthquake with this stuff?"

"Not predict, exactly, but record action in the area, which helps to predict. Two years before the Loma Prieta a Stanford researcher set up a very sensitive instrument to measure low-frequency electromagnetic waves in the Santa Cruzes. He put it up near where the epicenter was, later. He was actually tracking submarines. For two years there was no big change, but then, a few months before the quake, he noticed a moderate change, and then hours before a really big jump. Of course he only noticed that after the quake, but it shows you that movement and waves can be monitored. What we can't do, even with the best and newest stuff, is predict just when, or precisely where. I depend on my feet to do that. I don't wear shoes much up here."

"What else do you have?"

"You *are* hard to impress, aren't you? Nothing, really, except some books and magazines. I've got *Elementary Seismology*, by the grand old man himself, Charles Richter. He published it in nineteen fifty-eight, and it's still the bible for the profession. I've practically memorized chapter fifteen, Seismograph Theory and Practice. I still read it for fun. I've got *Peace of Mind in Earthquake Country*. It mainly covers how to build structures to withstand quake motions. Most of the pros have it. Of course, Kobe showed us how much use *that* was. And I take a bunch of magazines that the U.S. Geological Survey puts out, and some other stuff. Want to curl up with one of them while I shower and change?"

"No," I said. "I want to shower with you. I guess you mean that showerhead sticking out of the tower leg just above Curtis's water bowl, don't you? I want to take a long, no doubt bone-chilling shower with you, and then I want to go up and fix that damned bouillabaisse at last and put it on to simmer, and *then* I want"—and I reached over and pulled the band of his shorts away from his back and reached in and squeezed both his muscular buttocks—"then I want to see how many times in one day you can do it. Get cracking, T.C. We've miles to go before we sleep."

"Merritt, I do believe I have created an insatiable sex monster. When are you going to get enough of it?"

"When the fat lady sings," I leered, and ran back across the yard and turned the spitting, rusty stream of the shower on, and ducked under it. I was right. It was as cold as glacier water. We stayed under it only long enough to lather up with T.C.'s desiccated soap-on-a-rope, and then dried ourselves off vigorously and gratefully on the thin Fairmont towel that hung on a peg beside the soap. My skin was tingling as I ran up the ladder to the top of the tower, and the trapped heat in the glassed-in aerie felt good. Behind me, T.C. checked the answering machine again, found it still empty, and fetched a bottle of Glenlivet from a cubbyhole under his counter. He poured two healthy shots into squat, heavy glasses of cloudy old crystal, and handed me one. He plopped himself on the bed with his, crossed his legs at the ankle, and propped his head on the piled pillows. He had not dressed after his shower, and except for the strip of white where his shorts usually were, he was red-brown all over, felted with glistening black hair, and, to me, a very beautiful and serviceable man.

"Cook, woman," he said, sipping single malt. "Your reward will be lavish and long."

"In hours or inches?" I said, dragging the bouillabaisse ingredients out of the crowded under-counter refrigerator. They still smelled sweet and briny. I thought we were safe.

"However you want it," he said.

"Just like you said. Lavish and long. *Real* long."

"How about an incentive, instead of a reward?" he said, and I turned to look at him, and saw that despite the cold shower, he was erect once more. I laughed with pure, greedy joy, deep in my throat.

"If I don't get this stew on we'll have to throw it out and order in. But by all means, hold that thought."

"Do you know the one about the old earl whose manservant came in and found him with a hard-on for the first time in years, and said, 'Do you want me to call her ladyship, m'lord?' Well, the old earl said, 'Her ladyship be blowed; ring for the car. I'm going to smuggle this one up to London.' Tarry too long with that stuff and I'm going to take this one into Palo Alto."

"What's a few minutes to a bunch of fish?" I said, and went over to him and fitted myself down upon him, looking down at his brown face in the last of the sun.

"Mmmm," I said, moving slightly, leaning back. "I'm powerfully empty without this. What would you think of a life cast?"

"About what I'd think of a board with a bearskin nailed to it and a hole punched through it," he said, beginning to rock with me.

"What's that?" I laughed, gasping through the laughter.

"The traditional refuge of the Hudson Bay trapper after months in the Arctic without a woman," T.C. said, closing his eyes. "Slow, Merritt. Take it slow, my love . . ."

We ended up eating Brie omelettes, much later. The bouillabaisse boiled itself dry, and we did not notice until the reek of scorching metal filled the tower room.

The fat lady sang at 8:30 P.M.

We were lying together on the bed, propped up on pillows, loosely touching at shoulder and hip, and he was playing his guitar. Actually, he was accompanying Sunnyland Slim, who was rolling out *Do Nothin' Till You Hear From Me* on a plinky old piano. It was one of T.C.'s oldest records, and he handled it as a knight errant might the Grail. He had been instructing me on the movement of the blues from Mississippi to Chicago, and we had gone through Muddy Waters, Howlin' Wolf, Elmore James, and Walter Horton. I was absurdly happy. I loved the rich, wailing music; I loved the tall man who loved it too, and played it. I thought we might listen to it until the black mirror of the skylight grew pale, and then we would sleep. And tomorrow . . . tomorrow there would be more. Of everything.

When the phone rang I did not know what it was. T.C. stopped playing and sat very still. Sunnyland Slim went on plinking. Then T.C. got up and went slowly across the room to pick up the phone. On the way he pulled on his red-and-black checked shirt. It was that gesture that cut through my heart and down into my stomach. Only then did I realize that the phone had rung.

He stood with his back to me, leaning on one knuckled fist on the desk as he held the phone to his ear in the other.

"No need for that," he said pleasantly. "She's right here."

I knew then that the days of gold were over. Whoever it was who sought me—Glynn, Laura, Pom, even Amy—it was that other woman who must answer.

"No," I whispered aloud, tears of pure grief filling my eyes. "I'm not ready."

He held the phone out, not looking at me, and I got up and pulled on my shorts and T-shirt and went slowly across the floor. I understood then his gesture with the shirt. Eden had been breached and we must now cover our nakedness.

I took the phone and tried to speak, could not, and cleared my throat.

"Hello?"

"What are you doing up there?"

It was Glynn's voice, fussy and querulous. I had not heard that tone since she left childhood.

"I'm listening to Sunnyland Slim and fixing to wash dishes," I said, trying for lightness. My voice sounded like dull old sandpaper in my ears.

"What's up with you? You having a good time?"

"No. I'm having a shitty time. I have to leave, tonight, right now. You have to come get me. When can you be here? I have to tell Marcie's stepmother—"

"What on earth? What's wrong?"

"What's wrong is Marcie's horrible, shitty mother," my daughter snapped. "She just called and said Marcie and Jess have to come home first thing in the morning, on the eight o'clock plane. She didn't get her child support check and Marcie's dad promised it would be there by now and he says he sent it and she says he's lying and if he doesn't put them on that plane she's calling the sheriff. Of course I can't stay. So when will you get here? I want to tell them—"

I could not think. My ears were ringing and my mouth was numb. The other Merritt had gone far away indeed; I could not seem to find her. Finally I said, "Let me ask T.C."

"Why do you have to ask him, for God's sake? He's not your keeper. Why can't you just come yourself and let's get this over with? I don't want to have to talk to him and laugh at his stupid jokes."

Pure, red rage swept me like wildfire.

"Your tone stinks, Glynn," I said, trying not to shout at her, "and I will ask T.C. because it's his Jeep and because he has been extraordinarily nice to both of us, and because I do not want to drive down the mountains in the dark by myself. Not that it's any of your business. We can start . . ."

I looked over at him. He sat slumped bonelessly on his spine on the desk, studying me, his face closed and calm. He held up five fingers.

"We can start in five minutes," I said. "We'll be there

when we get there. Have your things out on the porch ready to go. And get your act straightened out. Neither one of us wants to cope with you in that mood."

"Well, that's just too bad about neither one of you," she said nastily. I could hear the tears under her voice, and my anger abated, but only somewhat. But then she added, "What would please either one of you? For me just to vanish and let you keep on doing . . . whatever it is you've been doing up there?"

The red anger soared.

"You are way out of line," I said coldly. "Be ready."

And I slammed the phone down, and stood there, thinking that I had no idea what move to make next.

He came over and stood in front of me, but he did not touch me.

"I'm sorry, Merritt," he said softly. "I wasn't ready, either. I thought there would be more time. . . . "

I began to cry, dully and hopelessly, the tears running down my cheeks and dripping off my chin.

"T.C.," I sobbed. "T.C. . . . I wanted to know what your second-grade teacher was like. I wanted to know where your folks went on vacation every year. I wanted to know if you hate boiled okra—"

"We knew from the beginning that it wasn't going to be one of those loves, didn't we? That kind of context, that kind of resonance—that's for the long loves, baby. That's for the loves that raise children and pay income taxes and look after old people and cuss the lawn service. We couldn't have had that. You already have one of those, a perfectly good one, and I already had one. This one is separate and different, and apart from that other kind. This one makes up in depth what it lacked in width. But I'll tell you this. Whenever you feel like you need to know something about me, stop and think a minute. Whatever comes into your mind will probably be right. Because I'll be there telling you, always, and all you have to do is listen."

I put my arms around him and scrubbed my face into his shirt and cried and cried. It was a soundless, wrenching sort of crying, endless, uncathartic. He held me very close, but softly, and kissed my hair and my wet face.

"You'll have to stop crying now, Merritt, because I simply can't stand it anymore," he said presently.

So I did. I still don't know why it was so easy. I suppose that there just has to be an end to tears sometimes, even when there is no end to pain. I looked up at him, and his dark eyes glistened wetly, and he let me go and turned away. I think it was then that my heart truly broke. After that there was mainly dullness and loss, and that was better than the raw grief. But only just.

We put Curtis in the backseat of the Jeep and went down the winding, dark mountain road in silence. It was still very hot and thick; Curtis panted restlessly in the backseat, and kept turning around and resettling himself, as if he caught the sense of pain. Once or twice he whined, and touched his nose to the back of T.C.'s neck. I felt the tears prickle again both times, but knew that I would not cry anymore. We did not speak until the lights of Palo Alto lay below us.

"We could meet," I said. "You're coming East in October, aren't you? To see your boy in his season opener? We could meet somewhere in the middle; I could come over to . . . where? Birmingham, maybe."

He was silent so long that I looked over at him, and saw that the white ghost of a grin flashed in his dark beard.

"A night in the Birmingham Days Inn? Dinner and a drink and a song or two around the piano bar? Condoms from a machine in the men's room? Would you want that, Merritt?"

"It might be better than nothing."

But I knew that it would not be; that it would be terrible past imagining.

"Don't settle, love," he said mildly and took my hand, and we rode the rest of the way in silence again, joined only by our intertwined fingers.

Glynn stood on the porch of the big Victorian. Her duffel and several shopping bags stood around her. She was alone. The yellow porch light spilled down on her, and even from the driveway I could tell that something about her was very different. Then it hit me: her hair. She had cut her hair, and it was curled around her small head in a medusa-like tangle of stiff-sprayed curls and whorls. For a moment she looked as if she was wearing a strange hat, a bright, complicated straw. Then I realized that she had bleached it, too.

"My God," I said, and T.C. laughed. It was nearly the old laugh.

"How you gonna keep 'em down on the farm after they've seen Palo Alto?" he said, and to my surprise I laughed, too. There was more pain in it than mirth, but it was a laugh. I thought in sudden, swift agony that laughter was going to be his last, best gift to me. He had saddled me with a new sense of absurdity.

Glynn picked up her bags and duffel and stomped toward us. She was wearing pink sandals that tied around her ankles and had very high platforms, and she teetered perilously. It spoiled the effect of what might have been a fine, angry prowl. She wore spandex tights down to her knees and a T-shirt cropped so that it cleared her waist. Every bone and knob and rib and hollow showed, and automatically I assessed the thinness. It was less than it had been, but it was still grotesque under the straw curls and the cerise spandex. When she got close to the car we could see that she wore vivid vermilion lipstick, and slashes of mauve blush, and her eyes were so thick with makeup that I could not see anything but spiky lashes and violet shadow in the dim light. I did, though, catch the gleam of gold in one of her nostrils. A ring. My daughter had a ring in her nose.

She should have looked entirely ludicrous, but in an odd, eerie way she was beautiful: instead of a young medieval martyr, a painted Mexican madonna, a hectically theatrical actress from a forties play. I could not speak.

"Well, go ahead," she said grumpily. "Tell me I look like some kind of whore. That's what Marcie's dad said we looked like. Tell me I belong on the wrong end of Sunset Boulevard."

"Hello, darling," I said. "Nice language. I'm not going to tell you anything, except that you look thirty years old and it's going to take me a while to get used to it. Hop in. Where are Marcie and Jess? Did you remember to thank Marcie's stepmother?"

"Oh, God, of course," she said. "Marcie and Jess are in Marcie's room blubbering." She got into the backseat, slamming the door. She did not speak to T.C. He lifted his eyebrows quizzically, but did not say anything. My face burned; the anger was starting up again.

There was a joyous woof from the backseat as Curtis recognized her, or perhaps it was her smell. I did not see how he could have found much else to recognize.

"Oh, Curtis; oh, hello, you old dog," Glynn said in an entirely different voice, one that was soft and so vulnerable that my very womb seemed to turn over at the sound of it. I looked back and saw that she had her arms around him and her strange new face buried in his neck. I turned back and stared straight ahead as we drove back out of town.

"He's missed you," T.C. said amiably. "He asked when you were coming back so often that we had to promise him he could spend the night with you when you did get back."

Glynn was silent a moment, and then she said, "Well, that should work out just about right for everybody, shouldn't it?"

I whipped my head around, but T.C. touched my thigh and I fell silent. For almost the rest of the trip we did not speak.

He drove past the tower and down to the lodge and cut the motor. We all sat still for a moment, and then he said, "I'll take you up to San Francisco whenever you're ready. You ought to give yourselves two and a half or three hours if you have to get a flight after you get there. Or I can call the airport for you tonight—"

"We're not going anywhere," Glynn said sharply.

"I'll come back up when I've gotten everything down here squared away," I said formally. "I need to make some calls."

"I'll just bet you do," Glynn said under her breath.

She got out of the Jeep and slammed the door.

"I'm sorry," I whispered to T.C. "I'm going to have to figure out how to handle this."

"You want me to come in and talk to her?"

"No, she's in too shitty a mood. I'm not going to let her talk to you this way."

"I wish you wouldn't let her talk to you that way either," he said, "but that's between the two of you. You really coming back up? You think you should?"

"I think I have to. I can't just . . . I have to see you one more time."

"I'll put on some coffee, then. But if you change your mind and think it would be easier just to . . . let it stop here . . . I'll understand. It might be, at that—"

"I have to, T.C. Don't you want . . . a little more time?"

"Oh, my God," he breathed. "What do you think?"

Curtis whined from the backseat and T.C. reached back and opened the door. "You still want him?" he called out to Glynn, standing rigidly by the lodge door with her back to us.

"Yes," she said in a low voice, and T.C. said, "Go, Curtis. Carpe diem."

Curtis took off out of the backseat like a heat-seeking missile and flew to Glynn, jumping up and down beside her, licking her knees and her hands. She knelt and put her arms around him and stayed there, motionless.

"Shall I bring him when I come?" I said.

"Whatever, he'll let you know what he wants to do. If he wants to stay with her, let him. Merritt—"

"I'll see you in a little while," I said, and closed the door and crossed the lawn to where the girl and the dog were.

We went inside in silence, and Glynn vanished into her room, Curtis loping beside her grinning his red-tongued grin. She closed the door with a small, ugly slam, and I opened it and went into her room.

I stood with my back against the door, arms crossed over my breasts as if to ward off blows.

"I think we'd better talk about this," I said tightly. "I think you better tell me what's gotten into you. The way you're behaving is not acceptable."

She was lying on her back, her arms around Curtis, who had flopped on her bed with her. She sat up abruptly.

"Oh, really," she said furiously. "Oh, well, excuse me, Emily Post. By all means, tell me from your vast store of acceptability just what it is that you'll accept from me."

"Glynn, what is it? Is it because you were having such a good time and you don't want to leave? Are you worried about your father? Do you think he's going to jump all over you about your hair and the nose ring and all? Because I promise you, I won't let him do that. How you look is your business; you're sixteen years old now—"

"You're goddamn right I am! And I'm old enough to decide for myself where I'm going to be, and I'm not going home! I'm not! I'm going to stay out here; they're holding the Joan part for me, and I'm going to do it, and you can't stop me—"

"You know you cannot do that movie. You know we agreed on that. I told you that from the beginning; you said you understood that—"

"But that was before we knew for sure they were going to do it! And they are, and they want me, and we've already made plans for it; I've already told Mr. Margolies I could stay; he's sent me some early scripts, and all kinds of presents, and flowers every day. *It's going to happen! You can't stop it! I've told everybody!*"

My head felt as light as if I were about to faint, and my pulse raced in my wrists so hard that I could feel it out to the ends of my fingers.

"It's not going to happen and I can stop it, so fast it will make your silly yellow head swim," I said through a red mist of rage. "What on earth has happened to you in just three days? Have you completely lost your mind? How did Margolies know where to get in touch with you? What kind of presents?"

"Aunt Laura told him!" she screamed at me. "Aunt Laura told Caleb, and Caleb told Mr. Margolies, and they've both been in touch with me, and it's a done deal, and we start shooting in September, and if you try to stop me I'll run away. I'll starve myself. I swear to God I will."

Oh God, Laura, I thought in dull grief and defeat. You just aren't capable of not wrecking things for me, are you?

"Where is Laura?" I said tiredly. "I haven't been able to get her anywhere, not at her place, not at Stuart's. . . . You'd better tell me. I need to talk to her. If you don't, I'm going to call Margolies this minute and tell him the deal's off. And it is off, kiddo. We're on that noon plane home tomorrow whether or not I've talked to your precious aunt. Don't think that's not going to happen."

"I don't know where she is," Glynn said sulkily, dropping her awful, spiky lashes. "I can't get her, either, and now nobody else knows where she is. I can't get Caleb, either, and Mr. Margolies isn't at his number . . ."

She looked back up at me, and there was a kind of wild radiance in her painted face.

"Listen, Mom," she said. "You know you can't go home without knowing where Aunt Laura is. You know it would just . . . haunt you. You know how you are about taking care of her. Well, why don't we go down to L.A., and you can find her from there? She's bound to let somebody know eventually; Caleb, or Mr. Margolies; somebody. We can ask around, and you can talk to Mr. Margolies and Caleb, they'll make you see how wonderful all this will be for me. I know they will. We can stay at Stuart's; he's not there—"

"How do you know he's not there?" I said.

She dropped her eyes again.

"He called me the other night," she said. "He was going into the hospital, and he wanted to talk to you about Aunt Laura. He said he'd tried to call you up at T.C.'s, but nobody returned his message. I asked him and he said he'd be very pleased if we'd stay at his place and try to get ahold of Aunt Laura."

"Why didn't you call me and tell me that?" I said slowly and clearly. "Why didn't you, Glynn?"

"I was afraid you'd make me go home, all right? I was afraid you'd find out something had happened to her and we couldn't stay."

She was shouting, her eyes screwed shut with anger and desperation.

"That was a very terrible thing you did," I said evenly. "It was truly an awful thing. I hope you never realize how awful. What hospital is he in?"

"I don't know. He didn't tell me."

"And you didn't ask?"

"No! I didn't ask! So what does that make me, a monster? Okay, then! I didn't ask and I'm a monster!"

"You're not anybody I know," I said softly, in misery.

She came surging off the bed and ran up into my face.

"Do you think I know who you are? You aren't my mother; you aren't that awful saintly shit who keeps telling me what the right thing to do is, who keeps falling all over me to keep me a baby, who always, always knows the good, kind, wise, saintly thing to do."

"I've never on earth tried to tell you what was right," I whispered. "I've never told you how to live your life—"

"No, but you've always *done* the goddamn right thing! Always, *always!* You've always been oh, so dutiful and good and pure; you've always taken care of everybody; you've always showed me what to do even if you didn't tell me! And I've always tried to do it, and it doesn't work; it doesn't get you anywhere; that fucking old woman still runs our house; I can't take the one good thing somebody's offered me that was all mine alone; you're always there with goodness shining out of you—"

"Glynn—"

"I want you to get out of my head! I'm not you! I'm me! You're not *anybody* anymore; you're just some cat in heat who's up here fucking the hired help."

"What the hell are you saying? How can you say such a thing?"

"*I can smell it on you!*" she screamed, and began to cry, hard and loudly, like a child. "*I could smell it on you when I got in the car! Do you think I'm a baby? You think I don't know what come smells like?*"

She whirled and ran back to the bed and threw herself down onto it, her face buried in Curtis's neck. She cried loudly. Curtis whined and nosed at her and licked her face. I put a hand out toward her, and then dropped it.

"I'm going up and try to get hold of Aunt Laura one more time," I said tonelessly. "And I'm going to make us a plane reservation. I'll be back after a while. Try to sleep. We'll see if we can start to sort all this out in the morning. I'm sorry you feel badly. I feel badly, too."

She did not answer, only lay there sobbing. I went out of her room and closed the door. I did not think that the part of me her words had hit would ever come alive again.

"*I will starve myself!*" she screamed after me through the closed door. "Starting right now! At least you can't stop me doing that!"

Then do it, I said, but not aloud. I can't be your reason to live. You have to find that.

I went out into the hot night and up the gravel path to T.C.

*   *   *

Much later we sat upon the sofa on his veranda and looked at each other. We had not made love; we had wanted to, and started it, but then we had known that after all, we could not, and neither of us had pushed it.

"Not after that business with Glynn," he said. "I don't want you remembering that when you remember how we were together. Remember the last time instead. Remember letting the stew burn, and you sitting on top of me, laughing like a hyena."

I had told him about the scene with Glynn. I kept nothing back. He'd listened without comment, and then said, "Poor you. Poor Glynn. You've started down that awful road of her growing up. I remember some of it from Katie, before I left. My grandmother used to call it starting up fool's hill. I wish I could help you with it, but that's for you and Pom to do."

He spoke freely and naturally of Pom. I knew that I could not have.

We were holding each other tightly on the sofa. We had lain there together for what seemed a very long time, kissing very gently now and then, but mostly just holding each other. He had broken it off to try Laura for me, at the Palm Springs house and at Stuart Feinstein's condo, but there was no answer anywhere, and I had no idea how to reach Caleb Pringle. T.C. had called the number Caleb had given him long ago first thing and gotten only an answering machine, and I knew that it was fruitless to try and reach Leonard Margolies. Finally he had called and made a reservation for Glynn and me on the Delta noon flight the next day. We had had to take first class; tourist was full.

"Good," he said. "Drink champagne. Eat steak. Stretch out and sleep. Soften the princess up with macadamia nuts and maybe get her a little drunk. And then tell her very firmly to shut up; she knows nothing about love. She'll be lucky if she ever does. Don't be a doormat for a spoiled mall punk. Don't be a doormat for anybody."

"She's not that."

"I know. I remember her when she first got here. But you mustn't let her start that way. On the other hand, maybe you should. Maybe now's the time to start letting her make her own mistakes. Do you think you could find it in you to let her do this movie? If you or somebody you trusted came along to look out for her? Maybe it would do her dad good to do that—"

"No," I said. "He couldn't. He couldn't if he wanted to. I see now that I have to let up, but I'm not prepared to let her go in harm's way. I haven't changed that much, T.C. I don't think I ever will."

"No. That part of you won't change," he said.

We lay there a while longer. The thin moon rode up the sky and diminished; it had risen a great orange crescent, apocalyptic and awful. I was glad when it shrank. The light it spilled down on us on the veranda sofa was thin and urine-pale, not the radiant cold silver it had been before. We were stuck together with perspiration, but neither of us moved.

"I won't see you again, will I?" I whispered at last, tasting the salt of his skin on my tongue, against his chest. "I mean, I know you'll take us to the airport, but I mean . . . see you."

"You'll see me," he said. His voice was very low. "Whenever you see redwoods in the *National Geographic*, or fog, or watch Shamu on TV, you'll be seeing me. Whenever you smell pine and spruce and day-old socks, that's me. Whenever you hear wind in the tops of trees, that's me, and whenever you taste crab and wine and Brie that's me, and whenever the wind blows your hat off or you get under a cold shower, that's me. Whenever you read about an earthquake, that's me, sure as gun's iron. Whenever you smell wet dog, that's Curtis and me, and whenever you see a *Rattus rattus*, that's Forrest, and I'm right behind him. Never see me again? You'll never not see me. And I'll never not see you. I've got you whole and real, just like you've been these last few days, in my brain and heart and the part of me you profess to want to make a life cast of. As long as I live, the Merritt of Merritt's Creek does, too. Didn't I say I'd always be your same stars? If you get to missing me, just look up."

"I can't stand this," I said. "I think I'll never . . . T.C., how can you ever go to bed with anybody else again? I don't think I ever can—"

"Sure you can. It's just the woman you leave up here that can't. And that woman won't, not ever with anybody else but me. Don't worry about me, baby love. If it gets too bad I'll just haul out my board with the bearskin—"

"Don't! I love you! I love you! I can't leave you! There's no way I can leave you."

"There's no way you can stay," he said, and stood up, pulling me up with him. He held me against him for a long moment, so hard that I could not breathe, did not want ever again to breathe. . . .

He stood back and looked at me in the mean light of the flinty stars.

"Get out of here, Merritt," he said, and his face twisted and tears sprang into his eyes and ran down to meet the black pirate's beard. But he did not turn away.

I turned and ran. I ran out of the yard and past the boy's earthquake inventions under the shed, and past the dusty Jeep, and started down the gravel path toward the lodge. I needed no flashlight tonight; the very path seemed to glow with pale, tired heat. I ran and ran. Above me, off to my left over the lower ridges of still redwoods, Arcturus slid down the sky, going home. It looked fake, a painted star, a burned-out star in a cardboard firmament. Dead, as dead and cold as the space around my heart where, for the past small lifetime, T.C. Bridgewater had lived.

"Be my same stars, T.C. . . ."

"I will. I always will. . . ."

I stopped on the path and turned and cupped my hands.

"Carpe diem," I shouted.

"Carpe diem," came his voice, a small flag in the vast, dead night.

I turned back and jogged on down the path. I did not cry for him again until much, much later.

11

I was given a gift that night, one that you often receive in childhood but seldom later. It was as if a good fairy had realized she missed her appointment with me when the gifts were being passed out around my cradle and came bustling back to make up the oversight. It was the gift of sleep. Sleep as panacea, sleep as opiate, sleep as oblivion. Forever after, I have been able, when pain becomes overwhelming, simply to sleep. It has rarely failed me.

When I got back to the lodge the night before I walked straight past Glynn's slightly opened door, saw the still mounds of girl and dog, went into my bedroom, and went to sleep. I would have said, in that dull red mindlessness of loss, that I would never sleep again, but instead it was as if I would never wake. I slept without moving until the pale first light of morning fell on my face and finally brought me back.

I lay there like someone who has wakened after a bad accident, a collision. Every muscle in my body hurt, and my limbs felt as heavy as cast iron. The thought of even moving them made me sick with exhaustion. For what seemed a very long time I lay there immobile, trying to assemble the thoughts I would need to get us through this day: this day of great distances, of tearing endings, and dreaded beginnings.

My mind flailed tiredly in all directions: Laura. What should I do about Laura? T.C. had said he would keep trying to trace her after we had gone and would let me know when he heard something, but I did not want that. I did not think I could pick up a telephone and hear his voice speaking neutrally of my sister from under the great, lost-to-me trees. I simply wanted Laura out of my heart and off my hands.

Glynn. About Glynn I could only feel detached anger and pain, and a kind of abstract shame. I did not feel like coping with this hurtful and hurt new daughter, either. There was nothing left in me that could meet this dangerous complexity. If I could have gotten home without exchanging another word with her, I would have done it with alacrity. These two creatures, both of my blood and both so much of my making—at that moment I loved them not.

Pom. I did not even know how to think about Pom. I did not, in that bled-out moment, know who Pom was or what he was to me. What he might be from now on was simply unimaginable. There wasn't any from now on. There was scarcely a now. *Carpe diem*, T.C.'s voice said in my head, and I felt agony rush at me, pecking. Oh, T.C., you seize it. I don't want this day.

T.C. For a long, still moment I lay there so filled with the reality of T.C., of the actuality of him, that it was as if he had entered my body and lived under my skin. My heartbeat felt like his; my fingers touched the cloth of the coverlet and knew how it would feel to T.C. It was as if a conduit, a major vessel, ran from his body on the veranda sofa down through the earth to the lodge and into my own.

I can't do this day, T.C., I said to him in my mind, and his answer came clear and true: Yes, you can. Get up. I go with you.

At that moment I heard the sound of china clinking in the kitchen and the gurgle of coffee being poured into a mug. I sprang up. It was him; he had come for me after all, he would heal this awful day somehow; he was waiting for me.

I flew into the kitchen, still in my underpants and bra. Laura sat on a stool at the kitchen table, a steaming cup beside her, her head in her hands as if she slept sitting there.

The disappointment was so profound that I closed my eyes against it. Then I took a deep breath and opened them. Here is Laura, I thought witlessly. What does this mean? I don't know how to think about this.

She raised her head and looked at me. She looked terrible. Her tan had faded and was flaking off the miraculous cheekbones in mustardy patches, and there were deep, incised blue circles under the slanted amber eyes. Her gilt hair was lank and lifeless, and she had simply jerked it back seemingly without combing it and pulled it tight with a rubber band. Somehow that rubber band spoke more vividly of damage to me than anything else about her desiccated face. She had often scolded me for using rubber bands in my hair.

"It breaks the hairs off and makes them thin and scraggly," she would say. "I would no more do that to my hair than I would pour tar over it."

"You're going to ruin your hair with that thing," I said stupidly, and she smiled, and then laughed. It was a spectral, shadowless little laugh, but it lit her face a little. She did not look dead anymore.

"Can't have that, can we? Hello, Met. You look like shit."

"It runs in the family," I said, and went and hugged her. Her ribs felt like separate ridges under my hands, almost like Glynn's. Not at all like the warm solidity of T. C. Bridgewater. Never again, I would never feel that again.

"I wish our family ran to fat," I whispered against her shoulder. "I get so tired of hugging bones."

She put both her arms around me and rocked me against her, and we stayed that way for a bit, both needing each other's body warmth simply to live. I could not ever remember needing Laura's arms. Wanting them, but never needing them.

"Go put on some clothes; you must be freezing," she said. "I'll pour you some coffee. Then I'm going to sleep for twenty-four hours. You look like you could use some more sleep, too. Then we'll talk. I'm glad to see you, Met."

"We can't sleep anymore," I said wearily. "We have to talk now. I have to take Glynn home in . . . what time is it? Eight? We have a noon flight. I can't leave without knowing what's going on with you."

She leaned her head far back and closed her eyes.

"Nothing, not anymore," she said. "I don't know. I can't seem to make my mind work. I thought you might help me. You could always see so much more clearly than I could see myself."

I can't see anything but the shape of my own pain, my mind wailed peevishly. Go away and take all your pretty fragments with you. The one thing I've got to do in this world is leave here and take my daughter with me, and right now I don't see how I'm going to do that.

"Tell me," I said aloud, or rather the old Merritt said, popping up like an indestructible jack-in-the-box. Get out of here I told her furiously in my mind; stay out of my head until I'm back where you live. This is not your place. I don't want you. I want the one who came after you. . . .

"Tell me," I said again to my sister. That was when I knew that the woman T.C. and I had created was not going to survive the trip home. It was the worst moment of all. I have felt no pain since that has even come close to that moment.

She took her coffee cup and went over to the sofa and sprawled out on it, putting her booted feet up. I followed her stiffly and sat in the facing wing chair. On the way I lit the half-charred logs and pulled an afghan around me. The cold felt as though it was sucking the life out of me.

She did not speak, and I said, "Did you see Caleb?"

"Oh, yeah. I found him right off, at his place. It was close to dawn, but he had company. They went out the back way; I never saw them. I don't know if it was a man or a woman, but I can't imagine any man friend of Pring's sneaking out his back door when I happen by. None of them thinks I'm important enough for that. And as it turns out, I'm not. I never was. I don't know now why I couldn't see that."

"I'm sorry, Pie," I said, and I was. Sorry, sad, but at a remove, as if through a pane of glass. I didn't know what else to say to her. I could not make this right.

"So things didn't go well about *Arc?*"

She stretched mightily.

"There's not going to be any *Arc*," she said. "I killed *Arc*. I'm glad I did. It was a monstrous thing, an abomination. It would have been even if I'd played the grown-up Joan, I can see that now. The whole concept is . . . obscene. He didn't change his mind about my doing the Dauphine; I thought at first he would, but in the end he wouldn't. It was no mistake, of course. That's what he wanted me for all along. That and for Glynn. When I realized he wasn't going to budge about that I called Margolies and told him there was no chance and you were taking her home. He pulled the plug on the picture that day. Pring was furious and oh, so wounded; he said he hadn't thought I had it in me to hurt him like that. *Can you believe it?* After the *Arc* business, after the baby—"

She stopped and dropped her face into her hands. She did not weep, just sat there, hidden behind her long, thin fingers.

"Oh, love," I said, sadness pouring into the crater in my heart I had thought empty forever. "He didn't want the baby?"

"Oh, God, no. Of course not. Caleb Pringle with a baby? A wife and a baby? Met, I was such a fool; I thought he would want it; he always had such a special thing with children. But the only children Pring can relate to are the ones on the other side of the camera. The only way he can see them is through a lens. It was that way with the kid in *Right Time*; it would have been that way with Glynn in *Arc*. Beyond that she wouldn't have existed to him. It would have destroyed her. I was too selfish to see that before."

"What did he say about the baby when you told him?"

"Well, let's see. He said was I absolutely sure it belonged to him, and that at this stage in his life a baby was *not* a priority, and then he said he'd take care of things financially for me, and he wrote me out a check for fifty thousand dollars and gave me the number of a man in Santa Monica he said would take care of . . . things. I don't know if he's a doctor or not, but he must be good, or Pring wouldn't have anything to do with him. I gather the problem has come up before and has been settled satisfactorily."

"Laura, you didn't—"

"Not yet. I was going to, but then Stuart tracked me down, and came flying over and spent two straight days trying to change my mind, and what with one thing and another . . . oh, Met. Stu's dead. He died this morning at three; I've been driving ever since. I came straight here from the hospital."

"Dead . . ." It was a whisper. Shock and swiftly following grief took my breath.

"He was sick when he got to me. I was still at Pring's; the morning after our little chat he took off for the Bahamas, whether with his mysterious visitor or not I don't know. He knows a guy with some loose money down there. He still thinks he can get *Arc* going, but he can't. Stuart was coughing horribly when he came, and he had a high fever; you could tell without even touching him. He wouldn't let me take him to a doctor, but after nearly two days of begging me to have the baby and let him help me take care of it, he just . . . collapsed. I called 911, but it was too late by then. He had pneumonia, that kind you get with AIDS; he was dead that night. Last night. This morning, whenever. The doctor said that all told, it was a fairly gentle way to go."

She began to cry. I moved over and sat next to her and put my arms around her shoulder. I simply sat there, holding her while she sobbed.

What a good man you were, and how much you loved her, I said to Stuart Feinstein in my head. She's never going to have anybody like you again.

Thank you, dollbaby, he said. But she still has you.

No, she doesn't, I said back. There's no me left. Ain't nobody home here.

"Do you know what he's done?" Laura said presently, around the sobs. "He's left me his condo and all his money. He had more than I thought. He's been saving it ever since he got sick and knew he wouldn't get well. He made his will then. He only told me the day he died. He never did think Pring was going to look after me. He said that no matter what happened to him, I'd still have a place to live and a little money to raise the baby with. He said he'd talked to another agent about handling me, and that I should call him."

"What a darling," I said, wishing for the ease of tears for Stuart Feinstein but knowing it was not going to be granted. "Will you do it?"

She raised her head and smiled at me. It was a terrible smile.

"Who in their right mind is going to take on a pregnant

thirty-eight-year-old Caleb Pringle reject, whose hot new vehicle just fell through? I did that to myself, Met. Remember that asshole Billy Poythress, the one who did the interview with me that day at the Sunset Marquis? Well, I got greedy and desperate and shot my mouth off about what a great love Pring and I had going, and about the sensational part I'd had in *Right Time*, and the even hotter one that was coming up with Pring and Margolies. . . . I didn't tell him about *Arc* exactly, but Billy's never had any trouble extrapolating. You wouldn't *believe* what he made of that interview. It was unspeakable. It ran the very day I saw Pring; the timing couldn't have been any worse. By now, of course, everybody knows that Margolies has killed *Right Time* and *Arc*, and if they don't know Pring has dumped me and taken off they'll know this time next week. There's not an agent in Hollywood who'd touch me. Stu must have known, but he gave it his best shot. It was me he was worrying about when he died, Met. The last thing he said was 'Take care of yourself, dollbaby!'"

"So what are you going to do?" I said. "I know you're hurt and shocked, but we've got to make a plan for you; I've got to know you're not going to . . . do something to the baby or yourself. Come home with us, Pie. What's holding you here? Leave the car in long-term parking, or with T.C., and just get on the plane with us and come home. We'll look after you; we'll find you a good doctor, Pom knows them all; we can help you get settled someplace nice with the baby, and find good day care . . . you can do all the theater you'd ever want to do in Atlanta; you'd own the city. You can do commercials there, you can do movies; they're always making movies in the South now . . . you could make a very good life for both of you. You might even enjoy it. It's a good place to live, a great place to raise a child. . . . "

And I hate it, I thought. Right now I hate it.

"I can't have this baby, Met," she said dully. "I can't look after a baby. I can't even look after myself. Do you think I want to screw up a baby's life the way I've screwed up mine? No, I thought I might go to New York. I still know some the-ater people there. I know I could do character parts, and the television there is always good. You know, after . . . I get things taken care of here. I'll have enough money to get start-ed. Pring was generous; he must know fifty thousand is way beyond the going rate for abortions, even in L.A."

Her face twisted and I took both her hands.

"I can't let you do that. You'd never forgive yourself. I'd never forgive myself. Neither would Pom. You know he'd tell you not to do it; he's always saying you've got to cast your lot with the living."

She smiled again, and it was no easier to look at than the last one.

"Met, I'd say you're going to have a hard enough time going back without bringing a pregnant sister with you. Can't you just see it? Maybe that horrible mother of his could baby-sit while you and Pom go to marriage counseling."

I looked at her.

"I know about things up here, you and T.C.," she said. "Glynn couldn't wait to tell me. She jumped me the minute I walked in. Listen, I don't care, for God's sake. I hope it was wonderful for you. I just wanted you to know that I know about it, so you don't feel like you have to talk around it. You're hurting; any fool can see that. I gather it wasn't . . . a small thing."

"No. Not a small thing."

"I'm sorry. I really am. Your time to talk now, if you want to. Listening to man trouble is one of the things I do best."

"I can't," I said briefly. "Laura, what did Glynn say? I need to know. . . ."

"Not much, other than you'd been screwing him behind her sainted daddy's back and she hated him and you and couldn't wait to get home and tell on you."

I could feel what was left of the color drain out of my face. This time she was the one to reach over and take my hands.

"I don't think she's going to do that," she said. "I gave her total hell. I'm quite sure nobody has ever talked to her like that in her entire virginal little life. When I finished she was bawling like a baby. I think she retired to her room with that big old dog of T.C.'s, to lick her wounds. Not before she washed that goop off her face and out of her hair, though. I told her she looked like every other little mall tramp on the face of the planet. Among other things . . . My God, that nose ring! When will they learn how silly they look with them? Like cattle just waiting to be led around."

"She said . . . she said she could smell it . . . you know . . . smell it on me," I whispered. "It was a horrible thing to say. I don't know which was worse, that she said it or that she could recognize it."

She laughed. It was a better sound, almost an old Laura sound.

"Don't worry that she's been doing it, though she'd probably love for you to think she has," she said. "That was my fault. Before I went to pick her up I stopped by to pay the guy who's been taking care of the Mustang; he's this beautiful kid, a real hunk, and completely gone on me; wants to be an actor, of course, and anyway, one thing led to another and I had some time, and so . . . I thanked him. It really had been a long time. As they say, I needed that. And then I was late, so I didn't have time to shower. Anyway, she sniffed around and asked me, and I told her. I think I set her sexual development back at least a decade."

"Laura, you are incorrigible," I said, and then began, incredibly, to laugh. After a moment she joined me. We hugged each other and laughed until the laughter slid perilously close to tears, and then we stopped, and looked at each other.

"Did you?" she said. "Sleep with him?"

"Yes," I said. "I did. Every time I could. All day yesterday. She can tell Pom or not, I'm never going to be sorry about that."

"She won't tell. She's too ashamed for that. Ashamed and scared."

"Ashamed of what? Scared of what? What on earth else did you tell her?"

"Ashamed of the way she behaved to you. Afraid she's driven you away. Afraid you'll leave her dad for T.C. Afraid she's lost herself now that she's turned herself into a perfect mall mouse. One of the things I told her was that she'd taken the most special thing she had—that real innocence and sweetness—and sold it to buy nose rings and platform shoes. I told her her looks and presence were the only reason they'd wanted her for *Arc*, and she'd totally destroyed those. I think she already knew that; I think she hated the way she looked and hated herself for letting her little buddies talk her into it. That's where a lot of the anger came from. Before she even got in that car she was angry, and being angry makes you scared when you're very young. I know. I took my anger and fright out on you for thirty-eight years. I just realized it when I lit into her."

Tears I did not know I had left stung my eyes.

"Poor Glynn. Poor Pie. You really let her have it, didn't you?"

"Damn straight. That's not nearly all. I told her *Arc* was dead as a doornail and just what it was she'd lost by losing it— the chance to be chewed up and spit out and hardened into somebody she'd hate, somebody she'd be stuck with the rest of her life. I told her what Pring had done to me and that he and every one of the others wouldn't hesitate a New York minute to do it to her, and that it wasn't acting that made you special; you had to make yourself special before you could really act. I told her there wouldn't have been a damned thing for her after *Arc*; that she wouldn't have done anything to deserve it. That acting wasn't that easy. That it wasn't easy at all; that you had to earn it hard, and be ready to be savaged for your pains. I said did she want it enough for that. Because that had happened to me, and I wasn't at all sure it was worth it. I just realized that, too."

"What did she say?"

"Nothing. She'd started to cry by then. I seized the home court advantage and pressed on. I told her I didn't ever want to see her take the troubles she'd gotten herself into out on you again; that she could tell you when she was angry or scared, but she must not treat you badly. That you loved her enough to take it, but that you'd spent your whole life taking other people's loads, and the time had come when you just couldn't do that anymore, and I wasn't going to let her grow up into the kind of person who took advantage of love, because that's not growing up, is it, Met? It's just growing older and staying the same, and what's the point of all this shit if you don't change into something better as you go along? That's another thing I didn't know I knew until I yelled it at her."

"Pie . . . Laura—"

"No. I need to tell you the rest of it. Most of the rest of it is about me, and I've never told it to you. I've been a worry and a grief to you most of my life, Met, and I can't take those years back, but I can try to see that Glynn doesn't get started down that road. And I can tell you how much I love you for standing behind me all those awful years. I couldn't then; somehow it just made me madder and scareder. But by God, *she's* going to tell you. You should have jerked a knot in me and you should jerk one in her if she does it again. And she will, because she has finally become, God help you both, a seminormal teenager, with all the special little delights that entails. I don't think you should lock her up, but *don't* let her devalue you. Real love always runs that risk."

Don't settle, Merritt. Don't ever settle . . .

Oh, T.C., don't you see that not settling is the hardest thing in the world?

I got my trembling lips under control.

"Dearest Laura, you will never know what this means to me," I said softly, reaching out to brush a strand of the wounded hair off her face. "But about Glynn being normal, being a normal, healthy teenager is what we always wanted most for her. We used to pray for it in church . . ."

I thought of Pom and his dark, troubled face, of the pain in his electric blue eyes when things were worst with Glynn. Pom . . . when it came to Glynn, he was the "we" of me. Where in this new equation did that fit?

"How can I punish her for being normal?" I said, feeling thick and stupid and tired again, utterly unable to cope.

She sat up on the sofa and smoothed back the straggling hair, and made a small face of distaste.

"Listen and let Mother Teresa tell you. What you do is make a deal. She gets to be a real teenager with all that entails, and you get to be a real person. A real woman, with all *that* entails. It's going to be harder for her to honor a deal like that than for you. She's already had a taste of what you're like when the woman and not the mommy takes over, and it terrified her. She's going to want to keep the mommy. And I'm here to tell you, that act has always been a bitch to follow."

"Have I really been that sanctimonious and smug?" I said.

"No. Just perfect. Just selfless. I used to wish you'd do something so sleazy and slutty that you could never jump on me again; I used to daydream that I'd come home and find you screwing the UPS man. And now you've screwed the caretaker and I find that I love you even more for it. It's turned you into somebody who knows what it means to want the wrong person so bad that your fingers curl and your teeth ache. And that there's a whole, greedy female woman in there. That's what's been missing all along."

I said nothing, but bowed my head in case the stinging tears ran over. They didn't, though. There weren't enough left. Presently I said, "He wasn't the wrong person, Pie. There's never been a righter person for me. It's just that the me he was right for isn't the one who's going back home today. I know that's not rational or consistent. But I know that it's okay, too. If I could have stayed that woman, I might not be going home, but in the end you go home, because it's your place and it never works for long when you leave your place. Just like he might have come back with me if he could have, but he couldn't because this is his place. So what we had was us, here, now. Like he says, 'Carpe diem.' I wish there could have been more of it, but what we did have was as near perfect as I'll ever know about. Laura, I didn't know how on earth I was going to get us home. Since I woke up this morning, I've thought I simply couldn't do it. But you've made me see that maybe I can, and even a little bit of how to start. And you've made me see that maybe, just maybe, I haven't driven my daughter away permanently. If I can find the right words when I talk to her—"

"The hell with the right words," she said, fishing a cigarette out of her pocket. "Use the words you feel like using. Don't lie to her. Don't ever do that. Let her see you whole. It's your job now to drive her away; it's what comes next, I think. How else will she get out into the world? She needs that real bad, Met."

I smiled at her. It was a watery smile.

"You'd make a wonderful mother, Pie. You know that?"

"No I wouldn't," she said heavily. "I can talk it but I can't do it. I'd probably let my daughter catch me screwing the UPS man; that's the difference between you and me. I can't be a mother. I just can't. Don't start on that. What it boils down to is that I flat just don't want to do it. The thought bores and horrifies me. You'd probably get stuck with it, and then I'd hate you and me, too."

We sat silent for a while. I knew that I should get up, get dressed, get going. Time was bleeding out of the morning. I knew that it was useless to try and persuade her to keep the baby, to come home with us. But I could not seem to move. I was reluctant to let her go. She was, in this moment, well-loved friend and peer, as well as my sister. I did not know if I would ever get that back.

"*Are* you going to leave Pom?" she said presently, and I said, before I even thought about it, "Of course not."

She raised an eyebrow at me.

"I had an idea he had a little something going on the side," she said. "I thought that might be one reason you hooked up with T.C."

"He may," I said slowly. "I keep hearing about a doctor who used to be with the clinic. Amy, of course, told me she's back in town. And when I called home the other night, she answered. . . . I know it was her. But it could have been nothing; I don't know about that. Pom has brought colleagues home before. It's not really the reason for T.C. and me, but I guess it . . . hurried things along a little. How did you know?"

"I've always thought he would, eventually. Men like Pom are superglue to women. I never thought it would amount to anything, but I've always thought it would happen."

"I never did," I said. "I may be stupid, but I really never did."

"Are you going to tell him you know about her?"

"I don't know."

"Are you going to tell him about T.C.?"

"I don't know . . . no. That didn't have anything to do with him. That had to do with me, and it's over now. I don't want Pom to turn it into something it wasn't, and I don't want to use it for a club or something. No matter what happens with Pom, I'll never do that again. I couldn't. There isn't anybody else like . . . him."

I could not say, T.C.

"You really are in love with him."

"Yes, I am. All of the me I am now is. I don't think it will be that way when I get home, not after a while. Or I would die. Speaking of which, I have to get going, darling. We have a noon flight. I've got to wake Glynn and get her started."

"How are you getting to the airport?"

"He's going to take us. T.C."

The name cut like glass on my lips.

"Isn't that going to be awful?"

"Beyond imagining," I said.

"Oh, hell, I'll drive you," she said. "I can make better time than that Jeep. Don't put yourself through that. I'll go up and tell him. You get it together with your daughter."

"Where will you go after that?"

"Home, I guess. Palm Springs. Then I have to close up Stu's place and get it listed. I've got a bunch of loose ends to take care of, before . . . I go to Santa Monica. I'll call you."

"How can I let you go through that alone?"

"I won't. I'll take a friend with me. There's one who's gone through just the same thing. It really isn't bad this early, Met. This guy keeps you overnight, puts you up in a very pretty little bed and breakfast next door, and sends a nurse with you for the first night. Just like a facelift. It's not back streets and coat hangers anymore, you know. It's been legal a long time."

"Oh, Pie, I hate this," I said, and swallowed the bitter, scanty tears and went, finally, to wake my daughter. Behind me, I heard Laura get up and walk slowly to the door, heard the click of her boot heels as she went to tell T.C. that we did not, after all, need him.

It was a monstrous, killing lie.

Glynn and Curtis were still mounded under the covers, but they were not asleep. Glynn lay staring into space and slowly stroking his blunt head, and he lay on his back, eyes closed, as blissful as a sybarite in the sun.

"You two look like an old married couple," I said, with what normalcy I could muster, and she looked at me. Her swollen eyes filled with tears and she began to cry again. Curtis stirred and looked up at her and sat up and began to lick her face.

I sat down on the bed beside her.

"Don't cry, love," I said. "No matter how either one of us has behaved, nothing calamitous is going to happen."

"Oh, Mama!" she wailed, and threw her arms around me, and I held her very tightly while she cried. I had been right last night; the ribs were not so sharp. She had washed the excelsiorlike frizz out of her hair, too; it was still damp under my fingers and smelled of apple shampoo and stood up at the back of her head like a rooster's comb. It was still thick and silky, and beneath it her neck felt so vulnerable and young that I wanted to wrap it swiftly in something to protect it, like a thick muffler. The nose ring cut into my shoulder.

Curtis jumped down from the bed and looked at us, and whined.

"I think you better dismiss your roomie," I said into the damp hair. "He hasn't been outside since last night, and he must have to go awfully bad. He's just too shy to tell you. He probably wants to go home to breakfast, too. And you need some yourself."

"Oh, poor Curtis," she gulped, still sobbing. "Go on, Curtis. Go home. Carpe diem. I love you."

Curtis woofed softly and trotted to the back door, looking back at her. I got up and went to let him out. Behind me I heard her sniff loudly and go into the bathroom and turn on the water. Curtis put his nose into my hand and then loped out into the morning. It was just like the last two: white-bled and hot and still. Only inside the lodge did the chill of night linger. Curtis stopped still and sniffed and looked back at me and then toward the trail that led to the tower. He held himself rigidly, as if he might come to a point.

"It's okay. I'll take care of her. Go home, Curtis. Carpe diem, dearest dog."

He trotted away springily, still stiff-legged, looking into the woods on either side of him as though he smelled something in them. Perhaps he did. T.C. had said there were deer often, and once in a while bear . . . *T.C. Curtis*.

I closed my eyes and stood very still against the sickening wash of pain, and then it receded and I went back into the lodge and started breakfast for my daughter.

She came into the kitchen a little later, red from scrubbing, mouth still quivering. She looked so strange to me for a moment that I simply stood staring, and she began to cry again.

"I know it looks awful. I don't know why I let Marcie and Jess talk me into it."

"For the same reason I dyed my hair red when I was a sophomore," I said. "It turned out fuchsia. I thought my father was going to kill me. Yours is different, but it's not bad, sweetie. The color can be toned down with a rinse, and the length is becoming, very smart. You have the features for it. You might even want to keep it short. As for the ring, well, if you get tired of it, Dr. Pierson can take it out in a second. Nothing's broken that can't be fixed."

She came to me and put her arms around me and laid her head on my shoulder. Once again I held her.

"Really, really?"

"Really, really. I told you that."

"I was awful to you. I said terrible things. Aunt Laura is furious with me. How can that not change things?"

I took a deep breath into her hair.

"I did things you thought were awful, too. I did sleep with T.C., and more than once. And I can't ever be sorry for that, Glynn. But it ended last night, and it won't happen again. We're going home this afternoon, and unless you want it to, the way we live at home will not change."

"You aren't going to leave Daddy?"

"No. Not because of this. Things between daddy and me probably will change some, but that doesn't have anything to do with what happened up here. And they won't change between you and Daddy, or us as a family. At least, I don't think so. To be very honest with you, no, I would not leave your father, but I am going to have to insist on things he may not be able to do, and he may not be able to stay. I don't think that's going to happen, but I can't say for sure. I do know that we both love you more than anything in the world. And that will *never* change."

"Do you? Do you really?"

"I wouldn't be going home if I didn't," I said simply.

She pulled back and looked at me blearily. The nose ring jarred, but the scrubbed, shiny face was Glynn's. I had told her the truth; the short, soft hair around her face was striking. It was just the cut they probably would have given her for *Arc*, without the unspeakable curls.

"You love him, then." She jerked her head toward the tower.

I nodded.

"I do. I can't tell you I don't. But I can tell you that it doesn't mean I can't love your father, too. It's a totally different kind of love."

"Sex, you mean."

"No. Much, much more than that. But that, too, yes."

She shut her eyes.

"I hate all of this," she said. "I don't see how you can love two people. I just don't see how you can do those things with two people at the same time. I don't see how it can not change things."

"Glynn, you can love a great many people at the same time, for a great many different reasons. I don't know how to explain this, because it's new to me, too. But I think love makes more love. To love, to love anything or anybody, is to start some kind of engine that makes more. The only thing is, you do have to choose what you will do about the loving; in the last analysis, I think you have to do that. I chose to have this time with T.C. for as long as I could, as deeply as it was possible to go. But I never meant to try and take it home, and he agreed with that. In fact, he's the one who made me see it. It is quite apart from what I have always had with your father, and will not spill over into that. But you should know that I will always keep this time up here in my heart, and I will always treasure it. As far as I am concerned, it will not change our family life, but it will probably change me some, and I will need to act on those changes. I know this is hard. I don't understand it yet, either. But I'm not going to lie to you, and I'm going to try very hard not to hover over you anymore. You are your own person, and I'm going to try to see you that way, and it is going to be hard because you have been my little girl for all of your life. I will ask you to try and see me as my own person. That will probably be hard, too."

"I want . . . I want you just to be my mother," she said, beginning to sniffle again.

"I won't stop being that. I couldn't. It's just that you get a woman friend along with the mother. Two for the price of one. At least, I hope you'll let her be a friend to you."

"Will you tell Daddy?"

"I don't think so. Will you?"

"What if I did? What would happen? Would it matter?"

"Probably, to him. I don't know what would happen. Do it if you have to. I'm not going to let you hold me hostage with it. I can't do that."

"I can't promise I won't get so mad at you sometime that I'll just blurt it out."

"Yes, you can. You very well can promise that. You can and will get angry with me; I think we've just started with that. But you can decide not to blurt it out. That's your call. Like I said, it's up to you. You stopped being a child up here, much as I regret that. You're accountable to yourself now."

"I won't tell him. I never would have done that."

"I think it's good that you won't. But that's probably more for his sake than mine. We'll renegotiate things as we go along."

She looked startled, and then grinned. Some of the old Glynn was in it. Someone new and rather fine was, too.

"Can you do that? Is that allowed?"

"It better be," I said. "How on earth would people live together if it wasn't?"

"Do you and Dad do that?"

"We will now."

"He's not going to like that."

"Probably not, at first. But I think he'll come to see that it's necessary. Things just can't go on being all one person's way. I need some things for myself that I don't have yet. So do you. That's what I'll start with."

"Like Mommee."

"Like Mommee. God love her, I hope you'll be able to remember her the way she really was. All that life, and spirit . . . She can't help what she's become, Glynn. But she needs to be in a place where they can concentrate just on her and help her, and we need a place just for ourselves. That's one of the first things Daddy needs to see."

"Will he?"

"I have no idea."

"What about . . . you know, you said we could look at Lab puppies."

"You'll get your dog. Even if it and I have to sleep in the doghouse. That I can promise."

She fell silent, and I put my chin down on the top of her head and we stood like that for a while.

"I'm sorry about *Arc*," I said. "I know that was hard to give up."

"Yeah. But Aunt Laura made me see a lot of things about that. It's not a good life, is it? She told me about Pring. I wouldn't have believed it. Mama, she told me about the baby, too. Isn't there something we can do about that? I don't think she ought to just . . . kill it."

I felt her wince at her own words. I flinched away from them, too.

"Me either. But only she can make that decision. That's very much her own to make, any woman's own. That's one thing we don't butt into."

"She could have it and we could take care of it."

"Who? You? You want to raise a baby instead of finishing school and going to college and making your own life? Or do you want me to do it?"

"Well, you've done it before. Twice. Once with Aunt Laura, and once with me. You know how. We could get a nurse—"

"No. As you say, I've done that. I have other things I need to do now. The baby is Aunt Laura's responsibility."

"She isn't going to take it."

"No."

"That's awful."

"Don't judge, Glynn. You just don't know enough yet. It will be a while before you do."

"You said we're going home—"

"Yes. In about an hour. So let's get you fed and packed up. Aunt Laura's going to take us to the airport."

"Are you . . . are we going to stop by at the tower?"

"No."

"So I won't see Curtis again?"

"You can walk up and say good-bye, and we'll pick you up on the way out," I said. "And I'll bet T.C. will send you a picture of Curtis. Why don't you ask him?"

"I don't see how I can talk to him."

"It's easy. Just open your mouth and let 'er rip."

"What should I say?"

"How about, 'Good-bye, T.C.'?" I said, and felt the tears again, and turned quickly to the refrigerator to get out the eggs and bacon.

She came close behind me and touched my shoulder.

"Mama, I'm so sorry. About what I said, and about . . . T.C.," she said, and vanished into her room.

"Me, too, my little girl, who never will be that again," I whispered.

She had finished her breakfast and gone to repack her duffel when Laura came back. I had put on the blue traveling suit from a faraway life, stacked my bags at the back door, and was putting our bed linens into the washing machine. Laura had said she would come back to the lodge and spend the night and make sure all traces of us were gone before she started for Palm Springs.

"I can't stand the thought that his next . . . whatever . . . might find something I left behind and put it on," she said. "On second thought, maybe I should hide my dirty underwear where he'll never find it. Make him smell me every time he turns around."

Now she came and stood in the sun beside me and leaned comfortably against me. We stood that way for a bit.

"If I were you I would never leave him," she said

presently, and I turned to look into her face. Tears stood in her eyes.

"He's so torn up over you he can barely talk. But we did, a little bit. About you. I would give a whole lot for a man I loved to say the things he did."

I could not speak. I hoped desperately she was not going to tell me what he had said. She didn't. There did not seem to be anything at all to say, so I said nothing, either. We leaned together in the mounting heat, smelling the scent of sun-burned pine, feeling our shoulders press together. I thought that I could easily sleep standing there.

"But then," she said briskly, "I'm not you and he's not Pring, and if anybody did say those things to me I'd probably smart off at him and ruin it. Y'all packed? I guess we ought to get this show on the road."

The trunk of the Mustang was up, and the top was down, and we were ready for the road, and the wind, and the sun. But I did not think that this time we would sing.

Glynn came out with her duffel and slung it into the trunk. I put my bags in and Laura slammed it shut.

"Well," she said.

"Did you see Curtis?" Glynn asked Laura, and Laura nodded.

"He's up there with his daddy, helping him fiddle around with that junk under the shed. He said to tell you he's waiting for you to come say good-bye."

"Then I think I will," Glynn said, and looked at me, waiting. I nodded.

"Pick you up in a minute," Laura said.

Glynn started up the trail, and then came running back and hugged us both, hard. She looked cool and pure and young again, with her clean, shining skin and the palomino hair falling in a soft bang over her forehead. I could smell the soap and shampoo; she had showered again, I thought. Her cheek was still damp, and cool.

"We really are a family, aren't we?" she said, muffled in my hair. "We went through all this whole crappy week and we came out still a family. I'm so glad."

"Me, too," I whispered, and Laura hugged her hard and

said, "Cain't nothin' bust this act up, pardner," and Glynn
laughed and turned to the trail again.

As on the first morning when I had started up the trail
toward the tower, lost in fog, we heard Curtis before we saw
him. He was barking, sharp, steady, peremptory barks I had
never heard before. He barked steadily and did not stop, and
as he came nearer, the barking got louder, and we could hear
the thudding of his feet before he exploded around the bend
and shot toward us like an arrow.

"Oh, you old dog," Glynn cried, stretching out her arms.
"You couldn't wait!"

But he did not run into her arms. He danced before us,
staring hard into our faces, barking, barking. When we did
not, for a moment, respond, he jumped up and put his feet on
Glynn's shoulders and barked into her face.

"What?" she said helplessly.

I saw the note in his collar then. No bandanna this morning, just a scrap of torn paper stuck under his worn red leather
collar. It was perforated, and there were words scrawled across
it in red. The paper from T.C.'s homemade seismograph, the
pen from it.

I took it from Curtis's collar.

Get out now, it said. The red pen skidded off the paper in
a scrawl. I stared at the note, and then at Glynn and Laura.
Curtis barked and barked.

It smote me then like a great wave, cold and numbing.

"There's an earthquake coming," I said, forcing the words
through shaking lips. "We've got to go *now*."

Laura gave a small scream and instinctively crouched in
the doorway with her arms crossed over her stomach. Glynn,
white-faced, turned and headed for the house.

"*No!*" I screamed. "Not in there! Stay out in the open, lie
down!"

Curtis was a sleek, dark missile as he leaped at Glynn and
caught the tail of her shirt in his teeth. He pulled fiercely, and
she stumbled out of the door and down the one granite step.
He knocked her to the ground and leaped on her. I started for
both of them.

It hit then.

You seldom hear them, all the experts will tell you. You will, of course, hear the roar and crashing of falling masonry and collapsing beams if you are near man-made structures, and you will hear the whipping and long, tearing cracks of trees splitting, and the thunder of their falling, and later you will hear the shrieks of car and house alarms and the icy crystal tinkle of shattering glass, and even later you will hear the fire and rescue alarms, and perhaps the cries of those who still live. But you will not, in all odds, hear the quake itself.

But I heard it. I knew in that moment that I was hearing the very voice of the snake, and I know it now, though I am told over and over that I could not have. The quake was deep in the earth; its hypocenter was almost as deep as the Loma Prieta, and that was the deepest ever recorded on the San Andreas fault. No man-made drill has ever reached that black depth, where the earth is no longer solid. I heard its deep-buried war cry, like the long bellow of a great distant steer, and I felt its indrawn breath even before the ground began to move. In the instant that I felt my body come down over those of Glynn and Curtis, I thought, this is what T.C. means. This is what he hears; this is what he feels.

The shaking began then, a violent, furious, side-to-side heaving as if something unimaginably huge had taken the earth in its fist and shaken, and then the ground rolled like the sea, and we were flung from side to side so hard that we ended up on our backs, fully ten feet from the place we had hit the ground. I remember lying there with my arms stretched out over my daughter and the dog, watching the air thicken rapidly with swirling dust so dense that I saw the sun grayly, as if through morning fog, and felt a great hot wind driving particles of grit and bark and pinecone into my face and mouth. It was so strong a wind that even in that moment of blank terror I wondered at it. I had never heard of an earthquake wind. Only later did I hear someone saying that in the mountains the quake had been so severe that the whipping treetops stirred up a wild windstorm before they began to come down.

When they did begin to fall, the noise of their dying was louder than anything that had gone before: the long, shrieking cracks, the snap, the whistling of the hot wind, the great,

following booms of their collision with the ground, the sighing rustling of their last limbs and leaves and needles as they
settled into the treacherous earth. On top of their death cries
came a long, shuddering, rattling thunder; I thought, idiotical-
ly, of the great elephant stampede in *Elephant Walk*. Elizabeth
Taylor, hadn't it been? Whipping my head to the side I saw
that the lodge had settled in upon itself like those buildings
you see demolished on TV, by implosion. The dust was now
blinding. The screams of the redwoods went on and on.

Somewhere in there, the rolling and shaking stopped, but
the trees did not. I became aware gradually that I was screaming at them, a high, endless dirge of fury: "You will not! You
will not! By God you will not, you will not . . ."

I saw the one that would finish us. It was falling directly
over us, slowly; so slowly that it seemed to have been filmed in
slow motion. It came down and down, its scragged top denud-
ed of needles, growing larger and larger. Still I howled in my
rage, "You *will not* . . ."

Something like a great, black, scratching, spurring ptero-
dactyl settled down over my face and then my body, shutting
out the dust and the light and the sound of everything but my
voice, still screaming invective. I waited for the darkness to
swallow me, but it did not; there was a gigantic, shuddering
thud, larger than any that had gone before, and a screech of
tearing metal, and a great whistling of limbs, and the little
knives of needles and branch tips cutting my face, and a great,
diffuse weight sinking onto my body. But no more darkness
came. There was a last thud, and the earth shook with it, and
then there was silence. Nothing more. Just sun and dust and
silence.

Much later, I don't know how long, I felt a tentative
squirming beneath me, and heard my daughter's muffled voice
crying, "Mama? Mama!"

The redwood had come down sidewise across us, its top
striking the Mustang. The Mustang had flattened, but it had
held enough to take the main weight of the tree. The ptero-
dactyl had been its outer top limbs; they had been small
enough so that they cut my face and tore my pantsuit to
shreds, but their combined weight had not been enough to

hurt me badly. I pushed the branches off me, stood up on shaking legs, grabbed the longest one and pulled. It lifted, groaning, off Glynn and, beneath her, Curtis, just far enough for them to wriggle free. They did not, though; Glynn lay there looking at me with great, empty eyes, and even Curtis was still. I could see his eyes though, dark and bright, moving restlessly about him, and see his doggy, panting pink grin through the gray mask of dust that he wore. Glynn wore one, too. She was a gray child, a daughter of dust.

"*Move!*" I shouted, and she did, wriggling out like a snake, and Curtis followed her, shaking himself so that dust flew and needles sprayed around him.

I let go of the branch and it snapped back, and I sat down hard on the ground and closed my eyes. Later, they told me I could not possibly have lifted the branches, but I simply looked at them in their ignorance. I could have lifted them with one hand; the rage was that strong. I could not even tell where I left off and that red, boiling rage began.

Like the quake, the rage ended suddenly, too, and I simply sat on the ground with my daughter kneeling beside me and Curtis at her side, nosing her all over, nosing at me. I did not open my eyes. Later, in a moment, I would get up and we would go away from here. They were not hurt. I was not hurt. We would go away, we would go home. . . .

"Mama," Glynn was shaking me. "Mama, Aunt Laura! Help me get Aunt Laura out! I can hear her."

I could too, then. She was crying softly, from the heaped, dust-swirling mess that had been the lodge. We could not see her, the dust still swirled so thickly, but I could follow the sound of her, and led by Curtis, we ran to the pile of rubble and leaned down to it.

Like us, the treetop had saved her. The treetop and the doorframe, hewed all those years ago from thick, solid Western pine. It still stood, like a ruined but not vanquished arch of a fallen Greek temple, and beneath it, under tangles of bare black and green, Laura lay huddled on her side, her eyes screwed shut, crying.

She lay in a fetal ball, wrapped in her arms, and also like me, she was completely whitened with leprous dust, and runnels of shocking red blood cut down her face and arms, from the little knives of the needles and branch tips.

"My baby," she sobbed. "My baby, oh, God, Met, my baby."

It was a kitten's sound, with no breath behind it. I reached in among the branches and lifted her to her knees. Still, she cried. Still, her arms wrapped her stomach. Still, her eyes were shut tight. Glynn and I pulled the branches off her and stood her up between us, and I looked her over sharply. I could see nothing amiss but the scratches and the dust.

"Can you talk?" I said. "Open your eyes, Laura, and look at me. I think you're okay. The tree took the weight of the house off you. Open your eyes!"

She did, looking at me with white-ringed golden eyes. Her pupils were black and huge, but her breathing seemed all right, though shallow and very slow. Shock, almost surely; I had had all the right Red Cross courses. But nothing else that showed. Perhaps, after all, we would be all right.

"My baby," she whispered again, and I looked quickly between her bare, bloodied white legs, but saw no terrible, spreading stain.

"Are you in pain? Do you think you're bleeding?"

"No . . . no . . ."

"All right. Then your baby's probably fine. They're a lot tougher than we are. We just need to go slowly now—"

"Where are we going to go?" she said in the breathy whisper that had taken the place of her rich voice.

"I'm going up to T.C.'s," I said, sure of it in that moment. "I'll go up there and get him, and he'll take us out in the Jeep. Listen, this is wonderful; he's got a complete earthquake kit that he keeps in an old safe on the porch, with first-aid stuff and food and bottled water, and flashlights and blankets and . . . and everything. I know right where it is. I'm going to walk up there now, and we'll come back in the Jeep and get you. You all sit down. Glynn, sit your Aunt Laura down and put her head between her knees and keep her still, and if she starts to bleed take off your shirt and press it up there and hold it—"

"I want to go with you," Glynn began to whimper. Her eyes filled with tears, and they tracked down through the white dust, leaving snail-like trails. "Don't go off and leave us; what if it comes back; what if Aunt Laura's not all right; what if something happens to you—"

"No," I said calmly and firmly. A ringing, faraway peace had fallen over me, now that I knew just what to do, now that I knew where to go.

"You're perfectly all right but your aunt is in shock, and you cannot leave her. The earthquake is not coming back. If you feel anything else it will be an aftershock and will not hurt you. What on earth could happen to me? I'm just going a quarter mile up the trail—"

"Mama—"

"You are not a child, Glynn," I said, and she fell silent and looked at me out of her minstrel's face.

"All right," she said softly, and I gave her cheek a quick pat and started up the trail.

Beside me, Curtis whined and whined, dancing in place, looking from me up toward the invisible tower, and I said, "Okay, Curtis, you marvelous, darling hero, you. Go home. Carpe diem."

He was off like a shot, in silence, and I listened until I heard the thudding of his feet in the dust fade, and then began once more to walk. Only then did I realize that my left arm was hanging useless at my side, and that no matter how I tried, I could not lift it. It did not hurt, but when I tried again to move it a sharp, not-unpleasant shock rather like electricity shot up into my shoulder.

"Okay," I said aloud. "To hell with it. I don't care. It doesn't hurt. T.C. will fix it."

I talked aloud the entire time I was on the trail. It was chatty talk, with a sort of hilarity bubbling just under its surface. The path looked nothing like it had before; trees were down across it, and the spill of a small rockslide blocked it at one point, so that I had to climb over it, and far over to my left, at the edge of the forest, I could see that earth had opened in a great fissure that whipped off into the depths of the woods. Beside it, trees were torn off midway up their trunks. I could not see into the depths of the opened earth. But the long, golden rays of sunlight still fell, incredibly, though now on ruin. Ferns were pulped and most of the small flowers and bushes buried by a rainstorm of needles and thick white dust. I turned my head back and did not look again.

"What a shame," I said. "It's such a pretty place. Maybe it will be like those places in the wilderness where there is a wildfire; maybe the flowers and trees will come back even stronger."

But I knew that it would be far out of my lifetime before these redwoods stood tall again. The knowledge did not seem to pierce the shell of the peace, though.

"Well, so, this is what we'll do," I said. "We'll put a sling on this arm and put Curtis and the kit in the Jeep, and we'll take some food and water with us in case we can't get through for a while, and we'll pick up Laura and Glynn and we'll get as far as we can today. Maybe we can get all the way through with no trouble. If we don't, they'll be looking for us pretty soon, and they'll probably find us before we get to them. They'll patch us up and give us something clean to wear, and put us on a plane home. Laura will come with us, of course. No more of this silliness about not having the baby. Oh, wait, oh damn . . . Pring won't know yet there's been an earthquake. Well, then . . . no, Stuart is dead. How could I have forgotten that? Poor Stuart. But the forest service must know somebody's been at the lodge; but then, how would they? T.C. hasn't seen anybody this week that I haven't seen, and they sure haven't been the park service. Maybe Marcie's father and stepmother, then . . .

"Pom will know. Of course. Pom knows where I am. Pom will tell them, Pom will come . . .

"Pom will come.

"Won't he?"

I walked on in the sun, muttering busily to myself. The silence was larger and deeper than I had ever heard it. No birds sang. The great, surflike breathing of the redwoods was still. Nothing rustled in the undergrowth, nothing chirped or buzzed or clicked. It was hot and still and it seemed to me that I walked and walked without making any progress, and that the sun was frozen in its arc overhead, and that it was no time at all. My own chattering voice was the only sound that went with me.

And then there was a sound, and my heart dropped like a stone and froze as solid as black ice in my chest, and I stopped. It was a howl; a terrible, primal animal howl of pain and desolation, and it rose and rose and rose through the heat and swirling dust until I thought that my eardrums would burst with it. And then it stopped.

"Don't do this, T.C.," I whispered, breaking into a trot. "This is just too much. This is not fair."

I came into the clearing on rubbery, leaden legs and stopped. There was no tower, no shed, no Jeep, no surrounding trees. Only a huge, dust-whitened pile of rubble, like that the lodge had disintegrated into; only a swirling cloud of dust; only the stems of maimed redwoods; only their fresh-torn yellow flesh.

Only Curtis, lying at the edge of the rubble pile, his head on his paws, whining and whining.

I went across the clearing to him, stepping over branches and chunks of wood and metal and once a recognizable piece of T.C.'s earthquake machine, the part that had been, I thought, the hi-fi speaker. I knelt down at the edge of the monstrous pile and put my hand on Curtis's back. He thumped his tail, but did not move.

"T.C.?" I asked experimentally, and the answering silence was so terrible that I did not speak his name again. I did not look around for him, either. I sat down on the earth crosslegged, like a child playing Indian, and laid my hands in my lap.

I want you to come out from there right now, I said prissily in my head. This is not funny.

Then I said, thought, oh, of course, he's gone for help, to get a truck or a car or something.

But I knew he had not. He would have taken Curtis with him.

I looked down at the dog. It was only then that I noticed that his paws were bloody, and his muzzle, and that he had laid his head on something that he was guarding, for he would not lift his muzzle when I tried to see what it was.

"Are you hurt, sweet dog?" I said, and picked up his paws, one after another. He let me do that. The blood was damp-dry and I could scrape it off, and when I did I saw no torn flesh, no injuries.

"Oh, good," I said to him. "I couldn't have stood it if you'd been hurt. Okay. Good. Good."

He lifted his head then, and laid it on my knee, and I saw that what he had been guarding was a pair of metal-rimmed glasses, mended with tape, whole except for the lenses, which were spiderwebbed with cracks. I looked from them to the rubble pile. I could see then that Curtis had tunneled far into it, but that the debris had slid back down and filled it partly in. I did not move to clear it out.

I lay down on the earth beside Curtis, carefully, because my electric shoulder and arm spat and crackled at me. No pain followed, though. I stretched myself full out and laid my injured arm at my side and put the other one around Curtis. He wriggled until he had fit himself into my side, and we lay there together, silent and still. I worked my good fingers under his chin and picked up the shattered glasses and cupped them loosely in my palm.

At first, even in the pounding sun, my body was cold. The earth itself and the rubble and dust upon it were warm, but they gave no heat to my body. I was as cold and stiff as if it had been a long, terrible arctic cold that felled me. Only Curtis, in the curve of my arm, was warm. He did not move.

Very gradually though, so gradually that I was only aware of it after it had happened, warmth seeped up from the earth and into my body. It seeped into my stomach and flattened breasts, out to the end of my fingers and toes, into my cheek where it lay pressed into the dust. The cold and stiffness drained away, and my body seemed to melt into the very earth. I shifted to feel it even closer, and then lay still. Curtis still did not move.

Far below me the earth spasmed again as the great snake, sated, flexed itself voluptuously. Rage flooded back, but it was a dull rage, abstract.

"You fucking bitch," I whispered to her. "You seduced him. You talked to him and you sang to him and you made love to him, and then you never told him. You didn't tell him. He loved you, and you didn't tell him . . . "

But she had. Told him just far enough in advance so he could send his emissary flying to us: *Get out now.*

I closed my eyes again, and waited, and the rage gradually slunk away and the warmth came stealing back. It was as if his body lay beneath me, giving me its warmth through the broken earth.

"Hey," I whispered. "You there?"

Always, I heard, though not with my ears.

"You got your wishes, you know," I said into the earth. "All three of them. And now you won't ever have to leave. Only I have to do that. Don't worry, though. I'm not going for a while. Not for a long time."

Stay.

Maybe I will. Maybe I will.

And I lay there, not moving, joined to him through the earth as I had been above it, only a day ago. I closed my eyes and drifted in silence and time, Curtis heavy and warm against me, the earth softening below. This is not bad, I thought. This is good. Presently I felt the stiff, bloodied white mask on my face split with a smile, and I wondered if, when it happened, he had been dancing.

12

It was Glynn who led us out. Glynn and Curtis, walking side by side, she with a stout branch she used for a walking stick, Curtis padding steadily beside her, head and tail down, wearing the harness she had fashioned that carried some of our supplies. Forever after when I thought of valor, I thought of my tall daughter going before me, the dog like a patient wolf by her side.

I don't know when it was that she came to me at the ruin of the tower. I know I heard her calling me up the trail before I saw her, heard the anxiety and the last remnants of the child in her voice, and heard her cry of fear when she saw me lying on my stomach with the dog beside me, motionless. It seemed that the sun was higher, directly overhead perhaps, but the thick, sullen heat of the past few days was gone. It was as if the snake had loosed her grip on the very skies when she was sated, and let the winds blow free again.

Glynn knelt beside me, beginning to cry, and I made an effort far larger than I thought I was capable of and sat up. Curtis, who had lifted his head at her voice, hauled himself to a sitting position, too, and thumped his tail faintly.

"I'm all right, baby. Just resting," I said, my voice thick and cracked in my dry throat. It was as if I had not spoken for months, years.

"Oh, Mama! It's all gone! Oh, God . . . Curtis! Mama, he's got blood all over—"

"It's not his blood, baby. He's not hurt. I looked."

She was silent. Then she said, "Is he . . . under there?"

I nodded. I was afraid to look at her. If the frail, shining shell around me cracked I did not think I could survive what rushed in.

Another silence, and then: "We have to dig. Mama, we have to dig for him. Lots of people survive earthquakes; you hear about them being found later perfectly okay—"

"No."

"Mama—"

"*No*, Glynn."

"I'm so sorry."

I heard her begin to cry again, softly, and I touched her dust-whitened knee and said, "You can't cry, baby. I'm sorry too, but that's one thing that we just can't afford right now. Later, but not now. Now we have to think what to do."

But I could not think. I wanted only to sit in the sun beside the great, obscene mound of rubble and be very quiet and still.

Presently she reached down and took hold of my arm to pull me up. A great shaft of electricity shot up to my shoulder. I cried out.

"Oh, Mama, you're hurt!"

"It doesn't really hurt. It just sort of buzzes. But I can't move it. I think it may be broken. It's my left one, though. I can use my right one just fine."

She sat back on her heels, her arm around the big dog, who leaned against her, his eyes closed. She scratched his chin in silence. Then she said, "Okay. We're going to have to walk out of here. We'll need some things to take with us. Let me poke around in this stuff and see if there's anything. . . . "

It was not a voice I had heard before. I looked at her mutely. She looked back at me levelly, as if daring me to contradict her.

"I think we should stay here," I said dreamily. "It's warm right here in the sun, and the . . . wreckage makes a shelter from the wind. We're close to the road. Someone will come before long. Your dad will come. . . . "

She looked at me, hope flaming in her eyes.

"Does Daddy know where we are?"

"Sort of. He knows we were up in these mountains; I think I told him Big Basin."

She shook her head.

"That's not good enough. You're hurt. Aunt Laura is . . . I don't know. She just sits there holding her stomach and staring. I don't think we can wait for anybody to remember we're up here. They may not even be able to get to us. We don't know what the road is like—"

"Glynn," I said, "how are we going to get a shocked, pregnant woman and a one-armed one out of here? What will we do if we don't find our way to a town or something before it gets dark? We don't even know what's still standing; I have no idea how bad that thing was."

Her chin lifted. She looked like she had when she had been a four-year-old, haughtily offended when someone told her she was too young to do something she wished to do. In spite of myself, I smiled. I felt the mask crack again.

"I'm going to get us out," she said. "I've had eight years of scouting. I took that emergency course at school last semester. All I need is a few things for us to take along; didn't you say there was an earthquake kit here somewhere? In an old safe? I don't think I can get into where the lodge kitchen used to be, and the car trunk is . . . gone. But maybe a safe would hold."

I drew a breath to argue with her, and then let it out. I was simply too tired to talk. Come to that, I was too tired to walk. Let her find that out for herself, later; activity and planning would be good for her now. In a moment we would see about Laura. In a moment.

"Here," she said, "hold on to Curtis. I'm going to poke around in this stuff. There's all kinds of things sticking up out of it."

"Be careful," I murmured, and put my arm around Curtis. He moved against me and tucked his head under my arm. He was warm and solid, and I clung to him, smelling the dusty smell of still-hot dog hair.

It seemed a long time later when I heard her cry out, "Here it is! Hot shit! Part of the steps held the rubble off it! Oh, thank God, it's busted open, and there's all kinds of stuff in it."

Thank you, I said in my head to him. You're going to get us out after all, aren't you?

Told you, he said.

Glynn had her things together in about an hour. From the battered safe she took two Mylar blankets, so thin they folded to washcloth size, and a first-aid kit and packets of freeze-dried food and coffee and trail mix, and a flashlight and compass and spare batteries. She found a map and folded it into the pocket of her jeans, along with matches and a folding water cup. There were plastic bottles of water, too, but they were too bulky for us to carry many of them, so she set aside only four. She made a sling for my arm out of an ace bandage and snugged it tight. Then she fashioned a kind of harness that fit around Curtis's chest and neck and tucked the blankets and freeze-dried packets and trail mix into it. Curtis sat passively, but whenever she passed he thumped his tail, and she stroked his head. He had not moved from his position at the edge of the rubble pile, though.

Curtis and I sat together while she went back down to the lodge for Laura.

I'm so proud of her, I told T.C.

Kid's got good genes, he said.

The only thing left to say then was good-bye, and I could not say that, so we sat placidly in the sun, Curtis and I, in the same companionable silence that the three of us had often shared in the last days.

When Glynn brought Laura up I felt a bolt of pure fear go through me. She walked like a little old woman, bent far over, her arms crossed over her stomach, staring straight ahead of her. She was whitened and bloodied and her clothes, like mine, were shredded by the whipping branches. Glynn lowered her to the ground beside me and I reached out and touched her arm with my good one, and she put her hand over it, but she did not speak or look at me. Her flesh was as cold as death.

I patted her in silence. Surely Glynn would see that we must stay here now. This woman could not walk.

But Glynn shook out one of the blankets and tucked it around Laura, and started a small, wavering wood fire in a spot of clear ground, and opened one of the bottles of water and washed Laura's face and arms and hands gently with moistened gauze from the kit, and when she had cleaned most of the blood and dust and grit away, she put salve all over the scratches, and made instant coffee in the folding cup and held it to Laura's mouth while she sipped it, and then gave her more water and with it two aspirin. Then she did the same to me. When her own face and arms were cleaned and salved, and we had all had heavily sugared hot coffee and aspirin, she stamped out the fire and scattered the ashes, and tied two of the bottles of water to her belt and made a belt for me out of the twine from the kit and hung the other two from my waist.

She stopped and considered her handiwork, hands on hips, and then went back to the safe and took out a heavy Swiss army knife and dropped it into her pocket. Then she came back.

"We have to go now," she said. "It's the middle of the afternoon. According to the map, if we turned right on the road instead of left like we usually do, we'd come to a little town called Boulder Creek that's a lot closer than anything else. It's south, I think. That's where we'll head. If the road's clear we could maybe walk it by tonight. Or I could, and could bring people back for you, but we have to get on the main road. Nobody can see us in here."

Laura said nothing, and I didn't either.

"Get up, Mom," my daughter said and held out her hand, and I pulled myself up with my right arm. I swayed dizzily, unreality boiling over me, but in a moment I was steadier.

"Help me," she said, and together we got Laura to her feet. The coffee and aspirin seemed to have helped some; her eyes made contact with ours, and she smiled, the bleached ghost of her old smile.

"Merritt and Laura and Glynn's excellent adventure," she whispered. "Wouldn't *this* make a movie, though?"

"How do you feel?" I said.

"Queer. Okay. Nothing seems real. The baby feels all right. Have I bled any?"

"No," Glynn said. "I've kept checking. I think you'll be all right if we take it slow, and we'll rest real often."

Above me the trees sighed, the first time in days I had heard that great, elemental breathing. The wind touched my face and ruffled my hair.

Whenever you hear wind in the tops of trees, that's me, he had said.

Well, I have to go now, I said to him. I've stayed as long as I could. We have to take care of everybody now.

It's time, he agreed.

You mustn't worry about Curtis; Glynn will love him forever and ever. So will I.

I know.

I think I will die from losing you.

Who said you were losing me? Don't you remember anything?

I remember. About the pine and spruce, and the redwoods in *National Geographic*, and the crab and the wine and the cold shower and the wet dog and the day-old socks and the *Rattus ratti*. I remember . . .

Then . . . Carpe diem, Merritt.

Carpe diem, T.C.

"Come on, Curtis," Glynn said, snapping her fingers lightly. "Carpe diem."

Slowly the big brown dog got up from his place on the earth. He looked back and whined softly, and then came to stand beside her. She put her fingers lightly on his head, and picked up her staff, and we began to walk. No one but Curtis looked back.

We walked for about an hour before we stopped the first time. We soon found our natural order: Glynn and Curtis in front, Laura and me behind. We had started out single file, with me behind Laura so I could catch her if she wavered and swayed, but she looked around so often to see if I was there that I soon moved up beside her. She trudged along, her hand on my right arm, looking down at her feet. After a time I looked down, too. Not only was the going slow and treacherous, with fallen trees and tossed boulders to pick our way around, but the sight of the blasted redwoods and the litter of bark and needles and dust was simply too terrible. By the time we reached the place where the lodge trail cut off Highway 9, we were sweating and I was shivering and rubber-legged. So was Laura.

It was time to stop, and we would have in any case, but what really stopped us was that the road was no longer there.

T.C.'s fire tower sat on the very top of the ridge that defined the spine of the mountains. The road was cut into the side of it, about a hundred feet down the opposite side. That hundred feet of blasted earth was all that was visible now. The earth had simply let go and flowed over the patched, bumpy old road, obliterating it as certainly as if there had always only been raw, clawed earth and shattered trees and rocks. We looked straight out into a sea of devastation that swept down to meet the next ridge before it rose again in a series of corrugations that stretched toward the suburban sprawl around San Jose. We could not see the suburbs there for the sea of diminishing ridges, and I was profoundly thankful. I could not even imagine what the human places must be like. This was awful enough, this casual, bomblike devastation of the wild places.

As far south as we could see there was no road, only landslide rubble and the great, hovering cloud of dust. I sat slowly down on the earth beside the twisted sign that said "Pringle," which had somehow survived the slide, and drew Laura down with me. She leaned her head on my good shoulder and closed her eyes.

"Okay, let's take a break," Glynn said matter-of-factly, as if we did not stand in the middle of devastation and the very textbook definition of lostness.

She sat down and patted the earth beside her and Curtis flopped down panting, and she set about ministering to us once more. Water, and more aspirin, and a cup of water for Curtis, and spread out blankets for us to lie back on.

"Everybody put their feet up," she said. "I need to think a minute."

"Darling, I'm going to have to insist—" I began, but she shushed me impatiently.

"This can be figured out," she said, pulling out the map and spreading it out on the ground. "I just need to concentrate. You take care of Aunt Laura."

I was silent. On my shoulder Laura slept heavily. My other arm and shoulder throbbed savagely. I could not even remember when the pain had begun. I was somehow grateful for it. It focused me solidly in the now, kept at bay the river of grief and loss that waited up on the mountaintop to pour down over me. I refused Glynn's offer of aspirin for that reason. I needed this pain as I needed air to breathe. If whatever conclusion my daughter reached about what we should do next seemed unreasonable to me, I would simply refuse to get up from the earth. There was little she could do about that.

It was only much later, looking cautiously back at that time under the wing of therapy, that I could see how close to passive, inert madness I had been.

"I think this is what we can do," Glynn said later; I did not know how much later. "I think that if we walk along the ridge right where the landslide started, always keeping next to the edge of it, we'd be following the road, or paralleling it. You can tell where the edge is; it's where the trees have fallen and the rocks have come out of the ground, where the ground is torn up. It's as plain as if it had been marked. It may take us longer because we'll be going through underbrush and rubble, but it's just not that far to Boulder Creek. If we have to spend the night out, well, we've got all the stuff for it. We'll get there tomorrow for sure."

"If Boulder Creek is still there," I said lazily. The lassitude that had taken Laura was nibbling at the edge of my consciousness, too.

"It'll be there," Glynn snapped. "Earthquakes don't wipe out whole towns. What's the matter with you, Mama?"

I simply looked at her, and she colored and turned away, tears coming into her eyes.

"I'm sorry," she said.

And so we set off across the broken, strewn earth beside the invisible road, and Glynn was right: the going was much slower. And it was much rougher. It was as if we were struggling through utter, trackless wilderness, over rubble piles and around the tops of fallen trees and through ruined undergrowth and around boulders taller by far than we were. Even with the stout sticks that Glynn found for Laura and me, we only accomplished a few hundred feet before we had to stop and rest again, and we were soon footsore and striped with dozens of new branch slashes that bled down our faces and on our hands. Our shoes were tearing apart, too. Only Glynn wore stout running shoes; Laura had put on her smart, pointed-toe boots that morning and was limping badly, and my own much-maligned Ferragamos were simply ribbons of leather by now, as useless as stocking feet. My feet hurt viciously in a hundred places, and my face burned from branch whips, and I gloried savagely in each new pain. It meant that I was alive. There seemed, by then, no other way to tell.

When Curtis began to limp Glynn stopped us for the night. It did not seem to me that we had come any distance at all, only struggled in place in a malevolent, blasted forest, but she showed me on the map.

"See that high place, where the brown color is?" she said happily. "I think that's the highest point on the road; it looks over Boulder Creek, both the creek and the town, I mean. We could see whatever was there for miles and miles from there, and we should be able to see the town. I think we're only a mile or two from there. We can do that easy in the morning. Right now it's nearly six and the fog is coming in and we can't go anywhere in that, anyway. We'll find a spot and make a fire and eat supper and sleep, and then, when we wake up, everything will be okay."

She looked up from the map at me, and it was as if I was seeing her, suddenly, for the first time after a long absence. She was Glynn again, my beautiful, good child, who had done something she knew would please me and make me proud, and was looking into my face for the signs of my approval.

I reached out and brushed the dusty hair off her face, and spit on my fingers and wiped a dried runnel of blood off her cheekbone. Then I drew her head down to mine and kissed her, tasting dust.

"I am very, very proud of you," I said, my voice shaking. "You have done something today that your mother and your aunt could not do, and I doubt that many adults could have. You are a real hero, Glynn. I not only love you, I need you. It may be a long time before I say that to you again, but I can't not say it today. And I say it with shame, because I'm the one who's supposed to take care of you, and here it is the other way around. But I say it with more pride than you will ever know, too. Your father is going to feel the same way."

She laid her head down on my shoulder and let me hold her for a while, and I could feel the fine, birdlike trembling in her body and hear her breath coming in short, shallow little gasps.

"I can be as brave as it takes if you're with me," she whispered. "I don't think I could have come a step by myself."

We were quiet for a little while, and then we both said, together, "I love you," and laughed and pulled apart. She went a little ahead to find a campsite for us, and I went back to Laura.

We finally settled in a small hollow in the lee of a huge boulder, with dense encircling brush for a windbreak and a little level stretch of earth in which to make a fire. The fog was coming in fast, in scarves and billows, filling the world up to the tops of the standing trees with wet white cotton batting, and once again, as I had before, I tasted the salt of the sea. I had tasted it, I remembered, on Point Reyes, too. I realized then that I was crying silently, and could no longer tell the taste of my tears from the taste of sea fog, and swallowed hard. Later. The tears were for later; the tears must not start now. There would be time for them; there would be a whole lifetime for them.

Because we were in a small depression the fog did not sink completely down around us, and we could see what we were about fairly clearly, though as if through stage scrim. Glynn and I dragged dry twigs and limbs from the undersides of the fallen trees, and she lit the little fire with T.C.'s matches. It flamed up cheerfully, its rosy light dancing off the solid white blanket of the fog. Curtis lay down close to it and put his head on his crossed paws and sighed deeply. I went over and sat down next to him, drawing comfort from the small spot of warmth and the dog's solid body.

"It may not be the fire you want, but it will keep you warm through this night, and me too, and we will take care of each other. That's not nothing, dearest dog," I said. He thumped his tail a little harder this time and sighed again, leaning in against me. But his eyes followed Glynn as she moved about in the firelight. Behind me, Laura stretched and sighed and said, "That feels good. Are we stopping for the night?"

"Yep. Supper and coffee in a minute, and then we'll sleep. Do you think you can?"

"I don't think the united forces of hell could stop me," she said drowsily, and it was true. By the time Glynn and I had water boiling and food packets laid out, she was sleeping heavily on the spread Mylar blanket, her breath as deep and regular as the surf of the sea. It sounded so normal to me, so healing, that I hated to wake her, but I did, nevertheless. She needed food and water, and I thought another two aspirin might take her through the night. I took more, too. My arm was a column of pure pain. Laura was asleep again almost before she lay back down on the blanket.

After we had eaten and Curtis had had reconstituted beef stew and water, Glynn said, "I want to stay awake to keep the fire going. I'm going to stretch out for just a little while; do you think you can stay awake long enough to wake me in a couple of hours?"

"You bet," I said. "You and Curtis roll up in that blanket and lie down beside the fire. It's going to get cold before morning. I'll poke you in a little while."

"No longer than two hours," she said, and called Curtis to her and rolled the Mylar blanket around them both, and stretched out before the fire.

"Night," she mumbled sleepily, and I smiled in the darkness. I had no intention of waking her before dawn. I did not intend to let myself sleep. Now, now was the time to let go and sink down into it; to see how far I could go before I had to pull back before the howling pain and emptiness. Now, when no one else would have to bear the cost of it.

"Night, darling," I said to her. She did not reply.

I pulled the blanket more closely around Laura and put the trailing end of it around my shoulders. We lay close together, she breathing slowly, I staring into the fire and trying to unclench the frozen fist inside me. I was not cold; the fire warmed my body, but the space around my heart was cold once more as it had been when I had first lain down on the earth above T.C.

I don't know if I can let it go, I said to him. I don't know if I'll still have you if I do.

I said you would, didn't I? Didn't I tell you that?

It doesn't feel like it.

Then take it on faith.

T.C., you said I'd always have you and you'd have me as long as you lived. So now what? Damn it, have I . . . has— what did you call her? The Merritt of Merritt's Creek—is she with only you now? Do I still have any of her?

I said you still have me, didn't I? Well, if you have me, you have her. As long as you still have me, she'll be with you.

What am I going to do with her back in Atlanta, T.C.? Nobody there even knows who she is. Do I have to hide her; will she ambush me; what if I can't find her after all? Or suppose if I can. I don't think Pom would know what to do with her. I don't think she would know what to do with Pom. Not with anybody but you.

If you're smart you'll let her out and sic her on ol' Pom and let her just flat turn him inside out. You'd be a fool to waste that woman, Merritt.

He may not be able to accept her.

Then he's a fool too, a worse one than I think he is. Don't go hunting tomorrow's trouble. Carpe Diem. How many times do I have to say it.

I turned over restlessly, and Laura stirred.

"Who you talkin' to?" she said thickly.

"T.C.," I said. "Go back to sleep."

"Oh," she said, and did.

The thing is, you don't need to settle, Merritt. Use everything you were up here. Use it to get what you want back there.

What do I do with all that leftover love? That was yours.

Didn't I hear you say that love made more love? Didn't I hear you tell Glynn that yesterday morning?

Yes . . .

Well, then.

I must have slept after all, because presently the little fire fell in on itself and sent a shower of sputtering sparks up into the night like fireflies, and I started up. It was cold, but drier. Beyond me, wrapped in silver, Glynn slept on. But Curtis had lifted his head and was staring off into the black space beyond the wavering fire. As I watched, the hackles rose at the base of

his powerful neck, and I saw his lips go back, and caught the
gleam of his long white teeth, and heard his low, menacing
growl. It was soft and sibilant, and went on and on, and in
that moment there was absolutely no doubt in my mind that
something purely and simply evil waited just outside the circle
of the dying light.

My heart pounding queerly, I rose to my knees and
reached out very slowly and picked up the knife that Glynn
had taken out of her pocket and laid on the earth beside her,
so that she would not roll on it. I unfolded its blade, still staring at the place where Curtis looked. The growling went on
and on, soft and low and utterly terrible. I felt my own hair
prickle at the back of my neck, and felt the little puckering of
the fine hairs on my arms. I waited there on my knees, not
breathing.

Then it ebbed. Whatever it had been was simply not
there anymore. After an endless moment, Curtis looked
around at me, gave me a toothy, embarrassed grin and
thumped his tail, and laid his head back on his paws. He
closed his eyes. I felt sweat break out at my hairline and under
my arms, and then I got up silently and built the fire back up
and sank down again beside Laura. I don't know how long I
had slept before the falling of the little logs waked me, but
when I looked up at the sky the fog had gone, and the stars
burned huge and silver and gaudy in the sky.

*Didn't I say I'd always be your same stars? If you get to miss-
ing me, just look up.*

I take your point, I said, and pulled the silver blanket back
around me and slept without moving until dawn. When I woke,
it was to the huge, clattering sound of a helicopter that seemed
to hover directly over us, filling the cold morning world with
noise and wind and confusion, and we had been found.

I wouldn't have believed you could set a copter down anywhere in that scrambled wilderness, but the young National
Guard pilot did, and quite neatly. Soon we were spinning low
over the line of the landslide, heading south. From the air you
could see where the snake had thrashed and convulsed; in the

mountains there was devastation, but it ended with the far edge of the landslide that had obliterated the road. On the far side, the trees stretched away unbroken and unvanquished, and the small towns and suburbs that I could see beyond them looked fairly whole. There were many fires in them, though; I could see their smoke. Gas fires, the pilot said, from where the heaving earth had broken the mains and the winds had whipped the fires alive. Further north whole sections of San Francisco were burning.

"Looked like the start of Desert Storm from the air last night," the pilot said.

"How bad was it? The quake?"

"Don't know yet. Big as Loma Prieta at least," he said. "Hardly any towns and cities for about two hundred miles around that haven't taken a hit. Don't have any casualty counts yet. I been in the air since last night."

"Have you found many people?"

"Just you all. It's you I been hunting. Somebody said in Boulder Creek that they'd seen a fire up in the Santa Cruz's around Big Basin. I didn't see nothing, though, till the sun came up. Saw it reflecting off them blankets then. Don't know if we ever would've found you if it had been foggy."

He followed the now intact road down to Boulder Creek and set us down on a football field behind the high school. A welter of tents, large and small, had been set up, and from the air the big red crosses told us who would be succoring us. There were trees down on the earth here, too, and the school itself sat strangely askew, but it stood. I did not see much of the rubble that would have marked completely destroyed houses and buildings, but everything I did see leaned or canted slightly and horribly. The whole scene looked like a child with little coordination had drawn it, just awry enough to be unsettling.

"There's bigger aid stations around, but they're jammed," the pilot said. "You'll be better off here. They got a full medical staff just waiting. It'll be a while before the folks from the mountains start coming in. There anybody else you know of up there?"

"Yes," I said. "Up at the very top of the ridge, where an old fire tower used to stand. You don't have to hurry, though."

He winced.

"I've seen that tower from the air," he said. "I'll tell 'em back at base. You know who he is?"

"His name is T. C. Bridgewater," I said clearly, "and he has family in Greenville, Mississippi. I don't know the address. He wasn't close to them . ... "

I started to cry and he said, in distress, "I'm sorry, ma'am. We'll bring him in and find his folks. You don't worry about it anymore."

"Can't you just . . . leave him there? He's covered up . . . "

He looked shocked.

"Can't do that, ma'am. But we'll take good care of him. Come on, let's get you all into that tent. That arm don't look good."

I followed him toward the largest of the tents, still crying, and people ran out to meet me with a stretcher. There were two others, for Glynn and Laura. They never did manage to get Glynn on the one that was hers, and when they told her that Curtis would have to stay outside, her face was so terrible that they relented and brought him in, too. When I looked around for the young pilot so that I might thank him, he was gone.

It was late that afternoon before I got a phone line out. They had set my arm—something that I do not, to this day, care to dwell on even with the shot beforehand—and given me a pain pill that had knocked me swiftly and deeply out cold. When I woke, I was lying on a cot under the tent, an olive drab army issue blanket over me, and Laura was beside me on her cot, sitting up eating Jell-O and drinking a Diet Coke. On her other side Glynn slept like a child, on her back, her fists lying loosely beside her head, her mouth slightly open. She was snoring gently, and Curtis, beside her on a blanket of his own, snored, too. All of us had been bathed and dotted with antiseptic and given clean, slightly too large clothes to put on, and fed and watered, and given the pertinent information to kind, harried people who were, I assumed, the proper authorities. By the time my arm was set the tents were filling up, and around me now, in the dimming light, I could see other forms, inert on cots or sitting up, talking with one another.

"There you are," Laura said. "I thought you never would wake up. Do you feel better? When they set your arm you let out a howl they could hear back in Atlanta."

"I feel fine," I said thickly and crossly. I was hot and my mouth tasted terrible, and I needed to go to the bathroom. "Are you okay? What do they say about you?"

"The baby's okay," she said, and smiled suddenly, a smile of such simple, heartbreaking sweetness and delight that I felt my eyes tear up again.

"I'm glad," I said, smiling back. I could feel my mouth waffling.

"I'm going to keep him," she said, not looking at me. "I can't . . . you know. Not after this. If he could hang in there through all this, he ought to have a shot at it, don't you think? Oh, Met. I want this baby so much. I want to raise him, and love him, and make a good life for him; I want him to know all his people. I want his whole family at his birthday parties. I want to come home, Met. How much of a problem would that be? Not to stay with you, of course, and I'd get a job first thing, but would it be awful on Pom? Or on you, for that matter?"

"I thought you'd never ask," I said, feeling the stupid, loose tears accelerate. "Of course you're going to come home. Of course you're going to stay with us, until he's born, at least. It's all settled. It makes me very happy, Pie."

"Mommee, though—"

"Mommee is not a factor," I said tranquilly. "Mommee is not a player. As of this minute, we are everyone of us casting our lots on the side of life. Even those of us who don't know it yet."

Laura grinned, and then looked over at Glynn, who stirred in her sleep, blew a small bubble, turned her head to the side, and slept on.

"Look at her," Laura said softly. "She just walked us out of an earthquake and saved our asses for us, and she looks for all the world like a sleeping baby. Except, of course, for that ring in her nose. Such innocence . . . I don't think she'll ever get that back, Met, do you?"

I thought about that.

"No. How could she, after the past week or two? Any one of the things that she's gone through would have been enough. But you know, it's funny about innocence, Laura. I thought I wanted to keep her innocent; I thought that was the best thing I could do for her. I think it's what all parents want for their children, maybe most of all. But we're wrong. Innocence is a tool; I think innocence—a child's innocence—is what nature gives them so someone will take care of them as long as they need it. But past a certain point, to condemn that child to innocence is to condemn it to certain harm. It has to be able to take care of itself when the time comes, and innocence just doesn't cut it for that. I think maybe that's why all the old cultures had rites of passage into adulthood that hurt children somehow, or frightened them enough to change them. They had to lose the innocence. We don't have any real rites now, certainly not in our safe little suburban world. We keep our kids babies so long they don't have an inkling of what to do about the hard choices when they come. They literally don't know what harm is, until they hit it big time."

"Well, my innocent little niece has certainly learned all that, and didn't she come through with flying colors, though?" Laura said. "How did you get so smart all of a sudden, Met? I'd have bet you weren't ever going to let her go."

"I don't know," I said slowly. "It doesn't feel like smart to me. It just feels like somebody else beside me is thinking it. I guess maybe somebody else is."

She reached over and put her hand over mine. I looked at our hands together. They were puffy and pale, and dotted with yellow blotches and streaks of iodine where the scratches and cuts were.

"I know what you left up there," she said. "I hurt for you in my very heart. If you'll let me, I'll help you through it."

I opened my mouth to say something flip, but instead I said, "I'll need you everyday, Pie. Stay close."

I turned my head angrily away. I could not simply weep my way through the rest of my life. That was when the nice middle-aged woman who had taken my medical history came to me and said, "We've gotten you a line through to Atlanta now, Mrs. Fowler. Better grab it before somebody else does."

The phone in the house by the river rang for a long time. I did not think anyone would answer it and had the fancy that if someone did it would be the owner of that rich, flowery dark voice that had answered the last time I had dialed the number. But presently someone did. It was a man's voice, but not a man whom I knew.

"Who is this, please?" I said formally.

There was a long silence, and then I heard, "Merritt? Met? Is that you?"

"Jeff! Yes, darling, it *is* me. What are you doing there?"

"Oh, Merritt, thank God! We didn't know where you were; we couldn't find that stupid goddamned place you said you were staying at; we've all been out of our minds, Dad is crazy. . . . What I'm doing here is waiting for you to call. Dad called me and Chip home the minute he heard about the earthquake. He's out there somewhere; he commandeered a CDC Lear jet and he and Chip flew out yesterday; they've hooked up with the National Guard somewhere around Palo Alto, and they're flying every inch of those mountains, or trying to. He calls in every two hours to see if you've called. I don't know exactly where they are right now, but Merritt, wherever you are, stay there. Stay there! I'll tell him when he calls back, and he'll come get you. Are you all right? What about Glynn? And Laura?"

I remembered how crazy he and his brother had been about Laura when they were children, and what short shrift she had given them. They had adored Glynn, too. The stupid tears were back, scalding and inexorable.

"They're all right. They're fine. I'm at a Red Cross station on the high school football field at a place called Boulder Creek, not far from the top of the ridge where Big Basin starts. Where the lodge . . . was. Tell him that; the National Guard will find us. They found us out in the middle of the woods this morning."

I stopped, gulping and gasping, and he said, "Don't cry, Met. It's all over now. I promise he'll be there in a little while. God, he's been so upset; I've never seen him like that—"

Suddenly I was angry.

"Well, when you talk to him, you tell him something for me," I said. "You tell him that Mommee is going to a nursing home and no two ways about it, and that—"

"Met, he took Mommee and clapped her in the Alzheimer's unit at Sable not thirty minutes after that earthquake hit—"

"Well, then you tell him that black woman better be out of there and on the road to Morocco or wherever before I leave California airspace, or—"

"What black woman? You mean Ina? There's no black woman here but Ina, and she's been crying for a day and a half, she's so worried about you—"

"Ina's back?"

"Back? Where's she been?"

I paused for a long moment, getting my breath.

"Then you tell him I'm bringing a pregnant woman," I continued fiercely, "and a big dog, a *great* big dog, and I don't want to hear one word—"

"Met, you could bring a T Rex home with you and Dad wouldn't care. What's the matter with you? Are you really all right?"

"I don't know," I wailed, and hung up, and went back to my cot and cried for at least an hour. After tentative efforts to pat me and soothe me and cosset me, Laura went for the nurse and sought help, and the nurse said just to let me cry.

"Post-traumatic shock syndrome," she said. "You'll all have it sooner or later. Let her get it out. The sooner she does, the better."

So Laura let me cry, and I slid from the tears into a hot, restless, flailing sleep in which things roared and crashed and battered at me, and Curtis growled endlessly. I knew I was dreaming, but I could not wake, and when Laura finally shook me, and I woke to the cool gray of twilight, I still did not know where I was.

"I think he's here," Laura said, smiling. Tears ran down her face. "I keep hearing somebody yelling 'Fowler, Goddamn it, Fowler' and it sounds like Pom when he's pissed. Go on out there. I'll wait a little while before I wake Glynn."

I got up stiffly and walked out of the tent, still dragging my army blanket, blinking in the last of the sunlight. My arm throbbed hideously, and my mouth was dry, and dried sweat stuck my unchic, flopping new clothes to my body. I stared, trying to focus. I saw him then. He stopped and looked at me from midway across the football field. He was as disheveled as I had ever seen him even for Pom; his black hair hung in his eyes, and he had a rime of black stubble on his jaw that was plain even at that distance. He lifted his head a little, and I saw the startling blue flash of his eyes. I had once described them to Crisscross, I remembered, as the blue of the light on the tops of police cars. He had been waving his arms at someone, but when he saw me he dropped them to his side and stood, simply staring at me.

I did not know him. I literally did not know this man. He was a collection of parts, each somehow significant, yet that added up to nothing, just as T.C. had seemed to me on the path down to the lodge that morning, a million years ago now—a heartbeat ago. Who was this man who had come for me across a continent, who stood looking at me now as if he, too, saw a stranger? What was expected of me; what came next?

T.C., who is that? I said in my head. I felt him close all of a sudden, so close that he might have stood just behind me. I almost leaned back so that his body could take my weight.

That's Pom. That's what comes next. Go on, Merritt. It's what should happen now.

But I don't *know* him . . .

Yeah, you do. Look, Merritt. Just look.

Pom stood still. He moved one of his hands as if to stretch it toward me, and then dropped it. I saw his mouth make my name: Merritt. But I heard no sound. Neither of us moved.

Pom began to cry. His face crumpled and tears ran down from his blue eyes and left clean tracks on his filthy face, and he did not move, just stood there with his arms hanging at his sides, crying. Something inside me gave a great, swooping slide, as if the earth had moved again, and then I knew him. Pom. Of course. Pom.

"Pom . . ." I said, in a small voice with no breath behind it.

Go! T.C. said from his mountaintop. *Go!*

I dropped the blanket and began to run.

© Jack Alterman, 2003

ANNE RIVERS SIDDONS's bestselling novels include *Sweetwater Creek; Islands; Nora, Nora; Low Country; Up Island; Fault Lines; Downtown; Hill Towns; Colony; Outer Banks; King's Oak; Peachtree Road; Homeplace; Fox's Earth; The House Next Door;* and *Heartbreak Hotel*. She is also the author of a work of nonfiction, *John Chancellor Makes Me Cry*. She and her husband, Heyward, split their time between their home in Charleston, South Carolina, and Brooklin, Maine.

www.anneriverssiddons.com

Anne Rivers Siddons

BOOKS BY
ANNE RIVERS SIDDONS

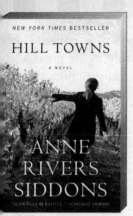

HILL TOWNS
A NOVEL

ISBN 978-0-06-171573-0 (paperback)

Making their way across the countryside of Tuscany, a couple soon feels themselves pulled in different directions, and the fabric of their marriage begins to unravel. Expanding beyond the bounds of a carefree trip, their journey takes them deep into the heart of their relationship . . . and becomes the ultimate test of their love.

NORA, NORA
A NOVEL

ISBN 978-0-06-187492-5 (paperback)

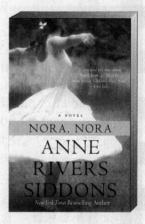

A free-thinking young woman turns the small town of Lytton, GA, on its ear one summer in 1961. She harbors a shocking truth that will stun the residents of the small, segregated town, and will forever change the life of the 13-year-old girl that looks up to her in every way.

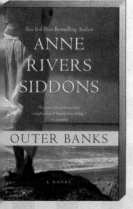

OUTER BANKS
A NOVEL

ISBN 978-0-06-053806-4 (paperback)

Four women who came together as sorority sisters on a Southern campus in the 1960s reunite to recapture the exquisite magic of those early years, to experience again the love, enthusiasm, passion, pain, and cruel betrayal that shaped their lives and set them all adrift on the Outer Banks.

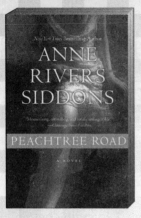

PEACHTREE ROAD
A NOVEL

ISBN 978-0-06-125624-0 (paperback)

When Lucy Bondurant Chastain Venable comes to live with her cousin, Sheppard Gibb Bondurant III, and his family in the great hous on Peachtree Road, she is only a child, never expecting that her reclusive young cousin will become her lifelong confidant and the source her greatest passion and most terrible need.

UP ISLAND
A NOVEL

ISBN 978-0-06-171571-6 (paperback)

Devastated by personal tragedies, Molly takes refuge on Martha's Vineyard where she tries to come to terms with who she really is. As her stay up island widens the distance between her and her old life in Atlanta, she lets go of her outworn notions of family and begins to become part of a new one.

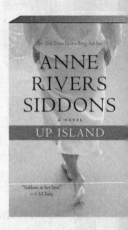

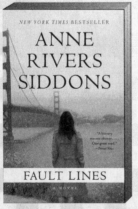

FAULT LINES
A NOVEL

ISBN 978-0-06-200468-0 (paperback)

A woman, her fragile daughter, and erratic younger sister struggle to see if the widening fissures between mother, daughter, and sister can be healed, as they search for the bedrock strength and courage that can save them whil traveling up the west coast . . . and through earthquake country.